J. D. PROFFITT

Manchester BLUFF

A CIVIL WAR NOVEL

Manchester Bluff is a work of fiction, an entertainment, and even though painstaking care has been applied to historical detail, occasionally a fact has been stretched or a truth bent for the sake of story.

To learn more about the author, go to www.jdproffittbooks.com.

ISBN: 1461173620
ISBN 13: 9781461173625
LCCN: 2011915230

To My Mother,

My Sons,

and My Siblings

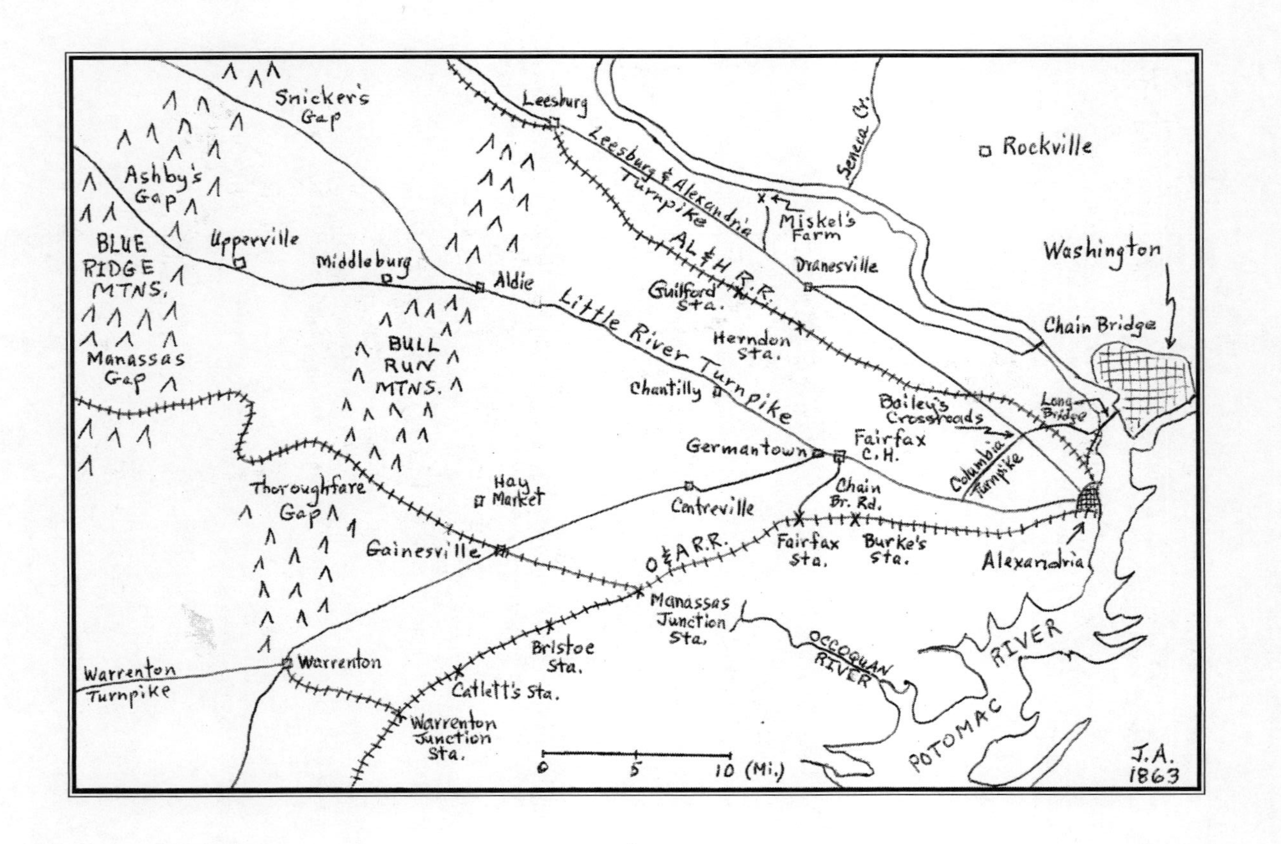

Snicker's Gap
Leesburg
Leesburg & Alexandria Turnpike
Seneca Cr.
Rockville
Ashby's Gap
Miskel's Farm
BLUE RIDGE MTNS.
Upperville
Middleburg
Aldie
AL & H R.R.
Dranesville
Washington
Guilford Sta.
Little River Turnpike
Herndon Sta.
Chain Bridge
Manassas Gap
BULL RUN MTNS.
Chantilly
Bailey's Crossroads
Long Bridge
Fairfax C.H.
Germantown
Columbia Turnpike
Thoroughfare Gap
Hay Market
Chain Br. Rd.
Centreville
Fairfax Sta.
Burke's Sta.
Gainesville
O & A R.R.
Alexandria
Manassas Junction Sta.
Bristoe Sta.
OCCOQUAN RIVER
RIVER
Warrenton
Warrenton Turnpike
Catlett's Sta.
POTOMAC
Warrenton Junction Sta.
0
5
10 (Mi.)
J.A.
1863

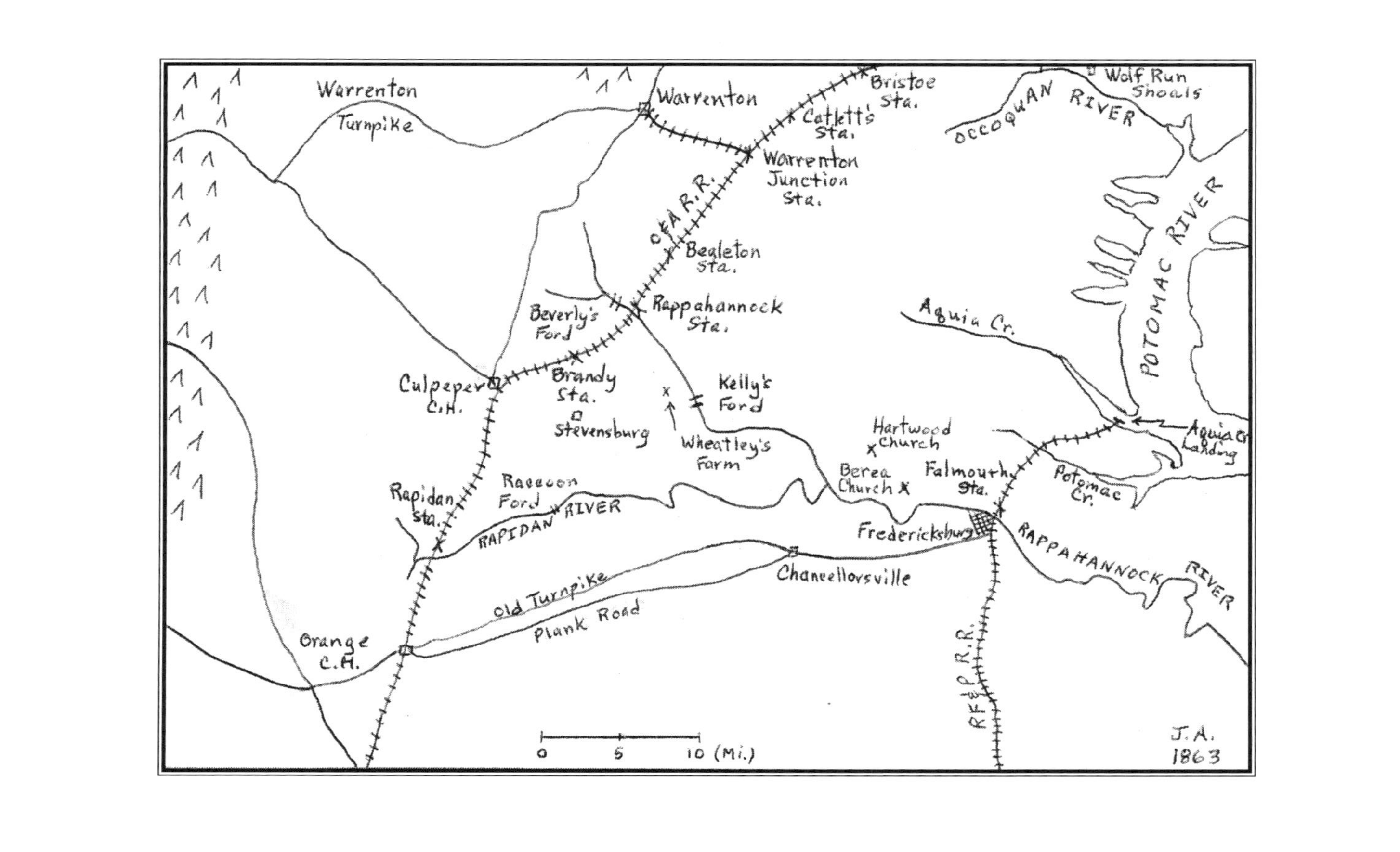
Warrenton
Turnpike
Warrenton
Bristoe
Sta.
Catlett's
Sta.
Warrenton
Junction
Sta.
O & A R.R.
Beàleton
Sta.
Rappahannock
Sta.
Beverly's
Ford
Culpeper
C.H.
Brandy
Sta.
Stevensburg
Kelly's
Ford
Wheatley's
Farm
Wolf Run
Shoals
OCCOQUAN RIVER
POTOMAC RIVER
Aquia Cr.
Aquia Cr.
Landing
Hartwood
Church
Berea
Church
Falmouth
Sta.
Potomac
Cr.
Raccoon
Ford
Rapidan
Sta.
RAPIDAN RIVER
Fredericksburg
RAPPAHANNOCK RIVER
Chancellorsville
Old Turnpike
Plank Road
Orange
C.H.
RF&P R.R.
0
5
10 (Mi.)
J.A.
1863

CHAPTER ONE

Alexander, Illinois
November 22, 1923

Is he dead?

I panicked when I saw the wicked fingers of flame reaching from the windows of Grandpa Alexander's house. My heart pounded—not so much from the run up the hill, but from my great fear of fire.

Just as I reached the porch steps, I hesitated and slipped in the snow. Suddenly, the front door opened, and a phantomlike form spilled out in a cloud of smoke. Stabbing at the porch floor with his walnut cane, Grandpa gasped for clean air. He saw me standing there looking up at him. "Hurry up, youngster…I need you," he sputtered.

I smelled burned hair when I reached him, and his old gray sweater was so hot that I had trouble keeping my hand on it as I helped him move away from the door. I grabbed a chair from the porch and dragged it along as we slowly made our way down the icy steps and onto the front yard.

He dropped into the chair, almost knocking me over with his wooden leg that jutted out at an awkward angle. He pointed a bony finger at the house, shaking it vigorously as he tried to choke out his words. "The box...you've got to get...the box." He dropped his hand and looked at me with empty eyes.

"I'll get it, Grandpa," I said. I knew what box he was talking about—it was the same one that my brothers and I had tried to investigate when we were younger—the box that he kept locked up in his desk drawer. We were sure that it was filled with gold coins.

"Pull that scarf up over your nose, and roll in that wet snow."

I did as he said and rushed toward the open door. Grandpa's study was on the main floor. Smoke rolled down the stairs like fog, and flames licked at me as I passed by. *Too late to save anything upstairs.*

I stumbled to the huge mahogany desk, which had served so well as one of my favorite hiding places. The drawer was locked, and I broke the handle when I tried to yank it open. I wanted to run out of the house right then.

I fumbled around for something that I could use to pry open the drawer. I spotted an old set of spurs hung near the fireplace. The tips were worn and rounded, but I managed to wedge a couple of them into the space above the drawer. It popped open.

The box was there, just like I knew it would be. I grabbed it and headed for the door, then stopped. *What else should I take? All of this will be gone soon, and it's up to me to decide what will survive. Probably time for two trips...maybe not. What else should I take?*

The pictures? Great-Grandfather John T. Alexander, Abraham Lincoln...The books? Rare collections that Grandpa had intended to pass on to Illinois College. The wooden carvings and bronze sculptures of horses and cattle that filled the walls and shelves? *The fire will destroy it all, burning up a lifetime.*

Swooping up an armload of the carvings and sculptures, and tucking my great-grandfather's picture under my arm, I escaped into the cold morning air.

Neighbors arrived, but not enough to form a bucket brigade. The horse-drawn pump that would soon make its way from town would only keep the fire from spreading to the nearby buildings.

"Did...Did you get it?" Grandpa couldn't move his eyes from the burning house.

"The box and a few other things...I'm going back for more." I saw my parents coming, and I hurried off before they could stop me.

Reaching the house, I discovered that the ceiling above the study had fallen, and it was now engulfed in flames. I helped a neighbor carry out the dining room table. A box of silverware and two silver trays rested upon it. *Grandma Alexander always served her special Christmas cookies on those trays.*

Grandpa held the box in his lap, and all of us stood around him, watching as the warmth of the fire on a cold November morning robbed us of any comfort.

The glowing shell of the house fell away as we slowly walked off.

⌘ ⌘ ⌘

We took Grandpa Alexander down the hill to our house, less than a mile away. He sat in the guest room well into the evening, taking only hot coffee. Late that night, I took some hot chicken soup to him. At first, he wasn't interested, but as the aroma filled the room, he gave in and began to eat. The box rested on the bed. We both glanced at it from time to time as he ate in silence.

That was the only time that I ever saw my grandpa cry—a single tear rolled down to the tip of his nose and fell gently into his soup. I tried not to notice, looking away to hold back my own tears.

"Sorry about the house, Grandpa."

"It's not the house," he replied. "The box is what mattered most, and you saved it. The house was gone years ago...after your grandmother died."

He was right. The place hadn't been the same since Grandma Alexander died. The old house had been filled with emptiness in these past three years as Grandpa slowly drifted away from the rest of us. Even so, I often visited him at the ranch, but we would just sit in silence as he looked out to the east from the large window in his study. Sometimes, he would look at me and ask me something just to acknowledge my presence, but his attention would soon return to the window, his portal to the past.

My thoughts returned to the present…and the box. I couldn't bear the mystery any longer. But before I could ask, Grandpa turned to me and said, "Inside the box, there's a *story*."

CHAPTER TWO

Jacksonville, Illinois
November 22, 1862
ante meridiem

Kinchelow's body was discovered on the same morning that I was called to President Sturtevant's office. While leading a Saturday morning working party of underclassmen who were cleaning up the cemetery grounds on the south end of Illinois College, I recognized my classmate Joshua Kumley running from the hilltop. Coming directly at me, Joshua closed the quarter-mile distance very quickly.

"Jason, they sent me to take over for you," he called. "You're wanted in College Hall...immediately." He paused for a moment to catch his breath when he reached me. "You think they want to talk to you about Kinchelow?"

"I suppose so," I said, "but I really don't know much about him."

"He was one of those troublemakers from Phi Alpha," Joshua said. "He probably picked an argument with the wrong abolitionist. They say he died from a stab wound...His body was in the alley behind King's Jewelry store."

"I heard the same thing early this morning. I didn't see much of him after he withdrew from his studies earlier this year."

"He was working for Mr. Ayers in the bank." Joshua didn't miss much of anything that took place in and around Jacksonville. His energies were focused upon exchanging information, and his classroom performance suffered as a result.

I left the work in Joshua's hands and started for the hilltop, slicing through the fallen leaves, some rich in color, but others dead dark. I didn't want to worry about Kinchelow. I only had a few more months to go to complete my studies, and if all went well, I might be able to find a teaching assignment. I stood at the top of the class, and I had worked hard to get there.

Large trees dotted the landscape—birch, cherry, oak, walnut, hickory, maple, elm, and hackberry. To the west, just past County Street, I could see Professor Jonathan Turner's Osage orange plantings—he sold them to ranchers like my father, John T. Alexander, to create hedges that were impermeable to cattle and horses, even pigs. Professor Turner also experimented in the area of animal health. His classes were very popular with students.

I was anxious to graduate, but I would surely miss this place. It had become my second home—the ranch would always be my first. I thought of the ranch as I walked past the stables, smelling the mix of horse and hay. I kept a horse here at the college in the warmer months, but I had just returned it to the ranch for the winter. Only a few carriage horses remained on the grounds for the underclassmen to tend to. Their other major duty included providing the firewood for the college living quarters, and I could see another work party off in the distance taking care of that.

Reaching the top of the hill, I paused to consider a quick trip to my room on Park Street to clean up a bit, but I noticed Governor Richard Yates descending the steps in front of College Hall. He was accompanied by a number of men and one woman, none of whom I recognized.

I met Governor Yates for the first time two years earlier, when he was honored at the Illinois State Fair here in Jacksonville for having been the first graduate of Illinois College in 1835. I saw him again just three months ago, when he visited our family to meet with my father at the ranch. A short man with a friendly, round face and a contagious laugh, Governor Yates was always neatly dressed and bore the stately demeanor befitting a governor.

When he'd dined with us, the discussion moved from horses and cattle to telegraph and railroads, and back again. Later that night, behind closed doors in my father's study, one could only guess at what was discussed.

Today, the governor and his party moved quickly past the magnificent red brick spires of College Hall and on toward West College Avenue, which bordered the grounds to the north. Just as I reached the steps, they disappeared into the two coaches waiting to rush them off to their next destination, most likely to be the railroad station to board the train to Springfield.

Perched on the hilltop like a small castle, College Hall was a well-known landmark. I climbed the steps and walked past the empty classrooms on the first floor and up the oak staircase to President Sturtevant's office. His tall, thin form stood in the doorway and motioned for me to enter and join him and Professor Crampton, who was warming himself in front of the brick fireplace.

"I see that Mr. Kumley promptly located you," President Sturtevant said.

"Yes, sir, he said that you wanted to see me right away."

"Please have a seat." President Sturtevant smiled at Professor Crampton and moved behind the modest hickory desk. Several chairs were arranged in front of it.

The office, about twenty foot square with tall, wide windows, offered a wonderful view of the south and west parts of the college grounds. Overflowing oak bookcases covered the inner walls, except for a spot occupied by a portrait of President Abraham Lincoln. The office smelled of a mixture of books, tobacco, and fireplace. Leather-bound tomes and sundry documents were stacked around the edges of the desktop, but the center was clear.

I took a seat, and Professor Crampton sat beside me. "I trust that things are going well, Mr. Alexander."

"Yes, sir, very well, thank you." *But why do they want to talk to me about Kinchelow?*

After graduating from Yale College in the fall of 1826 with honors, Julian M. Sturtevant had longed to extend Christianity and to establish a seminary of learning in the West. In a matter of days in 1829, he was ordained as a minister in the Presbyterian church, married Elizabeth Fayerweather, and received his master's degree. Shortly thereafter, the Sturtevants had set out on a long journey to join a rapidly growing community in Jacksonville, Illinois, at the country's western edge.

He quickly became a stalwart in the community and was joined by other deeply religious and patriotic Yale graduates seeking to create an image of their college on a 227-acre site purchased by funds raised from the local community and other sources throughout the country. Illinois College was formed in 1829. Julian Sturtevant became its second president in 1844.

One of the most important appointments that President Sturtevant made to his faculty during his first decade in office was that of Rufus C. Crampton, who in 1853 became Professor of Mathematics and Astronomy. A superb educator, Professor Crampton had a commanding demeanor despite his boyish features.

Anticipating the need to respond to future calls for support of the Union, Professor Crampton had recently formed Company

C of the 145th Regiment of Illinois Volunteers, largely made up of Illinois College students. The townspeople—an explosive mixture of Union abolitionists and Confederate sympathizers—were already calling the students "blueboys." Having just received his commission, Captain Crampton was conducting regularly scheduled drills at Camp Duncan, less than a mile north of Illinois College.

"Mr. Alexander, I'm sorry that we had to call you away from your duties this morning," President Sturtevant said as he took his seat behind the desk, "but we have an urgent matter to discuss." He removed his glasses and rubbed his eyes for a moment. "Jason, this is an issue of grave concern to your college, your state, and your country."

Just as in the classroom, President Sturtevant immediately gained my complete attention.

CHAPTER THREE

Jacksonville, Illinois
November 22, 1862
ante meridiem

The three of us sat there, and for a moment the room was silent. The only sound was the students chopping wood off in the distance. President Sturtevant's face reflected a mixture of soft and hard, happy and sad—he looked at me like my father looked at me. He broke the silence. "Mr. Alexander, you have studied the inaugural addresses of our country's presidents. What's your recollection of the words of Madison and Monroe?"

"I recall that Madison spoke of the responsibility associated with his office, and Monroe spoke of the obligations which it imposes."

"Excellent…and do you believe that the responsibility and obligation of a citizen are any less demanding?"

"No, sir, they are not," I said. I believed this, and I was sure that they did as well.

"I know that you've trained under Captain Crampton, along with the other students, in anticipation of serving your country after spring graduation," he said. "I'm afraid that we must alter that plan."

I turned to look at Professor Crampton. He was very still. He half smiled at me, but he deferred to his superior to continue the discussion.

"We have a special request that has come to us from the War Department in Washington by way of our Governor Yates. We received this request just this morning, and we have little time in which to respond." President Sturtevant moved a single sheet of foolscap from his right to the center of his desk, but he didn't look down at it—he was fully aware of its content. I detected a slight quiver in his hand. "Secretary Stanton is looking for help, and when we considered what he is asking for, there is only one person that comes to mind...and that is you."

I relaxed a bit. "That's not a problem at all. Once I graduate, I will go there instead of following Professor...I mean Captain Crampton."

"We would prefer that approach as well, but responsibility and obligation dictate otherwise. The secretary of war has asked for someone *immediately*," President Sturtevant said, tapping the paper centered on his desk.

My throat dried up. "But graduation is only a few months away."

"The secretary requires someone who is intelligent, someone who is able to ride with the cavalry when necessary, and someone who is trustworthy—in our estimation, you meet all three conditions."

Under normal circumstances, I would have been overwhelmed by the compliment, but in this case, I couldn't even force a smile across my face. Instead, I felt empty. My mind raced to the graduation that would not be—the goal that I had worked so hard for, the focus of my energy for the past five years.

I was angry with myself for feeling this way. Others would jump at the wonderful opportunity that had come my way, but here I was brooding over my personal loss...Perhaps they had chosen poorly. I almost suggested this, but my respect for my professors would not permit it. I would be going to Washington instead of graduating with my classmates in the spring.

Professor Crampton cut the silence. "Your ability to handle a gun, as well as your knowledge of the telegraph, will also serve you well in this position." He reached over to me, placing his hand on my shoulder. "Jason, only three young men have been chosen for this noteworthy assignment. We're honored that one of them will come from Illinois College."

My throat was still dry. "When must I depart?"

"You will meet a representative from the War Department at the train station in Springfield on *Monday*," President Sturtevant said.

CHAPTER FOUR

Jacksonville, Illinois
November 22, 1862
post meridiem

My mind raced with thoughts—my perfect future was coming apart. I would not graduate in the spring. I would not join Captain Crampton. I would go to Washington.

I walked aimlessly in the direction of my room on Park Street just east of Illinois College. After the dormitory burned down in the winter of 1852, students were forced to take up residence as boarders in the homes of Jacksonville's citizenry. I rented a room from Rufus and Adaline Crampton. Professor Crampton constructed the Octagon House in 1856 following the mathematically appealing architecture of Orson Squire Fowler. The two-story, eight-sided structure was surrounded by a double porch supported by massive pillars that extended down from the end of the roof, which was topped with a small octagonal cupola. Within the five thousand square feet of the home, I occupied a twelve-by-twelve bedroom on the second floor.

The pleasant scent of chicken soup hit me as I entered through the back door and walked up the circular staircase in the center of the house. I always joined the Crampton family for breakfast and supper, but dinner was usually taken quickly in the form of a bowl of soup from the pot that rested upon the flat-top cooking stove.

I sat down at my desk and looked out to the northeast, in the direction of West College Avenue. I didn't know where to begin… take my books back to the library in Beecher Hall…say good-bye to the professors and my classmates…But I didn't know what I could say about my abrupt departure.

I knew that I couldn't hide my disappointment. I decided to head home, even though it seemed like I was running from something. I longed to return to the work group back on the burial ground.

My books sat there on the desk, waiting for my attention—political economy, American law and rhetoric, natural philosophy, English literature, chemistry, and applied mathematics. I couldn't touch them.

I folded a few things into my soft leather suitcase and fastened the straps. I left a short note for the Cramptons. They had been so kind to me.

Quietly moving down the stairs, I opened the back door…

"Jason Alexander, you are not leaving here without a hug!"

Mrs. Crampton had been waiting for me since after hearing me arrive earlier. Professor Crampton had mentioned the meeting with Governor Yates, and she expected that the urgency of the matter spelled change.

"Is Rufus going with you?"

"No, it's just me," I said.

She didn't press for more information. With tears in her eyes, she gave me a tight hug and said good-bye. I thanked her for everything and rushed out the door before she could see my tears.

I headed for busy West College Avenue, leading to the train station about ten blocks away. Jacksonville, with its ten thousand inhabitants, was one of the largest towns in the state, and a thriving economy was attracting more people by the day. It was brisk, but not a bad day for a short walk. I was glad that I had not stuffed the suitcase.

When I reached 919 West College, I stopped to say good-bye to Meredith Montgomery. I looked up at the beautiful home constructed in the Greek Revival style. I had escorted her to a few dances in town, but I think she had her eye on someone else. I decided to write to her once I got settled in Washington.

I crossed over to West State Street, a block to the north, where the chance of gaining a ride into town would increase. Just as I reached the 800 block, Uncle Vince Richardson pulled up his wagon along the sidewalk.

"Heading home, are you? Hop in."

I didn't know why everyone called him Uncle Vince—I wasn't even sure if he was anyone's uncle, for that matter—but he filled the role quite well because he was friendly and willing to lend a helping hand to all of his adopted nieces and nephews. Uncle Vince had a small farm about three miles west of town, and he was a fine cook, his specialty being a thick soup containing special ingredients known only to him and his great ancestors from the Old Country.

"Thanks, Uncle Vince," I said as I tossed my suitcase into the back of his wagon amidst many other items.

"Say, I just saw J.Z. Scott as I came into town, and he tells me that one of your student friends was killed last night. I don't like to hear that. We don't need that sort of thing going on here in this town. Pretty soon people will have to put locks on their doors like they do down there in San Looiee."

I was quiet. One of the great things about Uncle Vince was that he would carry the conversation on his own if you would let him, and right now, that was just fine with me. *Maybe I should go back and say good-bye to Meredith in person.*

"J.Z. says that young Willie Kinchelow was killed by one of those abolitionists. Now I thought they was peace-loving folks, but like J.Z. says, they're the ones who started this war in the first place."

Uncle Vince seldom asked questions; he just made statements. I wasn't sure whether my lack of response implied agreement, lack of opinion, or disagreement. I wouldn't test that today.

"I want to pick up a copy of the *Illinois Courier* and see what it says about this," he said. "Have you seen it?"

"No," I said. *I don't want to worry about Kinchelow.*

Moving quickly along the tree-lined street, Uncle Vince guided his two horses past the massive Dunlap House Hotel and over to the front of the Heslep Tavern at 336 West State Street.

"I have a package to deliver to Charles Constable. They say it'll be *Judge* Constable someday soon, as he is favored for the judicial court seat here."

Heslep Tavern was a beautiful two-story, ten-room frame house with front and side porches graced with ornate cast-iron grillwork made at the Heslep foundry in Pittsburgh. It served as a boarding house for travelers, but Charles Constable had also used his large room as a law office. Thomas and Cassandra Heslep advertised that both Martin Van Buren and Stephen A. Douglas were former boarders.

"That's a busy man," Uncle Vince said as he returned to the wagon. "He was packing his bags and conducting business at the same time. It looked like Ham and Gil Green in there with him—I just left my preserves outside his door.

"Aren't those Green boys still attending the Illinois College with you?" he asked as we pulled away from the inn and headed east once again.

"As far as I know, they are," I said.

"I heard they were going to join the Confederacy," he said.

"That could be. I know they have a lot of relatives in Kentucky, and they have been critical of our professors," I said, trying to be careful and to avoid being pulled any further into the conversation.

"Well, they're not alone there, you know. A lot of folks around here haven't taken a fancy to those smooth-talking easterners. They don't have family in the South like a lot of us do."

"Yes, I know. My father has been worried about Uncle E.P. Alexander, who's fighting for the South under General Lee," I said.

We turned north on West Street, going past West Douglas, and stopped at the Jacksonville Woolen Mills near the railroad station. I knew that Uncle Vince raised some sheep, so I guessed that he was stopping to trade for shearing services that had been performed earlier in the year. Joseph Capps would barter or retain some of the wool as compensation.

"This stop should take care of the both of us," he said. "You be sure to tell John T. that I said to say hello—I haven't seen him since the burgoo festival on the Fourth of July."

"I'll tell him, Uncle Vince, and thank you for the ride."

It was time to leave Jacksonville.

CHAPTER FIVE

Jacksonville, Illinois
November 22, 1862
post meridiem

The next train that headed east to the Alexander station departed in thirty-four minutes. The Toledo, Wabash, and Western Railroad connected the Illinois River to Lake Erie, running on a regular basis between Meredosia, Illinois, and Toledo, Ohio. The many stops along the way included the stations at Jacksonville, Alexander, and Springfield.

The Jacksonville station had double sidings. The south siding ran up next to the woolen mill, and the north siding serviced the stockyards. Much to the gratitude of the local populace, the prevailing south winds of the summer months carried the smell away from town.

The station agent, Byron Pickford, was working the ticket window. Before I met him, I had communicated with him via telegraph from the Alexander station after reaching a satisfactory level of training as determined by my good friend and station agent Edward Hinrichsen. Growing up, I had utilized all available time away from the ranch to learn about telegraphy and railroads, and Mr. Hinrichsen knew a lot about both. My father had already accepted the likelihood that I would not follow him into ranching.

My ten-fare pass was not used up, so I had no need to go to the window and start a conversation, but I waved at Mr. Pickford as he tended to a small line of travelers. I knew that he would wire ahead to Mr. Hinrichsen that I was headed home.

I sat down in the waiting area and picked up a copy of the *Illinois Courier* lying nearby. I scanned it for information about the murder. There wasn't much. It didn't appear that Willie had been robbed, and he had been dead for several hours when he was found. The paper reported that he was a student at Illinois College even though he was not. *But then, neither am I.*

I loved the smell of the railroad. Steam-powered locomotives were so impressive. In the language of the railroad, they were called "hogs," and their engineers were called "hoggers." They were identified by name, number, and wheel alignment. We were leaving town on the Ridgely, engine number six, an American type 4-4-0, meaning that there were two pairs of small wheels on the leading truck, two pairs of large driving wheels, and no wheels under the cab. Approximately eighty thousand pounds of weight rested on the four driving wheels, and this hog could easily pull forty times that weight in freight.

I boarded the train as soon as it arrived. This was a passenger train, so the Ridgely hardly knew that we were here. The configuration of the train was typical for this route, with the tender behind the hog, followed by the baggage car, the gentlemen's car, and the ladies' car. A gentleman traveling with a lady would ride in the ladies' car; otherwise, a gentleman rode in the gentlemen's car, which was where all of the smoking occurred, much to my dislike.

The poorly ventilated passenger car was filled with bench seats in rows with an aisle down the middle. A small stove was located in the center of the car. Its heat seemed to cook the smoke from the tobacco into a choking cloud of mind-numbing amalgam. I pulled down my small window in a feeble attempt to escape from the oppression being created by just a dozen or so additional passengers.

The terrain rolled off ever so gently as we moved a bit to the southeast before heading due east to Alexander. The single pair of iron rails paralleled the turnpike road that had connected the towns for as long as I could remember.

Together the road and the railroad carved through pockets of trees and patches of wide-open areas. Brilliant fall colors splashed the line of windows and hypnotized me. Gently rolling carpets of fading green played touch with small creeks that meandered like loose string.

This land was an immense prairie once thought to be good for little, if anything. But my father had discovered that it was perfect for ranching, or more specifically stock-raising. His was one of the few large ranch-farms amidst a greater number of smaller ones covering Morgan County, the standard claim being 320 acres according to the unwritten law of the frontier.

John T. Alexander and Company sprawled across many thousands of acres. A lot of land was required to raise a lot of cattle. My father shipped more cattle to the East than any other rancher in the country—over a hundred thousand beeves a year, and he had been doing it for almost five years. It so happened that the second largest rancher was Jacob Strawn, whose large spread was just west of Jacksonville.

The Ridgely stopped briefly at the Arnold station for water. Such locations were called jerkwater towns by the railroaders because a quick tug on the downspout hanging from the water tower released the steam locomotive's resuscitative lifeblood.

Shortly after getting underway once again, we crossed into our ranch, which extended to the town of Alexander and well beyond. I looked to the north when we reached a point about three miles from the Alexander station and recognized our house off in the distance.

On the bright side, it would be nice to sleep in my own bed tonight.

CHAPTER SIX

Alexander, Illinois
November 22, 1862
post meridiem

Edward Hinrichsen was standing on the station platform as the train slowly moved into position. All of the men in my car remained seated, their destinations being further eastward.

I wore a trail of smoke like a cape as I descended from the car. Mr. H. gave me a formal handshake followed by a warm hug. *Mr. H. knows.*

"Well now, this is a great surprise," he said with a smile.

"It's good to see you, Mr. H. How are things going?"

In small towns like Alexander, the station agent was the collector and disseminator of information, running the railroad, the telegraph, and the post office. Mr. H. had also established his own mercantile trade business, which was very successful.

"It's been relatively quiet, Jason. James Brown over in Island Grove lost his top bull about two weeks ago, and Alma Berchtold gave birth to her fifth yesterday—a healthy boy."

"I need to check the schedule for Springfield departures on Monday morning," I said.

"Springfield departures, you say. Let me get Number Six on its way, and then we will tend to that." Mr. H. went about his business. Only three passengers were boarding here.

I went inside the depot and into the agent's office and sat down in my favorite chair. The agent from the New Berlin station, the next one up the line, was clicking for Mr. H. I could have answered for him and taken the message, but I just sat there, momentarily drained of energy.

I wasn't very happy about the way that I had left Jacksonville. I guess I was feeling sorry for myself, but I quickly recognized this self-defeating condition—one which my professors identified as "an insult to God" when you considered all of the gifts that He had bestowed upon us.

I was beginning to feel better when Mr. H. entered his office. "I think we'll have to get that hog into the shop soon. Ben says he can't maintain operating pressure."

He acknowledged the signal from the New Berlin agent and sent the out-of-station message, referred to as an OOS, to register the departure of the Ridgely, and then he took the message from New Berlin. It was directed to someone in Jacksonville, so Mr. H. just passed it on down the line.

Tilting his head slightly downward and raising his eyes above the top of his glasses, he stared in my direction. "We would want to be checking the timetables all the way to Washington, wouldn't we?"

"Yes, we would...How did you know?" I knew perfectly well that he *would* know, but it was always interesting to find out *how.*

He just smiled. "We've had some interesting movement through here lately, and those folks who passed through here earlier today with the governor certainly weren't from around here. I just put two and two together, and it came up four again," he said.

I had heard that one before, but it still made me smile.

"Jason, these are times when plans are taken off of the woodpile and thrown into the stove. You must answer the call just like so many others—actually, the fact that they have tapped *you* for this assignment gives me some hope that we are headed in the right direction.

"Just like that locomotive that rolled out of here a few minutes ago, the mighty force of the North will not prevail unless it is guided by intelligent minds. President Lincoln, Secretary Stanton, and Governor Yates have seen this, and they are taking steps to put the right people in the right places. You are but one piece in the large puzzle, but without each piece in its place, the whole thing is not complete."

His address was a good one, and I knew that what he was saying was right.

He fumbled through the stack of timetables and continued, "We cannot allow a state or any group of states to withdraw from the Union. If this happens, the Union will disappear, leaving the door open for the British and French to return."

"Yes, I have read that they've already discussed how they would divide our country between them." Mr. H. had a way of engaging me in the conversation.

"Let's see here," he said as he studied the tables, "it would appear that your Springfield departure time will be eight thirty on Monday morning. Now that's the Number Three Express, but I can arrange a quick stop here at twenty minutes after seven."

Edward Hinrichsen was a man of action. He was the one who had actually laid out the town of Alexander in 1857, but chose to name it after its most prominent citizen instead of himself.

Nevertheless, Mr. H. was the hub around which the wheel of Alexander commerce revolved.

Next to the huge stockyard area located just south of the side rail, Mr. H. had constructed a large building that he used to store grain. *"Buy low, sell high,"* he would say. People said that he bought and sold over a hundred thousand bushels each of wheat and corn during the year.

"You'll have to spend the night in Toledo and then depart from there at six-twenty a.m. on Tuesday. That should put you in Washington at nine-oh-two a.m. on Wednesday."

He leaned back in his swivel chair and clasped his hands behind his head. His big, bushy mustache broadened to its full expanse as he tightened his lips together. "I'll package up the newspapers from time to time and send them on to you. Those will help keep you close to home. Speaking of close to home, if you get a chance, say hello to Honest Abe for me."

CHAPTER SEVEN

John S. Alexander Ranch
November 22, 1862
post meridiem

After arranging for the night agent to come in a bit early, Mr. H. gave me a ride out to the ranch. I would see him again before I departed, so we said good-bye quickly.

It was quite a surprise when I walked into the house. My mother hurried from the kitchen, rubbing her hands on her apron before she gave me a kiss and a hug, "*Jason!* You're just in time for supper."

Somehow, eating had skipped my mind for the better part of the day, but now that I was home, and the smells from the kitchen wafted in the air, supper sounded great.

"Go wash up," she said. "The others will be here before long... Oh, by the way, we have a guest staying with us for a few days. He's getting the grand tour of the place right now. You can meet him at supper."

I wasn't happy to hear that. I wanted to share all of the news with my family right away, but now I would have to keep that to myself for a while longer.

Soon we were sitting down in the dining room to enjoy one of my mother's finest meals. Many of my favorites were part of the menu—it was almost as if she was expecting me. I met our guest, Gustavus F. Swift, who had traveled from Massachusetts. He was about my age, and the family seemed to like him, especially my sister, Jeanine, who had made it a point to take the seat next to him. Gustavus was enjoying her attentiveness.

After saying grace, my father started passing around the ample dishes of food. I was grateful that he directed the conversation around our guest, instead of me. "Gustavus is looking into establishing a meatpacking business in Chicago. If it works out, we may no longer need to ship the cattle eastward."

My brother, Jerome, joined in. "The packaged meat would be transported to the eastern cities instead of the beeves. The trick is preventing the spoilage, and he thinks there is a way to do it."

"I have a lot of things to pull together to make it all happen, but it looks promising at the moment," Gustavus said. "For one thing, I'll need more ranches like this one to supply the livestock."

"I suppose that we could expand some, but people around here are buying land, not selling," my father said. "I did hear that the Sullivant Ranch over in Champaign County might be up for sale—that's about three times the size of this place in terms of raw acreage."

"It's about the same distance from here as St. Louis," I said.

My father looked at my brother and me and said, "Yes...it would require at least one of you to move there and run it." It was quiet as everyone contemplated his statement. My father broke the silence. "Pass those beans, please." He was a big eater, but his tall, thin frame didn't carry an ounce of fat. His brown eyes were alive and friendly. People said that my brother and I looked just like him.

"And then there's the whole problem of waste," our guest continued. "John T. here tells me that a cow consumes thirty pounds of food a day and leaves ten pounds of waste. My operation must limit the amount of time that I hold the cattle on the lot before they're slaughtered because the cattle's food supply and their waste buildup become a severe problem with my restricted space. On the ranch here, you are able to deal with these matters by moving your cattle around on a regular basis."

Gustavus Swift was full of energy, and it was obvious that he had thoroughly researched the business opportunity. Under normal circumstances, I would have enthusiastically joined in on the discussion, but I had other things on my mind.

"The bigger problem in my mind," Gustavus went on, "is the waste from the butchering, which amounts to almost half of the body weight of the cow! I have nightmares over this one."

Looking at me, he said, "I am, however, encouraged by work that your Professor Turner has done at Illinois College. I'm sure you know that he has experimented with grinding up the bones and feeding that back to the cattle in a mixture with their normal alimentation. Since most of the waste is in the form of bones, this may be the answer."

"He's only been working on this for a short time," I responded.

"Yes, I will be discussing the extent of his project with him on Tuesday next. My hope is that he'll have these things worked out by the time I build my plant, which is a few years away...at the moment.

"I expect that I'm not the only one thinking about something like this, so I know that I don't have much time," Gustavus said. "The interest in providing meat for our soldiers has helped move this along. If you could see the mess in Washington, you would understand why packaged meat is desired."

"Yes, that must be an interesting sight," my father said. "We've already shipped off well over a hundred thousand head, and I'm pretty sure that Jacob Strawn is close to that number himself. Hinrichsen could give you my exact head counts, as they all pass through the rail station in town."

"Are we all about ready for some apple pie?" my mother asked.

"I'll give you a hand, Mother," Jeanine said as she finally took her eyes off of our guest. It was hard for all of us to accept the fact that Jeanine Edith Alexander would be sixteen years of age next month; Jerome was only four years her senior, and I was six, but she was still our little baby sister.

Perhaps we had both made it a bit too tough for suitors to come calling. On the other hand, Jeanine's ability to both outride and outshoot her brothers may have been sufficient intimidation for young beaus.

Somehow, I got the feeling that Gustavus Swift would pass this way again even if his business venture failed.

After our guest retired for the night, I had my first opportunity to talk privately with the rest of the family. I had sensed that my father and mother knew something about my situation, but I was quite sure that my brother and sister did not.

I told them what I knew as they listened intently.

It would be the first time that any of us would go away for an extended period of time, and it was going to happen very soon.

Jeanine cried. Jerome stared up at the large oak timbers that graced the front room and shook his head slowly. The fire crackled in the fireplace, trying its best to soothe the moment for all of us.

My mother tried to swallow the tears, but as tough as Mary DeWeese Alexander had proven to be over the years, she could not hide her concern for her oldest son. "I have long feared that this war would spread its ugliness over this dear family," she said.

"I'll be working in the War Department, Mother, and unless Washington is attacked, I should be quite safe there." I looked over at my father. "Did you know about this?"

"Only that it *might* happen—I told them that they needed to talk to you directly about it."

At the age of thirteen, John T. Alexander had driven herds of cattle with his father from Ohio, over the Alleghenies, to Philadelphia, Baltimore, New York, and Boston. His father had taken him to Ohio from Virginia in 1826, when he was six years old. A good part of the Alexander family had remained in the south, but John T. had moved here.

Like many of the other ranchers in Central Illinois, John T. had supported the Whigs until the Republican Party was formed in 1856. He supported Lincoln and the Union cause, but he was sympathetic to the South, knowing that the vast majority of the Confederate soldiers had no personal interest in slavery and were being driven by a handful of wealthy, aristocratic plantation owners. It was this same oligarchic control that had driven John T.'s father out of Virginia.

My father had often pondered the thought of facing a family member, perhaps his own cousin, on a firing line and wondered what he would do; now his son could actually face this possibility.

Not much else was said. We were satisfied with the comfort of our own company, recognizing that life can pull a family apart at a moment's notice, and perhaps never put it back together again.

CHAPTER EIGHT

Alexander, Illinois
November 23, 1862
ante meridiem

In the morning we went to the little Christian church in town that served the entire community. The children attended Sunday school while the adults worshipped together.

It was uplifting. I was able to put things in proper perspective again. It was like the pastor had prepared the sermon just for me. "You don't own your life. Your salvation was purchased at a great cost. It's your duty to make the most of your life in His honor. Our problems begin when we turn our attention inward, fostering a condition of prideful self-worship that is unfulfilling and detrimental to the common good."

The congregation remained afterward and socialized. Jerome and I fell in with a group where the conversation moved to Willie Kinchelow.

"That boy never hurt anyone." Charlie Drury, a hired hand who worked for my father, was angry. "He's my sister's boy, born in Kentucky, but no secessionist, and I'll put down any man that says he is."

"They'll find out who did it, Charlie," Franklin Kaiser, justice of the peace, said. The JP also ran the general store in Alexander, and his generosity had allowed many newcomers to get established by running up a good tab of credit.

"I know they will—it's just not fair to make my sister and her husband hear all this stuff. You'd think he was a damn slave owner the way those abolitionists are talking."

Charlie was one of my father's best men. I enjoyed riding with him. He'd taught me how to handle a horse amidst a herd of cattle. One of his sons had died from a horse-kicking, but that hadn't caused him to lose any love for the animals.

He had great respect for nature as a whole. Charlie was uncomfortable when confined by the constraints of buildings and crowds. He once told me that since we humans return to the earth along with all of the animals when we die, we should always treat both very well.

Like many others, Charlie Drury was confused by the war. The ravaging of the land, the cruelty to animals, and the loss of human life were unwarranted when it was unclear what the war was all about. He was sure that Willie Kinchelow was a victim of the war, even though he was far away from a battlefield.

I sidled over to another group nearby. Gustavus Swift was describing the mood of the people in the East. "Baltimore and New York are the areas of greatest concern. Both places have many people that openly support the South, and they are often belligerent about it. Many Union troops are stationed there in attempt to keep order.

"I would say that all of the cities, including Washington, are filled with sympathizers ready to carry bits of useful information southward," he continued. "As more people are killed and maimed, the bitterness grows. There's already a scar that will never fully heal no matter which side wins."

"Both sides will probably make a big push this coming spring," my father said.

"There's great concern that General Lee will attack Washington," Gustavus said.

My mother frowned noticeably.

"I don't think that is at all likely. Lee will not mire his army down trying to hold a city like Washington—his West Point training belies that," Edward Hinrichsen quickly retorted. "Look for Lee to fall back toward Richmond and lure Burnside to follow. That way, Lee can fight a defensive war on his own ground."

"That is certainly a possibility. General Burnside will be very anxious to demonstrate his ability to lead the Union army after replacing McClellan a few weeks ago," I said.

"That's true, that's true," Gustavus mused.

"Come with me and meet some of my friends," Jeanine said, whisking Gustavus away before he could continue the discussion.

The others seemed more than willing to change the topic to more mundane matters like the weather...but my mother was still frowning.

CHAPTER NINE

John S. Alexander Ranch
November 23, 1862
post meridiem

After returning to the ranch and excusing myself quickly after our Sunday dinner, I headed for the stables and saddled up my Morgan named "Dandy." We had a number of these great horses on the ranch; I received Dandy as a gift for my nineteenth birthday. He stood just over thirteen hands tall—short, even for a Morgan.

Dandy was ready for a ride. The gelding dashed across the range so quickly that I began to wonder if I had cinched his saddle adequately. I rode northeast to join up with some of the men who were gathering horses for another shipment to the Union cavalry.

Dandy's thick, silky mane glistened in the sunshine and muscles rippled across his shoulders like waves as he ran. Dandy was showing off, and we were both enjoying it.

His dark brown coat, almost black, sparkled with beads of sweat as we arrived at the scene of the roundup. The horses had been clustered, and some of the taller ones were being sorted out. The herd was in a cooperative mood.

Suddenly, a mare bolted from the group and headed in my direction. At my first ever-so-slight movement, Dandy responded and moved aggressively into the horse's path, stopping the mare in its tracks. Dandy moved so quickly that my hat flew off my head, and the runaway was stopped even before it floated to the ground.

After exchanging pleasantries with the men, I rode over to Spring Creek. As kids, my brother and I used to jump back and forth across Spring Creek, passing repeatedly between the counties of Morgan and Sangamon, which the creek divided at this point. I could almost hear us laughing just as we had then, and the fond memory brought a smile to my face. Did the tears that welled up represent joy or sadness, or both?

This was one of my favorite places on the ranch. I had camped near here with Charlie Drury to protect the herd from the wolves. They would come in at sunset, and then again at dawn. If they'd ever learned to attack at night when we couldn't see them, we would've had a serious problem. At first, I would load for Charlie since he was a much better shooter, but after he taught me how to focus on each step of the process and not to rush the shot, I was on my own.

The land here had a nice gentle roll through which the creek meandered in lazy fashion. The grass was thick and a rich green even this late in the year. Thousands upon thousands of cattle were driven to this part of the country to feed on the lush grasses. The cost of feeding the cattle from May to October was only a dollar a head. Over a period of four years, the total cost to prepare a beeve for market was about six dollars. With a market price of twenty-five dollars a head, the business case was compelling, and John T. Alexander had discovered the key to making it work year after year.

In October, corn is added to the cattle's fare—a small amount at first. More is gradually added until they become accustomed to the change—too much corn too soon results in gorging, and the cattle will eat themselves to death.

Once the grass disappears from the range, the cattle are moved into the feed yards for the winter. Here they're fed a mixture of straw and corn, which are moved directly from the fields to the feed yard until the snow cover is too heavy. Hay and corn are also moved into storage so that they'll be available when needed later. Perfect timing clears the fields just as the heavy snow begins to fall. If winter appears to be coming early, John T. will bring on extra help to clear the fields more quickly.

A good portion of the land is used for this process. A cow will eat about half a bushel of corn each day in the feed yard for roughly five months, and the typical field of corn will only produce forty bushels per acre.

The feed yards take on a character of their own as the winter progresses. The wagons etch out a trail that is bordered on both sides by a thick mat of cornstalks, providing a warm and dry bedding ground. The team of horses quickly learns to pull the wagon along the trail at just the right pace, allowing the driver to spend his entire time pitching out the feed.

The cattle will often add two hundred pounds to their weight during this feeding period. In the spring, John T. will introduce some pigs into the feeding area after it's vacated by the cattle, and the pigs will remove all remnants by summer. Many of the fattened pigs find their way to the Alexander household's table and those of the helpers. Some of the pigs are sold for a nice profit.

My musing was interrupted when I noticed three riders in the distance. I made them out to be my brother, my sister, and Gustavus Swift. Jeanine broke from the group, challenging the others to catch her, but there were no takers.

It didn't take long for her to reach me. "Did you get in on the roundup, Jason?"

"You might say that," I said.

"Father was with us, but he spotted a downer and rode off to have a look. Let's go back there," she said, pointing back to the northwest.

Jerome and Gustavus arrived. Gustavus looked uncomfortable in the saddle. "Miss Alexander, I am quite amazed at your ability to handle that horse."

"I could ride before I could walk," she said, winking at me.

"You still don't walk very well," Jerome joked. Jeanine's ability to trip over her own feet was the subject of considerable family banter.

Her Morgan was a buckskin named Star, standing at over fourteen hands. "Off we go," she called back over her shoulder. The others followed closely behind, but I paused for one more look at this part of Spring Creek.

Dandy managed to catch up quickly as the group moved slowly to accommodate Gustavus. It wasn't long before we spotted Father in the distance, waving as we came across the hilltop.

Having abandoned any further attempts to rise up, the Shorthorn was content to rest upon its tucked legs. The downer condition was not well understood. Many cows, like this one, showed no signs of injury or sickness. If the rate of occurrence rose beyond the usual numbers, the only thing the ranchers could do was to spread the herds across greater distances, if possible, to reduce contact. Professor Turner had examined many downers as part of his research, and he had recently begun to voice some concern about the common practice of eating them.

"Jerome, tell Alfred," Father said. "And ask him to take a quarter over to Kaiser's place in the morning."

Alfred Casson was the best butcher on the ranch. He would bring out a wagon and quickly dress and quarter the cow. The coyotes would remove what remained. The quarter of beef that would be taken to Kaiser's General Store was in exchange for various supplies already taken or to be taken, depending on the current balance on the trade ledger.

As Jerome rode off, Father looked at the cow and said, "We've been doing pretty well. This is the first one in over a month. Strawn had a problem in September that didn't spread to us, and I'm thankful for that. He was keeping Professor Turner pretty busy for a while."

"I remember that," I said. "His laboratory was full of downer skulls. Some had to be moved to a shed south of the campus because of the smell. Professor Turner worked all night to complete the examinations and record the results. He is an amazing person."

"I am quite anxious to meet this gentleman," Gustavus said.

"You will be most impressed, I assure you," Father said.

CHAPTER TEN

John A. Alexander Ranch
November 23, 1862
post meridiem

After supper, I went up to my room to pack. Thinking that I might be required to wear a uniform in Washington, I decided to pack lightly. Winter was coming, so I selected some warm clothing, and fortunately, I had taken little of it to my room near the campus.

I thought about taking a pistol and ammunition with me. I had always carried a pistol on the cattle drives that we used to make before we started transporting by rail. I decided that the added weight was too much of a burden.

Most of my books were in Jacksonville, but I tossed in a yet-to-be-read copy of Napoleon's *Maxims of War* that I had received as a gift from my uncle, E.P. Alexander. I needed something to read on the train.

I looked up and saw my father standing quietly in the doorway. I didn't know how long he had been there. "They will give you what you need when you get there, son," he said. "Now it would be quite different if you were heading off to join the Confederacy—you'd have to bring your own mount. Rebel raiding parties are coming closer and closer to gather horses."

"How long do you think this war will go on?" I asked.

"It should be finished now, but the Confederacy has the best of the generals. I'm afraid that it will go on until the Union is able to strike in a meaningful way, and nothing even close to this has happened yet. President Lincoln is searching for leadership."

"Do you think I will get to meet him again?" I had the pleasure of meeting Mr. Lincoln when he made a speech at Illinois College in 1859. He came at the invitation of the Phi Alpha Literary Society and spoke on the topic of discoveries and inventions.

"If you're going to be working in the War Department in Washington, I can't see how you wouldn't end up meeting him at some point along the way." My father had met with him on several occasions prior to the election of 1860.

"I think you know that I could tell Governor Yates that I need you here on the ranch, and he would accept that without any hesitation."

"Yes, I do know that," I said. It was a tempting thought, but it didn't seem right to me when so many others were making great sacrifices. I had already made up my mind that I would go.

Putting his hand on my shoulder, my father said, "One suggestion that I have for you is that you limit your trust to those who have proven themselves to be trustworthy in your own eyes. This war has parted many friendships, and even families."

And then we embraced, and I felt closer to my father than ever before.

CHAPTER ELEVEN

Alexander Railroad Station
November 24, 1862
ante meridiem

Just before dawn, we left for town in the buggy. Gustavus stayed behind, feeling that this was a family matter.

It was a short trip, during which we were all lost in silence. I envied the others' ability to return home after the train departed. I would have been most happy to return to the comforts of my studies at Illinois College, which seemed only a short time ago to have had some degree of permanency associated with them.

The darkness of the early morning felt cold upon my face. Winter was approaching, and its element of surprise paled in the presence of what lay ahead for me.

Father broke the heavy silence. "Our horses will be following you on another train later today."

"I'll be watching for them out there," I said. The distinctive intertwined "JTA" brand was well known from here eastward. The possibility of eating Alexander beef and riding Alexander horses after reaching Washington was somewhat comforting, even if the likelihood seemed a bit remote at the moment.

Just visible with the aid of a pinch of light in the east, a shroud of smoke from the night fires hovered above the town like a protective blanket. The sleepy hamlet was beginning to awaken. It was quiet except for the distant sound of an oncoming train.

Mr. H. had received the OOS from Byron Pickford a short time earlier, when the Number 3 Express moved eastward out of the Jacksonville station. Prior to its arrival in Jacksonville, Mr. H. had reminded him to remind the hogger that a special stop in Alexander was required this morning. Such alterations in the schedule were a privilege afforded to station agents in good standing even though the express runs were tightly controlled, making far fewer stops than the standard runs.

Mr. H. greeted us at the station platform and tried to temper the somber mood of our party. "I would have rolled out the red carpet if I had a red carpet."

"Good morning, *Edward*," my mother said in a somewhat admonishing tone of voice as he lifted my bag from the buggy with one hand and offered the other to assist my mother.

Looking at me, he said, "The tracks are clear all the way to Toledo."

"I just hope that someone in Springfield remembers that I'm coming today," I said. I hadn't heard anything from anyone since leaving the meeting with the professors in Jacksonville on Saturday.

"I can assure you that the station agent in Springfield knows that you're coming," Mr. H. chuckled. "Perhaps the red carpet is there." A second look from my mother sent him shuffling off ahead of the rest of us. He placed my bag right next to the tracks.

The sound of the approaching train was more noticeable now. I had always loved that sound, but this morning it loomed like an approaching monster ready to take me into its inescapable clutch.

I knew that we'd have to rush our good-byes because the train would only slow to a passing crawl as it pushed to maintain schedule. The frenzy of hugs and kisses filled the moments remaining.

I fought back the tears by trying to stifle blinks and dry them with the aid of the cool morning air. I was unable to sleep last night, worrying about how I would handle this moment, knowing full well that I was likely to handle it poorly.

Time seemed to evaporate, and suddenly, the train was clearly in sight. The last, bone-crushing hug came from Mr. H., after which, he turned and signaled to the hogger with a simple wave of the hand. I spotted the conductor, or skipper, standing on the steps of the passenger car, ready to assist with my ascent.

In one quick motion, I grabbed my bag and jumped on board. Before stepping inside, I turned to wave good-bye to my family and friend standing back at the station. As we moved apart, the rising sun cloaked their diminishing exteriors with splashes of morning paint. It was 7:20 a.m., and my journey had begun.

CHAPTER TWELVE

Springfield, Illinois
November 24, 1862
ante meridiem

"Boy...you must be important!"

The voiced opinion came from one of the men in the first passenger car. I wasn't in the mood for a conversation, so I just sat down near the stove.

The trip to Springfield was a short one, all of forty minutes. About three miles out, we crossed the last vestige of the ranch. I had the urge to jump from the train right then, but I wasn't sure how I would explain it.

After a bit, I scanned the other faces. Knowing that they must have boarded in Meredosia or Jacksonville, I thought I might recognize someone, but I didn't.

The express run was on schedule, making good time over the flat terrain.

Springfield was a rapidly growing city, already twice the size of Jacksonville. The downtown station operated by the Toledo, Wabash, and Western Railroad was located at Tenth and Monroe

Streets and looked just like the station in Jacksonville. As we approached, I could see a large crowd of people gathered there.

I regretted that I hadn't paid closer attention to the men who were with Governor Yates on Saturday in Jacksonville because it was likely that one of them was the representative from the War Department. I scanned the crowd as we pulled into the station, but the smoke and ash from the stack drifted back just enough to eliminate a chance of identifying anyone.

"Well, Mr. Important, I thought for sure that you would be getting off here."

It was that same voice again. I turned to see a portly man rising from his seat and walking to the back set of steps. He stood there until the train came to a full stop and then disappeared into the throng of people at the station. I remained seated, along with the others in the car. With no need to depart, we were reluctant to give up our seats near the stove.

The unloading and reloading of the baggage car began immediately. A lot of items were stacked on the platform, indicating that the five passenger cars used for this morning's trip might be quite full.

Minutes passed as we watched the commotion outside. I continued to scan the body of people, looking for a hint that someone out there was looking for me. I fixed my gaze upon a tall gentleman with deep-set eyes who seemed to be looking intently along the passenger car windows. Our eyes met, but when he saw that I wasn't the person that he was searching for, he looked away.

Three handsomely dressed gentlemen were clustered closely together, pointing in the direction of my car. But again, their interest seemed to wane after a short time.

I thought about leaving the car...Maybe that's what the man from the War Department was expecting me to do. I stood up and started to move, but then I sat back down.

At 8:15 a.m. the skipper cried out the "all aboard" signal, triggering a mad rush to the steps of the five passenger cars. I continued to watch for someone who appeared to be looking for me.

Some modicum of order prevailed, and all of the people boarded the train. I began to think about what I might do when I arrived in Toledo *alone.*

Just then, I was startled by a strong female voice, "Mr. Jason Alexander?"

I turned and looked up at a pretty lady standing in the aisle. "Yes," I replied, wondering who this person could be.

She appeared to be alone. "My name is Anna Ella Carroll, and I'm the person that you're looking for."

I rose quickly and offered my hand. "It's a pleasure to meet you. I thought…"

"Yes, I suppose I know what you *thought,*" she said. "Why don't we walk on back to the *ladies'* car, if you don't mind?" She didn't wait for an answer and headed off in that direction. I followed.

The last two passenger cars on this particular train were reserved for the ladies and their guests. It was slow going as we passed through small clusters of people remaining to be seated. Anna Ella Carroll seemed to be at ease with the crowd as she pressed along at a steady pace. I stayed close behind. She spotted two seats near the rear of the fourth car, and we settled in. I was happy to be away from the tobacco smoke that would already be filling the first car.

"In case you were wondering, I chose the seats away from the stove so we could talk," she said. Her voice was quite pleasant, rather deep for a small woman, and a bit Southern. "I saw you in the car when the train pulled in, and I was hoping that you would stay put. Governor Yates described you to me, and your friend, Mr. Hinrichsen, wired ahead noting that you had boarded the first car."

As I took my first close look at her, I noticed that she was nicely dressed in contemporary fashion with a dark velvet coat edged in white ermine on the collar and the cuffs. When she removed her cloche, I could see the beautiful red hair.

"I didn't intend to imply that I was disappointed that it was you who had come to meet me," I said, hoping that I had not already ruined the relationship.

"It was a natural reaction and fully understandable...You meant no harm, and I accept it as such. I assure you that I can tell the difference between innocence and guilt." Anna Ella Carroll was very direct, and her communication was accompanied with bright, piercing blue-eyed contact.

"I just didn't know that there were any women working at the War Department."

"Well, I do plenty of work for the War Department, but I must say that they're very slow in paying their bills," she laughed. "I suppose they do have a few more pressing items to deal with at the moment."

As the train pulled out of the station, she asked me about myself. I provided a brief summary of my life, all twenty-two years of it, but I had the distinct feeling that she already knew quite a lot about me...certainly more than I knew about her.

CHAPTER THIRTEEN

Toledo, Wabash, and Western Railroad
November 24, 1862
ante meridiem

The T. Mather, an American type 4-4-0, was easily pulling a fuel car, a baggage car, five passenger cars, and a caboose. The engine was named after a Springfield resident, Thomas Mather, who had been instrumental in building this railroad line eastward. A full load of water and wood was taken on in Springfield, so the express train would push hard before its next stop some fifty miles away in Decatur, passing through many small stations that would normally be stops in the slower passenger and freight runs.

"You may address me as Miss Carroll, young Jason, and you will accompany me all the way to Washington." She paused to look at the passing countryside. "I've lived there for eighteen years, but I don't call it home. I was born on a large plantation in Maryland."

The morning sun and the heat from the stove warmed the inside of the car enough for us to remove our coats. The noise level within the car began to rise as many conversations challenged the steady clatter of the moving train.

"When I was fourteen, my father became governor of Maryland, and we moved to the State House in Annapolis, leaving the plantation in the hands of the family members that remained behind." Governor Thomas King Carroll was the son of Charles Carroll, the last man to sign the Declaration of Independence. Miss Carroll had studied law and counseled her father. "We would often meet with Senator Clay and Senator Calhoun, and occasionally with President Jackson. I even started writing small pieces for them, and I discovered that I enjoyed politics.

"Competition from the richer lands of states like Kentucky started to hurt the plantation, and soon the tobacco revenue wasn't even enough to feed our slaves. Ultimately, my father and I sold the plantation and most of the slaves to pay off debts. We freed many of the slaves, but they had no place to go and found it very difficult to make a living."

The Carroll family had moved fifty miles away to an old brick manor on the Choptank River. "My mother and sisters tried to maintain our former lifestyle there, putting further strain upon my father." She paused to dab a tear from her eye. "He never *truly* recovered from the loss of the plantation."

Her comment made me think about my father and how devastating it would be for him to lose the ranch. I couldn't imagine what we would do.

"I didn't join the family in the river home. Instead, I moved to Baltimore...That was early in eighteen-forty, a convention year. I was actively involved with the Whig Party, making many contacts that led to writing opportunities."

In preparation for the convention in 1844, Anna Carroll, Henry Clay, and an active organizer from Springfield by the name of Abraham Lincoln were the principle writers in support of Whig politics. "We avidly read the others' writings," she said.

After Henry Clay lost the election, Miss Carroll had followed one of her best clients to Washington when R.J. Walker, president of the Atlantic and Western Railroad, was appointed to the post of secretary of the treasury by President Polk. Walker, a Democrat, paid Miss Carroll to write a number of documents supporting the rapid expansion of the railroad and telegraph systems, a position which President Polk also strongly supported.

Miss Carroll and her lifelong companion and former slave, Leah, moved into a boarding house at 347 Pennsylvania Avenue. Anna Ella Carroll was quickly included in the Washington social circles of Senator Thomas Corwin's Ohioans and Senator Clay's Kentuckians. She was also included in the Maryland and Virginia social circles because of her family connection with the Carrolls and the Kings, her grandmother's family.

"I worked within and outside of these circles to garner support for both a northern and a southern route for westward expansion of the railroad and the telegraph," she said. "I met your father and Jacob Strawn in Council Bluffs, Iowa, when I was there for a series of meetings a few years ago. The Treasury Department was looking at this site as the starting point for the northern route across the Platte River Valley of Nebraska. Your father and Jacob Strawn wanted to ensure that this location would be connected to Keokuk, a point to which the Toledo, Wabash, and Western Railroad would be extended."

"I remember when they made that trip," I said. "They were excited about the possibility of shipping cattle to the West, but both of them doubted that the market would amount to much by comparison to the East."

"The successes of people like your father and Jacob Strawn have helped many understand the value that the railroads bring to this country," she said. "I have traveled most of the routes, both north and south, along the entire area just east of the Mississippi River, looking at ways to improve the connections to increase commerce. After the war started, it became obvious to me that the control of the railroads and the rivers was the key to winning the war in the Western Theater."

"Are you writing about that now, Miss Carroll?" I asked.

"Yes, but it's hard to get much attention about the Western Theater when most of the concern back east is much closer to home. You'll see what I'm talking about when you start working out there."

Her comment brought me back in touch with reality—I *was* on my way to work out there. I was setting out upon a journey that would take me far away from home, and now listening to Miss Carroll talk about the war, I realized that I would soon be a part of it, even if only shuffling papers in the War Department.

CHAPTER FOURTEEN

Solano, Illinois
November 24, 1862
ante meridiem

A common interest in railroads fueled the conversation that Anna Ella Carroll and I carried on as we proceeded eastward on the Number 3 Express. She promised to introduce me to Herman Haupt, who President Lincoln had appointed as chief of construction and transportation in the Department of the Rappahannock. As Professor of Mathematics and Engineering at the Pennsylvania College in Gettysburg, he'd authored a book titled *The General Theory of Bridge Construction*, which I had studied at Illinois College. I assured her that I would not forget her promise.

Miss Carroll enjoyed a bit of history that I had learned from Professor Crampton regarding the origin of the U.S. standard railroad gauge. "The English brought that standard with them when they built the first railroads in this country," I said. "They used the same jigs and tools that they used for building wagons of the same wheel spacing.

"The wheel spacing was that which was required for the wagons to fit in the ruts in the old long-distance roads of England—any other wheel spacing would result in broken wheels. The original ruts had been created throughout Europe and England by the chariots of imperial Rome, the wheel spacing being that which exactly accommodated the width of the rear ends of two warhorses, a spacing of four feet, eight and a half inches."

I was just finishing this account when the train began to slow for a stop in Tolono, a station which included a short spur coming up from Alton. I'd heard the footsteps of the brakeman atop our car moments before, and I knew the stop was approaching. Some trains have the good fortune of having a brakeman dedicated to each car, but apparently this one did not—a situation which requires a brakeman to run from car to car, applying the brakes in a serial rather than parallel fashion.

"Each brakeman can cover two to three cars at the most," I explained. "It's a tough job with a very high fatality rate."

The train came to a stop in front of the station, where a number of people were crowded together. Just like in Alexander, the people gathered at the train station for the scheduled arrivals during the day; some were there for business purposes, but others were just onlookers seeking to take a break from the mundane daily routine. In addition to the TW&W Railroad, the Illinois Central Railroad also ran through Tolono, affording the townspeople the opportunity to check out a lot of activity from many different directions.

Miss Carroll and I decided to take advantage of the twenty-minute stop and disembark. Some of the other passengers had the same idea. I grabbed my book and followed behind Miss Carroll as we slowly moved to the front of the car.

It was just as she began her descent when the sun's brilliance reflected on the blade of the dagger, catching my eyes. I suppose that it was natural instinct that took control at that point, as the next few moments passed in an instant.

"No!" I shouted, and with all the force that I could muster, I pitched the *Maxims of War* at the expressionless face of the dark-eyed assailant.

He turned slightly in my direction when he heard my voice, and he raised his left hand—the hand that held the dagger—in an attempt to deflect the blow. Now visible to others, the raised dagger elicited excited shouts and screams from some of those nearby.

I quickly pulled Miss Carroll back up into the passenger car, just out of harm's way, as the slim, bearded attacker belatedly thrust the dagger directly at her. While others stood by frozen with fear, one nearby traveler managed to strike the man across the back with a heavy suitcase, sending him headlong into the crowd. The people scattered, and the attacker landed face down on the ground.

Immediately, a heavy boot came down hard upon the assailant's hand, still clutching the dagger, and several others knelt upon his back, rendering him immobile. Tolono's justice of the peace, Abner Richmond, easily pulled the dagger from the hand that now rather limply extended from the fast-swelling wrist firmly pressed to the ground.

The husky Mr. Richmond lifted his boot, stood the attacker up, and asked if anyone in the crowd recognized him. No one did. He then roughly hustled the man off to the local jail, appearing to lift his feet entirely off the ground at points along the way as he tugged at the back of his jacket collar.

"Are you all right?" Incredibly, Miss Carroll appeared to be unharmed.

"Fine," she said.

After a few minutes, we disembarked as originally intended. After a while, Justice Richmond returned to ask a few questions.

Somehow, he had discovered Miss Carroll's association with the War Department, and he suggested that she inform them of the incident. She had already done so with a telegraph message a few minutes earlier.

"You shouldn't be traveling without an armed guard."

"Thank you, Justice Richmond, but I feel quite safe traveling with Mr. Alexander," she said, patting my arm.

"His quick action probably saved your life, Miss Carroll.

"Here, take this little two-shot derringer that I found on him," he said, handing it to me. "You can send it back to me when you arrive in Washington, and if I find out anything about this character, I'll forward that on."

Miss Carroll was anxious to get moving before any reply was received from Washington that might suggest that we remain behind until someone met us here to provide additional protection. We said good-bye and returned to our still-vacant seats in the fourth car. Moments later, we were underway.

We sat together in silence.

Who would want to kill Anna Ella Carroll?

I realized that this woman must be someone who was *very* involved in the inner workings of Washington, and I expected that there was more to learn about her. I was sure that I would soon find out how much more.

CHAPTER FIFTEEN

Fort Wayne, Indiana
November 24, 1862
post meridiem

After departing Tolono about an hour behind schedule, we gained back a few minutes here and there to the point where we were almost back on schedule a few hours later. Additional passengers boarded at Danville, Lafayette, Logansport, and Peru, and our car was now quite full.

I continued to learn more about Miss Carroll. Perhaps she was feeling that she owed me some degree of explanation following the incident in Tolono. I discovered that it was not at all unlikely that she would have some enemies resulting from her writings.

She had authored a book titled *The Great American Battle* in 1855. "I sold ten thousand copies," she said. As soon as she mentioned this, I recalled that we had discussed the book at Illinois College, and now I knew the author, A. E. Carroll. The book had created quite a stir because she strongly warned against foreign influence in American politics. Her many examples of corruption included the defeat of Clay by Polk as a result of immigrant votes bought by Buchanan.

"Both England and France sought to divide our country between the North and the South, hoping to create this civil war," she said. "These countries clearly recognized that a divided United States was a much weaker nation, and much more likely to fall back into their hands. I emphasized over and over again that the union of the country must not be broken.

"But the South cleverly played upon the emotions of the Northern abolitionists and brought us into war. It was so frustrating for me—I could see it coming, but I couldn't do anything to stop it."

It was difficult for her to go on, so she changed the subject. "I pressed hard for the continuation of the railroads to the West…I saw this as a power supplementary to sea power that could cut the clutch of European imperialism on the New World. A railway to the coast would save two weeks over the Panama route that's currently used to bring gold from California, a route which passes over foreign seas through foreign territory.

"I pleaded for the construction of sturdy bridges across the waterways," she said. "This angered the wealthy steamboat companies…They complained about the dangers that these structures brought to the navigation along the rivers. As fate would have it, in the fall of 1857, I did have to testify for the defense when the steamboat *Effie Afton* collided with the piers of a bridge constructed across the Mississippi River by the Rock Island Railroad. Abraham Lincoln was the counsel for the railroad. Of course, I never imagined that he would be able to carry his courtroom antics all the way to the Executive Mansion."

I remembered some of the newspaper accounts of this case because my father had been very interested in the outcome. "It wasn't long afterwards that I was working behind the scenes at the convention in Chicago to get Abraham Lincoln nominated," she said. She continued to fight with him against secession, accusing her many Southern friends of treason as they belabored the decision. "I used all of my Carroll family connections to keep the state of Maryland in the Union."

Both her political prowess and her writings continued to impress President Lincoln. Her *Response to Breckinridge*, a point-by-point countermand to the firebrand speech of the Honorable John C. Breckinridge in the U.S. Senate, was one of the president's favorites.

"I defended the president's right to suspend the writ of habeas corpus, allowing him to make searches and arrests without warrants as deemed necessary to protect the interests of the citizens of United States of America, a right which Senator Breckinridge claimed did not exist under the Constitution."

By the time we stopped at the Baker Street station in Fort Wayne, Indiana, I was thinking that Justice Richmond should have given me some extra ammunition to go along with this derringer. The station was brand new and very large for a city of fifteen thousand people.

The station agent handed Miss Carroll a telegram from the War Department, suggesting that we spend the night in Fort Wayne and proceed directly eastward from here on the following day. She responded with a telegram indicating that she desired to continue the trip as scheduled, taking a more circuitous route that included both Toledo and Cleveland.

"We will spend the night in Toledo and then travel to Cleveland by boat," she said. "I have some dear friends that I want to see in Cleveland. We will spend some time there before we go on. I refuse to let this attacker change my plans."

I nodded enthusiastically. Toledo, a city of about eighteen thousand people, was the end of the line for the Toledo, Wabash, and Western Railroad, and I wanted to ride it all the way to its last point. The boat trip to Cleveland also sounded interesting, and I wasn't ready to argue with Miss Carroll.

CHAPTER SIXTEEN

Cleveland, Ohio
November 25, 1862
post meridiem

The sun was shining brightly as the *Santa Maria* paddled across Lake Erie, churning the blue waters into a milky froth in its wake. My restless night in Toledo's Lake Erie Hotel made it difficult to tolerate the rowdy passengers. When two inebriated men who were engaged in a loud argument lost their hats to a gust of wind, Miss Carroll and I joined many of the cheering onlookers watching the hats slowly sink into the lake.

We stepped off of the gangway, onto Cleveland's Edgewater Pier, just before 4:00 p.m. and rode a carriage to a large brick house at 817 Buckeye Road. We were immediately greeted by two well-dressed men and several Negro servants. After Judge Lemuel D. Evans paid the carriage driver, we followed the rotund and graying Ohio Congressman Elisha Whittlesey into the spacious home.

Once inside, our bags were promptly delivered to the upstairs guest rooms. "The other members of the Whittlesey family are away visiting relatives in Pennsylvania," the congressman said.

Even so, it wasn't long before I felt that I knew them quite well, as their pictures adorned every wall in the home.

Both men were quite friendly and seemed genuinely happy to see us. I particularly liked Judge Evans, who described himself as a Tennessean who had served as a congressman from Texas, until its secession. I learned that he now reported directly to President Lincoln regarding dual matters of the conditions and military preparations of the South.

"There are many of us that are very happy that you traveled along with Anna," Judge Evans said. "Our country needs her to return to Washington safely. You'll soon learn more about the role that she plays there."

"I just did what anyone else in that situation would have done," I said.

"Not so, Jason, not so at all," he said. "Most people wouldn't have done a thing, and the attack would have taken place, and likely succeeded. You've demonstrated the ability to think and act quickly—qualities that will serve you well in the War Department. I expect that Secretary Stanton may expand his plans for you."

"Let's leave that to Edwin, Lem," Miss Carroll said.

We had a chance to relax a bit and freshen up before supper. My room was on the second floor overlooking a nicely manicured garden that had succumbed to the ravages of the fall weather. I felt comfortable here, and the bed invited a quick nap.

⌘ ⌘ ⌘

Shortly before sitting down to eat, we were joined by two men from Cleveland. Amasa Stone was a director and major shareholder in the Western Union Telegraph Company, and his former general superintendent, Anson Stager, had been commissioned a colonel earlier in the year and was now assistant quartermaster and superintendent of all telegraph lines and associated offices in the United States.

Miss Carroll was purposely checking out my reaction after meeting these two men. "If Washington ever falls, we'll be setting up shop here in Cleveland," she said.

Supper was excellent. Stuffed duck, corn, potatoes, and spinach topped off with rhubarb pie. The conversation was guarded to begin with, just catching up on the general news. Congressman Whittlesey asked about my studies at Illinois College and the state of affairs at the ranch. As the evening wore on and more wine was poured, I soaked up additional bits and pieces of information.

Former Congressman Whittlesey was now serving his second tour as comptroller of the treasury. He did not appear to be in the best of health, as he moved very slowly, and his breathing was labored. His past experience as a brigade major in the Army of the Northwest during the War of 1812 came out clearly as the topic of discussion moved to the specifics of the current war.

"Anna, I truly believe that your Tennessee Plan will work," he said.

"That goes for me as well," Judge Evans said. "I'll be heading to Alton on Saturday to meet with General Grant...I know you just came from there, Anna...Did things go well?"

"We will check details and update maps shortly," Miss Carroll said.

"Indeed, we will," Colonel Stager said, "but before we do that, let's have a toast to Benjamin F. Wade, the esteemed senator from Ohio who put Edwin Stanton in Washington." The glasses were emptied and promptly refilled.

This time it was Amasa Stone. "Let's not forget Edwin Stanton himself, a genuine secretary of war."

They discussed Stanton's recent efforts to stop the proliferation of sensitive information in the newspapers of the Union states. "It's so bad that Stanton claims there's no need for the Confederacy to deploy spies since they have all of the information they need to know made readily available to them in the daily newspapers," Congressman Whittlesey said.

"Things are much better now that he requires that *all* telegrams from the field come directly to the War Department, and from there the information is disseminated as *he* sees fit," Colonel Stager said.

After the toasts were completed, the four men and Miss Carroll excused themselves and went off to the study to discuss matters in private. I was happy to head off to bed. I suspected that they would be working well into the early hours of the morning.

CHAPTER SEVENTEEN

Cleveland, Ohio
November 26, 1862
post meridiem

We had a late breakfast on Wednesday morning, and then Congressman Whittlesey, Miss Carroll, and I went for a ride in the congressman's carriage. Cleveland was a growing city with a population of almost seventy thousand people, and there was plenty of evidence of active commercial enterprises. Congressman Whittlesey pointed out many new factories that had been recently constructed to support the war effort; railroad cars, guns, blankets, shoes, and saddles were just some of the products belching from the plants in Cleveland.

But Congressman Whittlesey also wanted to show Miss Carroll the growing number of tent communities that had appeared in Cleveland as a result of the Underground Railroad movement of former slaves to the North.

I'd heard about the problems of this nature in Washington, but I didn't realize that the crisis had moved to other major cities as well. I knew that the Underground Railroad moved through

Jacksonville, but the Negroes always moved further northward, choosing not to settle in Jacksonville or the surrounding area; however, President Sturtevant had recently told us about a settlement of former slaves in an area west of Jacksonville, which they were calling Philadelphia.

"It seems that the numbers are growing more rapidly now that President Lincoln has announced that he will move forward with the Emancipation Proclamation," Congressman Whittlesey said. "If only he'd followed through with us on your idea to purchase the Chiriqui tract in Panama. The massive coal deposits would have provided worthwhile employment for many of these freed slaves and avoided this calamity that is falling upon our cities of the North."

Miss Carroll pressed her lips together, and then said, "I was sure the president was convinced that this was a viable solution to the problem, but his attention was turned elsewhere at just the wrong moment. I fear that this problem will be here one hundred years from now as a result of our inaction."

"It was all so perfect—we even had many of the railroads and our navy pledging to buy the coal from Chiriqui," Congressman Whittlesey said. "Do you think we have a chance to make another run at this with the president, Anna?"

"I'm certainly willing to try, but I'm afraid that there are just too many hotter irons burning in the fire at the moment. You know how it is in Washington—the constant give-and-take, one agenda item traded for another. Even the Tennessee Plan must compete with the demands of the defense of Washington."

Congressman Whittlesey puffed slowly on his cigar. "It's much too late in the year for General Lee to undertake an attack on Washington now. I expect that he'll wait and make his move in the spring. That gives us plenty of time to build up the defenses there. And thanks to the likes of your father, Jason, we'll have plenty of food for those soldiers."

"A harsh winter or a rampant disease can have an impact, but we've been fortunate over the last few winters to have avoided both," I said. "The feed lots have lessened the blow of the harsh winter, but cattle will die of thirst even when surrounded by snow. Disease is the greatest concern. A whole herd can go down in a matter of days."

The congressman seemed to be deep in thought. "I remember reading something about one of your professors at Illinois College doing research about the relationship between the diseases of cattle and humans. One of your representatives was trying to get some funding for the continuation of the studies...I think the matter was tabled."

"Yes, that's Professor Jonathan Turner. All of the students end up working with him from time to time during the course of their studies. He visits many of the ranches in the area, acting as the local cattle doctor. I know that one of the things he's trying to do is to convince the ranchers not to eat the meat of the downers... the sick cows."

"Now that will take some doing, young man. I've seen some of those downer cows in the stockyards in Washington, and I know that they're being eaten," he said.

I was sure that this was true, just as it was true that most of the ranchers had continued to eat the meat as well. "A recent visitor to our ranch told us that some ranchers were discouraging support for Professor Turner's work because they feared that they may eventually be unable to sell the meat from the sick cows," I said.

Later, we had another fine meal with the congressman. I discovered that he would be traveling with us tomorrow on the train to Pittsburgh, and he convinced Miss Carroll that we should join him and his family for Thanksgiving dinner there. We retired a couple of hours after supper in anticipation of an early departure in the morning.

CHAPTER EIGHTEEN

Tolono, Illinois
November 26, 1862
post meridiem

Dark Eyes buried the anger that burned within him. He'd made the foolish mistakes of an amateur, thinking that the assignment was too easy for him. He'd picked the wrong location, and perhaps even the wrong weapon, although the dagger was still his weapon of choice.

He had planned to make the kill in Toledo, but the immediacy of the opportunity in Tolono had lured him into the act. It would have been quick and clean had it not been for that damnable Yankee abolitionist who was traveling with her.

Dark Eyes was concerned that his poor performance on this quest would diminish the newly formed connection of which he was a part. He didn't wish to embarrass his close circle of companions who had pushed so hard for the expansion of their involvement in the terrible conflict.

There would be time to settle this matter in the days ahead, but now he must deal with the immediate matter at hand, *and deal with it he would.*

His wrist was better than he had let on, only feigning that it was immobile, and he'd been the model prisoner for Justice Abner Richmond. Dark Eyes had given the justice a false name and claimed that his intent had merely been to rob the lady because she looked like she was wealthy and appeared to be traveling alone. *"I simply intended to lead her away from the crowd at knifepoint and take her valuables,"* he'd said. *"I've never done anything like this before, and I certainly wouldn't've hurt her."*

Justice Richmond hadn't readily bought the story. He'd wired a description of his prisoner to Springfield and was awaiting instructions. He had received word that the governor himself had been notified of the attack on Miss Carroll. The derringer taken from the attacker had been made by Frank Bitterlich of Nashville, Tennessee, and Justice Richmond knew that most of his weapons were being sold to those who sympathized with the South.

Even so, the man had been apprehended so easily, and, as a prisoner, he'd behaved so well that it was hard to believe that he could be a killer.

Dark Eyes suspected that they would move him to a place of greater confinement before very much longer, so he'd decided to make his move just after midnight.

He had befriended the young night deputy named Ben. Each night, Ben let down his guard a little more, believing that his prisoner had simply made a foolish mistake attempting his first robbery, and he had repented soon thereafter.

The justice would leave for supper at dusk, shortly after Ben arrived. He would return again briefly between 9:30 and 10:00 p.m. to check on things before heading back home and, presumably, retiring for the night. It was Wednesday, and the entire town would be fast asleep by midnight. Dark Eyes had closely observed it all.

The ham and beans and cornbread brought over to the jail from the local hotel's kitchen was as tasty as he'd ever eaten, but Dark Eyes managed to be sure that he was not finished when the kitchen helper returned to pick up the remains. Ben sent her away, indicating that the items could be retrieved in the morning, when breakfast arrived.

Dark Eyes made sure that he was standing at the front of the cell near the bars when Justice Richmond stopped in for his last visit, masking the fact that his supper items still remained with him in the cell.

After he left, Dark Eyes spoke to Ben. "Are you ready for some checkers tonight?" He'd let the young man win all of the previous games, praising his skills.

"I thought you'd've had your fill of me by now, Clifford."

Clifford Bates was dead and buried in Cincinnati, so it had seemed like a good name for Dark Eyes to use when questioned by Justice Richmond earlier.

"Not a chance, I feel lucky tonight."

"I'm afraid that you'll need more than luck to beat me," Ben said, smiling as he moved the small table over to the front of the cell. He didn't carry the keys to the cells with him. They remained on the peg next to the gun rack behind Justice Richmond's desk.

The night wore on slowly as Dark Eyes indulged Ben in game after game. Finally, shortly after midnight, Dark Eyes pushed back his chair, stood up and stretched. "I think I'll call it a night."

While Ben moved his chair and the table back into place, Dark Eyes shifted the supper tray from his cot to the chair, moved the chair near the door, and quickly turned in.

Ben busied himself in tidying up the place as he was accustomed to doing before settling in for his series of catnaps that would carry him through the quiet hours of the early morning. He noticed that Clifford had not pushed the chair containing the utensils from his supper close enough to the front of the cell for him to reach them. He could wait until breakfast arrived later in the morning…but it would just take a moment to retrieve them from the cell right now without waking Clifford.

He turned the key in the lock and quietly opened the cell door. Ben was completely unprepared for what happened next when Dark Eyes leaped from the cot and slammed his tightly closed fist into the side of Ben's head. The unnecessary second blow followed immediately.

That's for thinking that you could actually beat me at checkers or, for that matter, anything at all, you stupid Yankee.

Dark Eyes moved quickly—he'd played each step through in his mind so many times. He'd leave a message so they'd know they hadn't captured a fool, and that the war had reached Tolono.

CHAPTER NINETEEN

Pittsburgh, Pennsylvania
November 27, 1862
post meridiem

The news reached us as we sat out on the veranda overlooking the Monongahela River following a wonderful supper at the home of Congressman Whittlesey. Everything had gone so well up until then. The train had arrived on time, a carriage was waiting for us at the station, and the weather was perfect.

Word of Clifford Bates's escape was bad enough, but the hanging of the jailer was tragic. Justice Richmond's telegram indicated that he had been wrapped in our flag—an apparent warning, left for us to contemplate.

The joyous mood of the day had been broken.

The congressman was visibly disturbed by the news. He sent word of the incident in a message to Secretary Stanton, suggesting that an armed guard accompany Miss Carroll for the remainder of her journey back to Washington.

"What do you think we should do?" she said to me.

"Bates and his friends, whoever they are, will expect that you'll be heavily guarded from here on out, so I don't think they'll make another attempt on your life right away."

"My thoughts exactly." She looked me in the eye. "We will proceed as planned and depart on tomorrow's train to Harrisburg.

Congressman Whittlesey strongly objected. "We have no idea what this madman may do now. His attempt on your life was somehow connected to the rebellion."

"Perhaps he simply didn't like my choice of dress in Tolono."

"Anna, please don't make light of the matter," he said. "You are a guest in my home, and I have a responsibility to the secretary and the president to see that you return to Washington safely."

"I understand that, Elisha." She paused, and softened her tone of voice. "But I already have an armed guard in Mr. Alexander, one who has already proven himself up to the task. I prefer a single, unobtrusive escort—I will not be herded around with a group of soldiers. How can they fight the Rebels when they're busy guarding me?"

At some point, he realized that he couldn't change her mind about it. He compromised, insisting that I carry some additional armament. He gave me a .31-caliber Colt Model of 1849, which he referred to as the Pocket Model.

I looked it over carefully. I liked the feel of it in my hand. It was compact and perfectly balanced, and the cast iron was nicely blued. When I noticed that *E. Whittlesey* was engraved on the butt, I tried to return what he had obviously received as a prized gift. He would have nothing of it and included a nicely made leather shoulder holster with adjustable straps and a box of ammunition.

And so it was settled. We'd move on the next day—just the two of us. Then we made the best of what we could with the remainder of the day.

I could see how the war would impact even the most innocent of lives…I expected that *all* wars did as much.

Who would remember the poor jailer in Tolono?

I would.

CHAPTER TWENTY

Harrisburg, Pennsylvania
November 28, 1862
post meridiem

We arrived in Harrisburg at 11:05 p.m. after departing about ten hours earlier from Pittsburgh. The Pennsylvania Central Railroad stayed right on schedule all day long, even though the train was almost fully loaded and the stations along the way were quite busy.

It was apparent to me that as we proceeded eastward, the impact of the war increasingly permeated the daily routines of the general populace. I saw more men in blue and more interest in the accounts of the war as depicted in the many written circulars freely passed about after the initial purchase was made.

I was still adjusting to the Pocket Colt, now attached firmly to my chest under my loosely fitting woolen coat. There was no question that it did provide me with much more power to protect Miss Carroll, and I was perfectly willing to use it, but hoping that it wouldn't be necessary.

We had started the day consuming a sumptuous breakfast with the Whittleseys. The congressman had given up on the idea of changing Miss Carroll's mind about the trip, so the conversation at the table fell onto other topics.

"President Lincoln was as patient as any man could be," Miss Carroll said. "It was almost as if General McClellan was trying to force his hand."

"Miss Carroll, do you know much about General Burnside?" I said.

"He's a man of action...and a strong supporter of my friend Herman Haupt. General Burnside already issued an order on November tenth requiring all of the commanding officers in the field to detail sufficient numbers of men to promptly load and unload the railroad cars—before this, the cars would sometimes sit for days, and the food would spoil. He also made it clear that the field officers cannot interfere with the civilian superintendents of the railroads."

"I read the newspaper accounts back in May when *Brigadier General* Haupt received his appointment," I said. "I remember that he established the O and A Railroad and its offshoots as the major supply arteries for the Army of the Potomac."

"Yes, he quickly moved to reinforce existing bridges and build new ones as needed, and he established a reliable timetable," Miss Carroll said. "He has strong support from both the general-in-chief of the Federal Armies, General Halleck, and the quartermaster of the Army of the Potomac, General Ingalls—and let's not forget that the sitting commander in chief is a former railroad lawyer."

"I recall that Congressman Whittlesey was worried about the practice of using some of General Heintzelman's forces for the defense of Washington to guard the railways," I said. "He was afraid of an attack from Stuart's cavalry as evidenced by his earlier ability to completely ride around McClellan's army."

"Now what would General Stuart do with Washington if he was foolish enough to capture it?" She tilted her head slightly forward and raised her eyebrows in such a way as to convince me that there wasn't an answer to this question.

I was still thinking about this discussion when we arrived at the Harris Hotel on Front Street. The two-story brick structure was very much alive with activity, even this late at night.

A large number of people were clustered around someone, or something, in the lobby, enticing both of us to go and take a look. We found a small, slender, sickly-looking man dressed in Union blues sitting in a chair and hanging on to a long Sharps rifle. We soon learned that the man was "California Joe" of the U.S. Sharpshooters unit. He'd just been discharged because of an injury and failing eyesight.

"I'm returning to the West Coast," he said.

Someone nearby commented, "This man's the most decorated of sharpshooters...said to have shot a man out of a tree at two miles off."

Truman Head did not like all of the attention, but he was not able to shake the crowd. I looked at this man whose eyes told of many things that he wished to forget...things he knew he'd never forget.

As we walked away, Miss Carroll said, "This is what the soldiers have to look forward to, if they are fortunate enough to make it back."

"Wonderful," I said.

CHAPTER TWENTY-ONE

Baltimore, Maryland
November 29, 1862
post meridiem

Congressman Whittlesey had tried very hard to convince Miss Carroll to forgo the stopover in Harrisburg so that we might travel through Baltimore at night. She scoffed at the thought. "Maryland is my home. Baltimore was a part of my childhood—I won't skulk through the city like some thief in the night."

The station agent handed a telegram to Miss Carroll moments before the scheduled departure from Harrisburg. After reading it, she smiled and quickly tucked it away without saying a word. We departed on time at 11:58 a.m.

The trip to Baltimore on the North Central Railroad was much like the other train rides that I had taken over the last few days. The novelty had worn off for me now, and I was getting anxious to get to my new job. Or maybe it was because I had to pay more attention to what was going on *inside* the car than what was happening outside. The weight of the Pocket Colt was a constant reminder of my duty to protect Miss Carroll.

If Miss Carroll was afraid, it didn't show. I admired her ability to live her life, even in the face of evil. She was an interesting lady, and I felt like I had known her much longer than just a few days.

She continued to brief me on the recent developments in Washington. "Both sides are positioning for the spring. I venture to say that the history books will identify 1863 as *the* pivotal point of this war.

"Burnside is an improvement over McClellan, but Grant is the most competent of the Union generals. He spends more time fighting than strategizing. Strategy is set in Washington; tactics are the stuff of the battlefield."

We arrived at the Howard Street station in Baltimore at 6:25 p.m. Many soldiers were present in and around the train station—there were so many that I was quite confident that Miss Carroll would be safe here.

A conversation with the station agent resulted in another telegram for Miss Carroll. This time she responded with a reply. While she was taking care of this, I enjoyed the smell of the ocean that was in the cool night air. It made me hungry.

I purchased some biscuits that were being sold in the train station and loaded our bags in an awaiting carriage. I watched our surroundings carefully as we took the short ride over to the Camden station on the B&O Railroad, munching biscuits along the way.

"I met Henry Clay here in eighteen-forty," she said. "...He would have made a great president...Abraham Lincoln is cut of the same cloth...country before self-interests."

"It's too bad that Jefferson Davis didn't feel the same way," I said.

"Jefferson Davis gave up on the Union long before the war began. As secretary of war, he surreptitiously moved arms to the

Southern forts in anticipation of the rebellion. He tried everything he could to take Maryland with him, but my father and I prevailed."

"What would have happened to Washington if he'd been successful here?" I said.

"Washington would have fallen," she said. "There's no doubt about that, Jason."

I weighed her words for some time as we continued our ride to the Camden station. Miss Carroll was quiet now. Perhaps it was all of the clusters of Union blue that dampened her spirit a bit. "I feel like a stranger in my own home," she said.

"When General Lee's army entered Maryland in early September, he received much support from the local people. Many thought that he could've easily taken Baltimore, but his objective was Harrisburg. Fortunately, he was turned back by McClellan.

"President Lincoln seized the opportunity to proclaim the emancipation of the slaves in the Rebel states, and I headed west to tend to matters of the War Department. One of the things that I was asked to do was to find someone like you to help us out."

Miss Carroll was pensive. "A civil war strikes at the very fabric of a nation. It buries the beauty of a city like Baltimore below the ugliness of hatred that can only be washed away with years of time." Miss Carroll looked for, but could not find, the place that she knew because it was no longer there—Baltimore, like many other places in the country, was very different now.

CHAPTER TWENTY-TWO

Washington, District of Columbia
November 29, 1862
post meridiem

We arrived in Washington at the B&O station on New Jersey Avenue at 9:05 p.m. The first thing that I noticed as we stepped from the train was the smell. It was the smell of life packed much too closely together. People and animals, food and waste, dirt and smoke.

It was apparent that there was *some* order to the chaos as we managed to get our bags and find a carriage sent by the War Department.

As we worked our way through the streets of Washington, I noticed that many of the clear spaces between buildings were filled with tents. There were also a good number of people camping out in the open areas. It looked like they were bracing their structures for the oncoming winter.

Miss Carroll had informed me earlier that she would secure a place for me at the boarding house where she stayed as soon as one became available. In the meantime, I would stay at the Willard

Hotel on the corner of Fourteenth Street and Pennsylvania Avenue, near the Treasury Department.

The carriage driver took Miss Carroll to the Ebbitt House on D Street. She paused as he took her bags inside. "I'll be quite safe now, Jason. Thank you for saving my life in Tolono...You turned out to be quite a good traveling partner. Don't forget your invitation to supper here tomorrow night...good-bye."

"Good-bye, Miss Carroll," I said.

My first look at the Willard stopped me in my tracks. It looked like a group of six large buildings that had been pushed together—an oddly shaped beehive, full of life on a Saturday night.

I thanked the carriage driver, who refused to accept any pay, and entered at the ground floor, which was filled with small shops selling all sorts of things. I worked my way through a shoulder-to-shoulder crowd of loud men to reach the front desk.

The desk clerk confirmed my reservation, secured by the War Department, and gave me a key. "You'll be sharing the room with a gentleman by the name of Weathers, who's out of town at the moment." This was just fine with me.

I found Room B24 without much trouble, and after settling in a bit, I realized how hungry I was. I decided to seek out the dining room. I'd lost a few pounds traveling with Miss Carroll, who never seemed to eat much of anything. Her clothes were worn so tight that they seemed almost painful.

I smelled my way to the dining room, an immense place with tables of all sizes, most of which were occupied with seemingly happy men and women. After a few moments of scanning the room for an empty seat, I saw a man waving at me and pointing to an empty seat at his table.

Recognizing that eating alone was probably not an option, I joined him at his table. "Thank you, I was beginning to wonder if I would ever find a seat," I said.

"On Saturday night, sometimes you'll have a long wait. My name is Adams, Charles B. Adams, but my friends call me Charlie...and you are...?"

"Jason Alexander," I said shaking his smooth but firm hand. He was well dressed and looked to be in his middle thirties; his round face and friendly eyes were welcoming.

"I was seated only a few minutes before you arrived, and I haven't ordered as yet," he said. The rectangular table for six included two couples who were satisfied to remain isolated from our conversation. We took the hint and paid little attention to them.

We ordered steaks and beer. Charlie seemed to be looking me over very carefully, while I was paying more attention to what was going on around me—a habit.

"You're new in town," he said.

"Yes, but this is a big city. How would you know that?"

"Big in some ways, not so big in others. I'm a salesman. I know names, and I know faces. In Washington they even change sometimes."

"The names?" I said.

"The names *and* the faces," he chuckled, then became more serious. "You'll want to be careful here, Jason Alexander."

The beers arrived, and we toasted our mutual good health. The beer was good, and I guessed that the steaks would be as well.

"If I may ask, what is your line of work, Mr. Adams?"

"Charlie, please call me Charlie." He smacked his lips together, leaned his large frame back in the chair, and grabbed the lapels of his coat. "Actually, I work for several companies, small companies. The big companies can afford to have their own person here making sales for them, but the small companies cannot, so I represent a number of them. I sell about anything that's not alive—mostly to the government, but some to sutlers and general stores. How about you?"

"I'm here to get work. I'll know more about it next week," I said.

He looked at me and smiled. "Well, whoever your prospective employer may be, they chose wisely. This is a place in great want for tight lips. Why, I can find out about anything I'd want to know by spending an evening in the bar right here at Willard's."

I believed him. I wasn't at all impressed with what I'd seen of Washington thus far. I knew better than to pass judgment too quickly, but the sense of urgency that I expected to see in the nation's capital, facing a rebellion, wasn't here. I did like Charlie, and I appreciated his respect for my privacy.

"Have you been here long, Charlie?"

"I arrived here from Maine about the same time that President Lincoln arrived from out west. In fact, I was staying here at the Willard when he stayed here before moving into the Executive Mansion—what a time that was! Henry and Joseph Willard were really hopping. I heard that they even sent him a bill for the ten days that he stayed here. Can you imagine that? I guess it just goes to prove that *nothing* is free here in Washington."

We were laughing when the steaks and baked potatoes were served. We had a second beer and blueberry pie, but I passed on the coffee.

Charlie wrote down his boarding house address for me and suggested that I find such a place if I planned to be here long. I told him that I would, and we parted. I was ready to get some rest.

CHAPTER TWENTY-THREE

Washington, District of Columbia
November 30, 1862
ante meridiem

I had a fitful night of sleep at the Willard. Many of the residents seemed to enjoy the practice of drinking themselves to sleep, and they liked to make a lot of noise while doing it.

Breakfast was good, and I had my own table. The hotel's desk clerk was able to direct me to the nearest Congregational church, which wasn't far away. After the service, I was asked to join the flock for a picnic lunch on the church lawn. The people were friendly, but I felt like a stranger.

The afternoon went quickly as I walked around and explored Washington. I located the building that housed the War Department so I would know where to go tomorrow. It wasn't a particularly impressive structure by comparison to some of the other buildings that I'd seen, but it had a presence about it.

The four-story building was located on Pennsylvania Avenue, at the corner of Seventeenth Street, and according to the cornerstone, it was constructed in 1820. I was surprised that it was so lightly guarded. Only four soldiers paced around it.

Six large white twenty-foot columns fronted the building on Pennsylvania Avenue; they supported a terraced overhang that provided ample cover for the main entryway and part of the white-washed brick structure. Peculiarly, just to the left of the first pillar, I could see a Maltese cross centered between two of the second-floor windows.

A nicely kept lawn separated the War Department and the Executive Mansion, which appeared to be a bit more heavily guarded. From conversation that I overheard last night at the Willard Hotel, I knew that President Lincoln was out of town meeting with General Burnside.

I searched out the stockyards by first following the smell, and then sounds of the cattle and horses. Walking along F Street, I found them penned in an area that was not far from the railroad station. There were thousands of cattle and hundreds of horses contained in a very confined area. A number of Negro workers were busy trying to feed and water them and remove the dung to a nearby area where it could be dried and used for fuel. The whole process appeared to be very poorly managed from a rancher's perspective.

I suspected that a good number of Alexander cattle, and maybe some of our horses, were in the pens, but I turned my back on the mess and quickly walked away.

Along Pennsylvania Avenue, I noticed another very large hotel, the National Hotel, at the Sixth Street intersection. Some sort of a party seemed to be going on there. There was another hotel, the Metropolitan Hotel, located on the west side of Sixth Street.

The mood in the city was surrealistic—the presence of the troops and their habitat permeated the capital, but the efforts of the people were directed at attempts of denying that anything was different. It was as if their Sunday would not be held ransom by any uniform, be it blue or gray.

Back at the hotel, I wrote a letter to the family, and another to Professor Crampton. I asked them to keep me updated on things going on there; I knew that it was going to be very important for me to stay connected with something, because I wasn't feeling particularly comfortable in Washington.

⌘ ⌘ ⌘

After a short rest, I prepared to set out for the Ebbitt House for supper. The Willard was quiet during the day, much better for sleeping than during the night. Much of this city seemed to be upside down, and inside out.

The short walk was pleasant. A fresh breeze from the north mixed with the smell of cooking. I noticed that the Ebbitt Inn was located next to the Ebbitt House. I walked up to the inn and looked inside; there was a pleasant dining area adjacent to a large stand-up bar. It was well kept and quite appealing, especially the backdrop of dark wooden bookcases against the back wall.

Next door, a soldier was posted in the doorway, and after checking his list, he rapped on the door. I was greeted by Mrs. Abigail Ebbitt in the entryway. I followed her to the Red Parlor, where four people were conversing.

General Winfield Scott sat in a large leather chair. He was a mammoth of a man, even as he sat. I judged that he was well above six feet in height and weighed near three hundred pounds. Impeccably attired in full dress uniform, he was a sight to behold.

His large hand was warm, and his smile was sincere. His silver hair was ruffled, and his eyes were soft. He commanded respect, but he was not a bit pretentious. I immediately liked him.

I met Mrs. Mason and Mrs. Brown, who were also in the room, and the other lady was Miss Carroll. She wore a beautiful blue dress with white lace trim and seemed to have completely recovered from the rigors of the trip. It was nice to be near her again.

"My knight in shining armor has returned," she said.

The ladies chuckled, and the general said, "Yes, indeed, the news of your heroics has preceded you to the capital. We are most grateful to you for protecting our Anna."

"It was nothing really," I managed to say, still trying to take in the fact that I was speaking to the famous General Winfield Scott.

"And humility is one of your virtues as well," he exclaimed. "Now that is even rarer than valor in this city."

Just then, William Ebbitt, the owner of the establishment, joined us, announcing that the meal was ready to be served. He bore the well-dressed appearance of a successful businessman, which I was sure that he was, judging from what I'd seen of his two enterprises.

The twelve seats at the hardwood table were filled with a mixture of boarders and guests. I got the impression that considerable effort was made to ensure that all seats were filled for the Sunday evening meal at the Ebbitt House. Even before we started to eat, I hoped that I would be invited again.

The Ebbitts sat at each end of the table, Mrs. Ebbitt being closest to the door from which the servers regularly appeared, and Mr. Ebbitt with his back to the fireplace. General Scott, the center of attraction, sat squarely at the middle of the table.

The warm light from two large candelabra bathed the comfortable room. As we enjoyed our meal, the conversation was light and varied in pleasant topics, generally avoiding a discussion of the war.

"Perhaps we have your father to thank for this delicious prime rib," the general said, looking across the table at me. "I haven't met your father, but I know that he sends a lot of cattle this way.

I hope that we can keep the primary routes of transportation open for him."

"Knowing my father, I'm sure that he has a few backup plans in place if he needs them."

The general nodded thoughtfully. "Yes, he would certainly have the knowledge that would allow him to do this. And that, my good people, is what will win this war for us. We will ultimately know more about the enemy than they will know about us."

He looked into my eyes and smiled. "Welcome to Washington, Jason Alexander."

CHAPTER TWENTY-FOUR

War Department
December 1, 1862
ante meridiem

I arrived early. That's my nature, and it certainly had been reinforced with my Illinois College training—the students had to be in the classroom *before* the professor arrived. At 6:00 a.m. there was just one other person standing near the front door of the War Department along with the guard. He eyed me intently as I approached and handed my papers to the guard.

"I'll take him on up," he told the guard, part yawning and part talking. "Follow me."

As we walked to the stairs at the end of the entryway, David Homer Bates introduced himself as the manager of the Telegraph Office. His manner was direct. He turned to me and said, "I know *why* you are here, but I don't know *which one* you are."

I hesitated for a moment. "Well, Mr. Bates, I know *who* I am, but I don't know *why* I'm here. It would appear that together we have the answers. I'm Jason Alexander."

We both smiled, and at that moment, we established what would turn out to be a lasting friendship. "Just call me Bates—you're the one from Illinois, aren't you?"

I nodded, and we shook hands. I followed him into a room on the second floor near the stairs. "This is the library," he said, "but now, many are calling it the war room." There were five windows with a perfect view right through the six pillars that faced Pennsylvania Avenue. The interior walls were lined with full-length oak bookcases, and stone fireplaces were set in each of the two side walls.

Pointing to desks placed against the wall between the windows, Bates said, "I think that's where they are going to put you fellows. You'll certainly be in the center of activity here. The only busier spot in the building is right next door in the telegraph operators' room—that's where I work."

We walked through the open door on the right that led to that room. Bates introduced cipher operators Charles A. Tinker and Albert B. Chandler, who pleasantly looked up to say hello, but just as quickly went back to their work. This room was less than half the size of the library, with only two windows facing Pennsylvania Avenue. One desk faced the wall between these windows, and other desks and tables filled the room.

"We're pretty busy right now trying to stay in touch with the president, who is out of town," Bates said.

Listening to the clicks of the telegraph, I said, "Is every message in cipher like this one?"

Bates's eyes widened, and the others momentarily glanced up and smiled. "You understand the code," Bates exclaimed. "That will be very useful…and, to answer your question, most of our messages are sent and received in cipher to and from the generals' headquarters in the field. Messages with the telegraph operators at the railroad stations are usually in the clear."

"That makes good sense to me," I said. "It would be very difficult to protect the integrity of the cipher in the railroad stations because the night operators can be almost anyone."

"That reminds me," Bates said as he raised his arm with index finger extended and walked to one of the desks. "You have a message that came in yesterday from Station Agent Hinrichsen." He retrieved a piece of paper and handed it to me. "Let's finish the tour, and then you can take this back to the library and read it while waiting for the others."

I followed him over to another door that connected to the next room. He peeked inside, and noting that it wasn't occupied, we stepped in. The office was filled with stacks of neatly wrapped and labeled bundles of paper.

"This is Major Johnson's office. He is Secretary Stanton's assistant, and custodian of the military telegrams. The secretary is next door in the corner office." The door that connected to that office was closed.

I returned to the library, which was still empty, to read my message. The following was received:

Alexander, Illinois/November 30,1862/2:30 p.m.

All is well back home. Heard of your trouble in Tolono and reported to your family that you are all right. No word on Kinchelow.

E. Hinrichsen

CHAPTER TWENTY-FIVE

War Department
December 1, 1862
ante meridiem

There were three of us. Kenneth Landry, a graduate of Yale College, was from Philadelphia, and Robert Smith, a graduate of Middlebury College, was from Bangor, Maine. They joined me in the library at 6:45 a.m.

Smith seemed friendly enough, but Landry was standoffish. They didn't appear to know any more about what we were doing here than I did. We were all a bit nervous.

Precisely at 7:00 a.m., we were greeted by Major Thomas T. Eckert, chief of the telegraph staff. We rose from our seats to shake his large hand, and then he asked us to be seated. Major Eckert was a thick man with thinning hair and a stately manner. His bushy eyebrows moved in unison as his deep voice filled the room.

"Gentlemen, you've been called upon to serve your country in a time of dire need. Each one of you has been vouched for by a member of the president's cabinet as one who is intelligent and trustworthy. Today marks the beginning of a journey that will challenge your skills."

Major Eckert's serious demeanor set the tone as he continued, "You will be agents of the War Department...a title that won't carry a military commission. But it means that you'll be able to move about freely when in the company of the field generals." He paused a moment before continuing. "I will tell you, however, that it's not clear what treatment the enemy may afford you if captured...good incentive to stay out of their hands."

The room was feeling quite warm now. The thought of being captured had never entered my mind.

"We will begin with three of you and, perhaps, expand to additional numbers as time goes on. You'll be utilized by the War Department to provide the intelligence required to fill in the missing pieces of the many puzzles created from multiple sources of information. Of course, our primary source of information here is the telegraph, but we also receive a lot of information from the newspapers, as well as documents captured from the enemy."

He pulled up a chair and sat down with us at the table. "I'll do my best to match your skills with your assignments, but we will do what must be done. I have an identification badge for each one of you."

He handed each of us our badge. My brass badge was firmly attached to a fold-over leather wallet. *J. Alexander, Agent of the War Department*, was impressively inscribed on the badge.

"Let me stop here and give you a chance to ask some questions," Major Eckert said.

"Will we carry guns and make arrests...things like that?" Robert Smith asked.

"You may arm yourself as you see fit—the War Department quartermaster will take care of that for you. I see that Agent Alexander is already carrying a concealed weapon...I would recommend that.

There is a shooting range behind the armory—you might even see the president there from time to time. As far as the arrests, I would hope that you would be doing that, at some point...but check with me first."

"Where will we be working?' I said.

"We will probably keep you close by, here in Washington, at least for the start. You'll have a War Department pass that will allow you to travel on any railroad, and horses are available at our stable. As I noted before, you will go where you need to go to do what needs to be done." Looking at me, he said, "Your ability to ride and shoot, Agent Alexander, will most likely place you in the field quite often."

"Is there any certain place where we should stay?" Kenneth Landry said.

"The War Department will cover the reasonable cost of your room and board, both here and out of town. In addition, you'll receive a stipend of twenty-five dollars each month, payable on the first day of the following month."

Major Eckert waited for additional questions, then said, "If there are no further questions, I will give you a tour of the War Department, the quartermaster's commissary, the armory, and the stables. I'll introduce you to the people that you'll need to know. This afternoon, you will meet the secretary of war."

CHAPTER TWENTY-SIX

Secretary of War's Office
December 1, 1862
post meridiem

John Potts, chief clerk of the War Department, led us to the office on the southwest corner of the second floor shortly after we returned from our brief dinner. It was a moment of great anticipation. It would be an honor to meet Edwin M. Stanton despite his somewhat infamous reputation.

Most of what I'd read about him claimed that he was a difficult taskmaster who stormed the halls of the War Department making impossible demands of his people. It certainly was no secret that many of the Union generals disliked him, and it was also said that he didn't get along well with the president.

Major Eckert made the introductions. Secretary Stanton was forty-eight years old with thinning hair that looked a lot like Major Eckert's. His beard was unkempt, and I tried to imagine what he would look like without it.

His beady eyes seemed to peer into my soul—they were almost hypnotic. His dress was conservative, and his clothes were badly wrinkled. His office was modest and very orderly.

Secretary Stanton was all business. I would come to learn that he'd brought sanity to a situation that was completely out of control when he'd replaced his predecessor, Simon Cameron, in January. I sat with my two colleagues and Major Eckert in high-backed armless chairs across from the secretary's desk.

"Gentlemen, you have been selected very carefully to carry out your duty to your country as agents of the War Department. You will act as my eyes and ears as you seek to obtain information or resolve cases of conflicting information. You'll find that this will be very difficult to do because many will provide this information to you only with great reluctance, if at all. You must be relentless in your pursuit of truth. At times, you may find that your very life is in danger."

Every bit of our attention focused upon the secretary of war as we began to come to grips with what we were being asked to do.

"When we're finished here this afternoon, I will immediately send a message to the generals, making them aware of your charge. I expect their full cooperation and will tolerate nothing less. You will report any derelictions promptly to Major Eckert…Is that understood?"

"Yes, sir," we responded in unison.

"In my opinion," he said as his tone softened a bit, "the activities of the next few months will shape the outcome of this entire war. The right move here, or the wrong move there, could spell the difference between victory and prolongation. You will notice that I did not use the word 'defeat'—that is an unacceptable alternative and will not be tolerated at any expense."

We nodded in silence.

He continued. "Your assignments will come from Major Eckert. You will work individually or in group as he sees fit. You'll discuss your work with no one outside of the War Department... and within the War Department, only with those who have the need to know. Is that clear?"

"Yes, sir," we responded.

"That will be all, gentlemen," he said rising from his chair. "Congratulations and good luck."

We thanked him, shook hands, and promptly followed Major Eckert out of Secretary Stanton's office. I looked back at him as I walked out the door—I saw a man who truly needed our help.

CHAPTER TWENTY-SEVEN

War Department
December 4, 1862
post meridiem

After our meeting on Monday afternoon with Secretary Stanton, we read an assortment of newspapers, letters, notes, reports, and telegrams relating to various matters of concern to the War Department. Periodically throughout the day, we were taken aside by Major Eckert for a series of briefings designed to bring us up to date on the current state of affairs.

These briefings were productive. I appreciated the major's anecdotal commentary, which was perceptive and analytical. He also shared some information about himself with us.

In 1847, at the age of twenty-six, he traveled from his home in Wooster, Ohio, to the city of New York with thirty dollars in his pocket to see the Morse telegraph in operation. "I was so excited about this invention that I helped to build the first telegraph line on the Fort Wayne Railroad a few years later," he said. "I was its superintendent until just before the war." He left that job to manage a gold mine in North Carolina, barely escaping northward in time to avoid capture and imprisonment at the outbreak of the war.

Early that afternoon, he began to sort out some specific assignments for each of us. One of the things that he gave me to do was to follow up on the attempt on Miss Carroll's life in Tolono. I had intended to watch this investigation closely. Now it would be much easier for me to do because I would have direct access to the information. Before the afternoon ended, I was able to send a telegram to Justice Richmond in Tolono.

After supper, I returned to the War Department to continue going through some of the information that was pertinent to my assignments, or cases, as Major Eckert called them. I became particularly engrossed in one case, which was tagged as Case File 23: Secret Line.

The Secret Line was purported to be a sophisticated channel for the leakage of information from Washington to Richmond. Bits and pieces of information had been obtained, including a report from a paroled prisoner who'd spent time in Libby Prison in Richmond, where he'd heard it referred to as the Secret Line.

Another informant overheard a conversation at Bailey's Tavern, southwest of Washington, wherein the name of Charles Cawood was mentioned as a possible courier. Information from West Point indicated that Charles Cawood was trained to use Myer's Signal System, also known as the wig-wag system, by E.P. Alexander, *my uncle.*

I was still thinking about the irony of this when Bates walked in from the telegraph office next door. "Agent Alexander, you look to me like you're ready for a break."

"That's a very good idea, Mr. Bates," I said.

"Just Bates, please—we don't want to get too formal around here, especially at night when the bigwigs are gone," he said.

"That's fine, so you can go ahead and call me Alexander."

"Fair enough, Alexander," he said as he smiled, motioning with his head for me to join him next door.

Bates introduced me to telegraph operators Matthew Grimsley and Jacob Farnsworth, who were sitting at the table in the center of the room, across from the fireplace. The telegraph keys were silent—it appeared to be a slow evening for them.

Bates pointed to an empty chair as he returned to his chair.

"When time permits, we attempt to decipher enemy messages that are taken in the field," he said. "We also look for ciphers that are sent in letters, or openly in newspapers and pamphlets. Tonight, we're looking at some numbers that are printed in the weekly *New York Clipper* and the Sunday *New York Mercury* by a baseball reporter, Henry Chadwick."

The sport of baseball hadn't made its way to the West as yet, but I'd read about it in the *Illinois Courier*, and I knew that the game was somewhat fashioned after cricket and rounders.

"We know that some of the subscriptions to the *Clipper* continue to be sent to people in the South. The numerical information is collected for each game played...They're called box scores. They also accumulate numbers for things like total runs scored, hits per game, and total bases per game."

Grimsley and Farnsworth were plowing through the papers, trying to determine if a cipher was present in the numbers that were readily available to anyone who could get their hands on the newspaper. I didn't envy them, and I was quite happy that they didn't ask me to join them in their examination tonight.

"Alexander, it's important that you gather up any documents, of any sort, that you may find when working in the field and bring them back here," Bates said. "We may find certain words or sentences marked in some way, or we may notice the same newspapers showing up at different locations."

Bates leaned on the back legs of his chair with his fingers locked behind his head and pursed his lips. "If you're willing to endure a bit more of my free advice, I'll also warn you that you should be stingy with your trust of others. The Willard and the National are dens of Rebel sympathizers. I would try to get into a boarding house as soon as you can."

"Miss Carroll is trying to get me a room at the Ebbitt House on D Street, but that may take a while," I said.

"Speaking of Miss Carroll," he said, "did you know that she was your sponsor?"

"I thought our sponsors were cabinet members."

"Miss Carroll is the unspoken cabinet member," he said. "Her opinion carries as much weight with the president as any cabinet member, save that of Secretary Stanton."

Just then a message started to come in over the wire, and the activity in the office began to pick up. It was a good time for me to bow out, and I did. I walked back to my desk next door in the library and put my case files away for the night.

CHAPTER TWENTY-EIGHT

Cincinnati, Ohio
December 6, 1862
ante meridiem

Dark Eyes slowly worked his way back to Cincinnati after leaving Tolono very early on the morning of November 27 after breaking out of the jail. He moved from one safe house to another along the way, traveling the 250 miles at night and hiding during the day.

Two of the owners of the safe houses showed him posters that had been displayed in the nearby towns, offering a reward for his capture. But Dark Eyes had already removed his beard and cut his hair much shorter. His journey was relatively incident free, but he had occasionally come across the northward movements of escaped slaves, traveling between stations of the Underground Railroad in the dark of the night.

He reported the locations of these stations to his comrades, hoping that they would be able to get some local people interested in interrupting future activity. He knew that this wouldn't be difficult because many Union supporters didn't favor the Underground Railroad movement, believing that such activity would only prolong the conflict with the Southerners. In fact, local law enforcement was more likely to be interested in capturing escaped slaves than looking for Clifford Bates.

Nevertheless, the reception that Dark Eyes received upon his return to Cincinnati matched the weather perfectly as a light sleet pelted the city. A fellow knight said, "I'm pretty sure that it was Clement Vallandigham himself, the grand knight, who'd ordered the quest that you botched."

If this was so, Dark Eyes worried that it would be a while before they would send him out again, *if ever.*

It had all happened so quickly. After taking care of some earlier business in Jacksonville, he was passing some time in St. Louis after finishing business there. His stay was cut short when he received word that Miss Anna Ella Carroll would be passing through Toledo, providing an opportunity for him to assassinate her there. He had studied a picture of her, along with a few other *targets*, that had been provided to him some time ago by the Knights of the Golden Circle people in Cincinnati. The message indicated that she would probably be traveling alone. He didn't know anything about her, other than she was said to be a friend of President Lincoln.

Dark Eyes mused about how quickly his business had transpired in St. Louis with the local KGC groups. He'd simply passed on the message that had been delivered in Cincinnati weeks earlier by Major George Ritter from the headquarters of Jefferson Davis in Richmond. *"Continue to discourage enlistments and encourage desertions, but develop your own activities, as you see fit, to diminish the Union's ability to prolong the war."*

This recent turn of events had greatly pleased Dark Eyes. In the past, the Richmond elite had refused to acknowledge the KGC as a bona fide instrument of the revolution, believing that the KGC lacked sophistication and conducted itself in a manner unbefitting of the Confederate States of America. But Major Ritter's message was clear. *"Now that the Union has demonstrated its willingness to abandon the gentlemanly principles of civil warfare by engaging in such actions as refusal of paroles in the field, and attempts to assassinate CSA cabinet members, everything has changed, and the gloves have come off."*

Dark Eyes was on his way from St. Louis to Toledo when he happened to spot Miss Carroll on the train that had just arrived in Tolono, the same one that he was waiting to board to Toledo. His spur-of-the-moment decision to assassinate her there, rather than making the trip further into the north to Toledo, had been a poor one.

He'd been sure that he could meet her descending from the train, take her aside, and quickly drive the dagger deep into her torso. By the time they would find her, he would have easily slipped away through the large crowd and boarded the train for Toledo.

But all he could do now was to let some time pass. He hoped that he'd be given another chance to remove Miss Carroll, but soberly doubted that he would be sent to Washington to finish off the matter. That was probably for the best. He didn't want to run into the belligerent Congressman Vallandigham, who was in Washington representing the bifurcated state of Ohio at the 37th Congress. Dark Eyes knew that the grand knight's patience had its limits.

CHAPTER TWENTY-NINE

Bailey's Tavern
December 6, 1862
ante meridiem

On Saturday morning, it was cool and clear, and I decided that I would ride out to Bailey's Tavern. I was anxious to ride a horse and get out of the city for a while, if for no other reason than to simply get a breath of fresh air. The tavern was located at Bailey's Crossroads, about six miles to the southwest.

This location had surfaced in some of the documents that I'd reviewed earlier in the week as a possible exchange point for Secret Line couriers. In our briefings, Major Eckert had continuously emphasized the need to include *personal observations* in our fact-finding exercises.

After an early breakfast at the Willard, I walked over to the stable to get a horse. I had stopped by a few days ago to look at the available stock and became acquainted with a quartermaster by the name of Andrew Jones. He was a friendly man with thick red hair, who knew how to take care of horses. He was there this morning and helped me pick out a good saddle and horse.

"This sorrel'll take good care of ya," Jones said as he took a long look at me. "But ya need to go over to the armory next door and get ya some hardware."

"I have the Pocket Colt," I said, opening the left side of my coat.

"I see that, but ya may need more than that there peashooter. Sometimes it's just good to have something show'n. Mel Richards is working over there this morning—tell'm I said to give ya an Army Colt and a Henry Repeater."

"Well, that's some *hardware* all right," I said.

"Take a few minutes and go back to the shooting range and fire each one of them several times to get the feel," he said. "And if ya haven't fired that peashooter as yet, do the same with it."

I did as he suggested and ended up leaving the stables shortly after 9:30 a.m., well armed with a good horse and a detailed set of directions. I was glad that I'd made a friend of Andrew Jones.

There was a slight breeze from the northeast, so it took a while for the smell of the capital city to stop following me. I crossed the Potomac River on a ferry, departing from a point near the naval yard. There were a lot of people out and about this morning.

I traveled through the area that was under the control of General Samuel P. Heintzelman, commander of the Military District of Washington, whose sixty thousand soldiers were assigned to the interior defense of the Union capital. A one-mile perimeter had been cleared of all obstructions around Washington and Alexandria to provide an open field of fire in case of an attack. An additional force of five thousand infantry and three thousand cavalry soldiers patrolled outside the perimeter to a distance of about fifteen miles. Today, the general mood was quite relaxed.

I made my way through the checkpoint at Fort Runyon and proceeded in a southwesterly direction along the Columbia Turnpike. Although it was covered with crushed rock, the road was thick with dust that seemed to tag along in a nagging red-yellow cloud. Holstered on my hip, the Army Colt felt awkward and heavy. The Henry was snugly placed in the saddle sheath.

My first thought was to pose as a newspaper reporter, but I suspected that my armament would give that away. The use of a false identity wouldn't hold up for very long anyhow, once the existence of War Department agents became well known.

I passed a number of small farmhouses along the way. Most of the visible activity was given to the gathering and cutting of wood for the winter, the fall crops having been harvested. I was joined by other riders and wagons on the Columbia Turnpike, traveling in both directions with their accompanying dust clouds.

Bailey's Tavern was at a crossroad with a cluster of houses and a small general store. There were nine saddled horses, and one dual team harnessed to a small phaeton, tied at the long hitching post directly in front of the tavern. They drank from the trough that was full of clean water.

I tied up next to the phaeton, which contained a couple of bags, like those carried by a medical doctor. I shook off the dust and entered the tavern.

About fifteen pairs of eyes quickly glanced my way as I walked into the log structure through the open door. Most of the inhabitants quickly went back to their current business, but a few eyes lingered. Several tables were located on the right, near the large stone fireplace. One card game was in progress. Acrid smoke filled the room—one reason why I didn't like taverns.

I looked at myself in the long mirror hanging behind the bar, wondering if I blended in with the others. I ordered a beer.

I exchanged small talk with those near me. None of them asked me for personal information, perhaps not wishing to offer the same to me. I noticed nothing out of the ordinary. I turned to the big man next to me. "Is this place always so crowded on a Saturday morning?"

"This is purdy much normal. Ya get the regulars like me, and ya get the passersby like ya. It's all the same ta Shorty, the barkeep…the more the merrier." He paused for a moment, then continued, "Now Saturday nights can get a bit inter'sting when the troops come in here. I like ta watch the fights."

He looked like someone the troops would want to avoid. I bought him a beer, and a second for me. He loosened further. "Ya would act'ly be a new passerby, not a regular passerby." As two more men entered the tavern, he nodded in their direction. "Those would be regular passerbys."

We talked for a while longer, and then I decided to ride on to take a look at Alexandria. I said good-bye and went out the door.

Two men in dirty clothing stood by my horse, and one of them, with a big red nose, had my Henry Repeater in his hands. He looked up and said, "Would this be your rifle, by chance?"

"It is my rifle, and I would appreciate it if you'd put it back," I said.

"How much would you be want'n for this piece?" he said as the other man chuckled, and spit on the ground.

"It's not for sale," I said as I moved along the porch in front of the bar to a point where their hands were in clear view. Both men had pistols in holsters.

"Well, if you won't sell it, I'll just have to take it," the man with the big nose said.

I put my hand on my Army Colt.

Just then, a well-dressed man walked out of the tavern door and said, "I believe the man said that the rifle is not for sale. I suggest that you put it back and be on your way before something bad happens here." His right hand was inside his long coat.

The two men seemed to know him. The rifle was placed back in its sheath, and they quickly retreated to the general store. I was relieved, and turned to the stranger. "Thanks for the help. I wasn't sure how that would turn out."

Offering his hand, he said, "You're welcome. I'm Doc Rathbonne. You're new around here."

"Jason Alexander...yes, I am."

He paused, waiting for me to say more, but I didn't.

"Those two troublemakers are going to pick on the wrong person one of these days," he said. "God knows I've patched up enough of their victims. Which way are you headed?"

"East."

"Well, it's back to Washington for me, but I have a stop to make near Hunter's Chapel along the way. Perhaps we'll meet again."

"Yes, and thanks again, Doctor," I said. I expected that we would meet again, because I certainly intended to return to Bailey's Tavern.

⌘ ⌘ ⌘

I rode on to Alexandria along the Leesburg and Alexandria Turnpike. I wanted to see the roundhouse and the railroad yard at the famous Alexandria Station, where the Washington and Alexandria Railroad met the Alexandria, Loudon, and Hampshire Railroad and the Orange and Alexandria Railroad.

It was most impressive. I didn't even attempt to count the tracks and switches. I would write to Mr. H. right away about this.

I checked on the next departure for Washington on the W&A and found that I only had a fifteen-minute wait. I secured a spot for me and my mount with my WD pass.

I'd be back in the city before dark.

CHAPTER THIRTY

War Department
December 17, 1862
post meridiem

A week passed quickly as I continued to dig into my casework. I found that I was beginning to think more about Christmas as the decorations began to appear in Washington. I thought about the smells of my mother's baking that would be filling the house back home now.

Major Eckert instituted the practice of an 8:00 a.m. briefing on Monday, Wednesday, and Friday. This morning, he tried to provide some clarity regarding our roles in dealing with senior military officers. "You must learn how to report back your findings, without becoming unwelcome spies."

Simple enough.

It was a busy day at the War Department as news was coming in regarding a battle that had taken place at Fredericksburg, Virginia. Secretary Stanton was visibly disturbed, and I noticed that everyone tried to avoid him as much as possible. I kept my nose in my work.

Miss Carroll and Secretary Stanton worked together in the library around midmorning, going over some maps of both Fredericksburg and the Tennessee River. I overheard Miss Carroll making a strong point with the secretary that the river uniquely flowed *northward*, providing a strategic advantage that the Union must exploit.

After they were finished, she walked over to my desk. "I may have found a room for you at the Ebbitt Inn, shortly after Christmas."

"That's great," I said. "My roommate at the Willard has returned, and he snores loudly."

"Please join us for supper on Saturday night," she said, looking at me with those beautiful eyes.

"Actually, I need to look for Christmas gifts for my mother and sister."

"I'll have something for you to send to them, but you'll have to come to supper on Saturday night before I'll show you what I have."

"Fair enough," I said. "I'll be there, Miss Carroll."

After she left, I tried to catch up on my letter writing. I felt guilty because I seemed to be receiving more mail than I was sending out. Jeanine had written about the Christmas tree that stood in the dining room at the ranch. She noted that a large package for her from Gustavus Swift now sat under the tree. My mother forwarded messages from my father and Jerome. She also promised that my packages would arrive in Washington within the next few days.

After eating supper at the Willard, I returned to the War Department to finish a letter to Mr. H. I wanted to be sure that the posters of Dark Eyes were continuing to be circulated. I could've used the wire to check on that, but I wanted to add some personal notes to the letter. I appreciated and anxiously awaited his frequent letters.

It was getting late as I finished sorting through the information that I'd gathered regarding the Secret Line. I was eager to get out and look at some more places, including Bailey's Crossroads... at night.

As I was marking a date on my calendar, I heard Bates call from next door,

"Alexander, is that you over there?" He didn't wait for an answer. "Come on over here and join us. We need someone to settle this discussion!"

I was surprised to hear from him since the telegraph room had been a beehive of activity all day long, so much so that I had to adjust to the steady state of the clatter of the keys in order to concentrate. I was quite sure that all of the excitement had something to do with the battle going on in Fredericksburg.

I put my things away and walked into the telegraph room, where I found Bates, two telegraph operators, Samuel Brown and Taylor Mason, and *President Abraham Lincoln.*

I managed to say something, but I'm not exactly sure what it was. Bates was thoroughly enjoying watching my reaction to the shock.

"Ah, young Alexander, it's a pleasure to have you here," President Lincoln said. "It warms my heart to see someone from back home. I think about your good father every time I bite into one of those savory steaks."

I shook his large hand. "It was a good summer, Mr. President, so there will be many more beeves coming this way for the winter. All of the folks back there asked me to send their best wishes if I happened to meet you...It's much sooner than I expected!"

Bates and the others were really having trouble containing themselves now, but amidst the laughter, he managed to say,

"Alexander, I wasn't lying. We do have a question for you." He pointed to an empty chair and waited for me to sit down. "If *both* sides in this war pray to God in good faith for a victory, how can He satisfy *both*?"

I thought about it for a moment before replying. "It's a paradox that points out that we should pray for God's *will* to be done, rather than for something more specific that suits our individual needs."

There was a slight pause, and then the president spoke. "Well put, well put—I think that settles it. We put the reins back into the hand of our Maker, where they belong...Let Him decide the outcome." The others nodded.

I would later learn that these philosophical discussions with the president took place quite often, late at night in the telegraph room, when things began to quiet down. I would be fortunate enough to participate in a number of them during my time in the War Department.

The president turned back to Major Eckert's desk, where he'd been working, and slipped some papers under the ink blotter. He grabbed a gray plaid shawl from atop the door to Major Johnson's office and said to me, "If you're ready to leave, how about walking me over to the Executive Mansion? Secretary Stanton gets mighty upset if I go it alone."

"Certainly, Mr. President," I said.

We walked across the lawn between the two buildings. I had trouble keeping up with his long stride. The president looked down and placed his hand on my shoulder. "I want to thank you for saving Anna. She is a very special person...a great patriot."

"It all happened so quickly—I was just lucky."

"No, you were *blessed*," he said. "There's a difference."

I thought about what he said as we walked along. It struck me that I could be so comfortable being near such a famous man, but the president made me feel that way. We could just as easily have been walking the streets of Springfield.

He stared ahead. He already looked older than he did in the recent pictures of him that I'd seen back home. I waited for him to speak, but he said nothing until our journey was near its end.

When the soldiers on the west side of the Executive Mansion spotted us, they rushed out to accompany us for the remainder of the way. Just before going inside, he turned to me. "I've asked your President Sturtevant to travel to England to help educate the English people about the evils of slavery. I'm hopeful that such efforts will convince them to insist that their leaders avoid signing any agreements with the Confederacy. I think he's the right man for the job."

"He will get the job done, Mr. President," I said.

"The Illinois College people always do...Good night, Alexander."

He was gone before I could respond. My short walk with the president of the United States ended in a matter of minutes, but I knew that I would remember *this* day for the rest of my life.

CHAPTER THIRTY-ONE

Ebbitt House
December 20, 1862
post meridiem

As I walked to the Ebbitt House, my head was still in the War Department, where had I worked for much of the day. Saturday's dusting of snow provided a nice cover over the general filth of Washington. I'd watched through the windows of the War Department as the large flakes fell like feathers as I waited for responses to a number of wires.

In yesterday's agent staff meeting, Kenneth Landry reported that the activities of the Copperhead movements across the country appeared to be increasing in frequency, and becoming more violent. He was collecting names of known and suspected members from various sources.

This particular area was Landry's case, so it was important for me to closely coordinate my activities with him. I wired the sheriff in Beardstown, Illinois, regarding a person by the name of John Husted, and the sheriff in Meredosia, Illinois, regarding a man by the name of John Stokes—both had appeared on Landry's list.

They were from my part of the country, and I wanted to find out more about them.

I also followed up on several possible sightings of Dark Eyes. I doubted the reports indicating that he'd moved northward, so I focused my efforts on the sightings to the south and east of Tolono. My telegrams to St. Louis, Cairo, Pana, Cincinnati, and Columbus were yet to be answered. This was not at all surprising, because the wires were hot with news from Fredericksburg.

I greeted the guard when I reached the Ebbitt House. I was very much looking forward to seeing Miss Carroll again. I enjoyed being around her—what was it that attracted me to her, and perhaps, her to me? I suppose that she was just grateful for me having protected her in Tolono.

The guard remembered me. He brushed the snow from my navy blue suit and opened the door, announcing my presence. I was promptly greeted by William Ebbitt and escorted to the familiar Red Parlor, where a number of people were gathered. The house was festively decorated, and I could smell the fresh evergreen, and cinnamon wassail.

I was welcomed by Mrs. Mason and Mrs. Brown. I remembered them from an earlier visit. We chatted briefly, and then I spotted Miss Carroll walking across the room in my direction. She wore a beautiful green velvet dress with red trim in perfect Christmas spirit. Her smile was radiant, and my heart skipped a beat.

"I am saved...My knight has arrived," she laughed. Her warm hand took mine, and she quickly excused us, leading me off in the direction of some unfamiliar faces.

"It's good to see you again, Miss Carroll," I said as we shuffled across the room. She plucked a steaming wassail from a nearby tray and handed it to me just as we reached our destination.

"Gentlemen, I would like you to meet my good friend and agent of the War Department Jason Alexander," she continued, "and Jason, I would like you to meet Brigadier General Herman Haupt and Quartermaster General Montgomery Meigs."

As we shook hands, I managed to choke some sort of a response. Both men were in uniform. Haupt was rugged, tall, and slender, and Meigs was quite the opposite. Both wore beards.

They were wrapping up a discussion about the recent battle in Fredericksburg, which was the talk of the town at the moment. The news was not good. General Burnside had lost many men, and failed to take his objective.

We were called to supper, and I was seated near Miss Carroll and Brigadier General Haupt. I was asked to lead us in prayer. "Father, bless this food, these people, and this place in the name of Your Son, our Lord, Jesus Christ. Amen."

"Thank you, Mr. Alexander," Mrs. Ebbitt replied. A wonderful tomato soup was served, much to everyone's delight. The conversation around the table moved from topic to topic. I managed to briefly mention to Brigadier General Haupt that I had some knowledge of railroads and bridge construction. He seemed to be interested in discussing this more, but not at the moment.

As the main course of meatloaf, mashed potatoes, corn, and green beans was being served, Mrs. Mason said, "I've read that General Burnside is blaming the late delivery of the pontoon boats for his failure to take Fredericksburg. He seems to insinuate that the delays may have been intentional. Those responsibilities wouldn't fall in either of your areas would it, Generals?"

There was a short period of silence, and then Quartermaster General Meigs said, "I'm sure that the good general was caught in the excitement of the moment...if he actually made any such statement at all. There were some regrettable delays, which we will try to avoid in the future."

Mrs. Mason wouldn't let up. "General Burnside appears to be directing his annoyance at Secretary Stanton, who he claims resents his assignment to replace General McClellan...The secretary seems to have preferred someone else."

"I certainly cannot speak to that, but I will say that anyone with good sense should not put themselves on the wrong side of Secretary Stanton," Brigadier General Haupt said. Several people at the table nodded.

"Let's not forget that it wasn't just the Union that lost many soldiers. The losses of the Confederacy were significant...As a part of the whole, their losses were even greater than our own," Miss Carroll said, with a certain level of annoyance at Mrs. Mason.

Mrs. Mason seemed to be willing to let the subject drop there; however, I noticed that she continued to demonstrate a very negative demeanor throughout the evening, so much so that, with the exception of Mrs. Brown, most people tried to avoid conversation with her.

Brigadier General Haupt invited me to ride with him after Christmas to view some bridge work along the O&A Railroad. I looked forward to that, and I made a mental note to arrange this as soon as possible after Christmas. I wanted to get in the saddle and ride out to the picket lines, and I couldn't imagine any better escort than Brigadier General Haupt.

After a second glass of Burgundy and a dish of hot plum pie, I briefly joined the others back in the Red Parlor until Miss Carroll excused us. I followed her to her suite to look at the gifts that she'd selected for me to send to my mother and sister. I met Leah, her former slave, who she introduced as her friend. She was quite charming and intelligent, as well as being very skillful, for I learned that she made all of Miss Carroll's coats, dresses, and hats.

Leah had made the two hats that Miss Carroll had in mind for my Christmas gifts.

I was astonished at the level of detail and perfection in the two hats of similar style, but different materials and colors. They were hats of the latest fashion for the spring...perfect for Easter, and I knew that my mother and sister would love them. Leah placed them carefully in boxes, ready for shipment.

As I reached for my wallet, Miss Carroll pulled my hand away and admonished me for even thinking that she would accept any remuneration. She did, however, accept a snug hug and didn't at all mind when I hugged Leah as well.

I noticed that Miss Carroll had a large arrangement of maps tacked up on one of the walls in the large living room of her suite—she had a war room of her own. Anna Ella Carroll was an intriguing individual.

I departed shortly thereafter with the boxes, after being invited over for Christmas. *Should I have given her a kiss instead of a hug?*

CHAPTER THIRTY-TWO

Fredericksburg, Virginia
December 26, 1862
post meridiem

I sat in the Maryland Avenue depot of the Washington and Alexandria Railroad, waiting for Brigadier General Haupt to finish his preparations for the trip to Fredericksburg.

I had been working at the War Department on Christmas Eve when the courier delivered the message from Haupt, inviting me to accompany him on the day after Christmas. Bates was there with me, taking the duty so his men could have that night off. We were able to send a wire to Alexander to let my family know that I'd received the bundle of gifts, which I'd opened immediately to find much needed winter clothing items.

Christmas Day was a quiet affair at the Ebbitt House with Miss Carroll and a few others. I received a nice leather vest from her, and she seemed to like the woolen cloak that I'd found for her. She noticed my melancholy and did her best to try to cheer me up, and the nice hug that I received after supper went a long way in that regard.

After leaving the Ebbitt House, I stopped by the telegraph room at the War Department to check for messages. My packages had been received at home, and all was well. I also had a message from the sheriff in Beardstown, indicating that John Husted was believed to be a member of the Knights of the Golden Circle. The sheriff noted that Husted frequently traveled southward, but he reported that there was little point trying to track Husted's trips since almost all of the law enforcement south of Beardstown was sympathetic to the Confederacy.

I left a message on Major Eckert's desk that I would be missing tomorrow morning's staff meeting to be with Haupt. I was sure that the major would approve.

It was almost 7:00 a.m., and Brigadier General Haupt stood with arms crossed, ready for Friday's departure of the Rapidan, a hefty 4-6-0. My quick count indicated that there were about eighteen cars on this train, all freight except for one passenger car.

"Are you ready for a good long day, Agent Alexander?" he asked, wearing his civilian dress of a long-tail coat, high jackboots, and a wide top hat.

"I am, General," I said. "I estimate that we have over fifty tons of engine here."

"Near sixty tons to be exact," he said. "Let's get boarded so we can get moving. I want to show you how we've arranged to get supplies to the front lines at Fredericksburg."

The short seven-mile jaunt to Alexandria began by crossing the five thousand feet of the Long Bridge. We talked about trains and bridges, and some of the problems that the Brigadier General had encountered. I was shocked to find out that he had just as many problems with our own troops as he had with the enemy.

The soldiers took baths and washed their clothes in the water tanks, a process that fouled the engine boilers and caused long delays. More disturbing was the fact that they also took timbers from the tracks and bridges for their campfires.

I'd seen the railroad yard at Alexandria once before while on horseback. This time, I was at the center of it all, right up next to the enormous roundhouse, which seemed to have tracks emanating from all directions in a complex maze that defied the imagination. Engines and cars were moving in all directions, sometimes in confusing order. We proceeded through the tangle to the 840-foot-long wharf.

It was here where the cars were detached, and pushed one by one onto a pair of barges, which had railroad tracks laid across them in such a way as to allow the cars to be pushed across a railed gangway and loaded in parallel onto the barge by a small yard engine.

"This was my idea," Haupt said. "What do you think of it?"

He waited.

"Fascinating," I said. It truly was; the train was going across the water without a bridge.

We rode along on one of the two barges, each of which carried eight fully loaded railroad cars. We were towed by a steamer on the Potomac River down to Aquia Creek, where the cars were off-loaded onto another large wharf using the same process as before.

"General Burnside has ordered an expansion of this landing," Haupt said. "It'll be doubled in size and called Burnside Wharf."

The transfer was done efficiently with very little lost time. The cars were then attached to what appeared to be a brand new 4-4-0, the E.L. Wentz, for the ride on the Richmond, Fredericksburg, and Potomac Railroad.

Brigadier General Haupt took in a deep breath. "Eighty fully loaded railroad cars are being transported to and from Fredericksburg each day...We will increase the number to twice that, by spring."

I was amazed at what I'd seen today. This trip marked the moment when I came to the full realization that it was just a matter of time before the Union would win this war. Contrary to the popular opinion of the time, I could see that any delays in the final outcome of the war could only work in *favor* of the Union, allowing the full potential of this powerful war machine to be realized in a way that could not be matched by the Confederacy.

Our eighteen-car train promptly departed the Aquia Creek Landing, and after a few miles, the road rose up and made a steep turn to the left, where we stopped atop a bridge that stretched across a deep ravine.

"This four-hundred-foot truss bridge was just constructed over Potomac Creek to replace an earlier bridge that was roughly thrown together from nearby timber," Haupt said. "The first bridge was destroyed by our own forces during the retreat from Fredericksburg two weeks ago."

As we looked out from the bridge, I could hear hammering below and realized that the construction was not yet completed! I could see a large number of tents just beyond the next hilltop, and I knew that we must be near General Burnside's camp.

Our last stop on the ten-mile railroad ride from Aquia Creek was Falmouth Station, which sat amidst the sea of white tents. The flames from the nearby campfires made the tents appear to dance like some strange apparition. Here the boxcars would be unloaded by the soldiers, and then the engine, the cars, and the caboose would all be redirected, one by one, on the turnaround, reconnected, and returned to Alexandria. Brigadier General Haupt was busy responding to messages immediately after we arrived, but I was able to take a brief look at the encampment. The soldiers had created some comfortable-looking structures, and it was obvious that they were planning to endure the winter here.

I returned to the station just as Haupt stormed out with a fistful of telegrams. "The local quartermasters continue to raid the stores as they're removed from the cars—I can't track the inventory. The generals let the loaded cars sit too long before they're unloaded, and then they don't send them back afterwards."

I followed along as he hurried to climb aboard one of the many wagons that were headed to Fredericksburg. A few of the soldiers that recognized him rushed a lazy salute as we passed by—I wondered why he didn't wear his uniform when he was out like this.

"If Burnside doesn't pick up the pace, I'll never be able to get more supplies to him," he said. "He even holds one train back on a special sidetrack just in case he needs to make a quick trip to Washington! Well, Agent Alexander, we'll just take that train back ourselves when we leave tomorrow."

The wagon driver coughed over a quick laugh when he overheard that comment.

It was only a half mile to General Burnside's tent, and we arrived a full ten hours after departing Washington. General Burnside's tent stood at the end of a street lined on both sides with the tents of his officers. I noticed that one of the nearby tents was the telegraph station because the pole and attached wire pair were visible in the light of the campfires.

Brigadier General Haupt moved swiftly in the direction of General Burnside's tent and went right in. I stopped at the entrance, but soon I was called in by the brigadier general and introduced to General Burnside. He seemed to look me over very closely with his piercing eyes. I admired the spacious tent, which included a fireplace, two beds, and a large table with plenty of chairs.

"At last I'm able to meet one of the secretary's agents," General Burnside said. "I'm surprised that there are only three of you, with all of the work that there is to do."

"I suspect that more may be added in the future, General, but Major Eckert wants to be sure that we can closely coordinate our efforts," I said.

He pursed his lips and furled his thick eyebrows. "I suppose so," he said as his voice trailed off. "You and Haupt are welcome to spend the night in the tent that we have prepared for the president, and of course, you will join me for supper in about an hour. In the meantime, Haupt and I have a few more things to discuss in private."

I excused myself and stepped into the telegraph station tent and introduced myself to the operator. "You're the agent who understands telegramese," he said. "Tinker and Mason are on duty in Washington...They told me you were coming." He promptly sent a short message to the War Department, letting them know that we had arrived. Tinker responded that all was quiet.

At supper I was able to meet Generals Sumner, Hooker, and Franklin—they commanded General Burnside's three Grand Divisions. The mood was optimistic, and there was some talk of mounting another offensive *before* the dead of winter set in.

CHAPTER THIRTY-THREE

Fredericksburg, Virginia
December 27, 1862
ante meridiem

The president's tent was outfitted with a plank floor, a large stove, and two comfortable beds. I slept quite well even though Brigadier General Haupt tossed and turned all night long.

We were up early and took breakfast in the officers' mess, which was spacious and warm. I met General Smith, in charge of the 6th Corps, and his 3rd Division head, General Newton. They seemed to be aware that the War Department agents existed, but they appeared to be surprised to meet one at Fredericksburg.

As we ate, we were joined at the large table by a jovial group of cavalry officers. Brigadier General Haupt identified them as Brigadier Generals Alfred Pleasonton and William Averell, and Major Henry Higginson. They were excitedly discussing a plan to make a cavalry attack upon the Confederates in early January.

"We will split off about a third of the force and openly send them in the direction of Culpeper—this will provide us with the cover for the main force that will cross the Rappahannock at Kelly's

Ford and move southward to cross the Rapidan at Raccoon Ford," Brigadier General Pleasonton said as he gulped down his coffee.

"When Stuart sees the diversionary force turn and head to Falmouth, it'll be too late for him to stop us from destroying the railroads feeding Richmond," Major Higginson said. "We'll be back here by the time Stuart is explaining things to General Lee."

General Smith and General Newton chuckled. "They aren't the only ones who would be surprised," General Newton said, poking General Smith in the ribs.

This remark quickly soured the mood of the cavalry officers. "We're finished being messenger boys for the infantry, General," Brigadier General Averell said sternly. Then, choosing to change the subject, he looked in our direction and said, "Haupt, who is your friend there?"

Brigadier General Haupt introduced me to them. I read the facial responses to be neutral, which was generally becoming as good as I could expect.

Brigadier General Pleasonton seemed to look me over more closely than the others did. "So what brings you out this way, Agent Alexander?" he said.

"Primarily my interest in telegraph and trains...Brigadier General Haupt has been kind enough to show me around," I said.

"I find it quite interesting that anyone in the employ of the War Department would be found this far away from Washington," General Smith said. Another chuckle came from General Newton.

"Well, General, I'm actually happy to see him here...and Agent Alexander, on behalf of the cavalry, I extend an invitation to you to join us anytime that you may wish to do so," Brigadier General Pleasonton said. "You'll be able to witness, firsthand, the transition that this cavalry will make as the new year begins."

"General, I've come to admire Agent Alexander's knowledge of the railroad in the short time that I've known him. Having come from a large ranch in the West, I'm quite sure that you'll find him to be an able horseman as well," Brigadier General Haupt said. "But now it's time for the two of us to be on our way...so Generals, I bid you a good day."

We left the officers' mess tent and headed for the telegraph tent. Brigadier General Haupt had messages...I didn't. He quickly responded to several of them with short notes that he handed to the telegraph operator.

Then he turned to me and said, "I would like to go take a look at the old bridge crossing before we head back—it shouldn't take long."

The two armies occupied the hilltops on each side of the Rappahannock River, overlooking the town of Fredericksburg. During the fighting, the bridge that had once spanned the river had been destroyed, severing the RF&P Railroad. We walked down the hill to the location where the bridge had stood, a point where the river was only four hundred feet in width.

As Brigadier General Haupt stared across at the support structure that still remained on the other side of the river, just at the outer edge of Fredericksburg, he didn't seem to notice that the Union soldiers who were nearby were crouched behind protective structures. Just as it occurred to me that we were in danger, a ball whistled above our heads, hitting a tree with a loud thump. We took cover as a few of our soldiers responded with return fire.

"It would take about a week," Brigadier General Haupt said.

"Sir?"

He turned to me and said, "The bridge...it would take about a week to rebuild the bridge." Haupt lifted his hat and scratched his head. I expected that the hat might be shot from his hand, but that didn't happen.

"If our cavalry rides through and destroys the railroads as they've suggested," he said, "it may force General Lee to pull back from Fredericksburg, in which case we will move back across the river."

We made our way back to General Burnside's camp, and after another short stop by the telegraph operator's tent, we started our trip back to Washington.

I'd grown to like Brigadier General Haupt. It struck me that he could be a man who would someday be recognized for his great achievements if he sought such acclaim, but I knew that he would not. He only needed to satisfy himself—a *much* more difficult task.

CHAPTER THIRTY-FOUR

War Department
December 28, 1862
post meridiem

There was a message for me at the desk at Willard's when I returned to the hotel. Miss Carroll informed me that a room had become available at the Ebbitt Inn. I stopped there immediately after breakfast, on my way to church, to make the arrangements with William Ebbitt. I would move in later today.

The thought of the change lifted my spirits, as I'd found myself avoiding the Willard as much as possible. I would have my own room at the Ebbitt Inn, and I was sure that I could make that room much more hospitable.

I stopped by the War Department on my way back from church. Tinker and Farnsworth were on duty in the telegraph office. They were working over an O&A Railroad map, which detailed the location of the telegraph line that ran along it.

"We heard that you had an exciting time in Fredericksburg yesterday," Tinker said without looking up from the map. "The telegraph operator passed on all of the details. This isn't the first time that General Haupt has encountered some very close calls. Rumor has it that he once wandered up to the enemy lines, and they took him to be one of their own and didn't fire at him."

I believed that. "What are you fellows up to this morning?" I asked as I walked over to the table in the center of the room where they were working.

"It would seem that we have some Rebel activity behind our lines—I think they have tapped into some of our transmissions between here and Burke's Station," Tinker said. Farnsworth nodded.

"How can you tell?" I said.

"It takes a long time before you develop an ear for it, but you can tell when an operator's keying is off. The operator at Springfield Station knows Ben Royal's signature, as we call it, and it's off this morning. He's sure that there must be a tap on the line."

"I'll take a ride out there and see if I can find the tap," I said. "Burke's Station is only a few miles out on the O and A line...I can be there and back in no time. Can you spare Farnsworth for a few hours? It would be a lot easier with a couple pair of eyes scanning the wires."

Tinker twisted his mouth to one side as he thought about it. "I doubt if Major Eckert would approve of it, but it has been real slow today...and only a few hours...I don't see why not. Go ahead, Farnsworth, you lucky guy. Get some fresh air."

CHAPTER THIRTY-FIVE

Burke's Station
December 28, 1862
post meridiem

General Jeb Stuart was fond of taking his Confederate cavalry behind the Union lines. His escapades were well publicized in the papers of both the North and the South, and his popularity was strong in both parts of the country.

He had chosen this cool and bright Sunday to ride along with a small detachment of riders from the 2nd Virginia Cavalry led by Captain John Demsond. They easily slipped through the gap in the Union screen near Centreville and made their way along the O&A Railroad, keeping a safe distance away so as not to be noticed. Their only encounter came when they overtook the drivers of two empty supply wagons, capturing the two teamsters and eight mules.

General Stuart was an accomplished telegrapher, who would occasionally climb the poles and tap into the Union communications on his own, but today that duty fell upon one of the privates. They tapped at several points along their journey as they moved eastward toward Alexandria, going all the way to a position just beyond Burke's Station.

Having noticed that only three Union soldiers stood guard at Burke's Station, which was only being used as a telegraph outpost, Stuart decided to return there in the late afternoon. The ten cavalrymen easily took the station, disarming the surprised Union soldiers. The prisoners were placed atop the mules, along with the teamsters.

General Stuart went inside the station, surprising the operator, Ben Royal, who recognized him immediately and offered no resistance. "General, you're kinda far from your lines."

"I ride where I please," he said, looking over the contents of the station with a keen eye. "I greatly admire your submarine clock, and I will take it." He took hold of the highly valued clock that Ben Royal had received as a gift from Samuel F.B. Morse, raising it high in the air to examine it more closely.

Stuart handed the clock to one of his men, and then he pushed Ben Royal aside. "I believe that I'll take this opportunity to send a message to your quartermaster general in complaint of the poor condition of these mules that we've captured. I expect better on my next trip this way," he laughed.

Just as General Stuart was keying the last words of his message, Captain Demsond stepped inside the station and announced, "General, *riders are approaching!*"

CHAPTER THIRTY-SIX

Burke's Station
December 28, 1862
post meridiem

Looking for the wiretap, Farnsworth and I rode along the telegraph line on a road that paralleled the railroad. A temporary tap is applied when someone climbs the pole and clips a keying device to the wires. We looked for a more permanent attachment, which could be well hidden. This kind of attachment is cleverly made at the top of the pole, often using clear silk to tightly hold the wires together. They are then draped down the back of the pole to a point at ground level, where the keying device can be easily applied and removed, thus allowing the interceptor to work some distance away from the pole.

As my eyes swept along the wire from pole to pole, I remembered stories that Edward Hinrichsen had told me about spots on the sun creating enough electricity in the wires to run the telegraph without batteries, and even harm the operators, and melt the keys.

We were unable to detect any taps, but we noticed some tracks that appeared to be quite fresh near one of the poles. We were still talking about this when we approached Burke's Station.

I caught a glimpse of a Union soldier sitting bareback atop a mule behind the station. At just that same moment, two Confederate officers charged out of the station and motioned for some mounted cavalrymen to move in our direction.

Unfortunately, Farnsworth and I simultaneously turned our horses inward, and we collided. By the time we recovered and pointed our horses to the east, three enemy riders were hotly in pursuit, quickly closing the fifty yards of separation that remained between us.

My first thought was that they would hesitate to fire upon two apparent civilians behind Union lines, but that assumption was shattered when a bullet blasted through Farnsworth's neck. He lurched forward, and his wild, wide eyes met mine as he fell to the ground.

At that instant, I whirled around, right behind Farnsworth's passing mount, and raised my Army Colt, taking dead aim upon the closest pursuer, who was charging forward with reckless abandon. A look of complete shock and horror came across the face of the enemy rider just as my bullet hit him square in the middle of his chest, sending him over the rump of his horse and directly into the path of one of the other Confederate riders.

Realizing that I was willing to make a fight of it, both remaining riders quickly pulled back on their mounts and fired in my direction with their pistols. Their bullets cut through air around me as I holstered the Colt and reached for the Henry. I instinctively braced for the impact of a bullet that I felt was surely coming as I leveled the repeater and picked off the two Confederates like target practice behind the WD stables.

Both riders seemed to stare at me in disbelief as the shots tore them from their horses in quick succession. I'd hoped to avoid an altercation like this, but somehow I'd known all along that it was coming. It all happened so quickly. Such is the condition of armed confrontation—there is no escape from it once the weapons are drawn.

The gunfire was sure to draw attention from the nearby pickets, so the Confederates settled for their prizes in hand and decided to quickly depart the scene. My heart was still pounding as I watched the young enemy officer study my face, etching it permanently into his memory before he rode away with the bearded officer and the others. I distinctively got the feeling that I would see him again before it was all over.

As they rode away, I looked over at Farnsworth. His frozen stare was still fixed in place. What had I done?

I sat there on my mount and didn't move. I was very tired, and shaking a bit.

Our cavalry arrived quickly, having been dispatched immediately after General Stuart's message to the quartermaster general was received in Washington. The Union riders were anxious to partake in the shooting—Stuart had recklessly tipped his hand that he was in the area. I motioned in the direction of the Confederates' departure, and the cavalry rode off.

I looked at the carnage strewn along the once-peaceful dusty roadway, where pools of red now shimmered in the sunlight. I began to feel sick to my stomach. I was immersed in the ugliness of war, and I didn't like it.

CHAPTER THIRTY-SEVEN

War Department
December 28, 1862
post meridiem

I will remember that night at the War Department for as long as I live. After accompanying Farnsworth's body to Alexandria, I received a message from Washington ordering me to return to the War Department immediately.

The soldiers fed the newspaper reporters in Alexandria with the news of the Jeb Stuart raid and the gunfight at Burke's Station. I avoided the discussion, still commiserating over the loss of Farnsworth. I was reluctant to return to the War Department.

When I arrived at 11:15 p.m., Major Eckert was in Secretary Stanton's office, behind closed doors. Bates and all of the telegraph operators were sitting in the telegraph room, talking about their fond memories of working with Jacob Farnsworth. I stuck my head in the door for just a moment and told them that I was sorry.

Bates came over and joined me in the library. "Major Eckert said to tell you that Secretary Stanton wants a full report on his desk before you leave tonight. Alexander, I have to tell you that the secretary was very upset when he learned that Farnsworth was with you."

I said nothing. I knew that Farnsworth should *not* have been with me.

"General Stuart made it back to safety," Bates said. "We think he slipped through our screen along the Little River Turnpike near Chantilly…He took Ben Royal back with him."

We sat in silence for a few moments listening to the soft voices of the operators, and the clicks of the telegraph keys in the adjacent room. "Go ahead and get started on that report. I'll get a cup of hot coffee for you," Bates said.

Bates was a good friend. He knew that I had made a serious mistake by taking Farnsworth out of the telegraph room, but he didn't blame me for his death. We were in a war, and death was a part of the expected outcome. Telegraph operators in the field faced it every day.

I finished the report and sat waiting for Major Eckert. I'd lost track of the time when he finally slipped out of Secretary Stanton's office and entered the library. He warmed himself near the fireplace for a minute or two before he sat down at the table near my desk.

"The secretary fired you," he said. "…He fired me once, too. But then the president came to my rescue…just as he did for you. The president knows just how to let him rant and rave long enough to vent his anger, but then things get patched up before mistakes are made with decisions that will later be regretted. You have your job back."

I handed my report to him. "It's all in here, including my admission that it was all my idea for Farnsworth to come along—Tinker should not be held to blame."

"You were in the *wrong* place at the *wrong* time…or perhaps, in the *right* place at the *right* time, depending on how you look at it. As the president pointed out to Secretary Stanton, we've lacked the backbone required to confront the enemy in many instances, so the last thing that we want to do is to get rid of someone who has the will to *do* it," Major Eckert said. "Us Yankees are expected to turn and run when we hear that Rebel yell, not fight back...You laid a heavy cost on Mr. Jeb Stuart's little trip to Burke's Station."

Major Eckert rose from his chair and returned to warm himself at the fireplace once more. He grabbed an iron poker and methodically stirred the burning embers.

"Stuart is known to be General Lee's eyes and ears, keeping him informed of the location of Union troops. As spring approaches, I think we can get a pretty good handle on what General Lee is doing by watching the areas that are probed by Stuart. I intend to get you involved in this effort since the information that we receive from *our* generals is still heavily salted to suit their taste."

I heard voices in the hallway, and shortly thereafter, the president and the secretary walked by. President Lincoln looked my way, smiling and ever so slightly nodding his head in approval.

Major Eckert saw it, too. "Go get some sleep, Alexander. It's been a long day."

It was then that I remembered that I was supposed to be moving into the Ebbitt Inn this very night.

CHAPTER THIRTY-EIGHT

Executive Mansion
January 1, 1863
post meridiem

Major Eckert suggested that I attend the president and First Lady's party bringing in the New Year...and Miss Carroll *demanded* it. Everyone who was anyone was going to be there. I managed to come up with a formal dress suit with the long coattails.

Miss Carroll had a new red satin dress that Leah had made specifically for the occasion, and it was stealing the show on this pleasant afternoon. I did notice, however, that Anna went out of her way to admire Mrs. Lincoln's dress when we passed along the greeting line—adulation that was only mildly acceptable to Mrs. Lincoln. I made a mental note that perhaps the two of them were not the best of friends.

The president seemed to be rather aloof. His cavernous eyes seemed to carry such sadness. I wondered if he, like me, wished that he was back home.

The ballroom had been elaborately outfitted under Mrs. Lincoln's direction. I couldn't even make a good estimate of how many people were here. I tagged along with Miss Carroll for a while, but then we were separated as a cluster of aggressive male pursuers muscled their way in.

Actually, this was fine with me because, by now, many had read about the incident at Burke's Station, and they wanted to talk to me about it. I preferred to dodge the topic, which was much easier for me to do when blending into the crowd.

"Jason, I was hoping that I would see you here."

I turned and immediately recognized my salesman friend, Charlie Adams. I hadn't seen him since my first night in Washington. "Hello, Charlie, it's good to see you once again," I said. "How are you doing?"

"Quite well, thank you," he said. "In fact, I now have a client from back in your part of the country...Jacksonville Woolen Mills, to be specific. Have you heard of the company?"

"Yes, of course, they're located in the same city where I was going to college."

"I'm selling their blankets to the army. They're good quality—just what the army wants now that Stanton is in office and Cameron is out. Say...I read that you're a big hero now."

"Not really, one of our telegraph operators was killed, and another was taken captive...nothing to celebrate," I said. "Are you still staying at the Willard?"

"When I'm in town, I do," he laughed, "but I'm out a lot, building up my clientele. Heck, I even visited your Jacksonville, but I wasn't aware of the connection until just now...sorry."

"That's understandable. I didn't say too much about myself the night we ate together. What did you think of Jacksonville?"

"Nice town...I stayed at the Dunlap House Hotel, I think it was," he said, "a lot nicer place than the Willard, that's for sure. I'll have to tell you that I was glad to get out of there, though. The hotel was full of those Copperheads, and they were raising quite a ruckus."

Just then, we were joined by Kenneth Landry and Robert Smith. I introduced them as my associates at the War Department, knowing that, by now, Charlie Adams was fully aware of my work from the recent newspaper accounts. Soon a couple of Charlie's friends came along, and they took him away to meet some people.

I seemed to get along well enough with Landry and Smith. All three of us were always very busy—the group could be tripled in size, and we would still have too much to do. Tonight, we were relaxing a bit, and it was nice to banter with them in this setting.

As we were talking, I glanced around the room and caught the eye of the gentleman I recognized as Dr. Walter Rathbonne from my encounter at Bailey's Tavern. We nodded to each other at a distance. He was talking to the secretary of the Treasury, Salmon Chase, and Senator Zachariah Chandler. Shortly thereafter, I noticed that Major Eckert joined their gathering.

A small group of Union officers, which included Brigadier Generals Averell and Pleasonton, and Major Higginson, made a point to stop by and greet us. Landry and Smith were impressed that I knew them.

After they moved on, I described the breakfast at Fredericksburg to Landry and Smith, but when I mentioned Generals Smith and Newton, Landry stated that he'd seen General Newton and two other men, whom he did not recognize, at Secretary Seward's home when he stopped by to leave one of his reports there, at Secretary Stanton's request.

"When was this?" I asked.

"Tuesday, I think..."

I was still pondering this when Miss Carroll came over and took me away to the dance floor. I warned her that I was a terrible dancer and proceeded to prove that I was telling her the truth.

"Dancing isn't everything," she said.

CHAPTER THIRTY-NINE

War Department
January 2, 1863
ante meridiem

The city buzzed with the news of President Lincoln signing the Emancipation Proclamation. According to the newspaper stories, he must have signed it just before he joined Mrs. Lincoln in the reception line at the Executive Mansion. The reports indicated that his cabinet had continued to debate specific points right up to the time that it was signed by the president.

I thought back to the discussion with Miss Carroll on the train, and her serious reservations about the ability of the freed slaves to integrate with the rest of the nation. The Emancipation Proclamation didn't address this issue at all, and from what I'd seen in Washington with the numerous encampments of former slaves who had fled from the South and lived on handouts, Miss Carroll's points were not to be taken lightly.

My thoughts on this matter were interrupted as Major Eckert entered the library for the beginning of our Friday staff meeting. He didn't waste any time in getting started.

"Gentlemen, this morning I'm going to begin with some comments that will hopefully provide some clarity with respect to questions that have been raised about your roles as War Department agents," he said. "Mr. Smith was recently rather rudely confronted by a Pinkerton operative, who accused Mr. Smith of interfering with his mission in support of the work of the government of the United States...or something to that effect. Is that right, Mr. Smith?"

"Yes, that's correct."

"I have confirmed it with the secretary that the War Department doesn't have any association with the Pinkertons, and in fact, both the secretary and the president have found them to be quite ineffective. That's not to say that there aren't other *legitimate* entities working for the government in various forms, but that should not be of concern to us. Secretary Stanton hopes to better coordinate all such activities at some point, but for now, we will continue to address *all* matters related, in any way, to telegraph communication. Having reviewed your case files, it's my belief that *all* of your cases satisfactorily represent such work."

Major Eckert was quite firm in the delivery of this message to us. I always felt that we had his full backing, and this was just further confirmation in my mind. I hadn't heard much about the Pinkertons, except that they worked for General McClellan, but I had read newspaper stories about government agents who worked for a secret service of some sort.

Before moving on to other matters, Major Eckert looked directly at Robert Smith and said, "Should another encounter with the Pinkertons take place, you have my permission to arrest the lot of them!"

We all laughed, and then we plowed into our briefings. Things moved along crisply until we came to Landry's report relating to a marked increase in the activities of the pro-South groups, such as the Knights of the Golden Circle. Major Eckert was concerned that there might be some direct connection between this organization and Richmond. He suspected that the free movements of the Confederate cavalry might be making the communication between the two parties much too easy to accomplish.

"Before long, our cavalry will be ready to actively confront the Rebel horsemen in a manner that they have not witnessed thus far," Major Eckert said. "Their reaction to this aggression will shape some of our future activities, particularly for you, Agent Alexander, as I plan to place you squarely in the middle of it all... but we'll talk more about that later."

I was honored that he would place such trust in me, but at the same time, I wondered if I was up to the task. I didn't really feel that I had accomplished much since coming to Washington—it was true that I was treated like a hero by the newspaper reporters for my involvement at Burke's Station, but the fact of the matter was that I had blindly stumbled right into the activities of a sizeable number of the enemy, and fortuitously lived to talk about it.

"By the way, Alexander, I received word from Justice Richmond in Tolono that the escaped killer used the name of a deceased laborer in Cincinnati...That was one of the locations of his possible sightings, wasn't it?"

"Yes, Major, it was. I wouldn't expect that he would return there after using that name, but he is the same person who tried to stab Miss Carroll in broad daylight, at a crowded railroad station," I said. "I will ask the authorities there to intensify the search in that area."

Major Eckert nodded his approval and continued on with the briefing session for a while longer. He reminded me a bit of Professor Crampton in that he was very organized and disciplined in his approach to the tasks at hand. It was a model that I preferred to emulate in my own life.

I took a short walk after dinner, as the weather in Washington was still very mild.

There were rumors that General Burnside might initiate an attack against the Confederate encampments at Fredericksburg. Based upon what I'd seen a few days ago, I doubted this, but the veracity of such rumors was quite remarkable.

The city didn't smell as bad now because a steady breeze from the northwest seemed to clear it out, but the visible signs of war were everywhere, and the walk did not lift my spirits. I had hoped that I would think less about being back home after the Christmas season had passed, but that hadn't happened. Maybe that's what led me to the familiarity of the stockyards.

Steam rose from the huge mountains of manure that were much too large to allow any drying to occur. The cattle and the horses were penned in so closely that much of their bodies were covered with manure, making it impossible for me to try to find the brand from home that I was looking for. I wondered if my father had any idea about what things looked like here.

I saw roughly cut piles of bones near the slaughterhouse. They were being picked through by some of the contrabands, hoping to find enough meat remaining to make a soup. I would eat a good meal tonight, but many people in this city would not.

CHAPTER FORTY

War Department
January 20, 1863
ante meridiem

The rumors turned out to be true—General Burnside was on the move. It was obvious that something was up when I entered the War Department building...There were a lot of people about, including the president. It was Tuesday, so there was no staff meeting scheduled today. I tried to stay out of the way as I cut a path to my desk.

All I had to do was listen to find out that General Burnside was marching north and west out of Falmouth with intentions to cross the Rappahannock at Banks Ford and attack General Lee's rear at Fredericksburg. The weather was still good, and if he could move swiftly, the plan just might work...although it didn't seem to me that General Lee would be caught by surprise.

Pontoons were to be at Banks Ford by tomorrow at dawn to build five bridges for the crossing; heavy cannon would be placed on the ridges for cover. Excitement and optimism abounded.

I buried my head in my paperwork, sorting my way through telegrams and newspaper clippings that were appearing with more regularity. Even copies of a subterranean newspaper called *The Constitutional Union* occasionally fell into our hands. Believed to be an organ of the KGC, it was edited and published by Thomas B. Florence, and endorsed by Clement Vallandigham, among others.

Occasionally, pieces of the puzzle began to fit together. For example, we had gathered enough evidence to clearly connect the KGC with the Secret Line, and Richmond. Secretary Stanton was very concerned about this—he even sat in on one of our meetings last week to get the details.

We suspected that KGC couriers were traveling to and from Washington by railroad and making connections with Secret Line operatives who were communicating with the Confederacy in Richmond. The cipher code that was being utilized appeared to be the same as that which was used by the CSA, which was a system of alphabetic substitution that originated in France. Professor Crampton had introduced a version of this cipher to his mathematics class at Illinois College, so I had seen it before. It wasn't a complicated cipher, but it did require the use of a confidential key word to encipher and decipher the messages.

The War Department instructed all of the station agents along the military railroads to forward any suspicious documents that might be collected in their areas. Likewise, the Union generals and their telegraph operators were also alerted. These efforts added a lot of paper to my daily workload—most of it was not useful.

When I walked back to the Ebbitt Inn for dinner just before noon, I noticed that the sky was quickly clouding over, and by the time I headed back to the War Department, it was raining heavily, and water was standing everywhere.

The mood inside the War Department had changed. Telegraph operators at Falmouth Station reported that the heavy rain was already slowing up General Burnside's efforts to get to Banks Ford.

As the afternoon progressed, the messages got worse. Supply wagons loaded from the trains at Falmouth Station were unable to move in the mud. The train shipments were halted because they couldn't be off-loaded, and also because the waters on the Potomac River were too rough for the barges. The nor'easter had blown in with full force and was not about to let up.

I returned to the War Department after supper. The rain was still coming down, and it was getting colder. The people were gone, and the building was quiet now. I entered the telegraph room and found Tinker and Brown on duty. They looked at me and shook their heads.

"How bad is it?" I said.

"About as bad as it can get," Tinker said. "They can't move. Soldiers are knee deep, and wagons are hub deep. If the weather doesn't break, it's over."

The weather didn't break.

CHAPTER FORTY-ONE

War Department
January 21, 1863
ante meridiem

The rain began to turn to snow as I departed the Ebbitt Inn for our staff meeting with Major Eckert. I could not help but think about the misery that General Burnside's soldiers were experiencing near Banks Ford as I entered the warm confines of the War Department building.

I met Tinker on the stairs as he was going off duty from his long night. "General Burnside wants to push on, but reports indicate that the Rebels have laid a plank road to Banks Ford, allowing them to quickly move cannon into place there," he said. "The secretary is not in a good mood, so you might want to avoid him this morning."

"I generally try to do that anyway," I said.

It was quiet in the building today by comparison to yesterday—an indication that Tinker's assessment of the situation was accurate. I was surprised to find that Major Eckert was already in the library preparing for our meeting. He had tacked up a couple of maps that I hadn't seen before.

We were all in our seats by 8:00 a.m., and Major Eckert started things off quickly. "Secretary Stanton wants us to break down the existing communication pathways to and from the Confederacy. I plan to propose two specific actions that will help to accomplish this."

Major Eckert read from his notes. "First of all, we will increase the number of Union troops at the major railroad stations so that we can start checking the passengers. Those with suspicious identities and questionable destinations will be pulled aside for interrogation and may not be allowed to continue on. A second measure will be to apply more pressure to the Confederate cavalry operating to the west and southwest of Washington, making it more difficult for them to connect to the civilians in and around Washington."

I was sure that both of these initiatives would be very helpful. In fact, one of them was a suggestion that I had made to the major just recently. Both actions would require the full cooperation of the military, and President Lincoln and Secretary Stanton would have to be involved in making this happen.

"The other thing that I would like to do is to close down the singular pathways that the couriers are using…by this I mean their equivalent to the Underground Railroad," Major Eckert said. "Alexander, I know that you have some thoughts as to where we should begin our efforts, and that will be helpful, but I want a lot more effort to be placed upon this, so I intend to bring in an additional agent to help."

I knew that I could use the help, as there were so many possibilities to be explored, and I had only been able to look at a few of them.

Major Eckert moved to the maps. "I've marked the routes that we'll start with. Military patrols will be increased in these areas, and we'll ask Union supporters who live there to be on the lookout for us. If we can shut down the enemy's primary links, the increased use of the secondary routes should help us identify those as well."

We suspected that many of the Confederate couriers traveled only short distances before they made a handoff with the next courier, a handoff that included materials moving in both directions. If the couriers had regular routes, they should be seen more often on these routes. But the Confederates would know that too, so we couldn't understand how they managed to avoid raising suspicion! We decided to try to identify the most frequent travelers of the most likely routes—gathering this information would be a challenge. We would need the help of the military, and it wasn't clear that they could be counted upon to gather this information for us.

Placing additional requirements upon the military checkpoints would solicit requests for additional troops, and such requests would be met with considerable resistance from the generals with responsibilities outside of Washington. The decision would fall to General Halleck, who was likely to defer to Secretary Stanton.

After the meeting concluded, I examined the new maps more closely. Roads extended like fingers from Washington, and they interlaced with crossing roads to create a cobweb like jumble of possibilities. Many of the crossroads also included railroad stations, where handoffs between couriers would be easy to accomplish. Major Eckert had placed pins on the map, identifying military checkpoints, and it was clear that they were insufficient in number to inhibit the free and easy movement of the couriers.

I stood there staring at the map, feeling cold and lonely.

CHAPTER FORTY-TWO

War Department
January 28, 1863
ante meridiem

All of a sudden, things were happening very quickly. On Monday, General Joseph Hooker took command of the Federal Army of the Potomac at Fredericksburg, replacing General Burnside. Immediately upon receiving word of this change, Major Eckert approached Secretary Stanton with a request to change the way the cavalry was utilized outside of the city of Washington.

Coincidentally, General Hooker decided to follow changes suggested by Brigadier General John Buford and Brigadier General Alfred Pleasonton, changes which had been rejected by General Burnside. These changes fit nicely with the new direction proposed by Major Eckert.

Somehow, it all came together. General Hooker's staff said that it would take about a week before they could "put it to paper" in the form of a general order, but Major Eckert presented the details to us in our staff meeting this Wednesday morning.

Nine thousand cavalrymen were placed in a single corps under Major General George Stoneman. He broke his command into four parts, three divisions and one independent reserve brigade, which was made up of the regiments of the Regular Army cavalry assigned to the Army of the Potomac. The First Division went to Brigadier General Alfred Pleasonton, the Second Division went to Brigadier General William Averell, and the Third Division went to Brigadier General David Gregg. Each of these divisions had two brigades.

Brigadier General John Buford favored cavalrymen from the Regular Army, many of whom were from the western states, so he was happy to take command of the Reserve Brigade, consisting of the 1st, 2nd, 5th, and 6th U.S. Cavalry regiments. His independent command was given the freedom to meet the *special needs* of the government. Major Eckert hoped to use Buford's help. He had arranged a meeting with the brigadier general this afternoon, and he asked me to join the two of them.

⌘ ⌘ ⌘

I rode out to the Soldiers' Home with Major Eckert in his carriage. Brigadier General Buford was to meet with us after his visit with a couple of ailing friends from his home state of Kentucky.

We covered the three-mile distance in about thirty minutes. The road stood amidst encampment after encampment of contrabands. The smell of the campfires failed to overcome the smell of human waste and bad water. Once again, I thought of Miss Carroll's warning that this problem could only grow worse. Major Eckert seemed to have his thoughts elsewhere.

My first look at the Soldiers' Home helped me to understand why the President and his family spent the summers here. Even in winter, the beautiful landscape and graveled roadways accented this special place. There was a quiet peace and tranquility about this location, nestled on a hillside overlooking the capital and surrounding countryside. We proceeded directly to a two-story brick house, which Major Eckert referred to as the Anderson Cottage.

Brigadier General John Buford was sitting at a large table in the library on the main floor, going through a large stack of newspapers when we walked in. A small fire burned in the large fireplace to his back. He motioned toward two empty chairs across from him at the table. We took our seats, and Major Eckert placed a roll of maps upon the table as we sat down. He waited for the brigadier general to begin.

Buford put down his papers, stroked his thick mustache, and said, "I understand that you need some help...and to the extent that I can help you, I will do that." His trusting eyes seemed to take both of us in at the same time. "Let's look at your maps."

Major Eckert spread the maps on the table, and he and the brigadier general used their pistols to hold down the rolled edges. "Secretary Stanton informed me that Major General Stoneman's three divisions will picket and patrol the area from Aquia Creek to Hartwood Church at the Ridge Road and the Warrenton Road," Major Eckert said.

"That's right, and my orders are to provide backup where needed," Brigadier General Buford said. He spoke slowly and thoughtfully. "I expect that the WD's greater concern will be from Hartwood Church northward to the Potomac, where Colonel Price is the screen commander."

Colonel R. Butler Price was responsible for screening Washington under the command of Major General Heintzelman. The screen extended in the form of a broad arc sweeping from Hartwood Church through Wolf Run Shoals, Union Mills on the O&A Railroad, Centreville, Chantilly on the Little River Turnpike, Herndon Station on the AL&H Railroad, Dranesville on the Leesburg and Alexandria Turnpike, to Seneca Falls on the Potomac River.

"It's too much ground for Price's force of just over three thousand cavalry and five thousand infantry—hell, I could go through there with a blindfold on," Brigadier General Buford said.

"It appears that the Confederate cavalry has already been busy probing points in the center of the screen, according to reports from Colonel Percy Wyndham," Major Eckert said.

"Fairfax County seems to be one of the major locations for courier activity," I added. "We have stacks of reports of Confederate sightings."

Brigadier General Buford nodded in reply and continued to study the maps. Then he looked up at me and smiled. "You spoiled Jeb's little party in Fairfax County a few days ago...I got a real tickle out of that." He took one more look at the maps, and then crossing the fingers of his hands behind his head, he leaned back on two legs of his chair and said, "I suppose I could give *Percy* a hand now and then, if he needs it. Of course, it might be easier for *you* to ask him...I understand that he spends a good deal of his time in Washington fraternizing with the newspaper folk."

I looked at Major Eckert. He said nothing. Colonel Wyndham's frequent visits to Washington were well known.

Major Eckert agreed to talk to Secretary Stanton. It would be up to the secretary to discuss the matter of overlapping areas of responsibility with the generals. I was not extremely optimistic that much progress would be forthcoming.

CHAPTER FORTY-THREE

Fairfax Court House
February 17, 1863
ante meridiem

Instead of sending Brigadier General Buford to support the Washington screen as we had hoped for, General Hooker decided to break up the heavy smuggling activity on the peninsula between the Rappahannock and Potomac Rivers. This was a suspected courier route as well, so I was not totally disappointed when I heard the news.

Nevertheless, recent information indicated that the activity in Fairfax County was rapidly increasing, so I decided to talk to Colonel Wyndham face-to-face. Bates had educated me regarding the military's tendency to control the amount of information that made its way to the War Department, and he believed that it was likely that Colonel Wyndham was already well aware of the situation.

I loaded my mount onto a boxcar in Washington and traveled to Alexandria, where I transferred over to the O&A Railroad for the trip out to Fairfax Station. Most of the trains were busy running supplies to General Hooker at Fredericksburg, and only one train a day was running out of Alexandria on the O&A, and that train departed promptly at 8:00 a.m.

My mount happily rode in one of the nine boxcars carrying forage. There was another car containing military supplies, and one carrying sutlers' supplies for sale to the troops. I rode in the passenger car with a few others. I wore my new WD armband to identify myself in the field, cooperating with the directive recently put in place by General Hooker requiring all of his people to wear such patches. Hooker believed that the measure would also help his soldiers to take more pride in their units.

We promptly covered the fifteen miles to Fairfax Station, making only one stop at Springfield Station. We passed by Burke's Station…

There was a fury of activity that commenced upon the train's arrival at Fairfax Station. All of the cars were quickly moved to a side rail, where they would eventually be emptied by the troops. I off-loaded my horse and headed north for my three-mile trip to Fairfax Court House on Chain Bridge Road.

I guessed that about four inches of snow coated the ground, but it was packed down pretty well on the narrow country road. I tried to ride in the middle of the road, avoiding the deep wagon-wheel grooves that were partially filled with loose, blowing snow. I soon spotted the town up ahead on a long, rolling hill.

Colonel Wyndham's headquarters was located in the home of Judge Henry W. Thomas, about a block south of the courthouse. I was surprised that there weren't many soldiers around. Lieutenant Colonel Robert Johnston of the 5th New York Cavalry greeted me at the door. We met Colonel Percy Wyndham in the first-floor library.

It was Colonel Wyndham's very large moustache that immediately gained my attention. It was thick like a beard and well combed. He had narrow, beady eyes and black, curly hair. His uniform was immaculate.

He spoke with a slight British accent, which remained from his homeland, where he had served in the Queen's 5th Light Cavalry. "It is a pleasure to finally meet the hero of Burke's Station. It is always such a welcome sight to see some of our Washington brethren pay us a visit here in the field, particularly in the bad weather."

"I suppose it's just part of my western nature...Thank you for seeing me, Colonel Wyndham. Major Eckert sends his regards. I won't take much of your time."

"Time is such a precious thing, isn't it?" he said as he carefully looked me over. "I find that I seldom have enough of it, and I have even *less* of it these days, as the outlaws are pestering me near to death." He seemed to know exactly why I was here to see him. "And I choose my words carefully, Agent Alexander. These attacks are not from Confederate soldiers, but from renegade outlaws. They make their raids in order to steal."

"You are speaking of Captain Mosby?"

"He is a self-proclaimed captain...if he is in the military at all. He is nothing more than a lowly private leading a gaggle of bandits for plunder," he said as his face began to turn to a light shade of red.

"Do you think that he serves as a connection with couriers out of Washington?" I said.

"If there is any kind of a reward in it, he does," Colonel Wyndham said. "This man does nothing for the sake of the Confederacy...It is purely profiteering."

"And you have noticed an increase in his activities?"

"Unquestionably," he continued, "this man becomes bolder with each success. I increase the size of my pickets, and he continues to attack them. I must now pull back the screen to points where I can place fifty men at night...fifty men who will rest uneasily."

"We tried to get you some help from Brigadier General Buford."

"So I heard," he said coldly. "I can do quite well without the help of George Stoneman's Reserve Brigade. I intend to set a trap for the outlaw Mosby, a trap that his greed will not permit him to avoid."

We continued the discussion, during which he passed on the names of several possible couriers based upon information gained at his checkpoints. I recognized a couple of them. I turned down the opportunity to join Colonel Wyndham and his staff for dinner because I wanted to ride all the way back to Washington, and I needed to get started.

As I rode along the Chain Bridge Road further into town, I noticed that Lieutenant Colonel Johnston's headquarters was located in a house close to Colonel Wyndham. Reaching the intersection with the Little River Turnpike, I turned to the east, but before doing so, I noticed that there was *another* headquarters for a high-ranking officer off to the northwest end of town.

I wonder who that could be?

CHAPTER FORTY-FOUR

War Department
February 18, 1863
ante meridiem

I made the sixteen-mile ride from Fairfax Court House to Washington along the Little River Turnpike and the Columbia Turnpike, arriving just after dark. There weren't many people out on the blustery winter afternoon. I came across a few Union soldiers, but it was apparent that the enemy could easily utilize the turnpikes if they were careful enough.

I reported my discussion with Colonel Wyndham at this morning's staff meeting. Major Eckert was very concerned about the situation out on the extremities of the Washington screen, but he held little hope for any relief in the form of additional cavalry support because General Hooker was not about to ease the protection around his flanks.

We felt that the best that we could do was to make the courier exchanges a bit more difficult, but we knew that we couldn't shut them down. Major Eckert informed us that Secretary Stanton had recently decided to take a more aggressive security approach by authorizing Lafayette Baker to arrest anyone under suspicion of conducting acts against the government. In the secretary's words, *"Baker's operation would continue to work independently of Eckert's."* But the major reminded us that we still had his permission to arrest any of them who get in the way of our work.

Just before our meeting was over, Bates entered the room with a telegram. He looked disappointed as he handed it to Major Eckert, who thanked him, and paused to read it.

For a moment, he was lost in thought, but then he said, "General Hooker has just ordered Brigadier General Marsena R. Patrick to form The Bureau of Military Information under the command of Colonel George H. Sharpe, who will be assisted by Captain John McEntree and John C. Babcock, a civilian. The bureau will not supplant the prerogative of the field commanders to hire their own spies or assign scouts. It's simply an attempt to organize and coordinate activities." Major Eckert looked up from the piece of paper that he held in his hands, rolled his eyes upward, and said, "Carry on, gentlemen." And then he left the room.

Things were getting more confusing by the minute. Certainly, there was more work to be done than what three agents could handle, but perhaps not enough for the heavy-handed Mr. Baker and the newly appointed Colonel Sharpe.

After the meeting, I spent some time with Bates in the telegraph room. It was quiet, so the telegraph operators were spending some time trying to decipher a few captured messages.

"It appears that the KGC and the Confederacy are using the same cipher system," Bates said. "That should increase our chances of capturing more messages...and eventually breaking the key...At least that's the way it *should* work."

"So Jefferson Davis thinks that it's more important to try to communicate with the KGC than it is to risk losing their military cipher?" I said.

"Apparently so…and it's a big risk since their communication system is poorly organized. If they lose their key word, it will take them a long time to get a new one established. If we can get our hands on a few more of their messages, I think we can break this."

"Maybe I can help some with this. In one of my mathematics classes, we would create simple ciphers and try to break them using an analysis based upon the probable occurrence of certain letters of the alphabet," I said. "We selected pages from books and newspapers and counted how often certain letters appeared. Then we applied our findings to the cipher text. Usually, it worked very well."

"We do something like that, but it is more guesswork," Bates said. "It would be useful to have that list, showing how often certain letters occur in normal text. Can we get that?"

"Sure, I'll send a message to Professor Crampton right now, and we should have it very soon."

CHAPTER FORTY-FIVE

Jacksonville, Illinois
February 20, 1863
post meridiem

Dark Eyes was churning inside as he stepped off the train in Jacksonville. The bite of the harsh winter wind cut to the bone. He had hoped that he would never return to this abolitionist hellhole of a city, but his visit was ordered by the grand knight himself, so he had no choice in the matter.

Even though his beard was gone now, Dark Eyes would stay away from the areas where his old poster might still be hanging. The dark winter clouds were bringing the night in early, and the Friday crowds were already spilling into the taverns.

Dark Eyes preferred to stay at the Dunlap House Hotel, where Confederate sympathizers congregated, but there were people there who might recognize him. He wanted to slip in and out of town as quietly as possible, so he opted for one of the rooms in the Heslep Tavern, where he would have to tolerate the abolitionist crowd. It would also be easier for him to meet with Charles Constable, whose law office was right there on the second floor of the same building.

The smug barrister was sitting at his favorite table. He didn't recognize Dark Eyes immediately. Charles Constable had to look twice because this wasn't exactly the same person, in terms of appearance, that he'd met back in November. A freshly stoked fire burned in the large stone fireplace, cooking the air that smelled of a mixture of beer and tobacco. Dark Eyes ordered a beer and stood at the bar instead of joining Constable at his table. They waited, scanning for recognizable faces.

It was a bit early for the larger evening crowd, and Dark Eyes knew that Heslep Tavern could sometimes get rather rough in the late hours. He'd replaced the derringer that he'd lost in Tolono, and his dagger was always at the ready, so he didn't worry about the local ruffians.

Local law enforcement was a different matter. As a precaution, Dark Eyes had taken a room that was available near the hotel's back exit, paying in advance for three nights.

He leaned against the bar and closed his eyes for a moment, letting the scent of tobacco carry him back to the days of his youth in Kentucky, when he'd handled wagonloads of the stuff, moving it from the fields to the barns for curing. But one by one, farmers like his father were forced to give up their places to the banks, which were run by the same abolitionists who saw to it that the slave workers were hustled off to the North in the dead of the night. Without them, the tobacco crop rotted in the fields.

His father had tried his hand at preaching for a while before he'd snuck back onto his former property and burned himself up in one of the barns.

Three beers and fifty minutes later, Dark Eyes was sitting across from the desk of Charles Constable, who sat gazing out of his office window facing West State Street, puffing away on his pipe. Without turning to look at Dark Eyes, he said, "So they want me to move forward, do they?"

"That's straight from Mr. Big, I'm told...You sure as hell don't think anyone else would have made me come back to this rat hole of a town, do you?"

"No, I expect not," the attorney said. "I suppose we can move things up a bit, but the plan will work better in the heat of the late summer."

"Your people are all in place, aren't they?" Dark Eyes was not in the mood for any resistance from Charles Constable, or anyone else in Jacksonville.

"You know they are...I reported that at the meeting you attended the last time you were here."

"I hope you've cleaned up your arrangement for allowing entry to your meetings since then," Dark Eyes said. "I'm not here to clean up any more of your messes. Next time you can get some of your farm boys to take care of it...'Course, you botch this up, Constable, you may become one of the messes that needs cleaning up."

Charles Constable did not like to be threatened. He turned to Dark Eyes and said, "I will soon be taking a seat on the judicial court here, so I'll be in the *official* business of cleaning up messes... It would be good for *you* to remember that."

Dark Eyes squirmed in his chair and shrugged.

"And another thing," Charles Constable said, "I don't expect to hear that there are any problems out on the Alexander Ranch in the next few days. Such a disturbance might interfere with my plan, and I won't tolerate that. Is that clear, Clifford Bates...or whatever your name is?"

Dark Eyes mumbled a response, but Constable stood and glared down at him. "Clear enough," Dark Eyes said.

CHAPTER FORTY-SIX

Morrisville, Virginia
February 24, 1863
post meridiem

Brigadier General Fitzhugh Lee had a jovial disposition to go along with the command presence on the field of battle—unique qualities that made it easy for him to lead his men wherever he wished them to go. Yesterday, he had received orders from General Stuart to probe General Hooker's right flank in the vicinity of Hartwood Church.

Fitz Lee's uncle, General Robert E. Lee, had learned that the Union cavalry was making it much more difficult to get information from sympathetic sources in Washington. The Union riders had concentrated their efforts upon very well chosen routes, but General Lee surmised that a probe of some authority would cause both Hooker and Heintzelman to pull back their cavalries and return them to more conventional duties. Hartwood Church was the perfect spot to get the desired attention of both generals.

Brigadier General Lee had set out this Tuesday morning from Culpeper Court House with four hundred men from the 1st, 2nd, and 3rd Virginia Cavalry with over eighteen inches of snow on the ground. The roads were in a terrible state, but the men were in generally good spirits, anxious to take out whatever frustrations they might have on the Yankees.

They crossed the icy waters of the Rappahannock with some difficulty at Kelly's Ford, and they knew that the return would be even more difficult, as the waters were rising quickly. The element of surprise would be in their favor, so they expected to make their strike and return before the Union could manage any sort of a threatening response. It was a matter of great debate amongst the Confederate cavalry as to how many Union riders were equal to one of their own, but many thought that it was as many as *five*, and if that was so, they knew that it would be quite some time before the Union could get two thousand horsemen to Hartwood Church. Of course, the Rebel officers reminded them of the equalizing presence of infantry stationed near there.

They settled in for the night at Morrisville, a small town about five miles to the east of the crossing. Brigadier General Lee was invited to spend the night in the home of Dr. Evan Cooper. He agreed to dine with the doctor and his family, but he would spend the night on the cold ground, enduring the same conditions as his men.

Even though the townspeople were quite friendly to the Confederacy, guards were posted to make sure that no one left town, *accidentally* giving away their position. Hartwood Church was only three more miles to the east of Morrisville. The Rebels would make the attack early on tomorrow's cold winter morning.

After supper, Brigadier General Lee, Lieutenant Colonel William R. Carter, and Captain John Demsond sat with Dr. Cooper in the comfortable confines of his library. The dark walnut bookshelves held an impressive accumulation. Some of the books were expensive collector's items protected with glass covers. A fire roared in the stone fireplace as the doctor poured a generous round of quality brandy into handsome goblets.

"I cannot begin to tell you how happy I am to see you coming back to this side of the river," Dr. Cooper said as he placed the bottle of liquor on the table near the officers. "The bluecoats have driven my couriers indoors...even more so than the harsh winter weather of late."

"I've heard that President Davis is concerned about the decline of information coming out of Washington," Brigadier General Lee said. "He wants to know what Hooker and Grant are up to, in particular, but it is obviously important to renew the ample flow of the streams of information, in general. General Stuart has assigned Captain Demsond here with the responsibility of identifying and remedying the major logjams."

Dr. Cooper smiled and raised his goblet in a toast. "Here's to the good captain's unbounded success in the endeavor." All glasses were raised in response.

At this point, Captain Demsond felt somewhat compelled to speak. "This won't be easy. Diligent efforts in Stanton's War Department have heightened the level of awareness throughout the area, making even simple courier activity much more dangerous. Some routes have been completely shut down."

He paused. "We've just introduced a second cipher key for improved security."

The full impact of Demsond's statement soaked in. It was going to be a rough spring. Each of them began to wonder whether the war effort as a whole was mirrored in these events...They hoped not.

"Personally, I don't see a meaningful threat," Lieutenant Colonel Carter said. "The Union cavalry doesn't pose a problem for us, and they never will."

"Carter, your optimism is only exceeded by your gallantry in the field of battle," Brigadier General Lee quipped. "Actually, I tend to agree with you...but if we cannot break their will to continue this war, the unlimited resources of our adversary worry me."

"All the more reason to keep filling their minds with the good news from Richmond," Dr. Cooper said. "Give them hell, boys."

CHAPTER FORTY-SEVEN

War Department
February 25, 1863
post meridiem

I had just returned from dinner after the morning's staff meeting. We went out together with the new agent, Simpson Dahlgren, who happened to be the nephew of Union Admiral John A. Dahlgren. The Philadelphian seemed to me to be quite forward and aggressive, and I wondered how well he would fit in with the rest of us. Our work required a lot of patience.

My concern about our new member was overshadowed by the messages that were beginning to arrive, detailing the events occurring in the vicinity of Hartwood Church. A Confederate force of unknown size had overwhelmed the pickets there and progressed along both the Ridge Road and the Warrenton Road toward Berea Church. This point marked the most distant extent of the telegraph line from Hooker's headquarters, where the chief of staff, Major General Daniel Butterfield, had already issued orders for Brigadier General Averell to fend off the Rebel attack.

The enemy's penetration four miles beyond Hartwood Church, in the direction of Falmouth, had greatly disturbed General Hooker. He alerted Major General Stoneman to prepare to personally lead a reserve force behind Averell to severely punish the brazen invaders.

The lines of communication were temporarily lost when the telegraph operators were forced to abandon their post at Berea Church, until Averell's forces permitted them to return just before 9:00 p.m. I was sitting in the telegraph room with President Lincoln and several of the telegraph operators when the messages resumed. The information was sparse and disjointed—Brigadier General Averell characterized the scene as one of *disorder prevailing*, and the size of the enemy force was estimated to be two thousand strong.

At 11:00 p.m. Averell held the position at Hartwood Church when orders were issued to Major General Stoneman to reinforce Averell and pursue the enemy all the way to their encampments beyond the Rappahannock. Butterfield also asked that Major General Heintzelman send forces as far as the Rappahannock Station along the O&A Railroad. Neither Stoneman nor Heintzelman responded.

President Lincoln left the War Department at midnight, shaking his head in disbelief. I walked with him in silence to the Executive Mansion and then went to the Ebbitt Inn to get some sleep.

Brigadier General Fitzhugh Lee returned to Morrisville for the night. He had lost six men during the day and taken 150 prisoners, approaching within five miles of Falmouth. By the time Brigadier General Averell and a reserve force led by Brigadier General Pleasonton would reach Morrisville on the following day, Fitz Lee would be safe at Culpeper Court House, writing his report to General Stuart.

Not being one to miss the opportunity to jab at his old friend, Fitz Lee left a message behind at Morrisville with his regimental surgeon, who remained there to care for the wounded Rebel soldiers. It read:

> *Dear Averell, Please let this surgeon assist in taking care of my wounded. I ride a pretty fast horse, but I think yours can beat mine. I wish you'd quit your shooting and get out of my state and go home. If you won't go home, why don't you come pay me a visit? Send me over a fresh bag of coffee. Good-bye, Fitz*

CHAPTER FORTY-EIGHT

Fairfax Court House
March 8, 1863
post meridiem

I had received reports of a gap in the Washington screen near Chantilly, on the Little River Turnpike. I passed this information on to Major General Heintzelman's staff, but the reports continued to come in from some of the locals, as well as from the telegraph operator at nearby Centreville. I decided to ride out there and take a look for myself.

It was another gray winter day, but there was very little wind, and it hadn't snowed for a few days. I was able to make good time on this quiet Sunday, arriving at Fairfax Court House before noon. Just like my last visit, the town was nearly empty.

Colonel Wyndham was away, leaving Lieutenant Colonel Johnston in charge of the three regiments of cavalry in the area. He informed me that the commander of the infantry at Fairfax Station, Brigadier General Edwin H. Stoughton, had established his headquarters in the home of Dr. William P. Gunnell on the west end of Main Street, over four miles away from his soldiers.

I accepted Johnston's invitation to spend the night with him and his wife in the home of Joshua Gunnell on Chain Bridge Road, near the courthouse.

"Colonel Wyndham placed two regiments of cavalry in Germantown, about a mile to the west of here, along the Little River Turnpike," Johnston said. "His third regiment is about six miles beyond there, at Chantilly. If you take the Warrenton Turnpike at Germantown, instead of the Little River Turnpike to Chantilly, you'll get to Centreville, where there's a brigade of infantry."

I walked over to the telegraph operator's tent, which was on the courthouse lawn, and sent a message to the WD to let them know where I was. Lieutenant Colonel Johnston saddled up and prepared to ride with me. We stopped by to meet Brigadier General Stoughton on the way out of town, but he wasn't available, so we rode on to Germantown.

Johnston pointed out the nature of the rough terrain on either side of the Little River Turnpike. I could see that the movement along the turnpike, even on a Sunday, required that he keep a sizeable force there, just to be able to check out the travelers in a reasonable amount of time without creating a logjam. He assured me that the situation along the Warrenton Turnpike was similar. It was very difficult to send the men out on patrols very far away from the main road.

It was another seven miles to Chantilly, where things were of a similar state. It was there that Johnston's own regiment, the 5th New York Cavalry, was placed. "I've already lost five men to bushwhackers," he said.

It appeared that the screen commanders were doing the best they could with what they had to work with, and I would report this back to Major Eckert.

We rode back to Fairfax Court House along the same route that had taken us out to Chantilly. As we rode along, I asked Johnston about the sentiments of the people in the area. He said that Stoughton had required them to take the *loyalty oath*...That answered my question.

I took supper with the Johnstons and the Gunnells, but before going to bed, I walked over to the telegraph operator's tent. I sent a message to the WD to inform Major Eckert that I would not be at tomorrow's staff meeting.

"By the way," the operator said, "you should know that the line between Chantilly and Germantown isn't working."

"That's odd," I said. "I rode by there in both directions today, and it was just fine." I returned to the house and went to bed.

I was having trouble sleeping. My stomach wasn't upset, but my mind was. Something didn't feel right. I gave up trying to sleep and dressed. I opened the window to get a breath of fresh air—it was pitch black out there, cool and quiet. In the distance, the light from the guards' small fire danced along the side of Stoughton's headquarters.

I went out to check on my horse in the barn, behind the house. It was very dark, almost impossible to see. I stood between the house and the barn for a bit, to let my eyes adjust before entering the barn. The horses were jittery, and I tried to calm them down. A dog began to bark outside.

The smell of the barn carried me back home. I tried to avoid thinking about home as much as I could, but it was this kind of setting that would suddenly do it. I didn't fight the thought, and fixed a picture of our big barn in my mind. I saw all of the stalls, and even the peg where I would hang Dandy's bridle—I knew that it was resting there right now.

It was then that I heard someone outside. I had left the door open, so I thought it was one of the guards checking it. I walked up to him, and when I told him that I was just checking on the horses, the man struck the side of my head with the butt of his rifle. I don't remember hitting the ground.

⌘ ⌘ ⌘

"What's happening?"

"Shhhhhh…it's me, Johnston."

He was dragging me back in the direction of the barn. My ears were ringing, and I could feel blood caked on the side of my face. I tried to help push myself along with my legs, but they were like butter. We got inside the barn—the doors were wide open, and the horses were gone. We stopped…Johnston sat me down and left for a moment, and then he returned.

Somehow, he managed to get me down through a trapdoor to a space below the floor of the barn. "Rebel raiders…Mosby, I think," he whispered. "They got the general. I got out through the bedroom window just in time…didn't even have time to put my clothes on."

"Here, take my weapons," I said before I fumbled around and found that both of my pistols were gone.

"They've rounded up all of the horses and taken a bunch of prisoners…All we can do now is to wait for them to leave…We'll stay here until sunrise." It was cold and dark, and my head hurt.

We waited for sunrise and slowly left our hideout. Mrs. Johnston and the Gunnells were shocked to see us. They were certain that we had been taken away. A few people were stirring about, but no one in military uniform. My legs were working better now, so I went to the telegraph operator's tent—no one was there. I tried to send a telegram, but the lines were out in all directions.

I went back to the barn and found my Henry leaning up against the back of the stall where I had placed it when I checked on my horse. It had been too dark for my attacker to find it. I looked around for my pistols, but they were gone.

A rider came into town, and he was sent southward to Fairfax Station to report the incident. There were troops and telegraph there. *Soon everyone would know.*

CHAPTER FORTY-NINE

War Department
March 11, 1863
ante meridiem

It didn't take very long for the newspapers in both the North and the South to try to make a legend out of Mosby's ride into Fairfax Court House. With help from thirty partisan rangers, including scouts from the area, he had snaked his way through the porous screen and made away with a brigadier general, a captain, a telegraph operator, twenty other men, and sixty horses. I was grateful that they failed to mention my two pistols.

I still wore a bandage when we met in the library on Wednesday morning. Major Eckert was in with Secretary Stanton, so we waited for their meeting to end before ours could begin. It gave me a chance to pour a second cup of coffee, which I badly needed.

Major Eckert soon arrived and started right out. "I think you're already beginning to make a difference, and I told the secretary so. The other side of that coin is that the enemy would love to get its hands on any one of you. However, we don't know whether they will treat you as a prisoner of war, or a *spy*."

We all knew what that meant.

"Of course, you may be here today, Agent Alexander, precisely because you were *not* wearing a military uniform in Fairfax Court House," he said. "I think you were taken for a civilian."

"It was too dark for him to see my WD armband," I said.

"I believe that Secretary Stanton will order Major General Heintzelman to pull back the screen to a distance where no known gaps are in existence. Commanding officers will be required to establish their headquarters amidst their troops...The smart ones would never think of doing otherwise." We chuckled.

"And as far as Mosby is concerned, we will just have to wait for him to slip up and make a mistake." Major Eckert paused a moment as if to think more about what he had just said. Then he continued, "Let's get on with the reports."

I had initiated a process for my Wednesday report that included a list of the ten most active courier routes, based upon available information. I was now receiving over two hundred pieces of information to review each week. My list was immediately sent from Secretary Stanton to Hooker, Heintzelman, and Sharpe. I could see where our increased attention in one area would immediately move more activity to another nearby route.

Suspicious characters were usually arrested by the soldiers, but Lafayette Baker also seemed to be increasing his activity. Major Eckert suspected that Secretary Stanton was giving my list to him as well. Reports were that his interrogation techniques were rather harsh.

After the meeting, I walked over to see Mel Richards at the armory. I was reluctant to tell him that I had lost my pistols, but I needed to get replacements. Much to my surprise, he seemed to take it rather matter-of-factly and quickly brought two pistols out for me to look at. He didn't ask me how I'd managed to keep the Henry.

"The Pocket Colt here is just like what you had before," he said.

"The other was a gift from Congressman Whittlesey," I said. "I will need to write him about that."

"Too late, my boy, I think he has left us."

"I didn't know." I was sure that Miss Carroll would have said something to me about that.

"Now I have something brand new to replace your Army Colt, and that would be this here *New Model* Army Colt. This one is right from my first shipment. It's got a solid frame that won't shroud the barrel threads, and a smooth cylinder, forty-four caliber with the eight-inch barrel...Take it back on the range if you like."

I did just that and returned to thank him before I left. The new pistol was very accurate, but after a few shots, my head couldn't take it any longer. I went to the stables to tell Andrew Jones about the stolen horse.

"She won't eat as well, but they'll take good care of her. Got plenty of other horses here for ya, but ya better let me know if yer head'n for a battle, 'cause I got some ready for that kinda action."

I knew that he was referring to horses that didn't shy away from a confrontation—a true warhorse even welcomed it.

Just then, a messenger from the WD rushed in. "Major Eckert wants to see you right away."

I found him sitting in the telegraph room. "General Hooker is going to send the cavalry to Culpeper Court House to run out the Rebels. I want you to ride along with them. You can meet up with Hooker's staff officer, Captain William Moore, at Morrisville on Saturday. This is a big operation, Jason. Brigadier General Averell will be leading three thousand men into this one."

The enormity of the situation hit me right away—it was Averell's opportunity to provide a payback to his old friend Fitz Lee. The timing was significant as well. This attack would set the stage for the summer of 1863, a time when President Lincoln hoped to put an end to the war. He was betting on Hooker and Grant to come through for him on their respective fronts.

It was a more aggressive approach, one that Miss Carroll had argued for in the cabinet meetings. She believed that the two generals who could execute such a plan were now in place. She had recently said to me, *"We need to strike while the iron is hot...to use a phrase that a cattleman like you, Jason, must appreciate."*

"What am I to do?" I said, looking right at the major.

"Just tell me what you saw out there, when you get back," Major Eckert said.

I was happy that he had not chosen to use the word *if.*

CHAPTER FIFTY

Kelly's Ford
March 17, 1863
ante meridiem

We moved out from Morrisville on the hard, frozen roads early on Monday morning. Devoid of any festive greenery in recognition of St. Patrick's Day, a mass of blue meandered in the direction of Kelly's Ford, thirty miles in the distance. Brigadier General Averell detached nine hundred men to protect his flanks, picketing the railroad between Bealeton Station and Catlett's Station and guarding the fords beyond the railroad. He also left some men to guard his rear at Morrisville. I was concerned to see such a large force peel off from the main group.

We had been unable to mask our approach, and the Confederates were waiting for us at Kelly's Ford when the head of our column reached there at 8:00 a.m. Two narrow gullies in the steep riverbank provided the only access to the crossing on our side of the river. Felled trees lay across the shallow riverbank and road on the far side. Confederate sharpshooters on higher ground quickly began to pick off our riders as they started to make their way across the river, being slowed almost to a stop by the formidable abatis. It was an ugly scene.

I watched from a distant hill with the senior officers. We helplessly sat atop our mounts with the cold breeze blowing in our faces. "Why would anyone in their right mind want to be a general?" Averell said.

Brigadier General Averell eventually sent his chief of staff, Major Samuel Chamberlain, to rally the troops and lead a charge, but he was wounded, and his horse was killed. Woodcutters from the 16th Pennsylvania were sent in with axes to clear away the trees. They worked courageously under heavy enemy fire from the rifle pits and eventually opened a few pathways, taking heavy losses. Riders from the 1st Rhode Island and the 6th Ohio were the first to make it across.

The Confederates held their position as long as possible, even allowing twenty men from the 4th Virginia to be taken as prisoners. It took about two hours for all of the remaining obstacles to be cleared out, allowing Averell's forces to cross in force and reassemble. The water was up to my waist where I crossed, forcing me to hold my guns and ammunition shoulder-high to keep them dry. The water was very cold, and the current was strong, but the river bottom was solid rock for most of the way. I rode through the little village of Kellysville to a clearing, where preparations for the battle ahead were being made.

In the distance, I could see an open field on gradually rising ground that led up to Wheatley's Farm, which included several buildings and a long stone wall. Beyond the farm, I could see the Rebels on a hilltop. Both sides were assessing the size of the forces that they faced. Averell's officers concluded that Fitz Lee was leading the 1st, 2nd, 3rd, 4th, and 5th Virginia Cavalry along with a battery of horse artillery. We later learned that they had also been joined by General Stuart, along with Stuart's Prussian aide, Major

Heros von Borcke, and artillery chief, Major John Pelham. Stuart had chosen to leave Fitz Lee in command at the battle site.

Closer observation revealed that a small group of dismounted Rebel cavalry occupied some of the farm buildings and crouched behind the stone wall. With some help from the 4th Pennsylvania and the 4th New York, Colonel J. Irvin Gregg's 16th Pennsylvania dislodged the Rebels, claiming their own positions behind the stone wall. Averell quickly sent more forces there to fortify the position. He also moved troops into the adjacent forests to flush out any possible Rebel flanking maneuvers. I moved with Averell and his senior officers to a command post on a small hill about a thousand yards from the stone wall, just out of artillery range.

As soon as we reached the hill, Fitz Lee attacked with his full brigade, charging down the far hillside in columns of four. The Virginians rushed headlong into the Union placement in the vicinity of Wheatley's Farm, but not before meeting with heavy artillery fire. Sabers glistened in the smoky sunlight, and the riders from both sides met in a fury of steel and lead. It was difficult for me to tell who was winning—at that moment, I recognized that *winning* was really just losing less than the other side.

Captain Moore was watching through his field glasses. "There seems to be a lot of flurry around one of their officers who just went down in the charge through the artillery. He doesn't have a beard, so it's not Fitz Lee."

I had studied pictures of the enemy's officers from West Point records, so I grabbed my field glasses for a look. I recognized the face right away. "It's Major John Pelham!"

"It can't be…His big guns aren't here," Captain Moore said.

"I'm sure that's him," I said. "For some strange reason, he was riding down the hillside with the others in the charge."

We watched as the attack was repulsed, and the Rebels rode back up the hillside to re-form their lines. Brigadier General Averell chose not pursue them with a counterattack; however, Colonel Alfred Duffié ordered a charge, leading the 1st Rhode Island, the 4th Pennsylvania, and the 6th Ohio. Although Averell was furious with the Frenchman, he immediately ordered two squadrons of the 5th U.S. Cavalry to join in on the attack.

Fitz Lee led the 1st, 2nd, and 4th Virginia Cavalry down the hillside to meet Duffié. They violently clashed at the base of the hill…The choice between the use of the saber or the pistol was the difference between life and death for many. The Union colonel's timing was perfect, as the Confederates were not completely prepared for the counterattack. If more troops had been sent in with Duffié, the day might have been won at that point, but a fresh squadron of Rebels was enough to halt the advance and allow time for an orderly retreat.

The Confederates withdrew to a point beyond Carter's Run, a small creek about a mile away, crossing under the road to Culpeper. They also brought up Captain James Breathed's four guns of horse artillery to face the six hundred yards of clear ground, bordered by woods on both sides, offering a good strategic position between them and Averell's forces.

Averell was quick to recognize the gravity of the situation, pausing to consider his next move. Captain Moore and I decided to ride down to inspect the buildings on Wheatley's Farm to see if anything of interest had been left behind.

I rode through the carnage of war, the fallen men and horses on the battlefield. The moans of the living, and the stone eyes of the dead, haunted us. As we neared the buildings, we saw both blue- and gray-clad combatants, some of whom had killed each other, now lying side by side in their mixed blood.

The farmhouse had suffered minimal damage, so we were able to safely move about its entirety. We found nothing, but I continued to search as Captain Moore checked the outbuildings. I paused for a moment to look at the family picture—father, mother, two sons, and one daughter—just like my family back in Illinois. Then I found a small bundle of papers, wedged under the bottom of a desk drawer in the library, and placed them in my saddlebag. Captain Moore came up empty. I informed him of my find and promised to share any discovery with him.

Averell moved his command post to a point just beyond the farm. Two of his six artillery guns were no longer operable, so the artillery firepower was now about even. It appeared that Fitz Lee was going to hold his favorable position and force Averell to press the fight. There was concern that Fitz Lee was setting a trap and preparing for a flank attack. Averell reluctantly moved forward, but with great caution.

Lieutenant Robert Sweatman of the 5th U.S. Cavalry led our advance, reaching the edge of the clearing where the Confederates waited, six hundred yards away. After a round of artillery fire, Fitz Lee attacked with a rush of force that brought the Rebels through our attacking forces and almost all of the way up to where we stood.

They rode with reckless abandon, seemingly expecting our troops to cut and run, but that didn't happen. We stood our ground. Instinctively, I grabbed the Henry from its sheath and opened fire on the attackers, as did the others around me. Strong fire from the 1st U.S. Cavalry, the 3rd Pennsylvania, and the 16th Pennsylvania turned the Rebels, only twenty yards away. Many were hit, dropping all around me, including Captain Moore on my immediate right.

The wounded moved to the rear, while the rest of us braced for another attack.

But only small attacks and counterattacks continued, until the Confederates permanently retreated to a point just beyond their big guns. They put down a field of fire that convinced Averell not to pursue any further. Chamberlain also reminded him of the possibility of fresh Rebel reinforcements that could be delivered by their side of the O&A Railroad located nearby.

At 5:30 p.m., after a long day of battle, Averell ordered the retreat back to Morrisville, by way of Kelly's Ford. Fitz Lee's forces did not make any serious attempt to attack Averell's rear, which was expertly protected by the 1st U.S. Cavalry. We were tired and cold and hungry as we made our way back along the same route that we had traveled earlier in the day.

At a farmhouse just on the outside of Kellysville, Brigadier General Averell left two badly wounded officers, and a surgeon with medical supplies. He also left a sack of coffee and a note for Fitz Lee. It read:

> *Dear Fitz, Here's your coffee. Here's your visit. How do you like it? How's that horse? Averell*

CHAPTER FIFTY-ONE

Elliott House
March 20, 1863
post meridiem

During our retreat from the battlefield near Kelly's Ford, I examined the small package that I had picked up at the farmhouse. I was concerned that there might be something of immediate military value, but I found only a coded letter wrapped in some newspaper clippings. I rushed to get this back to the telegraph operators in Washington.

On Friday morning I reported my observations of the battle at the staff meeting. I was fully aware that both the pro-Union papers in the North *and* the pro-Confederate papers in the North and South were claiming victory at Kelly's Ford. I thought a lot about what I was going to report…I truly believed that Averell's forces had represented themselves quite well at the encounter.

I couldn't help but offer the suggestion that crossing with the *full* force of three thousand riders might have resulted in a complete victory, taking us all the way to Culpeper Court House; however, it was difficult to question Brigadier General Averell's decision to protect his flanks. Had I been in his place, I would have done as he did, if I suspected a flank attack—my readings from Napoleon's *Maxims* supported Averell's approach.

I was satisfied that I could make this report in good conscience, because it was important that I be welcomed to ride amongst our cavalry again in the future. I could see why Major Eckert had added this assignment to my area of responsibility. It expanded the horizons of my sphere of knowledge far beyond what it would have been had I remained shackled to the restraints of my desk in Washington.

I understood how the freedom of movement of the Confederate cavalry directly connected to the communication flow in and out of Washington, making places like Kelly's Ford so important. I had a sense that I hadn't seen the last of that place.

I was able to get some badly needed rest before taking supper at the Ebbitt House. Miss Carroll looked great, as always, and she helped me deflect inquiries about my experience at Kelly's Ford. I had become much more sensitive to the seriousness associated with the loose lips around Washington. I preferred that those at the table be totally unaware of my involvement; however, that information seemed to be general knowledge at the Ebbitt House.

As usual, the sentiments around the table reflected the mood of the disparate North. Some lauded the victory attributed to the Union cavalry, and others were suspicious of it. I spoke in generalities, avoiding specifics, but I made it clear that I believed the mission to be a success.

Miss Carroll began a discussion about the poor quality of food in Washington, noting that it was not so unusual for this time of the year.

Abigail Ebbitt agreed with her. "We'll start to get the more frequent loads of beef from the West as soon as the weather breaks.

Jason, I expect that you will welcome this, and perhaps it'll bring you a little bit closer to home."

The letters from home had indicated that the corn-fed winter stock was generally healthy. "I'll admit that it would be nice to see the stockyards full of JTA beeves," I said. "My father said that he's going to send out some horses, too. I'm hoping to grab one of those for my own use."

"Quartermaster General Meigs frequently gets complaints from the field officers about the condition of their horses...He thinks that many of the riders don't know how to properly care for them," Miss Carroll said. "He has been working hard to get better quality horses, and more of them."

"Yes, that's true, and once we get them, we are able to feed them well, thanks to Brigadier General Haupt," I said. "The Rebels struggle to feed their mounts properly, particularly if they try to move northward, extending their supply lines."

"I can't imagine that General Lee would move from the advantage that he has at Fredericksburg," William Ebbitt said. "Eventually, Hooker will have to attack, and he will take heavy losses again."

"And the longer the war goes on, the more the North loses its appetite to keep fighting," Mrs. Mason said. "William, you're right. Lee will just sit tight, right where he is."

I really didn't have a strong opinion about the matter, nor did I wish to join this discussion. I was just enjoying the comfort of the Ebbitt House after being in the saddle for a few days.

After supper, Miss Carroll asked me to walk with her to the War Department, where she wanted to check on messages from out west. She told me that it had to do with the plans to take Island Number Ten on the Mississippi River, but she wouldn't say any more than that.

While Miss Carroll sat at Major Eckert's desk to read the messages, I sat with Albert Chandler at the telegraph room's center table. He was busy trying to break the Confederate cipher, working with the newest prize, the letter that I had retrieved at Wheatley's Farm.

"I'm pretty sure that this is the same cipher that we have seen before," he said. "We're getting closer and closer to this thing. David doesn't think they can change their key very often, so that should help us...By the way, he wanted you to look closely at one of the newspaper clippings." He pointed to it on the table.

I picked it up and moved closer to the fireplace. I could see what Bates had noticed. It appeared that someone had written something down on another piece of paper, and the ink had bled through to the newspaper clipping. It looked to me like it could be the name *Michael.* The first two letters and the last two letters were clear, but the middle letters were not.

As if he read my mind, Chandler said, "It's not the cipher key... I've tried everything close, and nothing works. We're sure that they use at least two words in their key."

"Can you ask all of the operators to take a look at the ink smudge and write down what they think it might be?" I said. "That will give us a good starting point."

"Will do."

Just then, Miss Carroll finished up her work and was ready to return to the Ebbitt House. She thanked Chandler; we said goodbye and departed.

She held my arm close to her as we walked in the gently falling snow as it neared midnight. Maybe it was because we had traveled together on the train from the West that made me feel like I was close to home when I was with her. We reached the Ebbitt House all too quickly. We looked in each other's eyes. She kissed me on the cheek and went inside. I felt all tingly inside. I had almost forgotten about Meredith Montgomery back in Jacksonville.

CHAPTER FIFTY-TWO

Toledo, Ohio
March 21, 1863
ante meridiem

Clement Vallandigham continued to raise his voice about the "wicked and cruel" war that the Republicans were waging upon the helpless victims of the South. The Ohio congressman, a leader of the Peace Democrats, also complained of the rough treatment that he had received at the hands of "Lincoln's stooges" in various encounters around the capital city. "It's no longer possible to speak up against the war...This wasn't the way America was supposed to be...What happened to freedom of speech?" he raged.

He sought to connect the activities of the KGC and the CSA, and it had finally happened. Regular courier routes had been established between the two groups to facilitate rapid communication. Vallandigham took personal interest in such joint ventures, particularly the ones that were larger in scope. He dubbed them with the knightly title of a "quest."

A plan to free twenty thousand Confederate prisoners who were being held in various locations in Ohio, Illinois, and Indiana was the first of these. It became known as Quest Number One, referred to as QI for purposes of security. The prison escapes were to occur at the same time, and the escapees were to be immediately armed and involved back in the war effort.

Even though all of the quests had met with his approval, Vallandigham had concerns that some of them would be very difficult, if not impossible, to carry out. In particular, he was fearful of those quests planned in or around Washington because he was acutely aware of the increase in the activities of the War Department there. His ability to communicate along the Secret Line between his Washington office and Richmond had been severely hampered of late. It had become necessary to use the Confederate cipher to protect these messages because the possibility of their interception had increased so.

QVII was a concern. The idea for this quest had fomented in the heart of the Illinois cattle country, or more specifically, at the abolitionist stronghold of a college that was located there. A Peace Democrat student had been poorly treated by the professors and most of the other students, prompting him to share the confidential findings of a science professor, with whom he had worked as a student, with the local KGC group in Jacksonville.

The risk of the plan being discovered before it could be carried out was great, but the enormity of the potential reward could not be denied, so QVII moved forward. As with all of these major quests, Vallandigham personally approved the selection of the knight in charge for each one of them, and QVII was no different.

He had just concluded the meeting here at his home on this Saturday morning with the man upon whom he had bestowed this quest. He knew that this choice wouldn't be popular with some of his knights, largely due to the fact that this man had recently demonstrated a bit of carelessness in the field.

But Vallandigham believed that it was only fair that the man who had saved the plan in its very infancy be recognized in this manner. After meeting with him face-to-face, Vallandigham was sure that Miles Palladin was just the man for the job.

Palladin was driven to see that a major part of the food supply in Washington was destroyed. It was the same man who had orchestrated the explosion at the Allegheny Arsenal in Pittsburgh not long ago—and the man had such *dark eyes.*

CHAPTER FIFTY-THREE

War Department
March 23, 1863
ante meridiem

As spring approached, I was beginning to get homesick. My mother must have noticed this when she read my most recent letter because she answered it yesterday, with a short telegram in advance of her return letter. It was my first spring far away from home, and spring had always been my favorite time of the year.

The ranch seemed to come alive in the spring, starting with a roundup of wild horses. A few of these became good for riding, but most of them were used to pull wagons. I could almost smell the JTA branding iron hitting the horsehide. It was a sure thing that some of the horses from this spring's roundup would end up in Washington in response to Quartermaster General Meigs's recent call to replenish the supply.

Strangely, I was reflecting upon a close call that I'd had with a branding iron years ago, when I bumped into Lafayette Baker as he was exiting the War Department building.

"Why, Alexander, I thought you would have been captured or killed by the enemy by now," he said.

"Fortunately not," I said. We'd been briefly introduced about a month ago just outside of Secretary Stanton's office, and our paths hadn't crossed since then. I'd heard the reports about his terrorizing the city, trying to flush out Confederate spies, but I wasn't sure if this had helped or hurt my endeavors here.

"I'll give you credit, Alexander, at least you aren't tied to that desk of yours all day long like most of the people in this building," he said, jerking his head in a backward direction.

"We prefer the use of brain over brawn, where possible," I said.

He shrugged, taking in a deep breath.

"That'll only get you so far with these Southern folks...They're playing for keeps, you know," he said, speaking through clenched teeth. "The sooner you guys figure that out, the better...Lead in the head is a bitter wake-up call, Alexander."

"I think you underestimate the value of our work," I responded, trying to remain calm. "We're working the whole puzzle, not just a piece here and there—the key to our victory is in the *sum* of the parts."

He just stood there looking at me. I was hoping that he was thinking about what I had just said.

"Good day, *Agent* Alexander," he said, turning quickly and walking away.

I watched him as he was joined by some of his men, who were waiting for him across the street. They were a tough-looking bunch, and made me think that the stories about them might just be true. Knowing that Baker reported directly to Secretary Stanton, I doubted that anything was going on that didn't meet with his approval.

I once overheard an argument in the bar at Willard's regarding how things would be different if Stanton was the president instead of Lincoln. I was grateful that things were not switched around, because I thought it was important for the commander in chief to lead with a combination of strong will *and* compassion, as President Lincoln did.

It was well known that the president would spend a good part of his day meeting with the people that would line up for hours to see him. They came from all parts of the country, and they knew that Abraham Lincoln would listen to their story and render a fair judgment.

I went to my desk in the library and continued to think about the mystery around the *Michael* ink smudge on the newspaper from Wheatley's Farm. I decided to apply some deductive reasoning skills that I'd learned in college. I assumed that if the name was actually "Michael," and it was a first name, then we would be in an untenable position with far too many possibilities to explore, so I abandoned that direction.

Instead, I posited that it was a *last name* of "Michael," or it was a word beginning with "Mi" and ending with "el" with the middle being two to four letters that looked like "cha" when combined. I further assumed that the word had something to do with a location because that would be of use to us, and little else would be at this point.

I was able to spend the entire morning on the task because our staff meeting was cancelled when Major Eckert was called away. I pulled the maps of Washington and the surrounding areas, going over them one by one. Tinker and Chandler provided some assistance when things were quiet in the telegraph room.

We came up with a list of thirteen locations that met the *Mi__el* requirements. There were eight residences, two taverns, two farms, and one road. Agent Simpson Dahlgren offered to help me check out these locations. We decided to leave Milrel Road for the end, since there were many locations along that road, including the Milrel farm.

I gave the Mitchel, Mitrel, and the two Michael residences, all of which were located in Washington, to Dahlgren. Remembering my experience at Bailey's, I decided to start out with Minstrel's Tavern at Ball's Crossroads and Miguel's Tavern at Hunter's Mills. We agreed to meet and discuss our findings prior to Wednesday's staff meeting.

Just as we were wrapping things up for the day, Tinker gave me a telegram.

Jacksonville, Illinois/March 23,1863/4:38 p.m.

> *Will arrive in Washington on Friday with Governor Yates at President Lincoln's request. Must meet with you for supper at National Hotel Friday night. Have news about Kinchelow.*
>
> *J. Sturtevant*

CHAPTER FIFTY-FOUR

Miskel's Farm
March 25, 1863
ante meridiem

Dahlgren agreed to report our findings at Wednesday's staff meeting. Even though we were discouraged because we had yet to turn up anything that was particularly unusual or disturbing, I knew that Major Eckert would want us to continue with an examination of the remaining sites on our list. The plan to do so was already in place.

Dahlgren and I had divided up the remaining locations, planning to explore them over the next two days. He would investigate three residences outside of Washington, and I would take Milrel Farm and Miskel Farm, both of which were out near the end of the Washington screen.

Early in the morning, I rode my horse to Alexandria, where I boarded the train on the Alexandria, Loudoun, and Hampshire Railroad, destined for Guilford Station, which was within riding distance of Miskel's Farm. The sun was peeking through some thickening clouds as I led my horse from the boxcar to a deeply rutted road called Church Road, starting me out in the right direction.

Before long, I turned to the left, taking a road that headed northward toward the Leesburg and Alexandria Turnpike, which I expected to be about three miles away, according to my roughly drawn map of the area. It was encouraging to see the trees that were budding out on this raw spring day, but I could still catch a whiff of the telltale smoke of the plentiful fireplaces and campfires continuing to warm those in the area.

I stopped at a farmhouse about a mile beyond the turnpike to check on directions to Miskel's. A young slave boy quickly came out to greet me as I turned in to the farm's entry road.

"Yassa, dis way sa," was the only response that I could get to my inquiries as he led me to the farmhouse, which was about a quarter of a mile from the main road.

A woman appeared from the front door. She waited for me on the front porch as I approached. A man that I took for her husband briefly looked up from his chore of chopping and stacking firewood at the side of the house.

"Oh, sure, the Miskels are the next place up the road, just two miles yonder," Isabella Reed replied to my query. "You can't miss them 'cause if you go any further, you'll be in the river." I noticed that she was studying me very closely. I hadn't worn my WD badge, nor had I ridden a saddle with the U.S. markings, so I believed that I was well disguised.

"Are you kinfolk?"

"No," I said, wondering if I should have answered differently, but her look told me that she knew that I wasn't a relative. I sensed that she viewed me as some sort of a threat. The woodcutter watched me closely.

She asked if I wanted coffee, or water for my horse. I turned down the offers. Surprisingly, she didn't seem to be in a hurry to send me on my way. The farm appeared to be well maintained, and there were a good number of horses feeding near the barn.

Before much longer, I rode on. About a mile out, I noticed the small slave boy off in the distance, running back to Isabella Reed's farmhouse *from the direction of Miskel's.* It appeared to me that he had been sent to warn them of my coming visit.

I carefully checked my weapons before passing through the gated entry to the farm, where Franklin and Angela Miskel stood off in the distance in front of the large farmhouse, awaiting my arrival. The farm was a collection of fenced-in areas connected by gates. As I rode along the long entry lane, I couldn't help but notice that the lane appeared to be well worn down by horses, but I could see only a few emaciated cows in the enclosure that surrounded the big barn west of the two-story house.

The Miskels looked like farmers. They were friendly, but very cautious. "We don't get many strangers on our road," Franklin Miskel said.

"There's no good place to cross the river here," Angela Miskel joined in.

I had a feeling about this place, so I quickly decided to try something different, not wanting to spook them by asking a lot of questions. "I'm beginning to think that I have come to the wrong place. I'm Jason Alexander from Washington, and I heard that your place might be up for sale, but that doesn't appear to be the case."

"Now where did you hear that?" Franklin said, lifting his hat and scratching his head in one swift motion.

"From a guy at the Willard Hotel last week," I said.

"You don't say...That floors me. We've never talked about selling...Have we, Ma?"

"Well, you sure haven't talked to me about it, but then I'm the last one to find out about things around here," Angela said. "I'm afraid you made a long trip for nothing, Mr. Alexander."

"You have a nice place here. I can understand why you wouldn't want to sell."

"We've been here almost fifteen years, isn't that right, Ma?" He didn't wait for an answer before continuing on. "We hope to be here for a good deal longer," Franklin said as he pulled a pipe from his pocket and began to tap the bottom of the bowl against the palm of his outstretched hand. "Well, if you don't mind, we've got chores to tend to."

"Certainly...I'll be on my way. I'm sorry for the bother."

"No bother...I hope you find the place you're looking for," Franklin said.

Later, I rode along Milrel Road and looked in on the Milrel farm. I found nothing unusual there. My mind was preoccupied with recounting my visit to Miskel's farm. It was an out-of-the-way location that provided great privacy, but it was also a place where one could become easily boxed in and trapped. I was sure that the Miskels had been warned of my arrival, and that was enough to raise concern in my mind.

I returned to Guilford Station just in time to board the last train to Alexandria for the day. I was hoping to get a wire off to Major Eckert before I departed, but there wasn't time. Light snow began to fall as the lights of Washington gradually appeared in the distance.

CHAPTER FIFTY-FIVE

National Hotel
March 27, 1863
post meridiem

A dusting of snow still remained on the ground as I left the War Department and headed to the National Hotel at Pennsylvania Avenue and Sixth Street to meet President Sturtevant for supper. I spent most of the day sorting through the numerous telegrams received from stationmasters across the country. We bundled and tagged these by subject matter, along with other sources of information, hoping to extract something useful. It was tedious work, and I was ready to spend my Friday night elsewhere.

President Sturtevant reserved a table for two on the east side of the main dining room, near the wall with the pictures of the country's presidents arranged in chronological order. He appeared to be as happy to see me as I was to see him, bringing memories of satisfying times from the past. To me, his warm eyes overshadowed the thin, stony face with the jutting jaw that pushed his graying beard forward like a short broom.

After we sat down, he ordered some wine for us. Then he looked at me across the table for a moment before he said, "Alexander, I must begin by telling you that you have formed quite a positive impression with President Lincoln…and I'm not just referring to your saving Anna Carroll and your exploits in the field, but the president specifically addressed your *organizational* skills. Such recognition certainly speaks well for Illinois College."

"I'm giving it my best effort, sir, and as each day goes by, I feel more comfortable with the contribution that I'm making to the War Department efforts…but I do long for my return to Illinois College, and graduation."

"We must go where we are needed," he said as our wine was delivered to the table. He appeared to be in no hurry as he waved the waiter off and lifted his glass, proposing a toast. "To Illinois College."

"To Illinois College," I repeated, and we took a sip of the dark Burgundy. We sat for a while in silence, enjoying the wine and the ambience of the place, with its perfect balance of comfort and class. All of the velvet-cushioned high-back chairs at the tables appeared to be filled with patrons.

"Professor Crampton sends his regards. The captain and some of your classmates have been ordered to guard prisoners of war in Alton, after helping to build a fort in Rolla, Missouri. I think you drew the most challenging assignment, Mr. Alexander."

"I think you're right," I said.

"Let's order some supper," he said as he opened his menu, "and then I want to tell you what's going on with me, as well as something about what is happening back home."

President Sturtevant ordered a round steak with stewed tomatoes, and I ordered game hen with smashed beans. The soup of the day was potato soup, which we received shortly after placing our orders.

As we waited for the soup to cool, President Sturtevant revealed that he was on his way to England at the request of President Lincoln, as an emissary for the Union cause. He was to depart for Liverpool on April 11 on the steamer *City of Washington.* He hoped to return before Christmas. His official designation would be that of a delegate of the American Congregational Union, but he would travel with a letter that he would receive from President Lincoln during his meeting with him next week.

President Sturtevant poured more wine. "The situation in England is enigmatic. The people despise slavery, but the politicians prefer a permanent split between our North and South, believing that they could then dominate and exploit the divided America in commercial matters." His charge was to gain support for the Union from the clergy and the academic community. Although he seemed eager to meet the challenge, I sensed that he was reluctant to leave Jacksonville at this time. *We must go where we are needed.*

After finishing with rice pudding and coffee, we began to talk about the developments back in the Jacksonville area. Mr. Hinrichsen kept me informed about many of the events taking place back home, but President Sturtevant carried some new information.

"Judge Charles Constable was just arrested for suspicion of being associated with the Knights of the Golden Circle. He had only been in his new office for a few days when he ordered the release of all of the men being held in jail for belonging to that abominable organization."

"I have heard that the sympathy for the KGC has grown in recent months," I said.

"It has grown to dangerous numbers," he said. "I fear that if the Union doesn't turn the tide of this war soon, the state of Illinois will swing to the Confederacy...It all hinges up at the central part of the state, since the southern third is already strongly supporting the Rebels."

"I think we're close to major improvements, particularly with regard to our cavalry," I said. "The mind-set that the Southerners are superior horsemen is waning, and we appear to be ready to take a more aggressive posture in this important area."

"I trust that you won't get yourself killed in the process," he said.

I shrugged.

President Sturtevant finished his coffee and motioned for a second cup. After waiting for the waitress to fill the cup and leave, he said, "Judge Constable was released shortly after his arrest, but I was told that he was immediately abducted by a local abolitionist group, and, after some rather rough questioning, Judge Constable stated that young Kinchelow was killed for attempting to carry information away from a local KGC meeting. He claimed that the killer was not from the Jacksonville area... Others came to the judge's rescue before any additional information could be obtained."

"If he was telling the truth, and the murder was done by someone from outside the area, the group might have been plotting something significant, something that reached out beyond the local area," I said. "We need to get to someone else who was at that meeting."

"That's exactly what the sheriff is trying to do," he said, "but you know that the law enforcement people are not likely to confront the KGC."

I invited President Sturtevant to stop by the War Department, if his schedule permitted it, before he left for

England. We parted with a hearty handshake, wishing each other well. I found that my spirits were greatly uplifted as a result of my visit with this wonderful man, and I was optimistic that he would convince the English to stay out of the war.

CHAPTER FIFTY-SIX

Miskel's Farm
April 1, 1863
ante meridiem

I was riding along the Leesburg and Alexandria Turnpike, hoping to meet up with the Union cavalry and get to Miskel's Farm by sunrise. Someone had reported to the picket that riders were seen in the vicinity of Miskel's Farm just after dark. When this information had reached Major Charles Taggart, who was in charge of the northern section of pickets, he'd wired his superior and the WD, following the special instructions that he'd received a few days earlier.

I was awakened with the news just after midnight, and rushed to the telegraph room. Major Taggart had denied my request to send troops to Miskel's Farm, but I'd contacted Major Eckert, and his telegram had yielded the desired result. But precious time had been lost.

I'd hurried to the stables and immediately departed for Miskel's, knowing that I would need to ride all night in the pale moonlight in order to get there by sunrise. If things went well, I could meet up with the cavalry on the turnpike and ride with them the rest of the way.

Major Taggart did not enjoy taking orders from the WD, but once committed, he wasn't willing to be embarrassed by a bad showing, so he ordered Captain Henry Flint to lead the battle-tested 1st Vermont Cavalry to Miskel's. The unit was stationed at a camp near Union Church, about five miles east of Dranesville.

Captain Flint divided his men into two squadrons. He would lead the first squadron of one hundred men, and he assigned Captain George Bean to lead the second squadron of fifty men. They moved out at just after 3:00 a.m., riding along the turnpike to Dranesville. Here they received confirmation from the locals that Confederates, possibly Mosby, were in the area earlier in the night. Having fought with Mosby before, Captain Flint was cautious and decided to inspect all of the buildings in Dranesville before moving on, not wishing to become Mosby's April fool.

I was not able to move quickly along the turnpike because of the darkness, so I didn't reach Dranesville until just before sunrise. I found that the cavalry had departed well over an hour earlier, giving them plenty of time to be at Miskel's by now.

Having just enough light to see, I was able to ride off at a gallop. The sun was beginning to creep up over the snow-covered ground when I heard the first shots in the distance. I knew that the shots were coming from Miskel's.

The noise grew louder as I came closer to the fight. From the sounds, I guessed that the Union cavalry had run into a sizeable group, but the lay of the land at Miskel's would significantly favor those who were outside the fences. I readied my rifle as I turned in to the lane, riding past Isabella Reed's place, and covering the next two miles in a matter of minutes.

What I saw next was not to be believed. The Union cavalry was *inside* the fences, engaging in close-in combat with a much smaller group of Confederates, most of whom were not yet on horseback, having been completely caught by surprise. I saw the flag of the 1st Vermont and noticed that the Union cavalrymen were flailing away with sabers, while the Confederates were using pistols with deadly results against numbers twice their own.

The Union leader made a huge tactical mistake, and the ground was littered, running red with men in blue. In a few more minutes, the battle would be over. Realizing this, a Union officer turned and headed for the outer gate. But for some reason, the gate had been *closed.*

The Union riders bunched up at the gate until it was pushed over by the sheer weight of the group. This delay gave the Confederates time to mount up and viciously attack the rear of the retreating 1st Vermont.

I could see that the whole mass of riders would soon be heading in my direction, because I was on the road leading to the only way out. I moved off the road and into a grove of maple trees, which provided good cover. I began to fire into the Confederates as the Union cavalry frantically poured from the outer gate and raced down the lane toward the turnpike. Six riders, who were no longer comfortable exposing their backs to the enemy, peeled away from the main group and joined me in the maple grove. Together, we were able to throw down a formidable field of fire, enough to convince the Confederates to ride on after the retreating cavalry, rather than remain in the open and face us.

We waited a bit before coming out from the trees after they passed. The six cavalrymen turned back to the farm to help their fallen comrades, and I rode down the lane. All the shooting had stopped. I rode on to Herndon Station to send a telegram to the War Department, knowing that they could get the necessary information out to the right people as quickly as possible.

I rode back to Miskel's Farm. More soldiers arrived, but I didn't see any of the original group, except for the six men who had fought with me in the maple grove. Franklin and Angela Miskel were taken away to the camp, presumably to be questioned by Major Taggart. They would claim that Mosby had threatened to burn their place down if they didn't cooperate with him.

The prevailing sentiment among the soldiers was that their comrades had been captured by Mosby. I suspected that this was indeed true.

The premises were thoroughly searched by the soldiers. I took a second look in the house after they were finished. The wounded were taken inside the house, and the dead bodies were stacked in a small wagon, with Captain Flint among them.

I was unable to find anything of interest, but one of the soldiers did tell me that a coded letter was found in one of the saddlebags that had been left in the house. It had already been taken to Major Taggart. I made a mental note to make sure that the letter ultimately made its way to the War Department.

CHAPTER FIFTY-SEVEN

Falmouth, Virginia
April 7, 1863
post meridiem

On the day following the battle at Miskel's Farm, I received instructions from Major Eckert to join him on a trip to Falmouth with President Lincoln and his family. The trip was Mrs. Lincoln's idea to celebrate Tad's tenth birthday.

We boarded the steamer *Carrie Martin* on Saturday at sunset, in the midst of a snowstorm. I was happy to find President Sturtevant amongst the guests. Because of the rough waters, we were unable to reach Aquia Creek, so we dropped anchor in a protective cove for the night. Tad was able to catch a small fish, which was promptly added to the supper menu.

On Easter Sunday morning, we reached the Aquia Creek Landing. We boarded a train, punching through sizeable snowdrifts all the way to Falmouth Station. We arrived at General Hooker's camp and discovered that President Lincoln's grand review of the Army of the Potomac had been pushed to the next day. Tents were prepared for us amidst the "officers' row" of tents that led to

General Hooker's elaborate structure. The president's tent was still in place next to the telegraph operator's tent, just as it had been on my last visit to this place, when General Burnside was in charge.

The sun was up on Monday morning, and the snow quickly began to melt, producing a thick mud by the time the grand review began at noon with the twenty-one-gun salute to the commander in chief. In full view of the Confederates across the river in Fredericksburg, the entire Cavalry Corps of twenty-five regiments passed by President Lincoln's reviewing stand, followed by the infantry, and then the artillery.

Twelve thousand blue-clad riders created an impressive sight, and I couldn't help but hope that the cavalry was ready to take the war to the next level. But the memory of Miskel's was still fresh in my mind.

That night, President Sturtevant, Major Eckert, and I joined the president and his family for supper in his tent, along with General Hooker, Brigadier General Averell, and Brigadier General Haupt. We talked about horses and railroads, two of my favorite topics. The mood was expectantly upbeat, and General Hooker was quite vocal about his desire to launch a spring offensive against General Lee.

Major Eckert said, "I can't help but think that if we could cut off Lee's supply lines from the Virginia Central and the RF and P Railroads, he would be forced to give up his hold on Fredericksburg." Brigadier General Haupt agreed.

"I can move up the Rappahannock, and cross beyond the Rapidan and take care of that, as long as Lee is distracted by a strong offensive at Fredericksburg," Brigadier General Averell said. "I know we've tried that before, but it'll work this time…if the weather clears." The cautious Averell was unusually optimistic tonight, almost haughty.

It was interesting to watch the senior officers posture themselves for recognition from President Lincoln—all except for Haupt, who remained the same, regardless of the audience.

"No doubt our ever-vigilant adversary is suspecting something," President Lincoln said.

"He can suspect all that he wants," General Hooker said, "but when I send one hundred thousand men toward the crossings at Fredericksburg, he will have his hands full." Fighting Joe Hooker was anxious to differentiate himself from his predecessor, General Burnside. "Bobby Lee's luck is about ready to run out."

I think several people wanted to respond to that comment, but everyone was mysteriously quiet. Brigadier General Haupt changed the subject. "Major Eckert, I see that your agents, like Alexander here, are putting some pressure in the right places."

Major Eckert acknowledged Haupt's positive comment with a smile and a nod. I did the same. "We have a lot more to do, but we're off to a good start," Major Eckert said. "We're concerned that the KGC has connected up with the Confederates, and they are now working closely together."

President Lincoln cleared his throat and said, "I intend to help with that problem by using my war power as president to harshly put down such treasonous acts. I will begin with Mr. Vallandigham." This statement met with loud cheer from all.

"Don't thank me," he said, "it is the work of Miss Anna Ella Carroll...She has thoroughly explored the legal rights of the president of the United States to take extraordinary measures to protect the Union during a state of war."

I was aware of this aspect of Miss Carroll's work. She was convinced that the business-as-usual mind-set would mire the Union down in a sea of paperwork and ultimately result in the loss of the war. She had worked hard to enlist support for her position amongst the president's cabinet. It was a shame that she was not adequately recognized for her work, just because she was a woman.

⌘ ⌘ ⌘

I returned to Washington on the next day along with President Sturtevant, Mrs. Lincoln, and young Tad. The president spent most of the remainder of the week with General Hooker, working on strategy.

The plan was to begin on Monday, April 13, with the movement of the cavalry, placing them into position on Lee's left flank. The cavalry would attack at the same time that the frontal assault began at Fredericksburg. Everyone was eager to put the plan into motion.

When the cavalry moved out on Monday, it began to rain.

CHAPTER FIFTY-EIGHT

War Department
April 17, 1863
ante meridiem

The reports from General Hooker's headquarters grew worse by the day. The rain didn't let up, and the spring offensive was stuck in the mud. The delay threatened to be costly because a large number of Union enlistments were due to expire very soon, and five thousand Union soldiers were deserting each month. A heavy cloud of disappointment hung over the War Department.

We were inundated with reports from all over the Union about the rising intensity of the actions of the KGC. In some places they were called the *Copperheads* after the Peace Democrats, and other names were surfacing, such as the *American Knights* and the *Sons of Liberty*. Clement L. Vallandigham was still recognized as their leader. He had returned to Ohio after failing to be reelected to Congress, and he was now running for governor of Ohio. A good number of people were encouraging him to run for president of the United States.

Major General Burnside had recently established the Military District of the Ohio and suspended civil rights therein, an action directed at Vallandigham and his associates.

I was trying to identify the communication paths between these subversive groups and the Confederacy. Secretary Stanton was particularly concerned about the flow of information out of Washington. He believed that we had leaks within the War Department itself, and he became more secretive than ever. His office door was always closed.

A good deal of my time was spent in the telegraph room because one of my greatest sources of information continued to be the railroad station agents. Their reports indicated that people sympathetic to the KGC cause were taking more trips on the railroad, probably because we were making it more difficult for them to use the roadways. Agent Kenneth Landry reported that KGC activities in New York City had reached an all-time high; he suggested that more troops be sent there in anticipation of riots.

A couple of the station agents had recently indicated that they suspected that *medical doctors* were acting as couriers between the KGC and the Confederates in their part of the country. This accusation struck a chord with me—a doctor is a perfect cover, freely moving about the city and the countryside, almost with invisibility. I recalled that I had encountered doctors on many occasions during my recent travels about the area.

I brought this item up with Major Eckert at our Friday morning staff meeting. He was immediately receptive to the theory, but after we discussed it, we were not sure *how* we would actually determine that a doctor was acting as a courier. Short of stopping each of them on a daily basis and doing a search, there was no way to know if they might be carrying a message.

Recalling past conversations with Miss Carroll, I knew that some sort of "probable cause" would be required before a prominent citizen like a doctor could be stopped and searched, even in conditions when civil rights had been restricted due to a state of war. I suggested that we require an armed escort for all doctors *for their protection.* Major Eckert really liked this idea. He promised to discuss this suggestion with the secretary as soon as possible.

In the meantime, I decided to spend more time checking out the taverns at the main crossroads as frequently as possible. These were good locations for information exchanges to take place, and I had already received a few reports of "suspicious actions" at some of these places from a number of the locals. I put these places at the top of my long list.

I had collected a few very specific names as well. Charles Cawood, William Farley, Channing Smith, Frank Stringfellow, Thomas Conrad, and Mountjoy Cloud were suspects, but no doctors were among them. I passed these names on to the other agents, hoping that they might discover something about them in their work.

Major Eckert reported that additional patrols, including cavalry and infantry, would be sent into an area that was becoming known as "Mosby's Confederacy" because of his dominance there. My brief interactions with Mosby had convinced me that his hit-and-run style of combat would *not* be subdued by this enhanced action. In fact, I suspected that Mosby probably *welcomed* the special attention, as he seemed to be quite the showman. He was a serious threat, and I always remained very alert when I rode outside of Washington.

I found it disturbing that many people, including some of our own soldiers, praised Mosby and actually cheered him on. Our Union soldiers were disturbed with the exorbitant behavior of many of the brigadier generals, fostered by the wealth of their military pay and abundant rations. Many of them were incompetent military leaders as well, being largely responsible for the Union's current predicament. Perhaps the soldiers wished that Mosby could take more of the generals away.

⌘ ⌘ ⌘

It was later that same day when President Lincoln walked over to my desk in the War Department library and asked me to walk to the Executive Mansion with him. It was perfect timing for me, as I was quite ready to wrap up for the day.

There was a break in the rain when we made the short walk, and he asked me to continue on with him, up to the second floor of the magnificent structure. We entered on the west side and walked into the president's office and cabinet room. The president placed a couple of items into the pigeonholes on the upper part of his desk. He noticed that I was admiring a handsome wooden paperweight depicting a horse rearing back on its two hind legs atop a majestic column.

"It was carved for me by a dear old friend in Springfield," he said.

"The horse reminds me of Dandy, my horse back home," I said. "I sure do miss him."

I followed the president across the hall to William Stoddard's office in the northeast corner; Stoddard wasn't there. I knew that he was often away, performing his military duties in the city. The president walked to a table that was stacked with guns of all sorts. "They come to me from their makers, hoping that I'll agree to order the army to use them as standard equipment," he said.

Most of the guns hadn't even been tested, but it was obvious to me that the president had looked them over very carefully, because he described several of them to me in some detail. "I like to look at the inwardness of the thing," he said.

After a few minutes, he picked up two pistols and handed them to me, and he selected a long gun for himself. After grabbing some ammunition, he said, "Let's go."

I followed him out of the room, down the stairs, and out of the building. But instead of heading off in the direction of the shooting range behind the armory, we went to the wide grassy area south of the main entrance known as the mall, or the President's Park.

We walked up to a stack of lumber in the middle of the mall. The president picked up some cans that were lying on the ground and set them up as targets. We walked back a hundred paces and loaded the weapons. The president took five shots with his rifle, which was manufactured by the Volcanic Arms Company. He didn't hit any of the targets.

He turned to me saying, "It may not be the gun...your turn." I took the .38-caliber rifle and fired it five times, hitting two targets on the last two shots.

"You adapt quickly," he said. "Jones in the stables tells me that you are one of the best shooters on horseback that he has seen."

"He hasn't seen my sister, Jeanine."

"Here...try these pistols," he said. "They're two different versions of Remington's New Model Army forty-four caliber...a lot like the Colts, but less expensive."

I fired six shots from both pistols, which differed only in the grips and the sights. The results from one were much better than the other. As we were discussing this, several soldiers were running in our direction, but they slowed when they saw the president.

It was against the law to fire weapons in the city, except at the shooting range. Our gunshots were bound to draw attention, and they had.

The president chuckled when he saw them coming. "I guess that's enough excitement for now," he said. "I suppose I'll hear about this from Secretary Stanton...Word always seems to get back to him about this kind of thing."

"I'm sure it does," I said.

The president laughed. "We'll have to do this again sometime."

CHAPTER FIFTY-NINE

Smithsonian Museum
April 27, 1863
ante meridiem

It was overcast, but no longer raining in Washington, when the war governors convened their gathering in the lecture hall of the Smithsonian Museum. Thirteen governors held the special title of *war governor* because of their unwavering support of President Lincoln's call for troops for the preservation of the Union. They came together on this Monday morning to discuss issues that they were dealing with in common, back in their home states.

War Governor Richard Yates of Illinois asked Miss Anna Ella Carroll to address the group regarding one of their key concerns, the growing activities of the organized societies that were hostile to the Union cause. The governors wanted to take actions against these groups; however, many of them, like Yates, had encountered stiff opposition in their state legislatures and were contemplating seeking federal help with a formal declaration of martial law.

"While I am sympathetic to your desire for heavy-handed action," Miss Carroll said, "I am also concerned that such action may cause those who have avoided taking a side on the matter to line up against what would be perceived as *big government.* This is an extremely complex issue, and we cannot afford to strengthen support for the Confederacy at this crucial time."

Governor Edwin D. Morgan of New York said, "Miss Carroll is right. The *New York Daily Tribune* just ran a story likening the acts of Governor Yates to those of Napoleon in December of eighteen-fifty-one, when he declared himself dictator and emperor of France. Martial law is out of the question!"

"The situation in Maryland is much the same," Governor Augustus W. Bradford said. "My state would fall to the South if such a move was proposed there. You all know what things are like in Baltimore." All of the war governors knew that Maryland remained in the Union only because of the intense political actions of Miss Carroll's prominent family.

"To be sure, we have two issues that present themselves in the minds of the people," Governor Oliver P. Morton of Indiana said, "On the one hand, there is the support of the Union, but on the other hand, there is the issue of emancipation. These do not line up well in my state, where people are strongly supportive of the Union, but they are indifferent with respect to emancipation. If emancipation was to be brought to the forefront as the primary reason for fighting the war, my constituents would withdraw from their units and return home." Several others immediately acknowledged this sentiment.

Governor Richard Yates stood. "The *New York Daily Tribune* article also pointed out that I defeated James Allen, the Douglas Democrat, in the eighteen-sixty election by a *mere* twelve thousand votes, but the fact is that I won...I am the governor, and that gives *me* the right to do what I believe is best for my state. Almost twenty thousand men from the southern part of the state of Illinois have taken up arms in support of the Rebels. What I am proposing is that martial law be declared in only the *southern half* of the state."

"I believe that General Burnside's recent action establishes clear precedent, so I support your proposed declaration, Governor Yates," Governor Edward Solomon of Wisconsin said. He was quickly followed by Governor Austin Blair of Michigan.

"Governor Yates, I can only repeat what I stated before," Governor Morton said. "If the reason is the right one, then it would hold up...However, it's well known that you have been a strong supporter of the abolitionist movement, and you've strongly advocated the use of the freed slaves in the Union army. I, for one, am not convinced that your heart is in the right place."

Governor Yates shrugged. There was a short moment of silence.

"Governor Yates, I suggest that you take the matter up directly with the president," Miss Carroll said. "It is well within his right to declare martial law in part of your state. Even so, I believe that he will be concerned about the backlash resulting from the fact that it is *his* home state as well, and such action could be construed as a sign of weakness...and next year, let's not forget, the president must seek reelection."

⌘ ⌘ ⌘

That night Governor Yates and Miss Carroll dined with Secretary Stanton and his wife, Ellen, at their home near Franklin Square. The beautiful brick-face home had been built in 1860 and was considered to be one of the finest homes in Washington. Earlier in the day, the secretary had received word that his assistant secretary of war, Christopher Wolcott, had died at his home in Steubenville, Ohio. Wolcott was married to Secretary Stanton's sister, Pamphila, and had taken ill over the winter and returned home.

"I will be leaving for Steubenville with my son on Wednesday," the visibly disturbed secretary said. "It is the first time that I will be leaving Washington since taking office."

"If you will permit us to travel part of the way with you, Miss Carroll and I were planning to leave for Illinois on Friday, but I believe that we can pull that up to Wednesday," Governor Yates said, noticing that Miss Carroll was nodding in agreement with him. "We must meet separately with the president before we depart, but I suspect that we can both accomplish that tomorrow."

"That would be just fine," Secretary Stanton said, "Now tell me what happened at the war governors' conference today."

Governor Yates proceeded to do so, drawing out the explanation in order to fully emphasize the emotions characterized by the participating governors.

Secretary Stanton listened intently. "Miss Carroll is right, Governor, the president will not support a declaration of martial law in southern Illinois...even though he would like to do just that. This business of the Copperheads does not sit well with him, but if he applies too much pressure to them, it can have dire consequences."

Secretary Stanton pushed his chair back from the table and smiled. "Governor, your concerns do not fall on deaf ears. I will help you out soon...*very soon*."

CHAPTER SIXTY

Dayton, Ohio
May 5, 1863
ante meridiem

It was past midnight, and now the special meeting had encroached upon his Tuesday morning—but the *meeting* hadn't even taken place as yet. Dark Eyes was still in the waiting room. He'd seen others come and go, and yet, he still waited his turn.

Dark Eyes suspected that it was Clement Vallandigham's way to punish him for his mistake in Tolono in November. No one else was waiting now, and there was just one other visitor left with Vallandigham and the others in the meeting room.

He'd been ordered from Cincinnati to Vallandigham's Victorian-style home in Dayton, but no additional information was provided. Dark Eyes scanned an article in the April 29 edition of the *Richmond Examiner* describing the request from many prominent Republicans for President Lincoln to countermand General Burnside's General Order Number 38. Suddenly the door to Vallandigham's study opened.

A man, who had introduced himself to Dark Eyes earlier as Johnny Powderhorn, departed the room and said, "They're ready for you now."

The study smelled of tobacco, whiskey, and moldy newspaper. A wagon-wheel gaslight chandelier provided ample light, and the fireplace glowed of embers hungry for a new log. Clement Vallandigham sat behind his large walnut desk, and the two others were introduced as Dr. George Bickley and Bryant Thornhill. Both men looked tired.

Vallandigham spoke first. His thick eyebrows seemed to dance with his words. "Mr. Palladin, or Mr. Bates, or whatever you are calling yourself these days, it has been a long day…or even beyond a long day, and we're exhausted…so I'll get right to the point. You are charged with the responsibility of an important quest—a quest which the three of us are quite excited about. Frankly, my friends here want to be sure that it has been entrusted to the right person."

Dr. Bickley was next to speak. "You may know that I organized the Knights almost ten years ago, when it was obvious that a state of civil unrest would expand into a full-blown war. It's now time for our quests to be stepped up. What you have proposed is *perfectly* timed, as far as I am concerned. Do you think it can be done?"

"I *know* it can be done, Doctor. The necessary resources are in place, and some of the *product* has already been moved eastward," Dark Eyes said with confidence, making sure to look each man in the eyes as he spoke.

Bryant Thornhill cleared his throat. Dark Eyes had heard about his attempts to brand the homes of Republican supporters in southern Illinois with a "K within a circle," effectively marking them as targets for the Knights. "I say we go forward with no further delay on the matter...and if you can take out Governor Yates in the process, please do so."

"Your mess-up in Tolono can't be a harbinger of things to come...You must understand this," Vallandigham said as he rose from his chair, placing his hands behind his back and pacing the space between his desk and the bookshelves on the east wall. "I still don't understand how you're going to get all of that material into Washington without it being noticed."

"We bring it in a little at a time and store it in the barns of the local friends until we need it. It goes unnoticed. Why...just a few weeks ago, the bags went untouched in the barn at Miskel's Farm, while the Federals swarmed all over the place, after giving Mosby quite a scare. I assure you that this plan will be successful, Grand Knight Vallandigham."

"I hope so, for the sake of the rebellion, and for *your* sake as well," Vallandigham said, staring at Dark Eyes. He paused a moment before continuing, as if he heard a noise outside the room. "...And how do you propose to keep the War Department out of your hair?"

Just then, before Dark Eyes had a chance to say a word, the door of the study burst open, and the soldiers of the 115th Ohio Volunteer Infantry poured into the room, knocking over unoccupied chairs and small tables, sending papers and small objects flying about.

Vallandigham and his three guests were held at gunpoint as Captain William Petefish read his orders for arrest. "Clement Laird Vallandigham, you are hereby under arrest and charged with *treasonable utterances* as outlined in General Order Number Thirty-Eight..."

Dark Eyes looked on in disbelief as the officer read the document in its entirety before placing Vallandigham in shackles.

One of the soldiers asked, "What about the rest of these Copperheads?"

"My orders are for the arrest of Congressman Vallandigham... The others cannot be detained," the captain said. And as quickly as they had arrived, the soldiers departed.

Dr. Bickley grabbed his hat and said, "We will want to spread the word of this atrocity as quickly as possible—there will be riots in the streets before this day is done."

CHAPTER SIXTY-ONE

War Department
May 5, 1863
ante meridiem

The War Department was alive with activity when I entered the building on Tuesday morning. Both President Lincoln and Secretary Stanton were going over the telegrams that were spewing from the telegraph room. A quick glance from Bates, as I passed by, informed me that I would be brought up to date *later.*

Several newspapers were scattered about on the table in the library. The headlines were filled with incomplete accounts from the battles around Chancellorsville, including a report that General Stonewall Jackson had been badly wounded. As I was reading a story in the *Washington Sentinel*, Taylor Mason slipped a note to me from Bates. It read: *Hooker in retreat, Vallandigham arrested.*

This bittersweet testimony left me motionless, until my stupor was interrupted by Major Eckert when he walked into the library. "The secretary wants to look at what we have on Samuel Morse and Amos Kendall."

I was quite familiar with these folders, having placed some of the information in them myself. I retrieved them quickly and handed them to the major, who hurried away.

Morse was the subject of much controversy, most of it due to his negative feelings about the abolitionists, and his mother's family's strong connections to the South. Morse had actually formed an organization in New York, known as the American Society for Promoting National Unity, which demonstrated to the South that there was strong support for their cause in the North. Kendall, a former postmaster general, was Morse's business manager.

Both men were quite popular, and I doubted that any connections that they had with the South would be of sufficient strength to have them jailed. Such was the nature of this conflict—if you dug far enough, you would find a connection through family, friends, or business associates.

My thoughts returned to Vallandigham. It would be interesting to see if any comments would come from Jefferson Davis, his old friend in Congress. Up to this point, Davis had pretty much ignored Vallandigham, attempting to establish the premise that Vallandigham's activities were entirely independent of influence from Richmond. I knew that Secretary Stanton didn't believe this, but President Lincoln's position on the matter was not clear.

When I returned from dinner, I found Tinker and Bates in the telegraph room alone. I learned that Vallandigham had been taken to Cincinnati to be tried by a military commission. Martial law had been declared there, and additional troops had been brought in to quell the riots that had broken out throughout the city.

In the meantime, General Hooker was blaming his defeat at Chancellorsville on Brigadier General Averell and had actually relieved him of his command late yesterday. I didn't think that this would sit well with the president, as he was quite fond of Averell.

Knowing this, Averell was likely to make his side of the story well known, and fortunately for him, he had been assigned to the adjutant general of the army, right here in Washington.

I spent the next couple of hours working with Tinker and Bates on the never-ending task of attempting to break the Confederate cipher. Two coded messages had been brought in by Hooker's courier, adding to our collection. We worked on code-breaking whenever we could, but we were fearful that the key would be changed before we could discover it.

Our methodology had become increasingly sophisticated. We analyzed linkages, including percentage of letter and word usage, syntax, sentence structure, and even metaphors.

We now believed that the key was made up of *two words*. We were also pretty sure that the same letter was not used in both words, but we thought that a letter might be repeated within the same word. We were very motivated by our suspicion that we were getting close.

Major Eckert kept the secretary informed of our progress, which was a well-kept secret. No one else, except the president, would be notified if we were to break the cipher. In fact, in order to hide the secret, we would continue with a charade, appearing to still be hard at work at the effort.

⌘ ⌘ ⌘

That night, I joined Miss Carroll and the others for supper at the Ebbitt House. She was in great spirits, and I was able to find out, as we spoke on the porch afterward, that General Grant had finally taken her advice to attack Vicksburg from the back, rather than from the river. Grant was moving into position, heading northeast toward the city of Jackson this very night.

"This is the beginning of the end, Jason. You just wait and see."

I knew better than to doubt her.

CHAPTER SIXTY-TWO

Globe Hotel
May 14, 1863
post meridiem

Grand Knight Clement L. Vallandigham's orders were clear, and all of the knights had followed them to the letter, clearing out to pursue their quests in earnest. Dark Eyes quickly made his way to Washington and took up residence in a rented room at 456 Sixth Street, between D and E Streets, not far from the stockyards. His changed appearance allowed him to move freely with little concern of detection, even in Washington.

The capital city's newspapers continued to be filled with news from Chancellorsville—Stonewall Jackson's death and General Hooker's excuses for defeat being the two top stories, with Vallandigham's trial taking a distant third place. There was talk that instead of being sentenced to the federal prison, President Lincoln would banish Vallandigham to some distant point beyond the Union lines, hoping to quiet the growing support for the Peace Democrats.

Dark Eyes felt quite at home in Washington, a city laced with anti-Union networks of all sorts. He was told that there were three hundred known KGC members in the city and nearby surrounding area. He would be directly involved with only fifteen of them, hoping to keep the number limited to avoid the chance that the quest would be discovered. Dark Eyes believed that there was a very good chance that the plan would go entirely undetected, but his greater concern was that its impact would be threatened by the large scale for which it was intended.

"We could neutralize the Union's ability to wage war in and around Washington," he had told Vallandigham just days ago.

Recent developments in Chicago had greatly improved the KGC's chances of success. Gustavus Swift had announced in March that he intended to use bone meal in his feed lots to supplement and enrich the beeves' diet before they were taken to the slaughterhouse. Ranchers were already collecting the bones and selling them to the mills, where they were ground up and contained in burlap bags for storage and transport.

It had been a simple matter for William Smith, the Washington stockyard's manager of forage and feed procurement, to engage the government in a contract to purchase a sizeable quantity of the new enriched bone meal feed-supplement product.

Dark Eyes and William Smith sat in the dining room of the Globe Hotel on the corner of Thirteenth and D Streets. Both were quite relaxed after the third round of drinks, enjoying the soft shades of blue that mixed with the oak and pine about the room. It was small in size by comparison to that of the Willard or National, but the room offered a more quiet and private setting.

"It's a shame about the grand knight," Smith said. "So much for the free country, or at least the free speech part of it."

"If they put him in prison, there will be an effort to break him out," Dark Eyes said. "We have our hands full here, so we'll let others worry about that. I don't expect our plan here to fail, and I want to know immediately if you see any problems whatsoever."

Smith had heard about the activities of Clifford Bates in Jacksonville and Tolono, so he knew that the one and the same, Miles Palladin, was no one to mess with. "The men that I'm working with on this end are all trustworthy. They know how to keep their mouths shut. I would be more concerned with the people on the *other* end of this thing, if I was you."

"You're not me," Dark Eyes said sternly, "and you don't want to be...and you don't need to worry about the men back in Illinois. They hate the Union more than the ones here do...or at least the abolitionist part of it. You only need to be concerned about taking receipt of the product once it makes its way here."

"I'm ready right now, if you could get it to me right now."

Dark Eyes smiled. "Actually, some of it is very close by, but I don't want you to get it and start mixing it in until there's enough of it available to create the results that we are looking for. Before the end of this month, you'll have plenty of it."

Dark Eyes was confident and didn't wish to discuss the matter any further with William Smith. "Enough of this for now...I'm hungry...Let's order. What would you like?"

"Steak...while I can still eat it," Smith said.

CHAPTER SIXTY-THREE

War Department
May 17, 1863
post meridiem

Miss Carroll had just returned from a quick trip to Illinois to meet with General Grant, and she asked me to join her for the Sunday morning Catholic Mass at St. Patrick's Church on Tenth Street. I had attended a Catholic Mass once before in Jacksonville, with Meredith Montgomery, and I enjoyed testing my Latin there.

St. Patrick's was a beautiful church, built in 1794 by and for the stonemasons who were building the Executive Mansion and the U.S. Capitol at the time. Miss Carroll told me that she alternated between this church and Georgetown's Holy Trinity Catholic Church, founded by the Society of Jesus around the same time. I accepted her invitation to join her at that church, next Sunday.

After the Catholic Mass, and dinner at the Ebbitt House, I slipped away to the War Department. I stopped by the telegraph room and briefly chatted with Albert Chandler. When I reached my desk in the library, I was surprised to discover three letters sitting on top of it. One was from President Sturtevant, another from

Edward Hinrichsen, and the other from Jeanine. I sat down to read them.

President Sturtevant had managed to get his letter on board a departing steamer shortly after his arrival in Liverpool, where he became a guest at the elaborate home of David Stuart, Esquire. He described his voyage across the Atlantic on the *City of Washington* as "trying," noting that he would plan his return trip when seas were calm.

Quickly getting to the purpose of his letter, President Sturtevant reported that he had met two gentlemen by the names of Arthur James Lyon Fremantle and Fitzgerald Ross. They claimed to be members of Her Majesty's Coldstream Guards, and on a night when they had "imbibed rather freely in the fruit of the vine," their conversation revealed that they'd made contact with a *Mr. Norris* of the Confederate Signal Service in Richmond. President Sturtevant wrote that both men seemed quite confident that England would announce its support for the Confederacy *by year's end.*

He noted that this information was included in his first formal report to President Lincoln, but he wanted to get it to me right away. I penned a quick reply to let President Sturtevant know that I had received his letter, and thanked him for it.

I opened Mr. Hinrichsen's letter next. I had always received a weekly letter from him, beginning immediately after I arrived in Washington. Recently, the letters had slowed a bit. His letter described the rapidly increasing eastward movement of horses and cattle, which he believed clearly signaled plans for a spring offensive. He noted that the railroad stock-holding pens in Alexander and Jacksonville had been doubled in size. My father and Jacob Strawn, and even some of the other ranchers, had taken on additional hired hands in order to keep up.

Mr. H. was wrestling with the need to provide thirty pounds of feed, and dispose of ten pounds of waste, each day for each cow retained in the holding pen...The horses were considerably less trouble. Out of necessity, many new sources of feed were being used, such as soybeans, cottonseed, flax seeds, bone meal, corn fodder, and cut grasses. Professor Turner at Illinois College was experimenting with several more. Mr. H. had already hired five more men to handle the additional demands on his own work as station agent.

He also wrote that the KGC activities continued to be troublesome, and in many of the surrounding towns, it wasn't safe for Union soldiers to travel alone. Open support for Vallandigham was commonplace, even in Jacksonville, where Judge Constable had made several speeches in support of Vallandigham and declared General Burnside's order as unconstitutional.

As an aside note, Mr. H. wrote that there was some rumor going around that the KGC was involved in Kinchelow's murder. He said that this seemed to be rather far-fetched for most to believe, but he decided to pass it on anyhow. I agreed with Hinrichsen's opinion, because I recalled that Kinchelow was a vocal supporter of the South, and unlikely to be a victim of the KGC.

I tucked Jeanine's letter into my coat pocket, deciding to save it for after supper. I dove into the pile of newspapers and telegrams that covered the rest of my desk.

I read that Major General George Stoneman had been ordered by General Hooker to move behind General Lee's lines and sever his communications with Richmond; however, by doing so, Hooker had exposed his right flank to Stonewall Jackson at Chancellorsville. The Federals had lost seventeen thousand men in the resulting battle, and the newspapers had not been kind to Hooker.

Stoneman had placed the Union flag on a hill within five miles of Richmond when he decided to turn back. Many believed that he could have easily taken the poorly defended Confederate capital.

President Lincoln and Secretary Stanton were furious. Stoneman was now seeking medical leave for a severe case of hemorrhoids, and Major General Alfred Pleasonton was expected to replace him. Like Averell, Stoneman was a close friend of McClellan's.

The *Washington Post* reported that President Lincoln would announce on Tuesday that he had decided to banish Vallandigham from the Union and have him delivered to the hands of the Confederates within the week. The newspaper was arguing that he should be hanged for treason instead.

One of the telegrams caught my eye. It was a message from Colonel George Sharpe in the provost marshal general's office. The chief of intelligence for the Army of the Potomac was reporting to Secretary Stanton that Union cavalry scouts had noticed a buildup in the Confederate cavalry near Culpeper Court House. Sharpe believed that General Stuart was on his way to Maryland. I interpreted this information as a clear indication that the courier traffic between the Culpeper area and Washington was likely to rapidly increase, so I set my plans accordingly.

Later that night, after a quick supper at the Ebbitt Inn, I was able to get to Jeanine's letter. She wrote that the spring roundup had gone very well, and now the purebred stock included Shorthorns, Jerseys, Devons, Ayrshires, and Herefords. My father was shipping forty carloads of cattle *per week* to the East Coast. A second bunkhouse and two additional barns were under construction at the ranch.

The family was well, but stressed by all of the activity brought on by the war. She noted that our father was negotiating the purchase of an additional twenty-six thousand acres of land in Champaign County. He had also offered to purchase some of Jacob Strawn's land to the east, since his activities had slowed a bit due to his poor health.

Jeanine wrote that Gustavus Swift had returned to the ranch for a second visit, after moving to Chicago in April. His plans for the meatpacking plant were going very well, and another gentleman, by the name of Armour, had recently announced plans to build a similar plant in Chicago as well. Swift continued to spend a lot of time with Professor Turner, who was trying to convince him that he should not slaughter "3D-cattle" in his plant—referring to those that were *dead, downed, or diseased.*

She ended her letter with a postscript note that I would receive a *surprise* for my twenty-third birthday, which was this coming Friday.

CHAPTER SIXTY-FOUR

War Department
May 18, 1863
ante meridiem

As an interesting point of debate, one may argue as to whether it is better to receive good news before bad news, or vice versa. I prefer the bad news first, and that is the way that it came out this Monday morning.

I arrived at the War Department early in order to prepare for our staff meeting. Bates was waiting for me at the door of the telegraph room—he had the bad news. "Our worst fears have been realized," he said. "They've changed the key...We're sure of it."

"How do you know?"

Bates motioned for me to follow him into the telegraph room, where a number of documents were spread out on the table. He showed me how some of the letters of the alphabet that we were sure we had identified had changed on the most recently coded message that was obtained from a captured courier, just yesterday. I could easily see that what Bates had said was certainly true.

I assured him that it wasn't as if we were starting all over again, because the techniques that had been established had placed us well along on what Professor Crampton would refer to as the *learning curve.* It was possible that we could actually discover the new key very quickly even though we had been unable to break the first one. "We should proceed on the premise that the new key will be two words with entirely different letters in each word, just as we had assumed before."

"I concur," Bates said. "I think it's still a variation of *Vigenéré*, with the twenty-six-by-twenty-six crossing pattern, or *matrix*, as you mathematicians call it. We need to get our hands on some newly coded messages as quickly as possible."

"I think I know just the place. Reports are that the Confederate cavalry is massing near Culpeper Court House. If we could get in there and take them by surprise, I'm sure that we could get to a bundle of messages before they have a chance to destroy them. Major General Pleasonton will be anxious to prove that he is the right choice to lead the cavalry," I added. I was already beginning to piece together my argument for this morning's staff meeting with Major Eckert, which was only a few minutes away from starting in the next room.

I soon learned that the timing was just right, as Major Eckert reported that Hooker would be meeting with Stanton tomorrow; the major knew that Stanton wouldn't order an attack for the sole purpose of gaining access to coded documents, but it would certainly be a good secondary objective behind the primary desire to disrupt anything that Stuart had in mind. Major Eckert said that he would meet with Stanton, right after our meeting, to discuss this matter with him.

The next item on the agenda was the top-ten report, the review of the list of the potentially most active courier sites based upon the information received from all of our multiple sources.

Because Stanton forwarded this information on to Colonel Sharpe and Lafayette Baker, who was now calling himself "Special Agent Baker," there was a chance that more than one of us was watching these places, perhaps even at the same time. So far, we had not gotten in each other's way, but it was bound to happen eventually. For the most part, Baker's and Sharpe's people knew me, but I didn't know very many of them.

Major Eckert reported that Baker was asked by Secretary Stanton to increase his arrests of "suspicious characters" in response to the unrest after the Vallandigham incident. Baker would follow the order with vim and vigor.

Before day's end, I hoped to get the opportunity to ride out to the number-one location on the top-ten list, Ball's Crossroads, which was about four miles due west of Washington. I generally tried to visit the top three on the list each week, but that was becoming more difficult to do as time went on.

After our meeting ended, I shuffled paper for another hour, and then Major Eckert asked me to join him in a walk over to the stables. It was a nice spring day, and the wind was blowing from the west, pushing the smell of Washington out to sea.

Major Eckert was a difficult man to get to know, as he seemed to keep to himself most of the time. However, he was in a rather good mood today. "Jason, you're doing a good job for us. I wish I had more like you," he said. "I think the weeks ahead are going to be the telling point for the outcome of the war...We're going to be very busy."

I sensed that he was right about what he'd said. "I think we're ready to turn the tables on them," I said. "From what I understand, we came real close at Chancellorsville...Maybe Culpeper will be the place for us to set them back."

"I talked to the secretary about it, and he will take it up with Hooker tomorrow. I'll let you know what the plan will be…I want you to ride along and make sure that we obtain some documents…and that they get back to the War Department *immediately*."

"Good, I was hoping that I could go," I said as we arrived at the stables. I followed him inside.

"Come here. Take a look at the latest addition to the stable," he said as he walked toward a stall about midway on the right.

Before I reached the stall, I heard the all too familiar sound… It was Dandy, my little Morgan from back home! It was such a joy to see him again, and now I knew what Jeanine's surprise was. "Wow, this is great," was all that I could say without choking up in front of my boss.

"We didn't think we could hide him here until Friday," he said.

"He came in on the train late last night," Andrew Jones said as he walked up from where he was observing the reunion at a distance. "I can't say that I've ever seen a finer Morgan in all of my days. If he's an example of what ya daddy is sending out here, I'm gonna head over to the stockyards and pick out some of ya stock right now."

"My father would only send good stock, so you should follow your instincts, Andrew."

"By the way, they also sent ya saddle…no sense putt'n a different one on his back. It's like new shoes are to us; they never fit right until they're about worn out."

"Thanks, Andrew, and thank you, Major Eckert," I said.

"Don't thank me…I think you might want to thank the president, though. I think he had his hand in this. He took note when you were admiring his wooden paperweight on his desk in the Executive Mansion a while back."

"I will make a point to do just that," I said as I hugged my horse. This was the good news that ended my day, after the bad news that started it.

CHAPTER SIXTY-FIVE

Ball's Crossroads
May 18, 1863
post meridiem

Wilson's Tavern was alive with good cheer, somewhat surprising for a Monday afternoon, but then the farmers were tired and ready for a beer after a hard day's work at planting. The English-style pub, with its heavy oak crossbeams and rough-stone fireplace, was the perfect setting for the small gathering of KGC activists, who blended right in.

James Wilson was too busy tending his bar, so he wasn't able to sit with them at the table, but all of the five captain's chairs were occupied with familiar faces, and Wilson filled their mugs for a second time during his hurried visit. "No need to wait for me…Go ahead and get started," he said.

They were all eager to do so and be on their way, so there was no objection from any of them. The four farmers from the surrounding area waited for the strange-looking man from Ohio to get things rolling. He made them feel uncomfortable, but they all knew that he was the fellow who was in charge, and they all supported what he was doing because it would help bring peace with their friends and family members in the South.

Dark Eyes was meeting these men for the first time, but he had carefully checked up on each one of them in advance of this gathering. All of them had been longtime KGC supporters, so his only real concern was that some of them may be being watched by the WD, but that was a risk that they would all have to live with.

"I'll start by saying that nothing has changed because of the grand knight's arrest in Dayton. The reason we're pulling things up is to time our event with General Lee's movement into the valley, which is about ready to start. When the Union forces follow, *we want to feed them right*."

That brought a chuckle from the others. Timothy Birch was the first to speak up. "So you want us to go ahead and move what we have into the city?"

"Yes, but be sure to mix the bags in with your other supplies so that everything looks normal," Dark Eyes said. "You all know the routes that are least likely to draw any attention, so use them."

"Even if the bags are checked, they don't look any different from the regular bone meal, so what's the worry?" David Wright said. "We'll go ahead and start spreading the word to the others."

"Yes, but only to those in the *circle*," Dark Eyes said.

"Are you sure that we're going to have enough product to pull this off?" Birch said, raising his bushy eyebrows.

"Our people have done a great job in contracting with all of the railroad station agents across the country to quickly take the bad beeves off their hands. We also have men working at all of the big cattle ranches. This isn't something we've thrown together in the last few days—this has been in the works for months now, so stop your worrying."

Dark Eyes was about to continue, but his thought process was interrupted when he noticed a familiar face entering the tavern.

The others at the table took note of the expression on his face and turned to see who he was looking at.

As they did so, Dark Eyes said in a hushed voice, "Gentlemen, there is the young War Department agent who messed up my plans for Miss Anna Ella Carroll in Tolono.

His name is Jason Alexander, and ironically, he comes from the very part of Illinois that gave birth to our quest...how fitting that he would be amongst us on this fine day."

Dark Eyes couldn't help but notice that Jason Alexander looked older and considerably more mature than what he remembered of him during their short encounter in Tolono. Taking note of the uneasiness that had appeared on the faces of the others in his group, Dark Eyes said, "There's no need to be disturbed. He won't recognize me now. I doubt that he even knows what he's looking for when he walks into a place like this...Maybe he thinks we'll all throw up our hands and surrender." Another group chuckle.

Dark Eyes watched as Jason Alexander carefully looked about the room. He seemed to notice that the group was looking at him, but then he turned his head and walked directly to the bar, where he remained. Dark Eyes let his attention to the enemy agent linger a moment longer. *I'll take care of you later.*

CHAPTER SIXTY-SIX

War Department
May 19, 1863
ante meridiem

I wanted to sleep a little later this morning after getting back late last night, but I knew that General Hooker was in the city to meet with Secretary Stanton today, so I wanted to be in the office if there was any news of interest. After stopping in at Wilson's Tavern at Ball's Crossroads Monday afternoon, I had ridden out to Bailey's Crossroads before returning to Washington after dark.

Dandy and I had enjoyed the ride, but he sensed the tension—in me and around me—very quickly. The pickets were all on edge because of rumors that Mosby was moving his raids closer and closer to Washington, so I had to be very careful when I approached them at each checkpoint in the darkness. I'd heard that the soldiers were even removing some of the planks from the Chain Bridge across the Potomac River at 9:00 p.m. every night.

The morning started weeping tears of rain when I neared the War Department, a far cry from yesterday's nice weather. General Hooker was already in the secretary's office when I walked into the telegraph room before heading to my desk, and he was still there when I left to check on Dandy before taking dinner at the Ebbitt Inn.

Late in the afternoon, well after General Hooker had departed, Major Eckert brought some information in to share with us. The cavalry was facing a serious shortage of horses after the events of the last week; many had been killed or badly injured in battle, and many were no longer serviceable because of bad backs or sickness.

Major General Alfred Pleasonton was now in charge of the Cavalry Corps. It was a temporary appointment, but most expected it to become permanent before very long. He was busy trying to find out what the Rebels were up to. Scouting reports continued to indicate that Stuart was gathering his forces in Culpeper, and Mosby was extremely active to the east of there. Secretary Stanton was very concerned about all of this, and he wanted to know what was going on.

Major Eckert said that Hooker would be returning to Washington in a week with a more detailed plan for his spring offensive. "I'm predicting that there will be an attack on Culpeper in early June," Major Eckert said, looking at me. "The secretary agreed that you should be present if there is any such action."

"That's music to my ears," I said. "There are several farms in that area that could be serving as headquarters for the officers—perfect places for coded documents."

"Do you think your horse can handle the battlefield?"

"I think so...He'll be more concerned about pleasing me than worrying about the noises. Morgan horses are pretty solid. Besides, he'll get mad now if he sees me on another horse."

⌘ ⌘ ⌘

That night I joined Brigadier General Haupt and Quartermaster General Meigs as the supper guests at the Ebbitt House. As usual, the conversation at the table was lively, augmented by good food and good company.

"Jason, you must take a trip down the O and A with me," Brigadier General Haupt said. "I want to show you all of the improvements that we've been making this spring."

"I'm prepared to do that at your earliest convenience, General," I said, knowing that some of the most recent work was done in anticipation of the likely Union assault on the Confederate cavalry at Culpeper.

"My supply officers have taken to refer to it as the *bottomless pit*," the quartermaster general said. "We just can't seem to fill the orders for livestock, and food for the livestock. I will say that all of the additional sidetracks that you've put in place at each station along the way have certainly helped with the matter."

"That, plus all of the reinforcement work on the bridges and road beds to support the heavier weight of the loads," Haupt said.

"Why all of the fuss?" the always inquisitive Mrs. Mason asked.

There was a silent pause before the brigadier general responded, "Oh, nothing more than the usual preparations for whatever might occur."

Miss Carroll and I exchanged glances with a smile after Haupt's response. I could almost hear President Sturtevant referring to that as a "textbook response." Was it silly for me to think that I could possibly be back in the classroom by the end of the year? I still held on to a bit of hope that that could occur—maybe I could saddle up one morning and ride west, and never return to this ugly place.

Mrs. Mason gave up on her earlier line of questioning and pursued another, looking directly at Meigs this time. "I've heard that there are a lot of sick animals. What's that all about?"

"The damp spring weather always causes some problems," Meigs said.

"I'm talking about more than just the damp spring weather," Mrs. Mason snapped back. "I read about all of the bad horses after Chancellorsville. Maybe we're getting bad stock from out west." She was looking at me now.

"My father only sends good horses and cattle," I said, feeling my face warming up and my ears turning red-hot.

Miss Carroll came to the rescue. "Let's talk of other things and give our guests a break from their work. I understand that the local stores have received the latest in fashions from Paris..."

After the other guests had departed, I sat with Miss Carroll on the porch, taking in the beautiful spring night, which was being helped along by the steady breeze from the west, blowing most of the foul smells away from us. I noticed that Miss Carroll was not in her usual pleasant mood.

"Miss Carroll, is there something troubling you tonight?"

"Oh, Jason, I am so disappointed with the way that I'm being treated by the establishment. I was promised appropriate remuneration for my writings, which have been highly praised by the president and many others, but I'm being treated in the same manner as a fifty-dollar-a-month clerk!"

I really felt bad for her because I knew how hard she was working, and I was sure that her opinion was no less valuable than any member of the president's cabinet—and for all intents and purposes, Anna *was* a member of that cabinet. I knew for a fact that she attended almost all of the cabinet meetings, and she was directing General Grant's campaign in the West, while Secretary Stanton cared for the eastern campaign.

I put my arm around her shoulder and pulled her close to me. We sat in silence for a while before I said good night and departed with some reluctance.

CHAPTER SIXTY-SEVEN

Chichester's Mill
May 22, 1863
ante meridiem

Shortly after dawn, a rider slowly approached Chichester's Mill, located about a mile southwest of Mill's Crossroads. He was nondescript, wearing a brown woolen coat and high black boots, which were exactly the color of his horse.

Dr. Walter Rathbonne waited nervously for his arrival, sitting in the upper room of the mill—a perfect vantage point. The doctor's horses and wagon were hidden under the wide expanse of the main level of the mill, where the large grinding stone was silent.

The rider stopped about a hundred yards from the mill and looked to the second floor. Seeing the agreed-upon signal from the doctor, he approached. Captain John Demsond was a cautious man, especially when he was riding in enemy-occupied territory. He'd managed to get a few hours of sleep, having arrived at the home of John Chichester, a short distance away, just after midnight.

Dr. Rathbonne had spent most of the night at Bailey's Crossroads, but he'd arrived at the mill well before sunrise, being aided by the light of a half-moon, even though it wasn't needed, since the doctor knew all of the roads quite well, as did his horses.

The handsome Rebel cavalry officer left his horse to share the ample forage on the mill floor with the other horses as he ascended the steep stairs to the next level. He had met the doctor once before, in Alexandria, prior to the start of the war. John Demsond was selling medical supplies then. They were meeting for a much different purpose now.

"Thanks for coming, Captain. I know it's dangerous."

"Not as bad as it may seem...the Union defense is quite porous."

"Perhaps...but many of our couriers are finding it to be much more difficult to operate these days...which brings me quickly to my request," Dr. Rathbonne said. "All of this can be remedied if you'll eliminate two key people at the War Department, namely Thomas Eckert and Jason Alexander."

Captain Demsond's face quickly registered his disturbance, and his soft blue eyes turned cold. "This is what you brought me out here for?"

"Not entirely...I have a courier pack," Dr. Rathbonne said, handing the leather-bound package to him. "Please don't take this request lightly...These men are causing us a lot of problems...and I understand they're trying to break the cipher as well."

"I don't doubt either of your points, Dr. Rathbonne, but we have our hands full in the field. General Stuart won't be expanding our activities into such endeavors as you propose. I suggest that you take this on with your own resources."

"That isn't practical...I don't have the resources necessary to carry it out."

"That's unfortunate, but unless we encounter these men in battle, we won't be harming them," Captain Demsond said. "I've seen Agent Alexander at Burke's Station *and* Kelly's Ford in the past, so I may be seeing him again...In fact, I hope that I do...but short of that, nothing else will happen."

The finality in Demsond's voice was clear, and Dr. Rathbonne chose to pursue matters no further. The two men parted company quickly, going their separate ways.

On the return trip, Dr. Rathbonne decided to focus his attention upon Agent Jason Alexander, whom he knew was out in the open much more often than Major Thomas Eckert. He also knew that Alexander periodically stopped in at Bailey's Tavern, so he could plan the attack on Alexander around that venue. The first opportunity would probably come as early as *next week*.

CHAPTER SIXTY-EIGHT

Columbia Turnpike
May 26, 1863
post meridiem

Dandy sensed it first...but then that was to be expected. He dropped his ears and turned his head back in the direction of Bailey's Crossroads, where we'd come from. Someone was following us.

It was dusk, and visibility was diminishing quickly as dark clouds rolled in from the west, with the accompanying lightning and thunder. We had just reached a point where the Columbia Turnpike cut through a heavy wooded area before reaching Arlington Mills Station. I quickly decided to ride up on the sloping ground to the north side of the road and hide amongst the trees, waiting to see what lurked behind me.

The hill was soft and very slippery, but Dandy managed to work his way up to a point about twenty feet above the road, where I turned him in the direction of the oncoming rider, and waited.

Flashes of lightning played tricks on my eyes as I watched through the intermittently appearing-and-disappearing maze of trees. The thunder masked all other noise, and very large raindrops began to softly pounce on my hat. Dandy and I waited in the darkness.

Dandy's flank twitched against my leg in the stirrup, signaling that he saw something that I couldn't see. I squinted to intensify my search, trying to sort something that was real from all of the imaginary figures that mysteriously emerged through the flashing shadows. *But wait...that last one...it looked so real...*A ghost had taken life form, and it looked like someone on horseback aiming a long gun in my direction!

The shot rang out and snapped off a large branch right above my head. *How could he have seen me?*

The rider's horse bolted and raced forward along the roadway. Dandy lurched forward as well, but we were on the hillside. As soon as his front legs reached the ground, we started to slide. Immediately, Dandy locked his front legs, pushed his hind legs under his body, and slid down the hill on his hindquarters. I managed to stay in the saddle by leaning forward into the crest of his neck.

Somehow, Dandy avoided the larger trees as we plowed our way down the hill. Lightning flash by lightning flash, I was able to determine that we were on a collision course with the mystery rider. Strangely, I was more afraid for Dandy than I was for myself.

At the inevitable point of impact, both horses were really moving, and in an instant, a gnarled mass of humanity and horse planted itself in the roadway. At first, I couldn't tell who or what was where. I had landed on a horse that wasn't moving. *Dandy was dead.*

But then, I heard Dandy. He was getting to his feet. I moved my arms and legs, and my body parts seemed to be performing well, but my left shoulder was hurting. I said something to Dandy, and he responded softly—I think he was checking himself out, just like I was. I walked over to where he now stood in the rain, and with the help of the lightning, I was able to see that he was shaken up, but surprisingly, unharmed.

The others had not fared as well. The ghost rider was pinned under the big horse, which appeared to be dead. I fumbled around, but soon I was able to place a small rope, which I carried in my saddlebag, over the horn of his saddle. Dandy pulled the dead horse off of his rider's body. I heard the man moan, so I knew that he was still alive.

With some difficulty, I managed to get the man up on Dandy and hold him there long enough for me to mount and ride the short distance to Arlington Mills Station. While the stationmaster, Millard Birch, sent his helper in search for a doctor, I was able to get a good look at the patient—it was the man with the big nose, the man who had tried to take my rifle at Bailey's Tavern during my first visit to that place.

Birch said his name was Thomas Hudson, and he worked odd jobs in the area. We bandaged up his injuries as best we could, but he remained unconscious.

When the next, and last, train bound for Alexandria arrived, we thought about putting Hudson on the train, but we decided that it was best not to move him until a doctor could see him. Birch encouraged me to get on the train, which would allow me to transfer in Alexandria, and take the train to Washington. I really wanted to do that, if for no other reason than to give Dandy a rest. I took his advice, and we rode the train back to Washington.

⌘ ⌘ ⌘

After I got Dandy settled in the stable, I walked over to the telegraph room in the War Department to check on the situation back at Arlington Mills Station.

The news wasn't good. Dr. Walter Rathbonne had not been able to save Thomas Hudson.

CHAPTER SIXTY-NINE

O&A Railroad
May 29, 1863
ante meridiem

Early on Friday morning, I met up with Brigadier General Haupt in Alexandria for our planned trip along the O&A Railroad. The morning sun rose into a perfectly clear sky, resulting in a beautiful day for a train ride.

I left Dandy at the stable in Washington; we were both still banged up a bit from the altercation near Bailey's. After asking me how I was feeling, Haupt didn't press the matter any further, and that was fine with me, because I was still not sure what to make of the whole thing myself.

We climbed to the second level of the caboose, where we could look across at the entire expanse of the train. Behind the engine's fuel car filled with wood, I counted nine cars of forage, two cars of commissary content, and one passenger car, all of which would easily be pulled along by the brand new 4-4-0 Chas. Minot. The train left the station promptly at 7:00 a.m., destined for Warrenton

Junction, with short stops scheduled for Fairfax Station and Manassas Junction Station.

Soldiers from the 15th Vermont Infantry rode atop the cars and in the passenger car, and the 7th Michigan Cavalry and the 12th Vermont Infantry patrolled along the track to a point just beyond Samuel Catlett's Station. Brigadier General Haupt excitedly pointed out all of the enhancements that had been made along the O&A as we moved along. It was obvious to me that the strategic importance of this railroad line had been well recognized and was being treated accordingly.

The countryside was a rich green in color, and its peaceful appearance belied the storm of war that could rain down upon it at any given moment. I could only marvel at the view from our great lookout point, and I suddenly longed for the similar beauty of the ranch back home.

Just as we arrived at the Manassas Junction Station, where the Manassas Gap Railroad met the O&A on the Tudor Hall Plantation, we saw Colonel William Mann and his 7th Michigan Cavalry heading southwest toward their camp at Bristoe Station, a short distance further down the line. Mail and some commissary items were dropped off before we moved on at 9:15 a.m.

We soon passed Colonel Mann's cavalry riders and then Bristoe Station, eventually reaching a point where the railroad grade rolled downward along a densely covered hillside, until it reached the road to Greenwich, where it leveled off again.

I saw the rail move, out in front of our locomotive, at the same time that Brigadier General Haupt did—and so did the hogger, as he hit the brakes and dropped sand on the rails in an impossible attempt to avoid the derailment.

I was amazed how abruptly the train slowed down, but the sharp incline made it impossible for the big engine to hold its position on the rails, and it came off to the right of the track, dragging a few other cars along with it as more track was pushed away by the sheer force of the iron wheels.

The engine finally plowed to a stop. It stood for a moment and shuddered before falling over on its right side. As it was falling, a loud cannon shot rang out, and the cannonball pierced the engine's boiler, creating a large and loud eruption of steam. I turned to look at Haupt, but he was gone.

Instinctively, he had left the caboose and run forward to decouple the passenger car from the commissary car in front of it, fearing that all of the cars would be toppled like a string of dominoes. As he did so, shots began ringing out from the woods on the right, where Mosby's raiders were hidden away.

They had cut down some telegraph wire and tied it to a rail, which they had loosened. Then they waited and pulled it away at just the right time to create the current mess. It was a good plan, and it was well executed by the crafty Mosby. But the cannon was something new for him and his small force of fifty men.

Union soldiers fell with the toppled cars, and others were easy targets as they stood atop the cars that were left standing after the dominoes stopped falling with the next-to-last forage car. The soldiers who chose to leave the passenger car from the right side also became easy targets. Another cannon shot hit the upper corner of the passenger car just as I took up a position behind it with some of the infantrymen. Haupt picked up a rifle from a wounded soldier and began shooting. I fired my Henry.

We were concerned that the Rebels might get in behind us, so we backed off into the woods on the left side of the track. Instead of pursuing us, the enemy's attention was drawn to the commissary cars, so we were able to hold our position in the dense brush as they stuffed oranges, lemons, fish, and leather goods into their ample saddlebags. They took the mailbags, and set fire to the hay in the forage cars, before retreating back to the safety of the woods with their plunder.

Colonel Mann heard the distant cannon fire from his camp back at Bristoe Station. He assumed that it was Stuart's artillery, and he proceeded carefully along the railroad tracks in the direction of the noise. Mosby was anxious to get away with his small cannon, so he retreated back along the road to Greenwich.

Mosby went less than a mile and encountered Lieutenant Elmer Barker's 5th New York Cavalry. They were ready to punish Mosby in return for the shame that they had endured as a result of their failure to protect General Stoughton back in March. The fight was fierce, forcing Mosby to use his cannon against Barker's forces to avoid being overrun by the larger force.

Leaving Haupt and a few others behind to help with the wounded, fourteen infantrymen and I ran up the road to see if we could catch any of Mosby's stragglers. When we heard the cannon fire, we knew that Mosby had been confronted by someone up ahead. We slowly worked our way into a position behind some fencing along the roadway and began firing into Mosby's rear.

Barker and his men were putting up a great fight, intent upon seizing Mosby's cannon. They recognized that Mosby was not skilled in the defense of the artillery piece that he now held in his possession. Nonetheless, the close-range canister shot from the lone cannon was taking its toll on the 5th New York Cavalry. Horses and men littered the roadway.

Our group concentrated fire on the men tending to the cannon. Eventually, the soldiers recognized the futility of their position and gave it up. For a moment, it looked as if Mosby might be captured. He seemed to be teetering in his saddle as he fought with his saber, but he managed to get away through the woods with some of the others, once it was obvious that the cannon was lost.

We joined the wounded Barker and his men and braced for a counterattack from the woods...but it never came. Mosby had had enough.

After Colonel Mann arrived with his men, I returned to the smoke-filled crash site. Brigadier General Haupt had borrowed a horse to ride back to the Manassas Junction station to begin making immediate arrangements for the repair of the railroad. We worked to keep the small fires from spreading to the other cars and the nearby woods.

After things settled down, I sat down and ate an orange that I found lying upon the ground.

CHAPTER SEVENTY

Washington, District of Columbia
May 31, 1863
ante meridiem

The streets of Washington were filled with people taking advantage of the beautiful Sunday morning. Dark Eyes walked to the stockyards, where he was pleased to find that the woefully crowded conditions had *not* improved. He smiled when he saw the downers mixed among the other cattle, seemingly going unnoticed.

He walked back to the place where he lived. He waited across the street and watched the entrance for a short while, as was his habit. Dark Eyes was careful to make sure that he hadn't drawn any special attention. He was satisfied that he was safe, but just to be sure, he decided that he would begin looking for a new place next week.

His next stop was the Ebbitt House. As he walked, Dark Eyes mused about the general lack of security in Washington—a situation that continued to amaze him. All of the attention was being placed on resisting an attack from the outside, and Mosby's recent escapades close to Washington had certainly added to that concern.

There were also stories in the newspapers about Stuart preparing his cavalry for a major attack on the Union capital.

Places like the Ebbitt House, commonly frequented by some of Washington's most prominent citizens, were virtually unguarded. Two of his *favorite* people would be there for Sunday dinner, and it would be a simple matter to walk in and *take care* of both of them at the same time. But no…that would have to wait…What mattered now was the quest.

Dark Eyes was concerned that the significance of his quest might be overshadowed by the New York draft riots quest, or by Morgan's raids into Indiana and Ohio. He would work hard to make sure that that didn't happen…very hard.

And things were going quite well. The fruits of their labor would soon be much more evident. His progress report had just been sent to the grand knight by way of Richmond. It would be even easier to communicate with Vallandigham once he went to Canada. It was so kind of President Lincoln to permit him to return to his duties, undermining the Union cause as the leader of the KGC.

The Union leaders made it so difficult to respect them as a worthy enemy…They were such fools. If Dark Eyes could have his way, he would hang them all, at the end of the war. Perhaps he would wrap them all with the Union flag, just like he did with the fool in the Tolono jail.

But today, his last chore, before returning to his room for a nice nap, was to closely examine the residences of each of the stockyard workers who knew about the KGC's plan. Dark Eyes had to be sure that they weren't being watched. He performed this task several times a week. These men were handpicked, so it probably wasn't at all necessary, but Dark Eyes wasn't taking any chances… especially when things were going so well.

CHAPTER SEVENTY-ONE

War Department
June 5, 1863
ante meridiem

All week long, reports were coming in from Colonel Sharpe's scouts regarding the current events in Culpeper. It was reported that General Stuart reviewed his cavalry forces on May 22 and that he was planning another review soon, with Jefferson Davis and General Lee to be in attendance. If such was to be the case, it was a clear indication that something of great importance to the Confederacy was imminent, and Secretary Stanton was deeply concerned.

Brigadier General John Buford assumed control of the cavalry forces in that area and camped at Warrenton Junction, leaving everything at the supply depot at Potomac Creek but pack mules and one wagon per regiment. Buford's frequent patrols encountered Rebel patrols at the Rappahannock River. His scouts reported that there were four brigades of Confederate cavalry at Culpeper.

General Hooker believed that Stuart's activities were designed to mask General Lee's push into the Shenandoah Valley, but

General Heintzelman believed that Stuart was preparing to attack Washington.

I watched these developments closely, and I was prepared to move quickly to join our cavalry if the attack was ordered. At this morning's meeting with Major Eckert, I learned that a member of General Hooker's staff would be riding along as well.

We were also informed that General Hooker would be abandoning Aquia Creek and moving his main supply line to the O&A, and no less than thirty men would be riding along to guard each train. Guards would be stationed at every bridge as well. Major General Julius Stahel's independent cavalry division of almost four thousand men was assigned to General Heintzelman to guard the O&A from Alexandria to Catlett's Station.

Mosby was antagonizing both Buford and Stahel. Reports claimed that Mosby now carried the rank of captain, but many Northerners still considered him to be nothing more than an opportunist who was using the war as an excuse to steal.

"Mosby's raids on the O and A at this critical time are of such strategic importance for the Confederacy that I can't help but believe that he's clearly taking orders from General Stuart," I said. "His actions will make it impossible for Major General Stahel to send any of his forces over to join Buford for an attack on Culpeper."

Major Eckert nodded in agreement. "Pleasonton will request the additional cavalry forces, but you're right, it won't be approved. He'd be better off pushing for some infantry support."

"But what if the target *is* really Washington?" Robert Smith asked.

"They'd've done it already," Major Eckert said. "God knows they've had many opportunities in the past. If they got in here, I don't think they could hold the city long, so why risk it? I think they're planning to move north into the valley."

"There's food for the men and their horses, if they go north," I said. "That allows time for a restocking of supplies in the South, so they'll be set when General Lee's forces return home."

"And any major victories would allow them to press all the harder for a settlement," Kenneth Landry said.

"But an attack on Washington would be a major victory for them, if it went well," Smith said, getting up from his seat to stir the logs in the fireplace.

"We'll find out what's going on soon enough," Major Eckert said. "Let's get back to our agenda."

We were able to finish things up before noon. Some of the pieces to our puzzles were beginning to fall into place, but there was so much yet to be done. Major Eckert assured us that Secretary Stanton was pleased with our work thus far, but at the same time, he reminded us that the secretary *expected* results.

Just as we were about to break up, Secretary Stanton walked into the room. "We just received information from one of Colonel Sharpe's people in Richmond that General Lee has reorganized his forces into three corps, each consisting of three divisions of infantry and five battalions of artillery. The corps commanders are Longstreet, Ewell, and Hill. Sharpe's man reports that Lee is headed back toward Richmond, but I find that hard to believe," Stanton said. "He's not about to spend the summer in Richmond."

Major Eckert nodded his head in agreement. "Are there any reports that he's pulling any of his forces back from Fredericksburg?"

"All of the prisoners taken in the area are saying that no one has moved out," Stanton said. "Hooker is going to send some of the Signal Corps up in balloons when the weather is right."

The secretary turned to leave the room, but after taking a step, he turned back. "We need to break their cipher, Major," he said.

"Yes, sir," Major Eckert said.

CHAPTER SEVENTY-TWO

Brandy Station
June 9, 1863
ante meridiem

Early last night, I received word that the attack on Culpeper had been ordered by General Hooker. I met General Hooker's representative, Captain Ulric Dahlgren, Agent Simpson Dahlgren's brother, at Alexandria, and we boarded a special train for Catlett's Station before midnight.

Because Hooker's Signal Corps had reported from their balloon observations that some of Lee's infantry forces at Fredericksburg had vacated their positions, there was concern that some of those men may have joined Stuart at Culpeper. As a precautionary measure, two veteran brigades of infantry, each with fifteen hundred men, were ordered to join Major General Pleasonton's cavalry corps east of the Rappahannock River.

By the time we reached Pleasonton's camp near Beverly's Ford, the attack force had been divided into two separate parts. Major General Buford's right wing, consisting of three brigades of cavalry and one brigade of infantry, was positioned near Beverly's Ford, and

Major General David Gregg's left wing, consisting of four brigades of cavalry and one brigade of infantry, was positioned near Kelly's Ford.

The plan was for each wing to cross the Rappahannock River simultaneously and join up on the other side, in the vicinity of Brandy Station, a railroad station located on the Confederate part of the O&A. The combined force would then move to the west for an assault upon the brunt of Stuart's forces at Culpeper. It seemed like a good plan, and there was a definite buzz of excitement at Pleasonton's headquarters, where the telegraph operators were sending off messages in quick succession. I was astonished to hear that a captured Rebel had stated that both the Confederate secretary of war, James Seddon, and General Lee had been present at Major General Stuart's grand review on John Minor Botts's farm near Brandy Station *just yesterday*. There was hope that they might still be at Culpeper with Stuart this morning.

Captain Dahlgren and I sent short messages to our superiors, reporting our arrivals, and after feeding and watering our horses, we tried to get some rest. Dahlgren seemed like a pleasant fellow, but we were both too tired to carry on a conversation...but much too excited to sleep. It seemed that my head had just found a comfortable place on the saddle when we were awakened by the order to take to horse. My pocket watch indicated that it was 2:00 a.m. as we saddled up.

We rode near Major General Buford in the dense fog, following the sweet scent of his pipe smoke as we slowly approached the crossing at Beverly's Ford. Once there, we waited for a short time, and then at 4:30 a.m., Brigade Commander Colonel Benjamin Davis led the 8th New York Cavalry through the narrow opening in the steep riverbank, and into four feet of river water, with the 8th Illinois and 3rd Indiana close behind.

The Confederate pickets immediately sounded the alarm and fell back along Beverly Ford Road. They were quickly joined by the 6th Virginia Cavalry, and the battle ensued. Major General Buford was disturbed to see that we had met with such resistance so soon, and then he received the report that Colonel Davis had been killed. The 7th Virginia Cavalry joined the resistance, and Captain Alpheus Clark, commander of the 8th Illinois, was badly wounded.

More regiments and artillery batteries joined the fray, and the Union advance was stalled about a mile from St. James Church, which was roughly two miles northeast of Brandy Station. Major General Stuart had ridden to St. James Church to take charge of the resistance there. Pleasonton was disturbed to receive the report of the stalemate, but he was even more concerned that he had received *no report* that Gregg had advanced at Kelly's Ford.

Pleasonton waited for that report as long as he could before joining Buford on the right wing front. It was obvious that he was upset when he rode up. "What in God's name is keeping Gregg?" he said as he came alongside Buford's gray mount.

"It's hard to say, General," Buford said. "Stuart's headquarters is *here*, not further out at Culpeper...That's thrown everything off. My guess is that Major General Gregg has run into Rebels at his crossing, just like we did...We've ridden into a bit of a bees' nest."

I could see that Buford was getting his artillery in position to fire back at the Confederates, and the cavalry forces were charging and countercharging across the wide meadow scarred with deep ditches. It looked to me like the confrontation here could go on for quite a while. "General, as soon as everyone has crossed the ford, I'll ride back across the river and down to Kelly's Ford to find out what's going on there," I said.

"That's fine," Major General Pleasonton said, looking closely at my horse. "I was about to send a message with a courier, but you can take it to the left wing commander."

Judging from what I could see, I wouldn't have to wait long to get back across the river. The three brigades of cavalry had already taken up positions across and on both sides of Beverly Ford Road, and the infantry brigade was rapidly forming up behind the cavalry. I departed as soon as the message was handed to me.

Dandy was eager to get back across the river, and after doing so, we quickly covered the seven miles down to Kelly's Ford. After passing through a small infantry force left to guard the ford, I rode through the Rappahannock River once again, and along Kelly's Mill Road, to a point where Major General Gregg had faced off against Confederate Major General Beverly Robertson's 4th and 5th North Carolina Cavalry.

After reading the message from Pleasonton, Gregg left a small force to hold Robertson in place, and then he moved directly toward Brandy Station. Colonel Alfred Duffié's division, consisting of two brigades, had already been ordered to Brandy Station by way of Stevensburg, a less direct route further to the west. Gregg hoped that Duffié could move through Stevensburg and take a position to the west of Brandy Station, cutting off Stuart's retreat to Culpeper.

Gregg ordered Colonel Percy Wyndham to take the lead directly toward Brandy Station with the 1st New Jersey and 1st Pennsylvania Cavalries. Wyndham motioned for me to join him, and I eagerly did so. We met no resistance at the railroad station, which was at the base of Fleetwood Hill, and when we stopped to look things over, we were amazed to see that Stuart's headquarters had been established on the hill right in front of us, and his tent appeared to be *unguarded*. Wyndham and I looked at each other in disbelief.

CHAPTER SEVENTY-THREE

Brandy Station
June 9, 1863
post meridiem

The two Confederate regiments that had been guarding Fleetwood Hill were sent to stop Colonel Duffié's advance beyond Stevensburg, leaving no defense at Fleetwood Hill. The sun was directly overhead when we rode up Carolina Road, which ran in a northerly direction from Brandy Station and continued across the top of the hill, where Major General Stuart's colors fluttered in the breeze.

The telegraph wire that was strung up on short poles, connecting Stuart's tent to Brandy Station, caught my eye immediately, and I was anxious to make the best of our good fortune.

I let Dandy break away from the others as I rode for the tent. I was there in a matter of minutes, and dismounted. With pistol drawn, I peered inside and found that the tent was empty. Not even a telegraph operator remained inside. I grabbed my saddlebags and went inside as the others surrounded the tent, raising a cloud of fine brown dust. Lieutenant Colonel Virgil Brodrick, who led the 1st New Jersey Cavalry, joined me inside, where the two of us scooped up messages and maps as quickly as possible.

I ripped away the telegraph key and wedged it into one of my bags, and Brodrick seized one of Jeb Stuart's magnificent plumes that often adorned his flop hat. There was no room for a fine banjo that hung from the tent's center support, or the magnificent dress uniform that was still laid out from yesterday's grand review. It was difficult for us to judge how long we'd been inside, but the sudden commotion outside was a clear indication that the Rebels had taken notice of our presence at their commander's headquarters.

Lieutenant Colonel Brodrick left first, while I stayed behind to take a quick look into some possible hiding places, but I found nothing. When I left the tent minutes later, Dandy was standing at the opening, patiently waiting for my return from the depths of the canvas. A thick shroud of dust now enveloped the top of the hill, and as I tied the saddlebags to my saddle, I realized that I was now alone on the hilltop.

Colonel Percy Wyndham and Lieutenant Colonel Brodrick had charged down the hillside in an eastward direction with the 1st New Jersey and the 1st Pennsylvania to engage parts of the brigades of Brigadier General William E. Jones and Brigadier General Wade Hampton, which were moving in from St. James Church, where they had fought against Major General Buford's forces. Major General Gregg ordered up a battery to the base of the hill, and they began firing in the direction of the Rebel advance.

Both sides were frantically calling more regiments and batteries into the area. I was ready to ride back to Gregg's position with my saddlebags when I saw it—the wire had been rolled back up onto a reel, but the poles were still lying on the ground where they had once stood—the telegraph line had recently extended beyond Stuart's tent! Having studied the maps of this area back at the War Department, I was quite sure that what was left of the telegraph line was leading out to Dr. Robert Welford's mansion, which was just north of Fleetwood Hill, behind Yew Ridge, and less than two miles away.

Welford's would be the perfect place for Secretary Seddon and General Lee to stay during their visit to the area. I had to have a look at it...but I had no idea what was going on at the far end of Fleetwood Hill, which stood in my way. I looked out in that direction, but all I could see was a mixture of dust and smoke. I mounted up and headed into it.

The top of the hill was clear, but I could hear a lot of movement to my right, at the base of the hill. I slowly moved forward, but then I decided that it was too risky for me to remain on Carolina Road, so I rode down the west side of the hill. As I did so, I could hear shells exploding on the top of the hill, back in the direction of Stuart's tent.

I dismounted and led Dandy through some dense brush at the bottom of the hill. We slowly worked our way around to the north side, and back to Carolina Road. Above us, on the top of the hill, the 9th Virginia Cavalry gathered, and prepared to charge across the top of Fleetwood Hill toward Major General Gregg's position. I waited for them to ride off, and then I mounted Dandy and rode off toward Welford's.

The two pickets on the north side of the hill saw me. For some reason, I waved, and they took me for a local civilian trying to get home without being killed. I wondered how long I could ride in enemy territory without paying the price.

Dandy was holding up well with all of the noise, but I could tell that he was nervous. I rode along, expecting to encounter another picket at any moment, but the path to the mansion was clear. When I reached the imposing structure, I waited for a few minutes before riding up. I went to the stable and rode inside the large structure. Leaving Dandy there, I walked toward the house. No one seemed to be around...which made me nervous.

There was a small stack of telegraph poles near the back door. I went in, and stood in the large kitchen listening for noises. It was quiet, so I went down the wide hall and into the library on the right. The elegant room reminded me of the library in Jacob Strawn's elaborate home outside of Jacksonville. The bookshelves went all the way up to the eight-foot ceiling, and there was a ladder with little wooden wheels on its feet that was hung on a rail that went all the way across the top. I looked around the bookshelves, behind the pictures, and in the desk drawers, but I didn't find anything of importance.

I didn't hear the two riders approach the house, even though I thought I was listening carefully. They rode ahead of the others in their group. Brigadier General William H.F. Lee's messenger had met all six of them at Welford's Ford on the Hazel River, where they were picketing, giving them the orders to pull the Confederate picket back to the south, as far as Yew Ridge.

The two dismounted, and entered the kitchen. They knew the Welfords had departed on the O&A with Secretary Seddon late last night, and they were hoping to find some food left over from last night's big supper...Instead, they found *me*.

At first, they thought that I was a member of the household when I walked into the kitchen. The dust covered my WD armband, but the alarm in their eyes moved me to action. Somehow, I sensed that gunshots were not in my best interest, so I grabbed a heavy frying pan from atop the stove, and with both hands, I hurled it at the tall soldier, hitting him soundly across his forearm as he shielded himself from the blow.

The other went for his pistol, but I ran headlong into him, burying my head into his chest, driving him into the wall and expelling the wind from his lungs. I rolled away from him just in time to avoid being kicked by the tall guy, who cradled his badly bruised arm across his chest. He rushed at me again, but I slid under his next kick, driving my shoulder into the knee of the leg that now held all of his body weight. I heard the knee pop as he yelled in pain and fell against a churn.

I grabbed a rolling pin and knocked both of them out, hoping that it wasn't hard enough to kill them. I tossed their pistols into a bucket of milk and paused for a moment to catch my breath. Through the kitchen window, I could just see the others off in the distance, moving in my direction.

Dandy sensed that I was in trouble as he looked out from the stable. I was afraid to shout for him, fearing that I would alert the oncoming riders, so I waved for him to come to me, and he did. In an instant, I sprang from the house and leaped from the small porch to the saddle, and we were off. I had to ride back in the direction of Yew Ridge, and I wasn't sure what I would find there.

Even though it didn't appear that I was being pursued, I rode quickly to the base of Yew Ridge. I waited, attempting to determine what ground was being held by each side before I moved any further. In a moment, Union riders came across the top of the ridge, riding at a gallop in my direction. I brushed the dust from my armband to make sure that they could see that I wasn't the enemy. They swooped down the hillside and rode past me. I promptly joined them.

I recognized one of Buford's staff officers, Captain Joseph O'Keefe, riding near me in a hail of lead that now came from the top of the hill, and when I looked back in his direction a moment later, he was gone from his saddle. It was impossible for me to turn back and look for him without being trampled by the rush of riders from the 2nd U.S. Cavalry. The 9th Virginia Cavalry and the 2nd North Carolina Cavalry descended from the hilltop in hot pursuit. I heard the *thump* as a ball of lead hit my saddlebag. I glanced at the top of the ridge one last time, and I thought I saw a gray-haired Confederate officer sitting atop a large gray horse…Could it be…?

I rode headlong with the others to the safety of Major General Buford's position along Beverly Ford Road, which was strongly supported by artillery and infantry, causing the Confederates to give up their chase.

Messenger reports were indicating that Confederate infantry forces were joining the battlefield. Hooker had given Pleasonton discretionary orders to withdraw if he deemed it necessary to do so. After almost fourteen hours of battle, Pleasonton decided to pull back across the fords on the Rappahannock River. There was no Confederate pursuit.

Reaching Pleasonton's staff, I discovered that Captain Dahlgren had been wounded, and Lieutenant Colonel Brodrick had been wounded and captured. Almost five hundred Union soldiers had been killed in the battle.

Both sides would claim victory in the Battle of Brandy Station. Major General Pleasonton would find that he was to be severely criticized for his withdrawal, while Major General Stuart would be chastised for being taken by surprise.

As for me, I was happy to be *alive.*

CHAPTER SEVENTY-FOUR

War Department
June 10, 1863
ante meridiem

I was very happy to return to the friendly confines of my simple office on the second floor of the War Department after traveling for the better part of Tuesday night to get back to Washington. I emptied my saddlebags onto the large table in the library, separating the messages from the maps, and a few newspaper clippings that were mixed in among them.

Bates, Tinker, and Chandler gratefully accepted the coded messages, and as I handed them out, I couldn't help but think about the others that had escaped our hands when Lieutenant Colonel Brodrick was captured. Bates saw the telegraph key that I had taken and asked that it be placed in the center of the mantel over the fireplace in the telegraph room. I couldn't think of a better place, and it wasn't long before it was appropriately identified with a small brass plate as: *Jeb Stuart's Telegraph Key, Brandy Station, June 9, 1863.*

I looked over the maps briefly and turned them over to Major Eckert in the staff meeting. I noticed that one of them very accurately represented the location of the Union cavalry screen around Washington. I placed the newspaper clippings on my desk for later reading.

The staff meeting began promptly at 8:00 a.m., and I described my involvement at Brandy Station, knowing full well that Major Eckert would be careful, when he made his report to Secretary Stanton, to avoid trumping any of General Hooker's reports, hoping to maintain our good relationship with him. Major Eckert and the other agents listened intently as I provided the details in advance of the newspaper reports that would appear within a few hours.

"Secretary Stanton will be upset with General Hooker when he finds that he didn't order Pleasonton to maintain the attack and push Stuart beyond Culpeper," Major Eckert said, "but when I listen to you describe the course of the battle, Jason, I wonder if Pleasonton would have been crushed if he'd gone any further. If it was General Lee that you saw, that could mean that strong infantry support wasn't far away."

"Frankly, Major, our cavalry was worn out," I said. "It was important for us to get back across the river before dark. I think Pleasonton knew that the Rebels wouldn't pursue us back across the fords."

"Does this mean that General Lee has moved his headquarters near Culpeper?" asked Robert Smith.

"It could," Major Eckert said. "I expect that our cavalry will earnestly probe the area over the next days to find out."

"All of this activity should make it much more difficult for the Confederate couriers to get in and out of Washington," I said. "I was thinking about this on the train last night, and I look for the couriers to move their activities to routes *north* of the Potomac.

The Rebels can cross the river west of Seneca Falls, where our screen ends, and work their way toward Washington on the north side of the Potomac and meet the couriers somewhere there."

"Perhaps we can extend our screen across the Potomac," Major Eckert said. "I will discuss the matter with the secretary."

I knew that Major Eckert would do just as he said, but I also knew that the cavalry would be unwilling, if not unable, to extend the screen. In fact, Major General Stahel had already made attempts to tighten the screen by pulling it back in, as there was still great concern about an attack on Washington.

After the staff meeting, I was able to get to my desk and take a look at the newspaper clippings that I had inadvertently collected from Stuart's tent. There were eight of them.

One article from the *Richmond Sentinel* noted that Secretary Seddon had recently recognized partisan rangers as part of the Confederate military, and *Captain* John Mosby's force was now Company A, 43rd Battalion Partisan Rangers; however, the reporter indicated that General Lee deemed the designation as "temporary" and that Mosby and the other partisan rangers would soon be brought into the regular cavalry.

Two other articles from Richmond papers described the devastation of the Virginia countryside, and its inability to provide adequate sustenance for the soldiers and the horses of the cavalry through the coming summer months. The ample provisions in the North were mentioned several times throughout the articles.

All of the other clippings were taken from Northern newspapers providing information such as train schedules, troop strengths, and changes in command. I knew that Secretary Stanton had attempted to address this practice of revealing too much information to the enemy, but he had run into considerable resistance from some civil liberties groups, and KGC supporters. In contrast, the Southern papers carefully controlled the information that they printed; moreover, they often worked in conjunction with the military to print misinformation for consumption by the Northern readers.

As I was reading along, David Bates left the telegraph room and walked over to my desk in the library. "Jason, I forgot to tell you that you had a visitor yesterday by the name of Charles Adams."

"Oh, Charlie the salesman," I said. "What did he want?"

"He wouldn't say. He asked that you contact him after you return."

"I'll do that...By the way, how do the messages look?"

"You picked up some good ones," Bates said. "I think they're going to help us a lot. All of them incorporate the Rebels' new cipher key."

CHAPTER SEVENTY-FIVE

Willard Hotel
June 10, 1863
post meridiem

"You're a hard man to find these days, Jason Alexander," Charlie Adams said as we settled into the seats at our table in the main dining room at the Willard Hotel. "I dropped by the Ebbitt Inn a couple of times before stopping by the War Department."

It looked to me like Charlie had lost some weight since I last saw him. "Yes, it seems that when I'm not at my desk, I'm in the saddle. How have you been, Charlie?"

"Well, even though I've been sick a lot lately, I've managed to make some good sales for my clients. Actually, I've established a solid reputation with the quartermaster general," Charlie said.

"That tells me that you're selling quality products," I said, "which is no less than I would have expected, knowing you as I do."

We ordered beers and steaks. I needed a good meal. It was the middle of the week, and the dining room wasn't real crowded, so the service would be good.

"I met your boss a few days ago...He's an impressive man. Major Eckert had just finished meeting with Quartermaster General Meigs, who spotted me in the waiting room. He called me into his office, and then he asked Major Eckert to demonstrate the poor quality of the government's fireplace utensils, or more specifically, the poker. You can imagine the shock when I saw him break it in half by striking it across his forearm!"

"I haven't seen him do that," I said, "but President Lincoln told me that he'd observed Major Eckert breaking one of those during a quiet moment in the telegraph office, and I can tell you that the president was quite impressed."

"If I can find a better supplier, I might get that contract, which includes the fireplace flue mechanisms as well," Charlie said.

We polished off our beers in short order and asked for a second one when our steaks arrived. I could tell that Charlie had something on his mind, but I thought it would be best for him to take the lead, so I waited for him to bring the matter up.

About halfway through the steaks, Charlie began. "Jason, I don't know if this means anything or not, and I don't want to seem like some kind of a nut..."

I waited for Charlie to continue.

"I spend a lot of time over at the government's main warehouse by the armory because I'm required to personally inspect a certain number of my clients' shipments. Of course, a lot of stuff comes in there that I don't have anything to do with, but I've noticed something that I wanted to tell you about.

"Well, anyhow...there are bags of ground-up animal bones called bone meal that come in there from all over the place. The farmers and ranchers save the bones from their dead cattle and horses and take them to the mills to be ground up, just like they'd grind up their grain. They bag up the bone meal in burlap and sell it to the government as some sort of a feed supplement for the cattle in the feed lots."

Charlie leaned forward and spoke more quietly as he continued, "Those bags are all stored in the same section of the warehouse, near some of my stuff, but I noticed that some of them have a small mark like an *x* or an *o* or something else like that on them. Well, one day I saw that the guy who was in there loading up some of the bags onto a wagon was picking out some of those marked ones like they were special. My inquisitive nature got the best of me, so I walked over there and asked the guy about it."

Charlie took another bite out of his steak, chewed briefly, and washed it down with a long pull on his beer.

"Well, to make a long story short, he about bit my head off, and told me to mind my own business or I'd be sorry if I didn't. And that's not all. A few days later, when I was back at the warehouse, the guy's boss, a Mr. Smith, stopped to see me and asked me a bunch of questions about my job. He was making me real nervous, Jason."

"You were right in calling this to my attention, Charlie," I said. "I'll take this in my own hands from here on out, so you should stay away from them and show no further interest in their matters."

"Gladly," he said. "I'd be careful with them if I was you, Jason."

"You can be sure that I will."

As Jason Alexander and Charles Adams left the dining room after their meal, Dark Eyes watched them from his table in the corner, thinking about a problem that he would need to take care of sooner, rather than later.

CHAPTER SEVENTY-SIX

Washington, District of Columbia
June 11, 1863
ante meridiem

I didn't waste any time in getting over to see William Smith, the man who was in charge of procurement of forage and feed for the Washington stockyards. He was a heavyset man with a bushy moustache, a small part of which appeared to have been burned away by his cigar stub. He made it obvious that he wasn't happy to see me.

"I'm a very busy man, Mr. Alexander," he said. "We'll have to walk and talk at the same time, if you're able to do that. If there're any delays in getting cattle and horses to General Hooker, I'm sure that Quartermaster General Meigs will be very quick to explain the impact of this interruption to the secretary of war."

"I won't require much of your time, Mr. Smith, and I'm perfectly happy to walk with you—in fact, I was hoping to get a closer look at your operation here. I grew up on a cattle ranch back in Illinois, so I have some experience with feed lots."

"That's impressive," he snorted, "but my feed lots are massive—there are some eighty-five thousand cattle in here right now. I need two hundred railroad cars of forage and corn *every day* to keep them fed."

"You didn't mention the bone meal," I said.

He turned to me with a furrowed brow. "The *bone meal* is something new...an idea from some guy named Swift. It's called a feed supplement...You mix it in with the corn...It's just a nuisance as far as I'm concerned."

"Then why bother with it?"

"If the cattle will eat it, I'm interested," he said, stopping at a watering trough that extended along the entire eastern side of the fence of one of the lots. "Tomorrow, we'll put feed in here, and water on the other side...It forces the cattle to move around some."

"Is there only one kind of bone meal?" I asked.

"It's ground-up bones, Mr. Alexander. There's only one kind that I know of...Bones are bones. The government pays fifty cents for a five-pound bag...It's enough to get some interest from the ranchers and farmers. They used to bury them to avoid attracting the wolves and coyotes, and now they can sell them."

"May I see a bag of bone meal?"

Smith shook his head. "I'll show you one, but now we're getting into that time delay thing that I was talking to you about earlier. While I show you a bag of bone meal, something *important* doesn't get done."

We walked to a huge building that stood alongside the railroad sidings that ran in from the main line of the B&O Railroad. Huge piles of forage and cob corn filled the better part of the building. Smith pointed to a large stack of five-pound burlap bags.

"Over ther're the bags of bone meal, alongside the bags of shelled corn. The bags of corn hold up better in the weather when we have to send corn out in the field, to feed the cattle held near the soldiers. The bone meal helps to fill the cattle up faster, and they eat less corn. This guy Swift claims that it's good for them, too."

Instead of walking over to the stack of bags, Smith led me to a wagon loaded with bags. He dropped the wagon's tailgate and pulled down a bag onto it. He drew a knife from his pocket and cut the bag open.

"You can see that the bone meal has almost the same texture as corn grits, but a little finer. This wagon will follow the corn wagon along the troughs, and this stuff will be poured right on the corn, and the cattle will gobble it all up without hesitation."

I didn't notice any markings on the bag that he opened, but I quickly scanned the other bags in the wagon. I saw a bag with *B* marked on it, and I yanked it down. "Let's look at this one," I said.

Smith was now very annoyed, biting down hard on his cigar. "I'll have to report this to the quartermaster general, Alexander. You're intentionally disrupting my work." He gave no indication that he was willing to open the bag.

"Just one more bag, Mr. Smith, and then I'll be leaving."

He stood there looking at me, trying to decide what to do. Then he looked away and exhaled deeply. "All right, one more bag, and one more bag only!" He cut the bag open, and the bone meal inside looked exactly like the bone meal in the bag right next to it. "Are you satisfied now?"

"Yes, I believe so," I said. "Thanks for your help."

"Help? How can I be of any help?" Smith said. "What on earth are you looking for?"

I looked him in the eyes and said, "The enemy, Mr. Smith, I am looking for the enemy." I turned and walked away.

⌘ ⌘ ⌘

After supper that same night, I sat with Miss Carroll on the porch of the Ebbitt House, out of earshot of the others. The news of General Grant's exploits in the back of Vicksburg was the sole bit of encouragement for the Union as the summer approached. I knew that Miss Carroll was often a participant in the frequent exchange of telegrams between the War Department and General Grant in the late hours of the night and the very early hours of the morning. I'd seen her in the telegraph room with President Lincoln and Secretary Stanton, enduring those long ordeals.

It saddened me to see how this true patriot and champion of the Union cause could be so mistreated by receiving no recognition for her work. From what I had seen with my own eyes, Miss Carroll was treated as a peer by the president and all of his cabinet members…behind closed doors.

"They're going to have a painting done of the president and his cabinet, Jason. It's supposed to commemorate the completion of the final draft of the Emancipation Proclamation. I was in that room when we finished it, but they can only paint in an empty chair to represent my place…an empty chair, Jason."

I sat there listening to her say this with such sorrow in her voice that I found it difficult to muster a response. After a moment, I said, "Why is it that the leaders of our country are afraid to tell the truth?"

Without hesitation, she said, "It's because the leaders of our country have long ago forgotten *how* to tell the truth. They live in the constant fear of having to justify their every move, so they only tell about the things that they can easily explain."

Miss Carroll paused. "In this particular case, they would have to explain that a *woman* sat in on the cabinet meetings and participated with a vote that was equal to that of that of their own. They know that the public doesn't have the stomach for that, so they are *afraid* to tell the truth."

"So, if they didn't have to explain it, they would tell the truth," I said, remembering something that Mr. H. had written in one of his letters: *You can tell me all you want that we are fighting the war to free the slaves, but I can tell you that we are fighting the war to preserve the power of the federal government over the states.*

"Yes, Jason, I think they would," she said.

CHAPTER SEVENTY-SEVEN

War Department
June 12, 1863
ante meridiem

I decided that, on the mornings prior to our staff meetings, I would take a walk over to the stockyards. My conversation with William Smith confirmed my suspicion that something was not right there, but I couldn't quite figure out what it was. After talking to Smith, I sent a message to Professor Turner with some questions about the use of bone meal, and I was hoping to get an answer back very soon.

The crowded conditions at the stockyard seemed to be causing some problems with the cattle. I noticed a larger number of downers than what I would have expected to see. The horses also seemed to be very agitated with their surroundings.

When I circled back through the railroad yards, I noticed that the tracks were filled with cars, and there were many engines in the station. I saw the Col. A. Beckwith, the Commodore, the Firefly, the Eagle, and the Vulcan all arriving at the station. One of the engineers told me that Colonel D.C. McCallum, the general manager of the U.S. Military Railroads, had ordered that all railroad stock be brought in within the defenses of Washington for protection.

I hurried back to the War Department for our Friday staff meeting, hoping to find out more about all of this. It turned out to be the first item on Major Eckert's agenda.

According to the major, there seemed to be some disagreement as to what General Hooker's next move should be. The general believed that the presence of Confederate infantry at Brandy Station was a clear indication that General Lee had divided his forces, sending Ewell's corps and Longstreet's corps away from Fredericksburg, leaving only Hill's corps there. Hooker began to move some of his forces to Manassas in anticipation of crossing the Rappahannock River to drive a wedge between Hill and the others. Hooker would then march all the way to Richmond, which he was sure that he could do.

Hooker's plan was strongly supported by Secretary Chase and others, who claimed that it was the fastest way to end the war. The plan was opposed by President Lincoln, Secretary Stanton, and General Halleck, who feared that Washington would be vulnerable. They wanted Hooker to stay between General Lee and Washington. In their opinion, Lee was still in Fredericksburg.

"Colonel Sharpe has assured General Hooker that an attack upon Washington is not part of General Lee's plan," Major Eckert said, "but Lafayette Baker has informed Secretary Stanton that this is not true. If we can break the Confederate code in the next few days, we may be able to sort out this difference of opinion."

I had worked with the telegraph operators for a while late last night, and I knew that we were getting very close. Unfortunately, some of the messages that were taken from captured soldiers in the vicinity of Fredericksburg appeared to be misleading—so much so, that Bates thought that they'd been intentionally planted for us by the Confederates.

"General Hooker has ordered Major General Pleasonton to probe the gaps in the Blue Ridge Mountains to prove that General Lee is advancing through the valley," Major Eckert said. "I suspect that Stuart won't allow Pleasonton to pass through the gaps and make this observation." He paused for a moment before continuing with a softer voice. "If Hooker becomes convinced that Lee has moved away from Fredericksburg, I think he may proceed with an attack on Richmond."

Major Eckert didn't pursue the topic any further, but he'd made it quite clear to us that he was convinced that "Fighting Joe" Hooker had no intention of remaining in his defensive position much longer.

We went around the table and reported out on our work. I recounted my findings at the stockyard.

Major Eckert listened with great interest, and then he said, "Jason, take it to the next level with this guy. Make sure that he sees you watching him and his operation, and talk to him some more...Remind him what happens to traitors. He's got a nice job, and he might just decide that it's worth keeping...We'll protect him if he talks."

"You'll take care of the quartermaster general?" I asked.

Major Eckert nodded. "Certainly...but if Smith has something to hide, I doubt that he'll go to Quartermaster General Meigs anyhow."

After the meeting was over, Major Eckert took me aside, and he said, "Jason, the secretary prefers that Baker and his men represent the *muscle* of the WD, but I think you may be getting close to a situation where you may have to make an arrest on your own. So here's a pair of handcuffs for you to carry. I'm giving them only to you, because I think the other agents aren't likely to need them...and I give them to you because I think you can handle the responsibility that goes along with them."

He didn't wait for any response from me, and I didn't have one. I realized that it was his way of telling me that I was ready for that *next level* that he had spoken about in the meeting.

CHAPTER SEVENTY-EIGHT

War Department
June 12, 1863
post meridiem

On Friday afternoon I went through the reports of "suspicious activities" and actual sightings of Confederates operating inside of the Washington screen. Much to my surprise, I wasn't seeing the movement of such events to the north as I had expected, but the action remained pretty much to the west of Washington. The most active location on my list for the past week was Mill's Crossroads, which was only four miles northeast of Fairfax Court House.

I had stopped in at Chichester's Tavern at Mill's Crossroads twice over the past few months, and it was quiet there on both occasions. Today was the first time that Mill's Crossroads made it to the *top* of my list, and I had to admit that it seemed like a good location for what I called the "far-end exchange," that is, the passing of the message between the last courier and the Confederates. Mill's Crossroads was only eight miles east of Chantilly, which was a location where the Confederates seemed to easily pass through the Washington screen.

Furthermore, I could see that Mill's Crossroads was within easy riding distance of an area that had become known as Mosby's Confederacy—an area bounded on the north by the Little River Turnpike, on the south by the Manassas Gap Railroad, on the east by the Bull Run Mountains, and on the west by the Blue Ridge Mountains. Many believed that Mosby and his men hid there among the locals during the day, before they gathered at night for their raids. I suspected all along that Mosby was involved in some of these exchanges with the couriers from Washington, and with the increased activity of the revitalized Union cavalry, more of this work was likely to fall upon Mosby.

My schedule for the next few weeks would force me to share time between Mill's Crossroads and the Washington stockyards. Ideally, I was looking for a breakthrough in both places, and I felt that Major Eckert, and perhaps even Secretary Stanton, expected it.

I was piecing together my schedule in my head when David Homer Bates pulled up a chair and sat down next to me at my desk. "You could cut the air around here with a knife," he said.

"I know what you mean," I said. "Everyone's anxious for some good news."

"The other night, the president told me that the First Lady is making plans for their return to Springfield...Imagine that," Bates said. "I guess it never occurred to me that he might not be reelected."

"My friend Mr. H., from back home, writes that President Lincoln may not even win Illinois this time. I'm certainly hoping that he's wrong."

"What're you going to do after the war, Jason?"

"I'm going to finish school...Then I'd like to teach or get a job with the railroad...Maybe I'll take over for Mr. H. when he calls it quits."

"I thought you might want to stay here in Washington," he said.

"No, I expect that I'll leave here...and I'm not likely to come back. I guess I'm like Dandy...He wants to go home, and so do I."

"Altoona, Pennsylvania, seems like a long way off at this moment, but I guess I really wouldn't mind going back there either," he said.

Next to Miss Carroll, David Homer Bates was my best friend in Washington. They were certainly two of the smartest people I'd ever met. I would put them right up there with my father, Professor Crampton, Professor Turner, and Mr. H. I thought how great it would be to be in a place with all of them at the same time.

Bates went back to the telegraph room, and I tidied up my desk before heading off to supper at the Ebbitt House.

⌘ ⌘ ⌘

I sat with Miss Carroll on the porch of the Ebbitt House after supper. "Do you think the president will be reelected?" I asked.

She was quiet for a bit, but then she replied, "May God help us if he is not. When I look ahead at the work that is to be done to rebuild the Union after all of this warfare ends, we will need the compassionate leadership of Abraham Lincoln. I have spoken with him at length about this. Without great care, we could easily end up with a situation that is much worse than what existed before...a situation where the Negro cannot find a home in either the North or the South...a situation where they will never fit in."

We pondered her words together in silence, until suddenly she said, "Do you see that man walking by, across the street? I see him walk by here quite often, and he looks familiar to me, but I have no idea who he is."

I took a close look at the man, who didn't look in our direction. "I may have seen him before, but I'm not sure," I said. "Perhaps he lives near here."

"Perhaps," she said.

CHAPTER SEVENTY-NINE

Little River Turnpike
June 18, 1863
ante meridiem

It was Thursday morning, and Major Eckert and I were riding along the Little River Turnpike heading for General Hooker's new headquarters at Fairfax Court House. The weather was beautiful, so we decided to ride the whole distance, instead of taking the train, from Alexandria to Fairfax Station. We were to meet with Hooker's chief of staff, Major General Daniel Butterfield, whose message to Major General Alfred Pleasonton was intercepted last night by Mosby near Gum Spring, along with two of Hooker's staff officers.

Secretary Stanton wanted us to find out exactly *how much* information was now in Confederate hands. We rode at a canter and arrived at Butterfield's quarters in Antonia Ford's large home on Chain Bridge Road in Fairfax Court House just past 10:00 a.m.

Major General Butterfield was not happy to see us. "There's no need for the two of you to ride all the way out here...We informed

Secretary Stanton as soon as we found out about the capture of Major Sterling and Captain Fisher."

Major William Sterling was a member of Hooker's general staff, and Captain Benjamin Fisher was the Army of the Potomac's chief signal officer. We knew that such officers would not be acting as couriers unless the message that they carried was of extreme importance.

"Secretary Stanton wants to know what information the message carried to the enemy," Major Eckert said in a firm tone of voice. "General Hooker keeps a copy of his orders, does he not?"

"Of course…I wrote the orders out for the general, and I have my copy right here," he said, handing the copy to Major Eckert, a lower-ranking officer, with a slight bit of hesitation.

Major Eckert read the message slowly and carefully. Visibly disturbed, he handed the message to me and said, "I want this *entire* message sent to Secretary Stanton immediately."

Butterfield did not intercede, but I was followed closely by one of his aides as I took the message to the telegraph operator's tent, which was just outside.

The reason for Major Eckert's reaction became clear. The message hadn't been coded in cipher, and it was intended to provide Pleasonton with detailed information about the location of Hooker's army. By now, General Lee knew that Hooker was headquartered in Fairfax Court House, Meade's corps was at Gum Spring, and Howard's corps was north of Meade's. The message included division strength for Hooker's entire army and revealed that Hooker was planning to keep his forces in these defensive positions indefinitely, while Pleasonton was ordered to probe the gaps to look for General Lee.

Secretary Stanton was sure to be furious. After seeing that the message was sent, I returned to Butterfield's office in the main parlor of the Ford home. The major general had excused himself for a moment to report to General Hooker.

As he sat, waiting for Butterfield's return, Major Eckert shook his head for a bit, and then he looked up at me and said, "Jason, there's no need for you to wait here...I know you'd like to ride over to Mill's Crossroads, so go ahead. I'll ride to Fairfax Station when I'm done here, and catch the train back to the city."

That suited me just fine, and I didn't delay my departure. I rode out the same way that we had come in, on the Little River Turnpike. About four miles to the east, I took a short road to the north, crossing Accotink Creek to Gallows Road, which led directly to Mill's Crossroads and Chichester's Tavern, where a delicious bowl of chicken soup was calling out to me.

Before one o'clock, I was leaving Chichester's quiet place and beginning the four-mile ride to Falls Church, located on the Leesburg and Alexandria Turnpike, which would take me directly to Bailey's Crossroads.

Dandy and I were enjoying the day in the sunshine and fresh air. About a mile from Bailey's, I noticed Dr. Rathbonne riding in our direction in his small phaeton.

I rode up next to him, and we both stopped. "Hello, Doctor, where are you heading?" I asked. Perhaps it was the slight bit of hesitation before answering, or maybe it was something else that I saw as we faced each other...Whatever it was, I reached down and grabbed the black medical bag that sat next to him on the seat.

"I'm going...What are...What are you doing?" he shouted. Instinctively, his right hand moved toward his coat pocket.

"I wouldn't do that, Doctor."

He believed me and relaxed his hand. "You have no right to take that bag. I have costly medicine in there. I'll see that you live to regret this, you young fool...I have many friends in Washington... You're making a *big* mistake."

As he rambled on, I made a quick search of the bag, pushing my fingers down through the medicine bottles and medical tools. Feeling around the edges of the bottom of the bag, I found the tab that I was looking for and pulled up the false bottom—and there it was, the piece of paper that I was looking for. It was a message coded in the *Vigenéré* cipher of the Confederacy.

I enjoyed a feeling of relief for just a moment, but then the reality of the situation set in…I would have to arrest the doctor…so that's exactly what I did. "You're under arrest, Doctor. You are now in the custody of an agent of the War Department. You must surrender any arms that you bear, and any attempts to resist arrest will not be tolerated. Sir, I suggest that you come with me peacefully."

The doctor correctly sensed that I meant what I said, so he handed over his gun, but he was not finished with his verbal tirade. "Young man, you'll be sorry that you ever laid eyes on me. I'll run you right out of Washington."

"That will be difficult, Doctor…You'll have to explain *this*," I said, waving the message at him. I checked his phaeton for any other guns and handcuffed his wrist to the seat. I took the reins of his two horses and led them back through Bailey's Crossroads and on to Fort Blenker, which was only a couple of miles beyond.

I saw that Dr. Rathbonne was placed in the brig at the fort, and then I rode on to Washington with the medical bag and the message. Dandy sensed my excitement, and he set a brisk pace back to the city.

Major Eckert was back at his desk in the telegraph room when I walked in at just a bit after 6:00 p.m. I reported the details of the incident to him. He looked at the message and turned it over to Bates, who'd just come in for the evening shift.

"I'll add this to our collection," Bates said, somewhat jokingly.

Major Eckert nodded as he explored the false bottom of the medical bag. "I shall report this to the secretary immediately. This is good work, Alexander." He rose from his chair and headed down the hall.

"You bagged a big one this time...so to speak," Bates chuckled.

"My, you're sure in a good mood," I said with a bit of a smile of my own.

"My sister just had her baby, so I'm Uncle David now."

"Congratulations, Uncle David."

Major Eckert returned, and interrupted our good-natured banter. "The secretary is tied up at the moment, but I'll discuss this with him before he leaves for home tonight. Jason, you've put in a good day...Go get a good meal and some rest."

"Thanks, I will, but I just remembered that I left Dandy with a soldier at the front door of the building, so he's first to be taken care of."

CHAPTER EIGHTY

War Department
June 19, 1863
ante meridiem

I knew that something important was going on when, soon after entering the building, I was informed that our Friday morning staff meeting was canceled. I realized that it had something to do with me when I was summoned to Secretary Stanton's office for a meeting with him and Major Eckert.

When I walked into the secretary's corner office, Major Eckert was sitting in one of the two chairs facing Stanton's large desk. Major Eckert nodded his head in the direction of the empty seat, and I sat down. I saw the medical bag sitting on the corner of the desk near the major.

Secretary Stanton had his nose buried in a fistful of papers. After a couple of minutes, without moving his head, his eyes raised up and peered at me just above his reading glasses, which were perfectly balanced on the end of his short, stubby nose. They were cold eyes, searching for something. "Agent Alexander, the major has been kind enough to tell me about your altercation with Dr. Rathbonne, but I would like to hear of it in your words."

I gave him all of the details, from the time that I spotted the doctor on the Little River Turnpike to the time that I left him in the brig at the fort.

"How did you *know* that he had the message that you found?"

"I *didn't* know, Mr. Secretary, but after reading all of the reports, and riding all of the routes over and over again, it all came together in my mind at that moment...I *felt* that he had it." As soon as I said it, I thought that it wasn't going to be what he wanted to hear from me, but it was the truth.

Secretary Stanton pursed his lips and nodded his head. "This afternoon's newspapers will report his arrest, and being the *fine* pro-Democrat papers that many of them are, they will claim that Dr. Rathbonne's constitutional rights have been violated and that he should be immediately released. The fact that he is a *spy* for the Confederates will be played down by the hysteria of fear that all citizens, especially doctors, are likely to be arrested by the War Department in the near future, for any reason that the War Department may choose." The secretary paused, and pushed his tiny glasses up, off the tip of his nose.

"Add this to the fear that the city may come under attack by the Confederates at any time," Major Eckert said, "and you have a city that is ready to come apart at the seams. Don't misunderstand us, Jason. You did exactly what we wanted you to do...You've eliminated a key courier and damaged the inner structure of their network."

"Major Eckert and I will be meeting with the president and his cabinet later this morning to discuss this matter," Secretary Stanton said. "In the meantime, I suggest that you get on with your good work...but doctors are off-limits, until we resolve this."

I excused myself and left the room. All eyes were on me as I walked into the telegraph room. There was a moment of silence, but then congratulations abounded from all, including the other agents.

Charles Tinker waved the apprehended message in the air. "This is a good one, Jason. A lot of numbers are mixed in here amongst the words...troop strengths around the city, we suspect... It'll help us figure out what we need to know to break their cipher."

I warned them about what was bound to be showing up in the newspapers this afternoon. They noticed my disappointment and toned down the celebration. "Surely, they won't let him go," Simpson Dahlgren said.

"I hope not," I said as I slowly made my way to the door to the library.

"Jason, I almost forgot...You received a message from Professor Turner last night," Matthew Grimsley said. "I put it on your desk."

"Thanks," I called over my shoulder as I left the room. I found the telegram right away. The following was received:

Jacksonville, Illinois/June 18, 1863/8:32 p.m.

I regret my slow response. All of my help is gone now. Bone meal is a good feed supplement for cattle. Most ranchers and butchers around here now sell the bones to the mills. Skull, brains, and spine are to be avoided.

Professor J.B. Turner

I immediately responded with the following message:

War Department/June 19, 1863/10:38 a.m.

What damage is done if the skull, brains, and spine are included? Can these be detected if they are mixed in with the other bones? Who else knows about this?

Agent Jason W. Alexander

CHAPTER EIGHTY-ONE

Washington Stockyard
June 21, 1863
post meridiem

Dark Eyes asked William Smith to meet him at the stockyards late Sunday night to discuss some new plans. The constant visits to the stockyards by the WD agent, Jason Alexander, had begun to disturb Smith to the point that Dark Eyes was no longer sure that he could trust him to keep quiet.

It was a black night, and a breeze from the south warmed the night air. Some of the soldiers who usually guarded the area had been pulled away to increase the forces on the perimeter of the city because of the threat that the Confederates might attack the Union capital. Dark Eyes welcomed the thought of such an attack, but doubted that it would occur. "Even Mosby wouldn't do it," he whispered to himself.

Dark Eyes saw Smith enter the warehouse and ignite a light in his small office near the main door. *William Smith is not going to stop this quest.*

After checking again to make sure that no one else was around, Dark Eyes entered the building. "Good evening, Mr. Smith, I'm glad to see that you could make it."

"We can dispense with the formalities...I see enough of this place without coming here on Sunday night," Smith growled. "Is this going to take long?"

"Not long at all, I promise you," Dark Eyes laughed, and in one swift motion he plunged the knife into Smith's heart. Looking into the eyes of his victim, Dark Eyes twisted the knife in his hand before pulling it out. He repeated the whole thing one more time just to make absolutely sure that Smith was no longer able to hinder his plans.

He quickly pushed the lifeless body away.

Blood began pooling on the floor. Dark Eyes had no intention of moving the body, so he took Smith's valuables to make it look like a robbery. Also, he didn't want any of the other KGC workers at the stockyard to think that the killing had anything at all to do with their subversive activities, being carried out under Smith's direction.

Before returning his knife to its sheath inside his pocket, Dark Eyes wiped both sides of the blade on Smith's rumpled coat. He doused the light and left the building.

As he walked back to his apartment, he thought about the other plans for killing Smith that he had abandoned in favor of this one. There was a chance that he could've taken Smith *along with* Jason Alexander, at a time when the two of them were together. But that would've been extremely risky, because it would have had to occur during the daylight hours.

There was no denying that Jason Alexander was his next target, and Dark Eyes also intended to make good on his attempt to take Miss Anna Ella Carroll's life as well. *This week* would be a perfect time to take care of the two of them...and they were often together. How convenient.

⌘ ⌘ ⌘

"There goes that odd-looking man again," Miss Carroll said. We were sitting on the porch of the Ebbitt House after a wonderful supper of ham hocks and beans with corn bread, one of my favorites.

"He seems to be in a hurry tonight." But just as I said it, he slowed down and looked in our direction. He was well dressed and clean-shaven, but something about this man was peculiar.

Miss Carroll shared the feeling...She reached over and took hold of my hand. "There's something about that man that just sends a shiver up my spine. I have no reason for saying this, for I know him not from Adam, but say it I will."

"Perhaps I will follow him one night," I said. "But then, he'd turn out to be a *doctor*, and I wouldn't be able to arrest him, even if I found him to be committing a crime against our country."

"Cynicism doesn't suit you, Jason Alexander," she chuckled. We had discussed the outrageous newspaper articles earlier in the night, and Miss Carroll was as disgusted as I was, but she didn't seem to be as discouraged. "A good number of the newspapers are in the hands of the Democrats, and they'll distort the facts to suit their needs. I expect that this will go on until the end of time."

"I just don't understand how they could be calling for Dr. Rathbonne's release after I found the message in his medical bag," I said. "What more proof do they need that he is an enemy spy?"

Miss Carroll squeezed my hand and said, "Jason, they don't care about the message. They only care about feeding the people's fear that any one of *them* could be arrested by agents of a War Department occupied by the sinister Republicans."

I didn't understand that, and I knew that I never would.

CHAPTER EIGHTY-TWO

Ebbitt House
June 22, 1863
post meridiem

Rumors of an impending attack by the Confederates continued to circulate around Washington, and the trains going north to Baltimore were packed with people leaving the Union capital. Even the officers were staying closer to their posts, as evidenced by the drought in the Washington nightlife.

I was tempted to pass on supper at the Ebbitt House, and instead take a walk through the now much quieter city, but the attraction of Mrs. Ebbitt's prime rib proved to be too much. Neither Miss Carroll nor I were able to steer the conversation away from the events of the day.

"Jason, I suppose that you're not happy that the secretary of war has released Dr. Rathbonne," Mrs. Mason said, "but even *you* would have to agree that the permanent military escort for him, and several of the other doctors in town, doesn't seem to make much sense."

Before I could respond, Miss Carroll spoke. "It makes perfect sense, Mrs. Mason. Our doctors are valuable, so why not protect them with a permanent military escort?"

I admired Miss Carroll's ability to keep a straight face as she said this. It was Miss Carroll who convinced the president to *mandate* the military escort for the doctors who traveled outside of the city, a clever act that immediately eliminated them as couriers for the Confederacy.

I knew that this action was going to create a need for the Confederate cavalry to get closer to Washington, because fewer couriers meant that the messages couldn't be carried as far. We knew that a good part of Stuart's cavalry was guarding the gaps in the Blue Ridge Mountains because of the fierce battles there over the last few days...perhaps leaving the matter of making the courier connections to the partisan rangers.

My thoughts were interrupted by the relentless Mrs. Mason. "I don't feel safe walking our streets at night any longer. You all heard about that poor man getting robbed and killed over at the stockyards, didn't you?"

I'd heard the unfortunate news about Smith's death early this morning, and I was quite sure that it wasn't a robbery, but I wouldn't discuss the matter tonight.

Mrs. Mason continued, "Why, this place is becoming a ghost town. I heard that the Willard was only half filled now. There are more blackies here than whites. I'm ready to leave myself."

I waited to see if someone offered to help her pack, but no one did.

"Mrs. Mason, I think we're all perfectly safe here," Miss Carroll said. "The city is surrounded by forts, and we have enough food to last us a lifetime."

"Anna Carroll, you know that those forts are practically empty, and as far as the beef goes"—Mrs. Mason paused, glancing at me—"it's tough!"

I wasn't going to defend the beef tonight either. She was right about the forts, though. The forces defending Washington were as thinly manned as they had ever been, and General Hooker had just talked Secretary Stanton into giving him control over the twenty-six thousand troops in Washington, as well as the eleven thousand at Harpers Ferry, so the situation wasn't likely to get any better.

After some of the best cherry cobbler that I'd ever tasted, Miss Carroll and I slipped off to the front porch. There was a gentle breeze from the west, and the smell of rain in the air on this Monday night. I noticed some pink lightning in the distance, reminding me of summer nights back home in Illinois.

"Mrs. Mason can be quite annoying at times," Miss Carroll said.

"That's an understatement, but her presence is a constant reminder for me to keep my mouth shut about anything that happens at the War Department, so in an odd way, she's helpful."

We were both laughing when I heard the two shots—one right after the other. Simultaneously, wood splintered just above me, and fragments of the Ebbitt House sprayed the back of my head.

I turned to assist Miss Carroll. She was lying on the porch floor, covered with blood.

CHAPTER EIGHTY-THREE

War Department
June 23, 1863
ante meridiem

Tuesday morning was a blur of activity. After spending much of the night waiting to hear about Miss Carroll, I went to my room and slept a bit before returning to her bedside. She hadn't lost consciousness and refused to be taken anywhere except to her room at the Ebbitt House. The bullet only grazed her shoulder, and the doctor said that the wound should completely heal.

President Lincoln and Secretary Stanton visited during the night, and a permanent guard was posted at the Ebbitt House. The news of the attack traveled quickly, and by midmorning, telegrams for Miss Carroll were coming in from all across the Union. They were stacked on Major Eckert's desk in the telegraph room.

Other telegrams were warning about the movement of Confederate troops into Maryland. One report indicated that the Rebels were as far north as Hagerstown, which was close to the Pennsylvania border. General Hooker was busy protecting Washington, with his forces spread out across three counties in Virginia. His right flank reached the Potomac, where he'd positioned pontoons in anticipation of crossing. As each day passed, General Hooker was becoming more and more vocal about his belief that he was missing an opportunity to attack General Lee's weakened rear, exposed as he moved northward.

It occurred to me that the Confederate riders in search of couriers from Washington would be forced to exploit the gaps in General Hooker's line in order to pass through to make connections. I could just as easily find these holes by riding along the line myself. Once I found them, I could make General Hooker aware of them…hopefully without upsetting him in the process.

After I cleared this plan with a somewhat reluctant Major Eckert, I walked in the rain to the provost marshal's office on Seventh and E Street to check on the status of the ongoing investigation into Smith's murder, as well as the attempt to murder Miss Carroll and me last night. I spoke with Inspector David Miller.

"We don't have much of anything on either case…no witnesses, no suspects. Do you think the attacker was after you, or her?"

"Two shots were fired. One hit her, and the other almost hit me…I would say that he was after *both* of us. Are you aware that there was an attempt on Miss Carroll's life a few months ago?"

"We know that. We also know that the man who called himself Clifford Bates in Tolono has *not* been captured. Do you think he came back here to finish the job?"

"I don't know…I doubt it," I said, "but what I *do* know is that *Smith's* murder wasn't associated with a robbery. I was trying to get him to tell me about something that is going on there at the stockyards, and I think he was about ready to spill the beans…He was killed by someone who stopped him from talking. Inspector Miller, the military guard at the stockyard has fallen off because of other demands. Is it possible for the police to patrol that area?"

"We are stretched thin as well, but I'll see what I can do."

I thanked him and walked out into what was now a downpour to return to the War Department. I had a good deal of paperwork to complete before I could ride out to inspect General Hooker's line. There were several telegrams to read, but the one that I was looking for from Professor Turner was not amongst them. Shortly after sending my message to him on Friday morning, I had received a message from the telegraph agent in Jacksonville, informing me that Professor Turner was out of town, trying to deal with the many issues associated with the Land Grant University Act that he had initiated years ago. A messenger was attempting to take my telegram to him.

I was intrigued by the most recent reports of the significant cavalry battles at Aldie, Middleburg, and Upperville, where the Little River Turnpike extended to the Ashby's Gap Turnpike, between the Bull Run and Blue Ridge Mountains. Over the past few days, the losses there on both sides were comparable to the more widely known battle at Brandy Station earlier in the month. There had to be a very good reason why General Stuart was fighting so fiercely to keep the Union cavalry out of the Shenandoah Valley.

A telegram from a local farmer reported that his son had climbed to the top of the mountain peak near Ashby's Gap and spotted massive Confederate camps in the valley. If this report was true, it would confirm General Hooker's suspicions that Lee was heading to Pennsylvania. I realized that the Confederate couriers would be forced to go well south of the Little River Turnpike to get their messages to their cavalry, who, in turn, would have to ride up into the valley to get the messages to General Lee.

I decided that I would look for gaps in General Hooker's line in that area. I would ride out there tomorrow morning.

CHAPTER EIGHTY-FOUR

Fairfax Court House
June 25, 1863
ante meridiem

On Wednesday I took the train out to Fairfax Station. Before riding out to look for gaps in the Union line, I went to General Hooker's headquarters at Fairfax Court House to meet with Major General Butterfield, letting him know what I was going to do. It wasn't necessary for me to get his permission, but I knew that it was important to maintain good relations with him, and for my own protection, it was good for him to know that I was out riding around.

He was still harboring ill feeling from the meeting with Major Eckert and me late last week, but he was so busy that he didn't wish to spend much time with me. It wasn't long before I was in the saddle, and Dandy was full of energy as we made our way in a light rain to Pleasant Valley, about four miles beyond Chantilly, along the Little River Turnpike. By the time we turned southward in the direction of New Market, the rain stopped, and the sun began to peek through the soft white clouds. Hooker's line appeared to be tight here, and I stopped to talk to soldiers from Webb's and Hall's brigades in Hancock's corps, which was concentrated in this area.

I rode almost all the way to the O&A Railroad's Manassas Station before turning around and heading back to Fairfax Court House. I spent the night in the telegraph operator's tent. I slept lightly and observed that several messages were traded between General Hooker and Secretary Stanton during the night.

Just before dawn, I was awakened by the telegraph operator. He informed me that Hooker was moving north immediately, because the signal station at Maryland Heights had reported that Confederate General Hill's corps was moving through Charlestown, toward the Potomac River. I was saddling Dandy, and trying to decide what to do next, when one of General Hancock's couriers rode in. He reported that some of Hancock's infantry had encountered Confederate cavalry on a road near Hay Market, just after they had begun to march northward, less than thirty minutes ago. I quickly mounted, and rode in that direction with the returning courier.

We covered the ten miles on the Warrenton Turnpike very quickly, but by the time we arrived at the road on which Hancock's corps was moving north, the short skirmish with the Confederates had ended. I was informed that the Rebels had backed off rather quickly, and appeared to move in the direction of Buckland Mills. Thinking that it was probably a small force looking to meet up with a courier from Washington, I decided to investigate.

Because of the size of the Union force in the area, I expected the Confederates to eventually move further west, so I headed for the Thoroughfare Gap. I rode along cautiously for about two miles. Suddenly, a rider appeared from the woods on the left, only two hundred yards ahead of me. He broke into a gallop, heading toward the Thoroughfare Gap. He wore the butternut uniform of a Confederate.

I immediately gave chase, keeping an eye on the wooded area to my left, just in case he had some friends close by. No one else appeared. Dandy quickly closed the distance between me and my quarry.

When I was only twenty yards behind the Rebel, I drew my pistol. Seeing this, he began to slow down. I thought he might swing around and confront me with a pistol of his own, but he did not. The Confederate rider reined in his mount and raised both hands, keeping his back to me.

I rode alongside him at a safe distance, keeping my pistol aimed squarely at his chest. I could tell that he wasn't sure why I'd stopped him. He looked curiously at my WD armband. "Are you a Yankee?" he said.

"War Department agent," I said.

His eyes widened. "You work for Stanton?"

"Yes, Secretary of War Stanton."

That seemed to concern him.

"Hand over your weapon...and that satchel that you're carrying," I said.

He cooperated, seeming to readily accept his fate. He was about the age of my younger brother, but the Rebel cavalryman was worn and tired. I cuffed his wrists, and, keeping him in front of me, we rode off in the direction of Fairfax Station.

Along the way, I found a coded message in the satchel. I immediately advanced our pace.

At Fairfax Station, I was able to place the Rebel courier and his message in the custody of the guards on a train departing for Alexandria at 11:00 a.m. The officer in charge assured me that he would get the message in the satchel to the War Department without delay.

The station agent warned me that the trains were being pulled back within the defenses of Washington, now that Hooker was leaving this area. He urged me to return on the last train, which would depart at 4:00 p.m. It was good advice, and it gave me enough time for a last look at the area where the Rebel riders had been seen earlier in the day.

CHAPTER EIGHTY-FIVE

Warrenton Turnpike
June 25, 1863
post meridiem

General Hooker's forces continued to move northward at a steady pace, occupying a good number of the roads crossing the Warrenton Turnpike. I worked my way through the rows of marching soldiers and horse-pulled artillery and wagons, finally passing through the last line on the road to Hay Market.

A nice cool breeze was blowing in from the north as I continued westward along the Warrenton Turnpike. I planned to ride as far as Buckland Mills and then return to Fairfax Station in time to catch the last train to Alexandria.

They seemed to come out of nowhere—six Rebel riders with pistols drawn. The big one with red hair and bad teeth said, "Well lookee here, boys, we got ourselves a Yankee spy. . .and we all know what we do with Yankee spies, don't we?" They quickly closed in, pressing their horses up against Dandy on all sides.

They grabbed my weapons, and as I tried to speak, the big guy drove the butt of his long gun squarely into my chest, knocking the wind out of me. Before I knew it, they had my hands tied behind me, and a gag placed in my mouth.

"There's a good tree right over here," one of them said. They led me off in that direction. It was all happening so quickly that I couldn't even begin to formulate a plan to escape. I tried to point with my head to my armband, hoping that one of them would recognize it, but they yanked my head up with the rope that they placed around my neck as they tossed the other end of it over the stout branch of a big hackberry tree, tying it off around the trunk.

They were backing away to make room to drive Dandy out from under me, when another rider approached with sword drawn. In one swift motion, he cut the rope above me. The end fell right across my nose like the trunk of an elephant.

"Can't you see that this man is an employee of Stanton's War Department?"

My rescuer was John Mosby. He looked squarely in my eyes and said, "You are my prisoner, and if you try to escape, I *will* shoot you." Turning his attention to the rider with the red hair, Mosby said, "Remove the gag, and tie his hands to the saddle horn. I don't want him falling off his mount if we need to ride quickly...In case you hadn't noticed, there are a lot of Union soldiers in the vicinity."

The big man reluctantly followed Mosby's orders, grumbling about my lack of proper uniform. Another rider approached and spoke with Mosby for a moment. Shortly afterward, Mosby sent two riders off to the east. Minutes later, another rider came in and gave his report to *Major* Mosby.

I assumed that I'd stumbled upon some sort of a rendezvous point, and from the short bits of conversation that I could understand, they were looking for someone who had not shown up on schedule.

I'd read the reports about Mosby's operation, and I knew that his band was made up of a very small group of partisan rangers, mixed together with other Confederates on leave due to injury or the need to find remounts. Looking at this group, I was pretty much able to sort them out. Their *uniforms* varied from the well-dressed Mosby, to a man whose badly worn gray pants and faded blue coat would have just as easily passed for the battered uniform of a Union soldier.

Mosby usually operated at night, with his men hiding out in various places during the day. Some argued that his men were involved in the war only for the contraband that they were able to seize, suggesting that they were nothing more than opportunistic thieves.

Though secluded by the wooded area away from the Warrenton Turnpike, these men weren't happy to be spending so much time in one place, but Major Mosby was reluctant to leave this spot.

He must be waiting to meet someone important. I thought about the courier that I had intercepted...but he was riding *away* from this area. Then I remembered the report from early this morning, a report that a Rebel force of unknown size was fired upon in this very area—surely that was it. Mosby was waiting to meet up with them. But why?

After dark, we moved off in a southeasterly direction, and from time to time on our left, I could see the Union campfires peeking through the fog that had lifted up from the warm, damp ground. Mosby and his men moved easily through the darkness, having full knowledge of the lay of the land.

At one point, Mosby rode up next to me, and in a low voice, he said, "What were you doing out here? This would seem to be a strange place to find a War Department agent." I could barely make out his slight form in the darkness, but his piercing eyes stood out.

Fortunately, I'd already thought about what my responses would be to such interrogation. "I'm embarrassed to say that I became separated from Hancock's corps, with whom I was riding for a short time."

"I doubt that," he said. "You're fortunate that I don't have time to pursue a stronger line of questioning. In due time, you will be taken to the prison in Richmond, and I will be taking this fine little horse of yours...You must be from Kentucky."

"Illinois," I said, "and after the war is ended, I will return to get him back."

Mosby just nodded and rode off. I wondered if he believed me.

The fog thickened into a heavy mist as we rode on. I wasn't sure how far we'd traveled when Major Mosby halted the group. "This is far enough," he said. "We'll rest here for a bit."

We dismounted, and the men pulled their raincoats from their saddlebags, along with jerky and biscuits. They offered me a biscuit and a drink of water, which I took. They fed some grain to their horses, and Mosby brought over a handful for Dandy. We seemed to wait for at least an hour before turning around and heading back in the direction from which we had come.

We were riding very slowly in single file now, and the mist was so thick that I could only see the rider directly in front of me—the one who held Dandy's reins. I knew that Mosby wasn't far behind me.

After a while, I found myself dozing off in the saddle. We were on some sort of a road now. I had completely lost track of time and place.

Suddenly, I realized that we were passing alongside a line of cavalry on our right. The heavy mist in the night, along with the dark raincoats, made any one rider indistinguishable from another, but I sensed that they were *Union*—two columns of them. Incredibly, they were paying no attention to us, assuming that we were just more of their own cavalry riding around them in the night.

Our pace began to quicken as our lead rider must have discovered what I had. I remembered Mosby's warning, and I was sure that he would shoot me if I called out, so I stayed quiet—waiting—and then I saw it...

Up ahead, there was a gap in the Union formation, where one rider had fallen back. Only my eyes were moving now. Any head movement might have warned my captors. My heart was pounding. My hands were useless, tied to the saddle horn.

Is the opening large enough?

And then in an instant, I nudged Dandy with my left knee. He responded immediately—just like he always did back on the ranch when my hands were occupied roping a steer. He pulled the reins out of the hands of the rider in front of me and entered the open space in the Union column in one swift movement, instantly adjusting to their slower pace. He did it without even touching one of the other horses.

There was no time for the rider in front of me, or the riders behind me, to react...and now they had no choice but to *neglect* to react, for they were greatly outnumbered...Nevertheless, I braced for the bullet that never came.

Out of the corner of my eye, I caught a glimpse of Mosby as he rode by, head slightly turned in my direction. Again, there was that slight nod of his, perhaps an acknowledgement of my new-found freedom, or perhaps it was his way of telling me that we would take this up again, sometime in the future. Frankly, I hoped that I would never see him again.

I turned to the soldier on my right and leaned in to speak to him. But I could only mouth my words.

The rider looked at me more closely and said "Are you all right?"

Finally, the words came. "I need to see your commanding officer right away."

CHAPTER EIGHTY-SIX

War Department
June 26, 1863
ante meridiem

It was my good fortune that we had blindly stumbled upon a small patrol led by a Major Remington…I never did find out his first name. We rode off after the Rebels, but after a short time, we gave up the pursuit. I knew that the patrol would never find Mosby and his men.

I went directly from the stables to the War Department. I entered the building just as David Bates was arriving. I told him about my ordeal.

"Alexander, you live a charmed life," Bates said.

"I pray that my good luck doesn't run out," I said.

Bates nodded in agreement. "Secretary Stanton is very upset that Hooker decided to move northward," he said. "I'm guessing that he'll be relieved of his duty, probably over the weekend."

Bates put his hand on my shoulder. "Miss Carroll is doing well…and that message that you were expecting from Professor Turner has arrived…It's on your desk."

The telegram was on top of the pile of papers on my desk. I had started to read it when Major Eckert walked in. "You look like you had a rough night...Tell me about it."

He listened intently as I provided the details. "*Something* is happening out there, but it'll be hard for us to find out, now that we've moved out of that area." Major Eckert turned, and looked out the window. "I don't want you riding out there anymore...We need you in here."

I heard what he said, and he didn't say any more. He stood in silence as the other agents came into the library, one by one, in anticipation of the start of our Friday morning staff meeting.

As we were about to begin, Bates rushed into the room. "We've got it!" he shouted.

I immediately knew what he was talking about...We had broken the Confederate cipher.

We rushed into the telegraph room, with Major Eckert leading the way. The operators were gathered around the table in the center of the room. Tinker held up the message that I'd sent back from Fairfax Station just yesterday. "Their code word is *Manchester Bluff*, and this message is from General Stuart to General Lee, informing him that General Hooker is moving northward."

"And if Stuart was in a hurry, and dispatched only one messenger," Major Eckert added, "we can assume that General Lee is not yet aware of General Hooker's movements...I must see the secretary immediately." Major Eckert took the decoded message from Tinker and headed to Stanton's office.

For a moment, I felt a great sense of relief as I stood there amongst the others—a group of fine young men who had worked so hard for the Union cause, and I was proud to be a part of it.

"You're a good man, Jason Alexander," Bates said as he offered me his hand.

"And so are you...all of you," I said.

It was then that things began to happen very quickly. I could hear Secretary Stanton calling out orders from his corner office. People were hurrying about, and the telegraph operators were handed messages to transmit.

Without saying so, Major Eckert canceled our staff meeting. He was now quite busy with other matters.

I returned to my desk, hoping to read my messages. The first that I read was as follows:

Jacksonville, Illinois/June 24, 1863/11:10 p.m.

Skull and brains and spine bone meal causes sickness in the cattle. Eating the sick cattle could kill humans. The bad bone meal cannot be detected. All farmers and ranchers have been informed.

Professor J.B. Turner

The second message that I read was as follows:

Alexander, Illinois/June 25, 1863/4:23 a.m.

Local abolitionist group seized Judge Constable and made him talk. KGC operative killed Kinchelow, who was ready to reveal evil plot to kill cattle. Killer was Miles Palladin, also known as Clifford Bates, believed to be in Washington now.

E. Hinrichsen

I sat there holding the two telegrams, one in each hand. I needed to see Major Eckert, but I knew that he wouldn't be available for some time. I placed the two messages on his desk in the telegraph room with a note that I would return soon, and then I headed for the stockyard.

It was a few minutes after 10:00 a.m. when I entered the manager's office at the stockyard. I was informed that a Mr. Mabry was now in charge as I stood on the bloodstained spot where William Smith had fallen. I found Mr. Mabry supervising the loading of well over one hundred wagons destined for General Hooker's forces. I told him that the bone meal should not be included in the shipment.

"I can't off-load the bone meal without permission from the quartermaster general," he said.

"You'll have that right away," I said. I rushed out the door.

As I rode off, I noticed that Dandy sensed that we were being followed, but I couldn't see that anyone was close behind. Just as I crossed Eleventh Street near the office of *The Star* newspaper, a shot rang out, and I took a bullet in my left leg.

I drew the pistol that I had borrowed from Major Remington, but I couldn't locate the assailant. Within minutes I was confronted by several soldiers who insisted that I drop my weapon. As I tried to explain things, I blacked out, and fell from my horse.

CHAPTER EIGHTY-SEVEN

War Department
June 28, 1863
ante meridiem

It was early Sunday morning when I fully regained consciousness as I lay in Leah's bed in Miss Carroll's suite at the Ebbitt House. Leah had taken care of me for almost a full day after the doctor had patched up my leg wound. According to the doctor, the lead ball had cleanly passed through my left leg, missing the bone.

Miss Carroll and Leah complained vehemently as I rose to dress and leave for the War Department at 9:00 a.m.

Albert Chandler and Matthew Grimsley were on duty as I entered the telegraph office. They were surprised, but very happy to see that I was up and around. They had heard that my wound was a bad one. I pressed them to bring me up to date on what had happened since my misfortune.

With the discovery of the *Manchester Bluff* key, the telegraph operators had been able to decipher all of the messages that had been obtained from the Rebels in recent days, including the one that I had taken from Dr. Rathbonne.

"That message clearly linked him to the doctor's line of communication between Washington and the Confederacy," Chandler said.

I asked them if Major Eckert had seen the messages that I placed on his desk, but they knew nothing about that. I looked on the major's desk and couldn't find them, or my note that I had left there.

"General Meade will be relieving General Hooker this morning at Frederick," Chandler said. "He will lead the Army of the Potomac northward to confront General Lee."

Just then, the telegraph operator at the first station southeast of Rockville reported that he was quite certain that the Rockville agent was no longer at the telegraph key at his station. In fact, the operator suspected that General Stuart was sitting there. Many of the Union telegraph operators were very familiar with Stuart's distinctive keying pattern, having received rogue messages from him in the past.

Chandler was distraught because he had been instructed to send a message to the military outpost located in Rockville to notify them that the wagon train of 135 wagons, loaded with supplies for General Meade, was traveling along the Rockville Road.

"I can't send that message now, or the Rebels will know that those wagons are coming and intercept them," he said. "I need your permission to cancel the message." He looked at me and waited.

After a moment, I said, *"Send the message!"*

"What?" Chandler was completely surprised, and visibly disturbed.

"I don't have time to explain it now, Albert, but I have reason to believe that those wagons are loaded with contaminated bone meal that will sicken General Meade's cattle, and perhaps his men as well. Let General Stuart take the wagons to General Lee instead!"

"If you're wrong, this could put us both in prison," Chandler said.

"I accept full responsibility, and Grimsley here is witness to this," I said. "That's what the messages were about that were on Major Eckert's desk. The same guy that tried to kill Miss Carroll in Tolono, Illinois, is here in Washington working as a KGC operative. He's trying to kill the cattle in the stockyard, and Professor Turner believes the people who eat the sick cattle could also become very sick, or perhaps even die."

The telegraph operators stared at me in disbelief, but then Chandler turned and transmitted the message.

I grabbed a piece of paper and wrote a note to Major Eckert. I asked him to request that Quartermaster General Meigs order that the bone meal at the stockyards be destroyed. "Chandler, send this to Major Eckert via messenger right away. I'm going to ride out to see what happens with the wagon train."

CHAPTER EIGHTY-EIGHT

Rockville Telegraph Station
June 28, 1863
ante meridiem

General Jeb Stuart arrived at the charming little village of Rockville just before noon on Sunday. The Rebels easily took the small military outpost located there without a shot being fired. The townspeople went about their business as if nothing had happened.

He wanted to attend a church service, but instead, General Stuart sat at the telegraph key at the Rockville Station, playfully sending on messages in place of the usual telegraph operator. He tried to think of something clever to transmit to Secretary Stanton. Once finished, General Stuart would order his men to begin destroying the telegraph and railroad lines between Washington and the Army of the Potomac.

He had come here with three brigades of cavalry and orders from General Lee to disrupt the Union's communications and supply lines. General Stuart wouldn't attack Washington, but he enjoyed making the Union *think* that he would. He'd undertaken the dangerous journey after discovering General Hooker's northward movement on Thursday, and after immediately dispatching a courier with an urgent message notifying General Lee of his discovery.

"By now, General Lee will have settled into a superior defensive position on high ground, where he will await General Hooker's attack and pick off the blueboys like a good old Virginia turkey shoot," General Stuart said.

His brigade commanders, Fitzhugh Lee, Rooney Lee, and Wade Hampton, all agreed, but they were tired and hoping for a bit of rest before they had to move further northward. They had departed at midnight on Thursday, leaving a larger force of three thousand men in Jones's and Robertson's brigades behind to guard the passes, protecting General Robert E. Lee's rear as he boldly moved his forces into the breadbasket of the Union.

Stuart and his men were late arriving at the rendezvous point near Warrenton Turnpike, and their intended guide, Major John Mosby, wasn't there. They couldn't afford to wait for him, so they pressed on with their journey, which had taken them through Fairfax Court House and Dranesville before making their difficult crossing of the Potomac River at Rowser's Ford last night.

The hope of rest disappeared when, moments ago, General Stuart intercepted a message from Washington, informing the military outpost in Rockville of the wagon train destined for the *newly appointed* General Meade.

"It's Meade's army that we're fighting now...So much for Fighting Joe Hooker...I'm not all that surprised since Stanton and Halleck didn't like him anyway," General Stuart said. "Let's go get those supply wagons that are heading this way. There'll be cattle too...We can use some red meat, and our horses can use some fresh grain."

"Those wagons will slow us down, General. We should take what we need and burn the rest," Brigadier General Fitzhugh Lee said. "We have a lot of distance to cover to meet up with General Early in York, Pennsylvania."

"Your uncle's supply lines are stretched far too thin, so I prefer to take the cattle and the wagons to him," General Stuart said. "Fitz, you worry too much...We have plenty of time. General Meade will dawdle around for days before making his move."

General Stuart paused for one last thought, and then he tapped his message to the Union's secretary of war: *Stanton, I'll drop in for supper at your place tonight. J.E.B. Stuart*

Just then, word came that the supply wagons had been spotted. General Stuart smashed the telegraph key, and immediately, he and his officers went to their horses.

They could already see the lead wagons when they'd ridden just two miles east of Rockville. The cattle kicked up a dust cloud that reminded the Rebel riders that they would eat well tonight. Several regiments were ordered forward to direct the attack, with the 2nd South Carolina Cavalry charging to the rear in an attempt to stop those wagons from getting turned and escaping back to Washington.

General Stuart's overwhelming force necessitated but few shots being fired, and 125 amply loaded wagons and nearly four hundred men were captured very quickly, but not before the drivers of a few of the rear wagons managed to reverse their path and frantically race away from their potential captors.

Ten wagons rushed headlong for Washington's defense perimeter, scattering the cattle in their way. Some wagons were able to get back on Rockville Road, but the frantic teamsters drove others on a rugged parallel path alongside the road. Some began to jettison part of their load to help increase their speed. The bags of feed and other discarded supplies also had the effect of slowing their pursuers; consequently, most of the Rebels gave up the chase as the wagons reached a small hill within a very short distance of Washington.

A lone rider, who had fallen from his horse after narrowly avoiding being trampled by the oncoming wagons, stood on the hilltop and fired in the direction of the few Rebel cavalrymen who were still giving chase. That was enough to turn the riders away—none of them were interested in taking a bullet at this early point in their journey.

General Stuart watched the exchange from a distance. "Where've I seen that guy before?"

CHAPTER EIGHTY-NINE

Rockville Road
June 28, 1863
post meridiem

It was just past noon when I rushed to the stables to saddle Dandy, but as I rode out of Washington, I remembered that I was only armed with a pistol. My bandaged leg was aching terribly, and I could see that blood had seeped through to the leg of my pants.

I had been informed that Major James Duane was leading the four hundred men with the wagon train, and I expected that I could catch up with them very quickly.

It was much more quickly than I had anticipated. Just as I reached a point on a hill along Rockville Road, about two miles from the Old Stone Tavern on the outskirts of Washington, I was driven off the road by several wagons racing back to the city.

Dandy was startled and reared, throwing me to the ground. Somehow, I managed to roll out of the paths of the oncoming horses and wagons. When I rose to my feet, I noticed that some Confederate riders were coming up the hill, giving chase to the wagons. Luckily, I found my pistol on the ground and fired all six shots in their direction.

I didn't hit any of them, but they instantly pulled up. After a moment, they decided to head back in the other direction. I was fortunate because I could have easily been captured.

Off in the distance I could see that the Confederate cavalry had seized all but the few wagons that had almost run over me. I estimated that there were as many as two thousand Rebel horsemen within striking distance of Washington, and they had easily captured almost all of Major Duane's men.

I raced back to Washington, quickly passing the returning supply wagons along the way. Although I seriously doubted that General Stuart would attack, I stopped at the first outpost and raised the alarm…just in case. After this was done, I rode into Washington, but instead of going directly to the War Department, I decided to stop to see Inspector David Miller.

I told him that I suspected that the person who attempted to murder Miss Carroll and me last Monday *was*, in fact, the same person who tried to murder Miss Carroll in Tolono, and the same one who shot me in the leg. "I also believe that Miss Carroll and I may have seen this man walk by the Ebbitt House, on more than one occasion, prior to the attempt on our lives," I said. "He may be using the name of Miles Palladin or Clifford Bates, but probably not."

"If what you say turns out to be true," Inspector Miller said, "I doubt that he's still in Washington."

"That's not the way that this guy works. I'm sure that he's still here, and I think he stays somewhere near the Ebbitt House. Can you give me a list of all of the known occupants of all locations within five minutes walking distance of the Ebbitt House? You can exclude the large hotels, for I'm sure that he wouldn't being staying in one of those places."

"Yes, I can do that," he said.

"I know what that man with the dark eyes looks like now, and I think I can find him," I said. I waited for the list, and then I returned Dandy to the stables.

I also stopped by the armory and picked up a replacement Pocket Colt to go along with the pistol that I had somewhat permanently borrowed from Major Remington. I wanted to be fully armed when I started my house-to-house search, and the idea of carrying a concealed weapon was particularly appealing at the moment.

The streets of Washington were filled with soldiers moving very quickly to their battle stations in anticipation of an attack. An expanded guard detail was in place at the War Department, and my credentials were carefully checked before I could get near the building.

I went directly to Major Eckert, who sat at his desk in the telegraph room. "I hear that you're out chasing the Rebels again," he said. A muffled chuckle emanated from some of the telegraph operators, working elsewhere in the room.

"I had to make sure that the wagons ended up in the right hands," I said.

"So I gather," he said. "That was a bold move...sending on the poison."

The tone of his voice was not all that convincing, but I took it as a compliment. Sometimes I forgot to acknowledge that it was Major Eckert who had to explain things to Secretary Stanton, and I certainly didn't envy him in that role.

"Our lines of communication with General Meade have been broken," he said. "I'm curious as to how General Stuart plans to join up with General Lee when he knows that General Meade blocks the way," Major Eckert said, pausing for a moment to ponder his own point. "What do you think?"

"He has about two thousand men with him, and I don't understand *why* he is *where* he is...It just doesn't make sense to me," I said. "When General Lee marches into enemy territory, he *always* uses General Stuart to lead the way. I think there was a mix-up of some sort."

Major Eckert leaned back in his chair and laughed. "Well, wherever he is headed, he'll be slowed down a while. Major Duane has been trained to ask for parole, and General Stuart, being the gentleman that he is, will grant it. That will take *hours*...and if he doesn't burn the wagons, he'll only be able to move at a snail's pace. Better yet, if they feed the bone meal mix to their horses, they may not be able to move at all!"

I told Major Eckert about my plan to search for the man with the dark eyes. He reluctantly approved. He had come to know that I couldn't be tied to the desk for a long period of time. He also relished the thought of bringing the dangerous KGC operative to justice.

I was relieved when I received his approval, because I knew that President Lincoln had purposely disallowed such practices as house-to-house searches, deeming them to be overly oppressive in nature and inconsistent with the freedom that is generally preached in the nation's capital. But, at the same time, I also knew that Secretary Stanton allowed Lafayette Baker to terrorize the locals in his search for the enemy.

Such paradoxical behavior in Union leadership wasn't uncommon. I'd grown to accept it and wasn't so disturbed by it any longer. I suppose that I wasn't the same naïve and idealistic Jason Alexander who had arrived in Washington just a few months ago.

I wondered if I could return to Illinois College and be the same *student* that I had been just a few months ago.

CHAPTER NINETY

Washington, District of Columbia
June 29, 1863
ante meridiem

I was eager to conduct the house-to-house search in the area where I believed the man, who I had come to refer to as *Dark Eyes*, would be hiding. Major Eckert was satisfied that a single person such as myself, who was not accompanied by a group of armed soldiers, would not draw a lot of attention to the matter...particularly when the city was bracing for a Rebel attack.

The process turned out to be much more difficult than I had expected. I was only able to investigate a dozen locations on Sunday afternoon. The list that I'd obtained from Inspector Miller wasn't complete, and people were generally suspicious regarding the intent of my visit, and often unwilling to reveal the identity of any boarders that they had taken in.

By the middle of Monday morning, I was almost ready to abandon the search. I decided to stop at one more place before checking in at the War Department. When I described Dark Eyes to the owner of the house at 456 Sixth Street, he reported that a man fitting that description had just moved out about ten days ago. I was both excited, and disappointed, at the same time. I had just missed him.

Since Dark Eyes had apparently been at work here in Washington within the last ten days, I felt that he was still around somewhere. I suspected that he didn't move very far away from his last location, so I decided to continue the search. I stopped at four more locations, with no luck, before going to the War Department.

The telegraph room was full of people, including the president, when I looked in. Bates saw me and stepped out for a moment to inform me that Secretary Stanton was in an uproar, having lost all communication with General Meade. All of the current activity in the telegraph room was now associated with General Grant's activities at Vicksburg. Telegraph communication with him was conducted by way of Memphis or Cairo, with couriers delivering the messages the rest of the way—a slow and frustrating process.

I told Bates about my search for Dark Eyes. He told me that Quartermaster General Meigs had ordered that no more bone meal was to be used until further notice; moreover, President Lincoln had mandated that tissue samples from autopsies of soldiers suspected to have died from any sort of disease be encased in paraffin and permanently stored in a warehouse.

I stopped in at the Ebbitt House to see Miss Carroll. She was now getting around quite well. She invited me to stay for dinner, so I did. Mrs. Mason and Mrs. Brown had left to stay with relatives in Baltimore, joining many others in the exodus from Washington. It was strange to see so many empty chairs in the dining room. The mood at the table was melancholy, but the food was great.

After dinner, Leah changed the bandages on my leg and warned me that I needed to stay off of it for a while. I knew that that wouldn't be possible, but I said nothing.

Miss Carroll offered a suggestion. "Jason, I know you don't like Mr. Baker, but why don't you talk to him to see if he knows anything about Palladin? I think he might help you."

"You know how he obtains his information...His captives are near dead when he is finished with them," I said.

"So I've heard...but will you feel better if this monster kills again and then runs off to never be found?"

"No," I said, "I wouldn't." I excused myself and departed, in search of Lafayette Baker.

⌘ ⌘ ⌘

My meeting with Lafayette Baker would establish a formal connection between our organizations. Major Eckert wouldn't like it any better than I did, but I knew that I probably didn't have much time to get Dark Eyes. It would be very easy for him to move to Baltimore, where he would find many more of his own kind to hide him.

Secretary Stanton had recently commissioned *Colonel* Lafayette Baker, and in his role as special provost marshall, he was now Inspector David Miller's boss. I found Baker in his office in the Navy Department building just south of the War Department. It was a large office with bookshelves with no books, and a mahogany desk with nothing on it except a dagger. I recognized the dagger right away.

He chased away the two men who were in his office. I recognized one of them as his thug cousin, Luther Baker.

Lafayette Baker was going to make things difficult right from the start. "How is your search going, Agent Alexander?" I took a seat in front of his desk without being invited to do so. "I trust that Inspector Miller is serving you well." His huge bulk reminded me of his former protégé, General Winfield Scott, and his words spilled out over his unkempt beard in an agonizing fashion.

"He has," I said, "but I want to make sure that I've been given *all* of the information that you have on this man."

"You're not suggesting that we are holding anything back, are you?" he said, studying me intently with his cold and piercing eyes.

I didn't look away. "I'm not *suggesting* anything. I'm searching for a killer, and an enemy of the Union. I need whatever information you have."

"Well, of course you do...but let's just suppose that I have some more information...I wonder what that information would be worth to you?"

"I'm not here to make trades," I said. "I expect to get what you have."

"Those are very strong words coming from a War Department minion. I expected better from the college-educated son of a rich cattle rancher."

"What you see is just what you get," I said, trying my best to remain calm.

Minutes passed as we stared at each other. Then he relaxed a bit and looked at the dagger on his desk. He ran the index finger of his left hand methodically across its hilt. Slowly looking up at me, he said, "His real name is Miles Palladin, not Clifford Bates. I don't know where he is at the moment, but if he's still here in Washington, he has been known to frequent Taltavull's Star Saloon, near the burned-out remains of John Ford's Atheneum."

Then he slid his chair back from the desk, signaling an end to the meeting. "Here...take this...You might need it for evidence," he said, pushing the dagger over to me. "I expect that he has a replacement now. I'm told that he keeps it in his boot."

Lafayette Baker squirmed out of his chair and walked to a window. He peered outside and said, "Frankly, I don't have the time to hunt down this man. I have my hands full with the spies that are trying to get information about the defenses of Washington out of the city and into the hands of General Lee."

I wanted to respond to that statement, but I did not. "Thanks," I said. The meeting had actually turned out better than I'd expected. He had given me a good lead. Things were looking up.

CHAPTER NINETY-ONE

Taltavull's Star Saloon
July 1, 1863
post meridiem

A bit of good fortune came my way when I told Major Eckert about my plan to watch for Dark Eyes at Taltavull's. Since I would easily be recognized inside the saloon, I needed to watch from a distance, and Major Eckert knew the gentleman who owned a house across the street at 453 Tenth Street. It was arranged for me to utilize the small attic above the three stories of the brick building.

I spent time in the attic in the evening, and at night. With the aid of field glasses, and the gaslights along the street, I could get a pretty good look at those who entered and departed Peter Taltavull's Star Saloon. Business was brisk, and my task was tiring.

During the day, I continued my door-to-door search, but I couldn't resist the need to check in on a regular basis with the telegraph room in the War Department, to find out what we knew about the movements of the Union and Confederate forces in Pennsylvania. Some information was coming in from Harrisburg by way of Baltimore, but it was piecemeal at best.

Concerns that Confederate General Ewell was moving down the Susquehanna River had forced General Meade to position himself to protect Baltimore and Washington. Major General John Reynolds was ordered to position his First Corps on Meade's extreme left, at the crossroads town of Gettysburg. It was his responsibility to make sure that General Lee didn't slip in behind Meade's army and make a run at Baltimore or Washington.

President Lincoln was visibly disturbed about the current situation. He feared that the need to guard Washington and Baltimore was going to allow General Lee to reach Harrisburg, and then perhaps Philadelphia. Bates told me that the president was now spending the whole night in the telegraph room.

Brigadier General Haupt was busy trying to restore the railroad lines that General Stuart had demolished as he moved northward. Stuart's forces had severely damaged a large section of the B&O Railroad, as well as numerous telegraph lines.

One encouraging bit of news had arrived within the last hour by way of a courier sent by Haupt. He reported that some of the local people had indicated that a good number of Stuart's riders were "doubled over in their saddles and looking to be very sick, and their animals were looking even worse." Haupt suggested that this impairment, whatever it was, had certainly hampered Stuart's progress.

This condition had not gone unnoticed by President Lincoln. He commented to me in the presence of Secretary Stanton, "Agent Alexander, I think your decision to send the wagons to Stuart was a good one. That dark-eyed fellow that you're after must've fed those beeves a bunch of that stuff before they left the stockyard."

"I'm sure he did," I said. "He was expecting to slow down our troops, but instead, he impacted his own. I would love to be the one who gets to tell him about his mistake...but I have to find him first."

I had already accepted the fact that finding him was going to be very difficult. Dark Eyes had proven himself to be a master of deception, and even though he'd been captured in Tolono, he wasn't likely to be taken so easily again. I was in the need for an additional bit of good fortune to come my way.

I arranged to pick up some fresh bread and a canteen full of tea at the Ebbitt Inn each afternoon, before I went to my watch station in the hot attic. I sat on a small wooden box, which put my head right at the window level. I tried to focus on the task at hand, but I found myself thinking about what I had been doing at this time one year ago...

We were busy getting a big shipment of cattle ready to send eastward prior to the Fourth of July. I recall that my father was very concerned about the heat of the summer and its debilitating effect on the herd. Mr. H. had double-checked all of the arrangements along the railroad route for getting water to the cattle, including a couple of extra stops that he had arranged.

At that time, I was anxiously anticipating starting back to school in the fall to finish up—the war hadn't really occupied my mind. It seemed so far away. How quickly things can change.

I was hoping for a change right now as well. The shadows created by the gaslights in the street danced in the darkness and blackened the faces of Taltavull's like soot. At times, I wasn't sure what I was seeing, or not seeing. The strain on my eyes gave me a headache that almost made me forget about the backache, but not the heat. I longed for sleep, but Taltavull's didn't close up until midnight.

I had already decided that if I saw Dark Eyes go in, I would move to the street level, and hide in an alleyway, so I could follow him out when he left. Otherwise, I would lose him in the time that it would take for me to get from the attic to the street.

Just as I was reviewing this plan in my mind, I saw him. He was wearing a large flop hat that helped cover his face, but the deep-set eyes gave him away. He stood at the saloon door for a moment, looking up and down the street. He looked inside the saloon. After a moment, he went in.

I have him.

I hurried down from the attic and out the back door of the house. I ran through the alley between the buildings. I waited at the end of the alley and watched for Dark Eyes to depart. It was just after eleven o'clock, so I didn't expect to wait very long.

I had a good view of the entryway for the saloon, and I watched very carefully as the patrons arrived and departed. One by one, the people departed shortly after midnight. But Dark Eyes wasn't amongst them.

I waited until Old Man Taltavull was beginning to extinguish the lights before I walked across the street. I peered inside and confirmed that all of the patrons had left.

I went behind the building and checked the back door. It was locked. I went back around to the front and walked inside. I asked Old Man Taltavull if he had any boarders living upstairs. He told me that only he and his wife lived up there.

I surmised that Dark Eyes had departed almost immediately after he arrived, and I had missed him when I was leaving the attic. He was being very cautious...or maybe it wasn't Dark Eyes after all...or maybe he saw me.

If he saw me, he wouldn't be back.

CHAPTER NINETY-TWO

Taltavull's Star Saloon
July 2, 1863
post meridiem

It was now Thursday night, and it was getting dark. The events of the day swam through my head as I sat on the hard wooden box in the hot attic, looking across Tenth Street at Taltavull's Star Saloon.

The city of Washington was buzzing with the news that was coming in from Gettysburg, where a huge battle had erupted. It was difficult to know which side was winning, because there wasn't much information coming into the War Department by way of the telegraph. In fact, the most reliable information seemed to be coming from the scouts that Thomas Scott had positioned near Harrisburg to report on the condition of the assets of the Pennsylvania Railroad.

Scott was doing his best to meet the requests of Brigadier General Haupt, who was busy building a railroad spur directly to Gettysburg for the delivery of supplies and the evacuation of the wounded. There seemed to be no end to the ability of this man to excel in the time of a crisis.

Just as I was leaving the War Department late this past afternoon, a report came in that a Confederate rider had been captured in the valley, carrying a message from Jefferson Davis to General Lee. The deciphered message indicated that Davis was confirming an earlier message to Lee, denying him permission to proceed with an attack on Washington.

With this message in hand, President Lincoln was ready to send all of the reserve troops in Washington to Gettysburg, but Secretary Stanton convinced him to hold off on that order. Even so, the mood in the city was noticeably more relaxed than it had been in the last few days. The soldiers had returned to their routine patrols, and the busy nightlife had resumed in the local establishments like Taltavull's Star Saloon, where the patrons were pouring out into the street, even before dark.

I'd lost the ability to keep up with the flow of activity. I had no idea whether Dark Eyes was in the crowd or not, but I thought I might have seen him. The only way for me to know for sure was to go down there and take a close-up look.

It didn't take much to get me out of the hot attic. It seemed like the heat was also making my leg worse. I worked my way through the crowd of drinkers in the streets to the big front window, where I had a clear view inside. Dark Eyes was standing at the bar in plain view, talking to a man who I did not recognize. He pulled a small piece of paper from the pocket of his short summer coat and handed it to the stranger, who departed shortly afterward.

After finishing his beer, Dark Eyes left some money on the bar and slowly moved toward the swinging doors at the entrance. I wasn't sure which direction he would turn when he came outside, so I moved back into the crowd on the street. He went south, in the direction of Pennsylvania Avenue.

It was easy to follow him because I could see the large flop hat that he wore, and he didn't seem to be in a big hurry tonight.

I was careful not to follow him too closely, but at the same time, I certainly didn't want to lose him, like last time.

When he reached Pennsylvania Avenue, he turned toward the capitol building and continued to Sixth Street. Once there, he turned to the north and headed for the National Hotel. But instead of going to the front of the building, he went around back to the service entrance, where it was very dark.

Immediately, I wondered if he'd seen me and intended to make his escape. I grew cautious as I approached the unfamiliar area behind the hotel. I could smell the stench of garbage as I waited for my eyes to adjust to the blackness. I pulled my pocket pistol from the shoulder holster.

Surely, he was going to escape from me if I didn't give chase immediately—standing and waiting would only serve his purpose if it was his intention to get away. I had to move *now.*

I did...and it proved to be a big mistake. I'd gone no more than five steps when I heard a noise to my left.

The blow to my head knocked me out before I hit the ground.

CHAPTER NINETY-THREE

James W. Pumphrey's Stable
July 3, 1863
ante meridiem

I awoke to the sound and smell of horses and with the pain of a sore head. My hands and feet were bound tightly with rope, and my mouth was covered with several layers of tight bandage. I could only breathe through my nose, and I was having some trouble doing so.

It was still dark outside, and even though my eyesight was fuzzy, a dimly lit lamp allowed me to see that I was lying on the floor of a room that appeared to be occupying part of a stable loft. I was able to roll over on my side to get a better look at the room, which contained a bed, a desk, a small lamp table, and two chairs. I was alone in the room.

My feet were pulled up and tied to my hands behind my back in such a way as to make it impossible for me to pound on the floor and make any noise. I noticed that my wounded leg was bleeding again.

I didn't know where I was, but I had a sense that it wasn't far from the National Hotel, where I had been attacked. I was wriggling around, trying to find a more comfortable position, when I heard someone beginning to climb some stairs that led up to the loft-room. I looked in the direction of the noise. Much to my surprise, I saw Miss Carroll's head pop up into the opening as she struggled up the stairs and into the room. I wasn't surprised to see Dark Eyes following closely behind her.

"Jason, are you all right?" Miss Carroll said as she rushed over to me.

I was able to feebly nod my head in response. She started to remove the ring of bandage that was around my mouth, but Dark Eyes immediately grabbed her hand.

"You'll do nothing of the sort, Anna Carroll!" His voice was not loud, but it was firm. "Sit down, and be quiet. I will do all of the talking from now on."

It was clear that he was not in the mood for any disruption to his plan. "You will both follow my instructions without exception…Failure to do so will result in the immediate death of your friend." He pulled a knife from his boot and waved it in the air.

"And it would be wrong of you to assume that death is inevitable," he said. "I don't intend to kill the two of you…but I *am* going to deliver you into the hands of President Davis in Richmond. He will decide what to do with you after that…so you see that your lives are entirely in your own hands."

I listened to what he said, but I got the feeling that he wouldn't be extremely upset if he was *forced* to kill us. I wondered how he planned to get us out of Washington.

"You may think that I am mad, but I am actually quite sane. The protectors of this city are worried about people coming in, not going out," he chuckled, "and they certainly won't expect us to be traveling during the *day*."

Dark Eyes walked over to me and cut the rope that held my hands and feet together, allowing me to stretch out my aching arms and legs. I sat up on the floor. I had very little feeling in my left leg.

Miles Palladin slipped the knife back into his boot. He looked at me and said, "Alexander, you will lead us out of town with your War Department badge. Your pistol will be in open view... unloaded, of course. I will sit in the rear seat of the carriage with Miss Carroll...with knife in hand, of course."

Daylight began to creep into the room, like an unwelcome guest. On the surface, his plan seemed to be ridiculous, but I knew that it just might work because of that. As we sat there, Dark Eyes made some changes to his appearance by donning a fashionable suit of clothes and applying a small moustache to his upper lip. He stuffed a pistol into the small of his back under his coat and placed another in a small carpetbag that he pulled out from under the bed.

"Mr. Pumphrey will have our carriage ready down below in the livery at daybreak, and we will proceed down the stairs and into the carriage in an orderly fashion, as if everything was perfectly normal. Is that clear?"

The two of us nodded in captive agreement. I began to visualize the possible routes that he might have me take out of the city. I needed to formulate an escape plan.

"Anna Carroll, would you be so kind as to remove the bandages from Alexander's mouth and rewrap that awful wound on his leg? I wonder how he got that?" he smirked. "Take some water from the bowl here, and clean up that stain on his trouser leg as best you can, while you're at it. We should try to look our best when we travel, don't you think?"

As long as he remained close to Miss Carroll, I wasn't inclined to stir up any trouble. I truly believed that he would kill her, and I couldn't bear the responsibility for the death of this good lady. So I would play along…*for now.*

CHAPTER NINETY-FOUR

Columbia Turnpike
July 3, 1863
ante meridiem

I followed the directions that Dark Eyes gave to me as I drove the two horses that pulled our landau carriage through the city. Dark Eyes was correct when he assumed that we would look so normal that we would be almost invisible. With the collapsible top in the upright position, it was difficult for anyone to get a good look at the two occupants of the backseat, and my WD armband was all that was needed to grant us *carte blanche* movement.

We went down Maryland Avenue and across the Long Bridge. I looked for my opportunity to get at Dark Eyes, but there was no way that I could do so without endangering Miss Carroll's life. I would have to wait for a time when the two of them were further apart.

Dark Eyes casually purchased a copy of the morning edition of the *Washington Constitutional Union* from the newsboy who ran alongside the landau. The killer glanced at the headlines, never taking his eyes from me for more than a few seconds at a time.

"I really get a laugh out of these Washington newspapers," he said. "Even when they know that General Lee will be victorious, they write about a Union conquest, just to keep Lincoln and Stanton happy."

"Your *General Lee* has gone too far this time," Miss Carroll said. "He would have been wise to hold his defensive position at Fredericksburg, instead of taking the offensive so far away from home."

"Oh yes, I forgot that I am in the presence of the omnipotent Anna Carroll, who sits with the president's closest advisors." He gave the paper to her. "Here, you can read the hogwash to us as we leave this awful city."

We passed through the Fort Runyon checkpoint, with but a glance from the soldiers there, and made our way onto the Columbia Turnpike, heading southwest. Because it was so early in the morning, the activity on the hard road was light—perhaps also because it looked like it was going to rain. Dark Eyes had picked a good day for us to make our exodus.

As Miss Carroll read some of the news from Gettysburg, I tried to paint a mental picture of the places that lay ahead, hoping to identify a point where I could best make my move on Dark Eyes. There was a tollgate about a mile away, and Hunter's Chapel was a mile and a half beyond that. A mile further, we would cross the Leesburg and Alexandria Railroad at Arlington Mills, and beyond that, there was Bailey's Crossroads.

I heard some thunder in the distance as we passed through the tollgate without the need to stop, my WD armband working its magic once again. I decided that I would take my chances at Bailey's, somehow trying to get between Dark Eyes and Miss Carroll, and hoping that the ruckus would raise enough attention to get some help.

As I faced forward, Dark Eyes was behind me, on my right side. He held the dagger in his left hand, very close to Miss Carroll's ribs. His right hand grasped the frame of the landau, helping to hold him firmly in his place on the bench seat. He watched me closely, so I knew that any move that I made would have to be quick, and certain.

"Alexander, I hope that Yankee mind of yours, as simple as it is, wouldn't be contemplating something stupid."

"You don't think that I'm that foolish, do you?"

"Yes," he said with some conviction, "and it would be a big mistake."

"I'm actually looking forward to meeting Jeff Davis," I said.

"I doubt that...but you *do* know that Anna Carroll here knows him *quite well*."

"At one time, he actually served his country with honor," Miss Carroll said. "Now he will be hanged for leading a rebellion against that same country."

"Dream on, Anna Carroll, dream on...We'll see who will be doing the hanging."

I almost changed my mind, and nearly turned on him as we crossed the rickety tracks of the railroad at Arlington Mills, shaking the landau with such force that I came close to leaving my seat.

That moment *did* give me an idea that I could implement at Bailey's Crossroads up ahead.

CHAPTER NINETY-FIVE

Bailey's Crossroads
July 3, 1863
ante meridiem

The rain was falling at a steady pace as we approached Bailey's Crossroads. The horses jumped at the boom of thunder, which was now in lockstep with the lightning. Dark Eyes and Miss Carroll were well protected by the landau's cover, but I was exposed to the weather, and in a very short time, I was soaked.

I was grateful for the cool rain because it seemed to awaken me, and my spirit. I also became aware of the dryness in my mouth, and I took in what rain I could lap up with my tongue. I wondered how much of a distraction the rain might be for Dark Eyes.

I could see Bailey's Crossroads up ahead. There was a heavy wooded area on our right, and open fields on the left, as we made our approach on the turnpike. The rain would keep the people inside, so my hope of getting help from the locals had dwindled.

"Take that next road up ahead on the right," Dark Eyes called from behind me, raising his voice above the persistent patter of the raindrops on the landau's cover.

I had planned on going into the heart of the little village, so his order caught me by surprise. *He must be meeting someone here—perhaps Mosby! I have to make my move now.*

As I started into the turn, I let the wheels on the right side of the landau fall off of the edge of the elevated road of the turnpike. This alone may not have been enough to tip the carriage, but when I turned abruptly and rolled out of my seat, I threw myself into Dark Eyes, legs first, shifting my weight just enough to complete the intended spill.

The landau slid a bit in the mud and then came to an abrupt stop. For a moment I had the killer's right hand pinned down with my two hands. His left hand, which held the knife, was held fast by my two feet, as my body lay on top of his. I looked into his red eyes as he frantically tried to wrestle free.

Miss Carroll was on top of his legs, which helped to keep him from kicking his way out, but he was beginning to work his knife-hand free. Dark Eyes was not a big man, but he was very strong. I could see that Miss Carroll and I would not be able to subdue him much longer.

The horses were slowly beginning to drag the tipped carriage through the drainage ditch, scooping in the soft mud all around us. My slippery feet were losing their hold on Dark Eyes.

His left arm came up with the knife in hand, and in one swift motion, he drove the knife into my left leg, just below the knee—almost in the same place where he had shot me a few days earlier. I just missed blocking his thrust with the boot on my right foot, but I did manage to kick his hand free from the dagger, just after it was thrust into my leg.

Everything was happening so quickly. I felt the pain in my leg. *Is that knife in my leg?* I fought the urge to pass out.

I had to keep Dark Eyes from getting the weapon again. I thought about trying to grab it myself, but I needed both of my hands to keep his right arm pinned down.

I moved my body up higher across his chest, trying to dig my left knee into his throat. I did manage to pin his left arm down again with my feet...but I was getting tired.

He began to wriggle away by sliding *under* my outstretched body. I realized that this was going to work...The mud was making it impossible for us to hold him down. When his face was directly under my left leg, I pressed down with all of my might to hold him there.

I shouted to Miss Carroll, "Hit the knife!"

She sat up, still on his legs, and froze.

"Hit the knife!"

And then, in an instant, with both hands, she drove the dagger to its hilt deep into my leg and into the skull of Dark Eyes, passing directly through the socket of his left eye.

I felt his struggle give way almost immediately, but I waited to see if it was real before I let up on him. Miss Carroll's hands were shaking, but still pressing on the end of the knife. She wasn't fully comprehending what had just taken place.

His body jerked one last time. "It's all right now," I said. "I think he's dead."

"But...but...*your leg*," she said, beginning to take everything in.

I lifted her hands from the butt of the knife and slowly moved my leg away from Dark Eyes. The mud poured into his pierced eye, filling the darkness one last time.

I was now more aware of my own predicament, but I couldn't bring myself to pull the knife from my leg. I just wanted to lie back and close my eyes...and that is what I did.

CHAPTER NINETY-SIX

Armory Square Hospital
July 6, 1863
post meridiem

The first person I saw when I opened my blurry eyes was David Homer Bates. He was sitting there next to my bed. When I turned my head, I could see that Miss Carroll was sitting on the other side. I didn't know where I was or why I was here...but then I remembered some of what had happened...but how long ago was that?

I was in a room with many other beds. The sun was shining in through the open windows, and it was very warm. I was tired, but I was glad to be alive. *What day is it?*

The look on their faces was one of concern for me. I could see a smile on the lips of David Bates and Miss Carroll, but there was deep sorrow in their eyes.

"Did we win at Gettysburg?" I said. My throat was dry, and my voice was raspy.

They looked at each other and smiled. *We did.*

I expected as much, but I also expected more of a celebration on their part. *Something's wrong.*

Bates finally spoke. "Lee's in full retreat...General Meade will destroy what's left of his army before he can reach the river. You'll be able to go home now and finish your studies...The war's almost over."

It was the way he said it that didn't sit right with me. Bates wasn't being Bates. I turned to Miss Carroll and said, "Tell me what's wrong."

There was a long silence. I could hear the music of a small band off in the distance...It was happy music. Closer, I could hear moans and groans of the men near me in the room. There were people talking in hushed voices. A strange smell was in the air.

"It's your leg, Jason," she said. "They had to take part of it off."

Part of it...

What was Miss Carroll talking about? My leg felt fine. Sure, it was a bit sore, but I expected that. Why would she say such a thing?

I turned to look at Bates. He twisted away to avoid meeting my eyes.

Oh no...

Part of it...

I slowly looked down at the sheet that covered my legs. There was a space under the sheet where the bottom of my left leg should have been. I didn't know what to do or what to say—I didn't even know what to *feel*—but the strange thing was that I thought I *could* feel my entire leg.

But when I looked again at the sheet that covered my legs, I could see that she was right...The bottom part of my left leg was not there.

I couldn't bring myself to lift the sheet to examine it more closely. *How will I live without my leg?* I began to feel a bit dizzy.

Just then, Major Eckert walked up to my bedside. He placed his hand on my shoulder and said, "Jason, you'll always have a place at the War Department, leg or no leg, but we think you should go back to Illinois and finish your studies. I'm told that Illinois College will be opening back up in the fall." He looked into my eyes and smiled.

"The doctor said that he can fix a wooden peg for your leg," Miss Carroll said. "He said that, with a cane, you will be able to get around just fine."

A peg...a cane...

"President Lincoln came by for a while this morning," Miss Carroll said. "He wanted you to know that you will be receiving a Presidential Award for foiling the KGC's plot to contaminate the beef in Washington, helping to break the Confederate cipher, and closing down the doctor's line."

"You're a hero, Jason," Bates said. "The next thing you know, they'll be naming a building after you."

We laughed...even me.

CHAPTER NINETY-SEVEN

Alexander, Illinois
November 30, 1923
ante meridiem

Grandpa Alexander died in his sleep a few hours after he finished the story. I was sitting at his bedside when he slipped away. He just didn't wake up anymore. I will always remember the smile that was frozen on his face when he saw God.

I've never seen so many people in our little town at one time. Some called it the largest funeral since Abraham Lincoln's—that's how the *Springfield Journal Register* described it. The headline read "Jason Alexander Laid to Rest—Local Hero Joins His Commander in Chief."

Most of Grandpa's old friends were gone by now. I did see a few older folks in the crowd, but I didn't know who they were. All of the local farmers were there. They now worked the property that was handed down to them from their fathers, who had received the land when my great grandpa was no longer able to pay them in cash.

There were delegations from Washington and the governor's office, and the railroad even stopped the trains during the funeral service. "They did that for Old Man Hinrichsen, but I never thought I'd see it again," my father said.

The entire town was filled with the people braving the chilly fall weather. They clustered around the front of the Church of the Visitation of the Blessed Virgin Mary. My Irish-Catholic mother had converted my father and my grandfather many years ago. We sat behind Father Corrigan, facing out to the large congregation gathered for this memorable funeral Mass.

I was in somewhat of a fog all day long, but I remember that Father Corrigan described my grandpa as "Alexander's grand knight." After listening to Grandpa's story a few days ago, I knew what he was talking about.

One of the people who stepped up to say a few words was my Auntie Jeanine, Grandpa's sister. She was retired now, but at one time, Jeanine had been a world-famous breeder of racehorses. She spoke about how her brother had worked with the doctors in the military hospitals to design wooden legs for the soldiers. "He constantly worked to make the designs better. He was able to walk for years without his cane, and his hope was that someday no one would be able to tell that a person was walking with a wooden leg."

I never really thought of my grandpa as *a man with a wooden leg*—he never let it stop him from doing anything that he wanted to do. My father told me that he even wanted to return to Washington after the war lingered on, but the governor had convinced him to stay here and help him deal with very serious local issues. He did make a trip to Maryland to see Miss Carroll just before she died.

After the Mass, we put my grandpa on the train that was waiting at the depot. It was an old steam locomotive that they had brought out of storage just for the occasion—it was the T. Mather.

Almost everyone filed into the passenger cars and rode with my grandpa on his last train ride to Jacksonville.

Jason Alexander was buried in Diamond Grove Cemetery, which sits on a small hill just south of Illinois College.

⌘ ⌘ ⌘

At the first opportunity after supper, I hurried to my room and pulled the wooden box out from under my bed. I had wanted to look at its contents earlier, but I'd made the decision to wait until today, the day that my grandpa was laid to rest.

I cleared a space on the top of my desk for the box. I sat there for a few minutes, looking at it. I knew that my father was aware of its existence, but he hadn't said a word to me about it. For some reason, I felt that my father wanted me to have it.

With both hands, I lifted the lid of the box and set it to the side. The first thing that caught my eye was the wooden carving of a horse. I was sure that it was the same one that President Lincoln had once used as a paperweight on his desk in the Executive Mansion. He had given it to my grandpa.

There was a thick lock of coarse black hair that had been braided to hold it together. It was the hair from the mane of a horse...*Dandy's.*

The WD armband was there. It was well worn. As I looked at it, I formed a picture in my mind of my grandfather wearing it proudly as he worked in Washington to preserve the Union.

There was a telegraph key with a brass plate—Jeb Stuart's—the same one that my grandfather had taken from General Stuart's tent and placed on the mantel of the fireplace in the telegraph room at the War Department.

A dagger was there—perhaps the one that had almost taken Miss Carroll's life, or the one that took the life of Miles Palladin... and my grandpa's leg. There was still some dried blood on it.

At the bottom of the box, I found Miss Carroll's obituary, which was cut from the *Washington Sunday Chronicle.* She died on February 19, 1894. The article seemed rather small for a woman of her stature, and I was sure that my grandpa had reacted in the same way.

And that was it. I returned the items to their place in the box and slowly closed the lid. I would keep it for my own children to hand down through time.

The box has a story in it.

Made in the USA
Columbia, SC
10 July 2021